STEFANIE LOZINSKI

Maker

Storm and Spire Book 4

To Dawson
In the time that it has taken me to write this series,
you've learned how to read!
I am so proud of you.

"A man must be prepared not only to be a martyr, but to be a fool. It is absurd to say that a man is ready to toil and die for his convictions if he is not even ready to wear a wreath around his head for them."

G.K. Chesterton

Contents

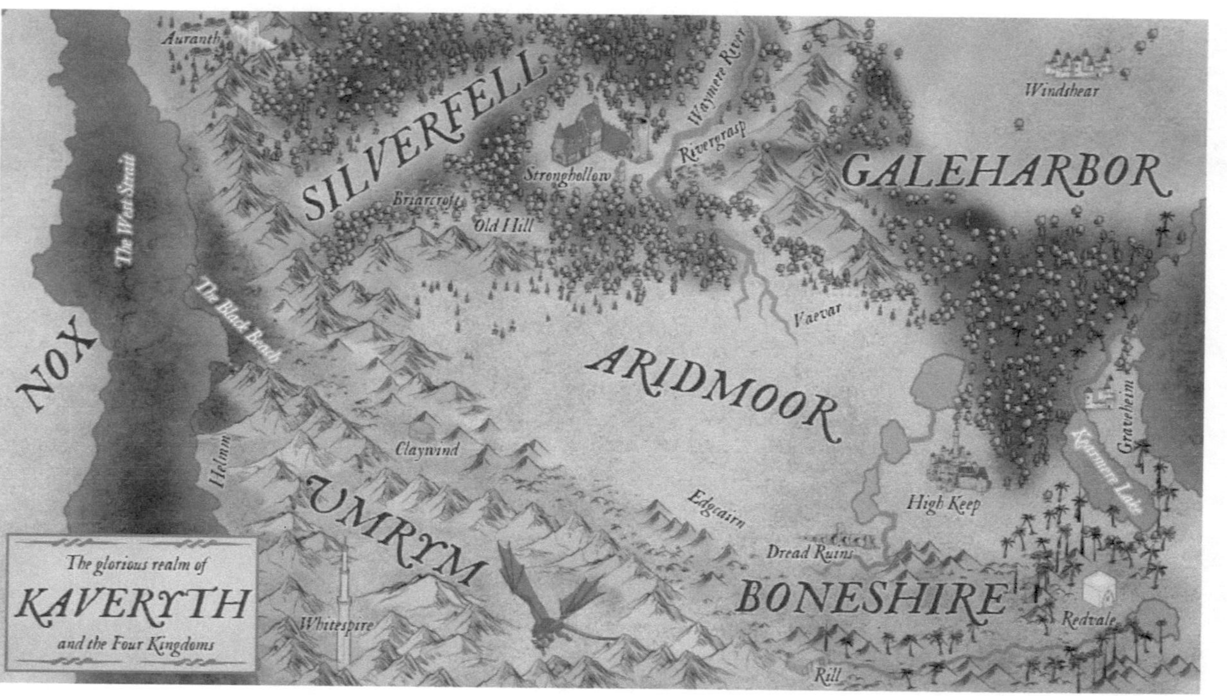

NOX
SILVERFELL
GALEHARBOR
ARIDMOOR
UMRYM
BONESHIRE
Auranth
Windshear
Waymere River
Riverguard
Stronghollow
Briarcroft
Old Hill
Vaevar
Gravebeim
Kearmere Lake
The West Strait
The Black Beach
Helmm
Claywind
High Keep
Edgcairn
Dread Ruins
Redvale
Whitespire
Rill
The glorious realm of
KAVERYTH
and the Four Kingdoms

Prologue

AELRIE
BEFORE

"We need to hide. It looks like there might be a small cave over there," Wes said, gesturing toward two huge rocks that rested against the mountain. For a moment, Aelrie could not see any place where a person could fit, but as they approached, she noticed that there was a narrow entrance bathed in black shadow.

In the distance, she could hear the sound of whispering voices and the touch of soft leather boots on stone. Her people could be silent when they wished to be, but it seemed that for the moment they did not care about being detected.

The dragon had noticed them first, of course.

Even her own superior senses could not match the nose of a dragon. Not that she could let Wes know that she knew who Celesyria was.

"Right," she heard herself say as they pushed their way inside, her ankle smarting as she tried to support her weight without the aid of his shoulder. Even with the strength of her elven eyesight, the darkness was deep, and it took her several seconds to adjust. She glanced over at Wes, noticing the whites of his eyes as he glanced around the space.

She reached out a hand and laid her fingertips on his forearm, trying to tell herself not to notice the firm muscles and wisps of hair that rested there. "Close them. Your sight will adjust faster."

He said nothing, but she watched as he closed his eyes, not pulling away from her touch. She let her fingers settle there a moment more, knowing that she should back away, but struggling to bring herself to do so. There was something magnetic about him, some unseen quality that made her want to stay, but she knew it was impossible.

She had only moments left.

I'll find them again.

I'll find a way to be free when the time is right.

Wes glanced over at her, and despite the darkness she could see the wary look in his eyes. She couldn't blame him. Elves did not deserve trust from men.

"Thank you for helping me," she said, wanting to smile but finding herself not quite able to. "It was very kind. I've never experienced kindness at the hands of a human before. Then again, I suppose my folk have never given you any reason not to hate us."

Wes did not respond straight away, clearing his throat as the silence stretched out several seconds too long to remain comfortable.

"Seems like you didn't need my help much in the first place," he pointed out, gesturing to her ankle. "I'm sure you would have been fine, had you waited for a few minutes."

He was right. She had gotten it stuck between the two rocks, and it had indeed been injured, but even now she could feel the pain subsiding. She couldn't help but to laugh a little, the sound pouring out before she could stop it. It felt good to laugh, especially there in the dark.

"I'm kind of a simple girl that way," she said quickly, hoping to get the words out before her own good sense stopped her. "When a handsome man offers to help me, I figure it's best to take it."

She could sense Wes blushing despite the shadows, and she decided that he probably looked all the more handsome for it.

Not that I will say another word about it. Not that I will think about him at all. I don't even know him.

They sat there another moment in silence, listening to the distant sound of running feet. She was out of time, she knew. She had stalled long enough.

"I need to go," she said, getting to her feet and narrowly avoiding smacking her head against a jutting stone near the ceiling. It seemed that the man's presence was not conducive to her usual grace.

"What?" Wes said, his brows folding together in puzzlement. "It's not safe. You can't go out there."

She could hear voices now, and laughter. Though she couldn't make out the words, she could guess at many of them. Jeers, taunts, cruelties. What else was there?

They were at least as close as the field of broken rocks now, but she was certain that her fellow elves would not be foolish enough to catch their ankles.

"I told you that I couldn't explain everything, and I really can't," she said, reaching out a hand and placing it upon his shoulder. He felt so warm, even through his tunic. "But I'm really glad to have met you."

She swallowed. She meant it, even though she was surprised by how much it hurt to leave him so soon.

Wes was up now, gently pushing past her and striding a few

paces toward the entrance. He peered out into the dawn light for a second before taking a quick step backward, blinking. Even near dawn, the light would surely be blinding after resting here in the dark.

She found herself touching him again, clasping his hand so that she could lead him back into the shadows. He sat down against the wall and she rested beside him, their fingers pressed together awkwardly for a moment longer until both let go.

"I have to leave now," she said. "Perhaps one day we will meet again."

Please.

Wes leaned back closer against the wall, his dark curls pressing against the stone.

"Can I ask you one thing before you go?"

"Yes. Anything."

I could not even bring myself to hesitate. Foolish.

"I believe you, about what you said," Wes continued. "I'm sure you're right. Some elves are innocent. But are you?"

Excuses and lies caught in her throat as silence filled the cavern.

She could hear blood rushing in her ears, her pulse ticking like a clock, demanding for her to give an answer that she so very much wanted to give. It would have felt so good to lie.

"No," she said at last, getting to her feet.

She did not wait for a reply before heading through the mouth of the cave, pressing her eyes into slits as the morning sunlight assaulted her vision.

She pushed the foolish, forbidden thoughts away.

The others were close.

She walked as quickly as she could across the rocks, away

from where Wes hid. She could not risk breaking into a run, not when they might crest the nearest rise at any moment. If she was going to keep him safe, she'd have to be convincing.

Some of the elves she had been traveling with disliked her already. She could see it in their faces.

She shook her head as a gust of wind hissed through the stones, sending a tendril of her long black hair into her face.

I must reveal nothing.

Aelrie sucked in a breath.

There, mere feet away, stood two elven women. Their long blonde hair glimmered in the sunshine, their pale eyes searching her face as she approached them.

"Where have you been?" One of the women, the taller of the two, asked. She did not smile.

Aelrie wanted to ask where the rest of their scouting party had gotten to, but she thought better of it. She could only hope that none of the others were near Wes.

"Forgive me, Ethraina. I was following the Envoy as I was commanded, but he got away. When I went after him, I got lost."

It was a half-truth, at least. Such were the easiest lies to tell.

"These mountains do play tricks," the other elf said, her voice kind, gesturing to the gray peaks that surrounded them on all sides. Aelrie could not remember her name. "It's hard even to tell which way is north when the sun is low."

Ethraina rolled her eyes. "You're elves. Figure it out."

Neither protested. Aelrie knew that she was right. Claiming navigational failure was a particularly flimsy excuse when one was endowed with elven abilities.

"I'll get used to it," the other elf said. "I suppose I'll have to. I've been assigned to one of the new Umrym settlements."

Aelrie forced a smile. "An honor."

Ethraina nodded. "You will get to see the seeds we have planted here beginning to bloom. Many would be envious."

For several minutes they walked in silence. Aelrie took several slow breaths, hoping to ease the racing of her heart. They did not suspect anything.

To her right, over a stooped-looking hill that could not quite be called a mountain, she could see the great spire that overlooked the city of Whitespire. Camp was near, and she suddenly found herself feeling very hungry.

How easy it is to slip back into the life that I claim I want to leave behind.

As if reading her mind, Ethraina spoke.

"Aelrie, I'm afraid you can't come to lunch just yet. It is your turn to mind the hatchery."

This surprised her. She had never even seen a hatchery, and she had certainly never been told that elves were being given guard of it.

"May I ask why?"

Ethraina gave a tight smile. "The council meeting is taking place today, in the obelisk room."

Aelrie had heard of the council, though she was surprised to hear it being spoken of so openly. She knew that it was an alliance of sorts between elves, dragons, and dwarves. They held their meetings around an obelisk that the elves had installed in the depths of Whitespire's cavern, brought all the way from Nox. Beyond that, she had no idea what these meetings entailed.

"A dwarf woman called Cingra is usually in charge of the hatchery," Ethraina explained. "But as of this morning, she has been imprisoned, and they've been scrambling to replace her."

"She was stealing the eggs," the other elf put in, her voice a whisper that all three of them could hear.

Aelrie's eyes widened. Surely the dragons would not take kindly to such conduct, and she did not blame them. Imprisonment was a tame punishment. In Nox, the dwarf would be lucky to escape execution.

"Anyway, there is another dwarf there now, taking an extra shift. She will instruct you on what you are to do."

Aelrie nodded. Ethraina gestured toward the west, where Aelrie could just make out a flat plateau at the top of a narrow path that wound between the mountains. "Someone will come to relieve you in a few hours. I know you must be eager to rest."

"Thank you," Aelrie replied, trying to reveal neither her confusion nor her biting hunger.

She watched for a while as Ethraina and her companion headed down into the valley toward Whitespire, before turning to the east and stepping onto the path that led to their camp. Ethraina walked as though she did not fear detection, her head held high as she avoided the cool shadows.

Umrym will be ours soon enough.

Aelrie felt her stomach clench as she walked toward the plateau. She did not want to be counted among her people. She did not want to be here when Umrym was swarming with elves, the dragons and dwarves living as slaves, if any were allowed to live at all.

Fools. Every one of them.

As she made her way along the narrow path, she forced thoughts of the settlements out of her mind. There was nothing she could do about the fate of this land now. She could only hope that another opportunity would arise where she could make her escape.

At least she'd be giving her soul a chance, however small.

What good would it do? You've turned back out of fear, over and over.

She kept walking, each step of her boot sending a small puff of gray sand into the air. The guilt never stayed away for long.

Gramnok Beastbane was only trying to protect the dragon, and you stood by as he was tortured.

She walked faster.

Finally, she saw the edge of the plateau. Her boots sank into the dirt as she climbed the final hill, refusing to slow. She could not dwell on all that she had done, all that she had failed to do. Today, she had returned to protect Wes Cervos. She refused to apologize for that, even to herself.

"They sent you?" a dwarf-woman said nearly as soon as her feet hit the smooth stone. She was rather round, with coarse black hair in a braid and jolly-looking pink cheeks.

"Yes, I'm Aelrie," she said, trying not to fidget as the woman looked her up and down. Mumbling something to herself, she headed across the plateau. Not knowing what else to do, Aelrie hurried behind her, blinking against the light as the sun broke free of a cloud.

"Were you told of your duties?" the woman asked as they approached the far edge of the great table. Aelrie watched in amazement as the dwarf-woman headed over to a circle of large stone bowls, where dragon eggs of all colors were nestled in amongst equally colorful quilts.

"No," Aelrie whispered, afraid to disturb the little hatchlings from within their shells.

"Right," the woman said, reaching into a nest seemingly

at random and picking up a purple egg. It was huge, but the woman carried it with seemingly no difficulty.

"It's simple really," she continued, walking briskly toward the cliffside. "We choose at random—from this allotment, anyway—unless there's someone with a crack, or someone smaller than the others, or something like that. You'll catch on."

She looked down at the egg in her hands, tut-tutting as her finger traced a small fracture.

Without another word, she turned toward the abyss and sent the egg hurling into space.

Aelrie stood there, openmouthed, unable to say a single word. A long moment later, she heard a sickening crunch, followed by silence. The dwarf woman was already bustling back toward the nests, adjusting quilts and looking up at the clouds as though disapproving of them for blocking the warming sunshine.

"W-what have you done?" Aelrie stammered, rage filling her chest as she approached the woman, no longer caring if she woke the peaceful hatchlings.

The dwarf-woman narrowed her eyes at her, her thick brows knitting together.

"The mother couldn't care for the egg, so she brought it here," she said slowly, enunciating each word so as to be sure Aelrie fully understood. "She knew that this was a possible outcome. Obviously, we don't have the resources to raise all of them!"

"The dragons are dying," Aelrie said, blinking back hot tears. "This doesn't make sense. How could you do this?"

The woman shook her head, sending her black braid flapping between her shoulder blades. "Times are difficult here in Umrym. I'm afraid that the living take precedence over the mush in an egg."

Aelrie said nothing.

The woman had referred to the hatchling as a *someone*, and now it was mush?

She could scarcely comprehend the words that were coming out of her mouth.

"If this troubles you, I suggest you take it up with the council," the woman added, her voice gentle. "Now, I will just show you–"

"I–I need a minute," Aelrie said, bile filling her throat. The tears were flowing freely now, and she turned back the way they had come. Without waiting for an answer, she strode calmly across the plateau, clasping a hand to her mouth to stifle her sobs. For a terrible second, she thought that she heard the smashing sound again, but when she glanced over her shoulder the woman had stayed where she was.

She forced her feet to move faster.

Finally, she could see the soft sand of the path and made her way down, stumbling on shaking knees as she pushed her way over the edge.

As soon as she was out of sight, she broke into a run.

She would find the Envoy and the dragon, and this time, she would stand with them and she would fight.

No matter the cost.

Chapter One

WES

Wes stared at the wall until his eyes began to sting.

It was made of wood, gray from years of sunlight and scrubbing. He followed each plank with his eyes, tracing each narrow shadow between the boards until it disappeared against the floor.

He did not want to close his eyes again, did not want to fall back down into the dark, cloying sleep.

He forced himself to turn onto his other side, his entire body screaming with effort. More gray boards along the walls. A still-mostly-brown ceiling. Heavy blue curtains hung over a nearby window, blocking out most of the light. He wasn't sure how much time had past, but they had to be well into the next day.

He blinked once, and then again.

I'm still here, it would seem.

He was in a bed with rather stiff white sheets, and across from where he lay he could see another just the same. There was a washstand beside it, and for a moment he considered trying to get to his feet to see if he could find some water. His throat was unbearably dry. He saw no pitcher, however, and he did not want to risk leaving the bed if he might not be able to get back into it.

Instead, he looked at the floor. It was even more gray than the walls, mopped a thousand times, every bit of newness worn away even in the corners.

His head swam, and his eyes fell shut again, tired with the effort of staying open. Moments and hours passed, he wasn't sure which.

He thought of a woman laying on another set of scrubbed gray boards, her cheek pressed against them, salt spray filling his lungs and peppering his cheeks as he watched her.

"Aelrie!" he felt himself screaming, the sound of it loud in the small room. "Aelrie! Aelrie, please, please!"

He was sitting now, his head hammering with pain, trying to turn his body so that he could plant his feet on the floor.

His eyes were open now, and the floor seemed to be moving again, a ship's deck, the same swabbed gray boards, the same pervasive taste of salt...

"Wes," a voice said from the door. He heard the latch click, and then Alder was there, rushing over to push him back down onto his bed. "Shh. It's okay. You're okay."

"Where am I?" he asked, swallowing against his dry throat. He blinked again, slowly, waiting for the world to make sense when he opened his eyes.

Alder did not answer for a moment.

As his friend sat there, rubbing his shoulder, he felt his thoughts coming together and making sense again. He thought of the ship, the monster, the storm. He did not recognize the house, but he knew by the smell that they were still in Kingsvier Landing. He had gone to look for Aelrie, he had reached out to touch her... and now he was here.

"Where's Aelrie?" he asked instead, rubbing a hand against his temples. A cough escaped his throat.

Alder got up without a word and headed through the door, returning a second later with a large mug. Wes grabbed the water and began to suck it down his throat in thick gulps, but Alder took it away again, warning him to drink slowly lest he throw it all up.

Wes pressed his fingers against the glass, forcing himself to sip slowly.

"Aelrie is fine. Everyone's fine."

"Thank the High One," he said, swallowing again, the cool liquid soothing against his scratchy throat. It was the most delicious thing he had ever tasted. "Where is she? I need to see her."

"You blacked out," Alder said, ignoring him.

"Just now?"

Alder's jaw went tight. "Perhaps. But I meant on the ship."

He paused for a second, remembering, trying to put together the details correctly in his mind. Although it couldn't have been long since it happened, the whole event felt very far away.

"As soon as I saw her moving the ice, I felt this strange pressure, like a tidal wave was ripping through me. When I tried to touch her hand..."

He struggled to find more words as his head pounded, the fresh pain of recent events mingling with the sickness that had already taken him captive. He had not yet told Alder of his headaches, and he was not sure how much he felt like explaining at the moment. He had worried his friends enough.

"I didn't feel anything like that," Alder said, raising an eyebrow. "I don't think anyone else did, either."

"I'm fine now," Wes said firmly, placing the mug on the floor next to his bed.

It wasn't entirely true. His head swam when he sat up, and he was afraid to even attempt to stand, but compared to the prior night he felt wonderful.

"We both need some sleep. There will be time to talk soon enough," Alder replied, climbing back into his own bed. "I took some punches. We both did. "

Wes nodded, laying back down.

When he closed his eyes, memories of the fight danced on the backs of his eyelids. The Gorok. The waves. The elves. Somehow, he had been able to hold his own against them. He could almost feel the jolting sensation in his nerves as he remembered the way that their swords struck his own.

Surely, the High One was with him. There was no other explanation.

KESSARA

The sea was quiet now.

Small rippling waves lapped at the shore, the white foam bubbling as it hit the sand. The sun had been out for most of the day, but it was not bright or warm enough to dry the wet ground from last night's rain.

Kessara looked out across Kingsvier Landing, leaning across the balcony rail and surveying the damage. Not long ago, she had been at home in Galeharbor, looking out across the same sea, awaiting doom.

She felt a smile pressing into her cheeks. Autumn was near, the unmistakable coolness of the approaching season touching the salty air, promising a future.

"The world continues on, much as we try to shatter it," she said aloud, content to speak only to the sea. After last night, she needed the quiet. Old worries bubbled to the surface of her mind again, now that the immediate threat had been vanquished, but she tried not to get lost in them.

She drew a deep breath, forcing herself to gaze at the harbor, where entire docks had been torn loose and ships had been smashed into pieces. She had a good view of most of the city from the top of the main city hall, with the exception of the stairs and the cliffs that lay behind her, and it was painful to consider the extent of the damage. Everywhere she looked was another home, another boat, another place of work that had been touched by the beast and his waves.

She hoped that the people who had fled Kingsvier Landing would return, but she knew that some who had left were leaving for good. As the menace of the elves touched their shores, many would move inland, searching for some place of refuge that they would never find.

"We can't outrun the darkness," she said again, her gentle voice swept up in a gust of wind. The shushing in her ears sounded almost like a reply.

She squinted at the huge piece of floating ice that was bobbing on the horizon, drawn away from the coast by the pull of the waves. The Gorok was there, imprisoned in the cold. Whatever Aelrie had done, it seemed that the monster would not be coming back.

At least, she hoped it wouldn't. Anything else was unthinkable.

A knock sounded at the door, and Kessara straightened, hoping that no one had heard her talking to herself. She had told her guards to go downstairs and rest, but they didn't always listen to her.

She strode back into the room—an office borrowed from the mayor—and drew the heavy door inward.

"Yes?"

One of the councilmen stood there, a short fellow with tanned skin and blonde hair similar in shade to her own.

"Your Highness," he said, bowing at the waist, waiting for a long moment until she gestured that he may stand again. "King Manta is here to see you."

She had not been expecting him so soon, but she tried to mask her surprise.

"Thank you. Please tell him to join me at his leisure," she said, leaning against the doorframe as the councilman scurried out of sight.

You could have listened, Father. Had we kept Galeharbor's navy here, perhaps we could have lessened the destruction. Perhaps Aelrie wouldn't have had to do... whatever it was that she did.

She swallowed the words, determined not to utter them. The people of Kingsvier Landing had been through an ordeal already, and they needed the support of their monarchs now. The past was past. Reminding her father that he'd been wrong would be of little use.

There was something else she had to tell him that would be much more difficult.

She thought of Alder, safe in a house nearby, keeping watch over Wes.

Tears sprang to her eyes. He had nearly died last night. For a terrible few seconds, she thought that he had. She pressed her eyes together, listening to her father's heavy footsteps as he made his way down the hall.

When she was confident the moment of pain could no

longer be read in her eyes, she plastered a smile onto her face, watching as the door swung open.

Her father stood beside Captain Drohma.

CELESYRIA

Celesyria nearly dropped the wooden board she held between her claws as Wes' voice sounded in her head.

"You're awake!" she said stupidly, turning and announcing the good news to Nazzan and Jaconial. They grinned back, their white teeth gleaming.

"I'm a little busy," she added, diving back down to pick up another piece of rubble. The three dragons were hard at work near the harbor, trying to clear the remains of a building that had fallen onto one of the docks. Three of the fishing boats were anchored at sea with nowhere to tie up, and if another storm swept in, they could be lost.

The water was still pooled beneath where she flew, farther inland than it should have been, but at least the North Sea was calm for the time being. Still, they would not risk taking too much rest. The weather here was never guaranteed to last.

"But thank the High One you're awake," she added. *"You worried us. I thought that–"*

"Where's Aelrie?" he asked quickly, letting her fears remain unvoiced. *"Alder promised she was alive, but wouldn't say more."*

"Which is wise, considering that you need to rest," she chided. *"You were unconscious for almost a full day."*

"I barely know what happened to me. I need to talk to her."

"She needs rest, too," Celesyria pointed out, picking up a huge piece of limestone with the aid of Jaconial and flying it out over the sea. *"I'm sure destroying the Gorok took a lot out of her."*

She thought of gentle Aelrie standing there, arms raised, commanding the sea and the ice to obey. A shiver coursed through her spine, and she let the rock go a moment too early, earning her a cry of protest from Jaconial.

"Sorry," she said. "I'm a little distracted."

"On to the next one," Jaconial said, wheeling around and heading back toward land, where her mate was struggling to lift a huge old anchor that had become embedded in the dock.

"I know her, Celesyria," Wes protested. *"She'll feel terrible about what happened. She'll want to know that I'm alright. I need to at least check on her."*

Celesyria shook her head as she dove low, skimming the surface of the water with the scales of her belly. It felt nice and cool against her skin after all of the work that they had done. They were all ready for a long rest, but she knew that the sooner they could show the townspeople that rebuilding was possible, the better off they would be. There would be time to sleep soon enough.

"Fine," she said after a long pause, watching with a familiar pang of jealousy as Nazzan bumped Jaconial's cheek with the tip of his snout. *"She's in the same house you're in, in the basement. We wanted to keep her from prying eyes. I'm not sure that the people here would take kindly to an elf in their midst at the moment."*

She hoped that the citizens of Kingsvier Landing would know what she had done for them eventually, but in the meantime, she needed privacy. So far as Celesyria knew, she had been sleeping for several hours, and probably still was.

"Thank you," Wes said. She could hear the relief in his voice. *"I won't keep her, I promise."*

"Be careful."

Wes said nothing.

The breeze picked up, and Celesyria gazed out at the sea, wishing that she could tell him more. But she knew that he would not listen.

I mean it Wes. She's dangerous. And not just because she almost killed you.

Chapter Two

ALDER

"Alder," a voice hissed from somewhere in the room. "Alder! Wake up!"

The dream he was having had been beautiful.

Already, it was fading away, the soft blooms of flowers and green moors passing away, fading into a boring gray room with boring gray walls. There had been words, too, words that may have been from the High One for all he knew, now gone and lost.

He shook his head, blinking. The High One had not spoken to him that way in quite a while. More likely, the dream had been nothing more than a peaceful gift from his exhausted brain. Still, he was annoyed. Somehow, he felt even more tired now than he had a couple of hours before.

"Morning," he muttered, forcing himself to pull off the warm blanket and step onto the cold floor. He padded over to the window and pulled the curtain back, and the soft sunlight filtered into the room. It had to have been well into the afternoon by now.

"Do you need more water?" he asked Wes, swallowing the sticky dryness that filled his throat. Whatever his friend wanted, he hoped that he could get it done quickly. Suddenly he was sure that he could sleep all the way through until tomorrow. The fisherman would continue to check on them and bring them food, Kessara was safe with her guards, and he wasn't any help to the dragons at the moment anyway.

"I need you to go downstairs and check on Aelrie," Wes whispered. Alder looked over at his bed, finding him staring up at the ceiling. "I lied, before. I don't feel well yet. I can't stop thinking about her, and I need your help."

Alder walked over to Wes' bed. "You need to be careful."

Wes rolled onto his side, his dark brown eyes staring at him so intensely that for a moment he wanted to shrink away.

"Whatever happened, she didn't mean to hurt me. She's on our side. You must believe that now."

"That's not what I'm talking about."

"What do you mean?"

His eyes were defiant.

For a second, Alder wished very much that he could slap him, could make him see sense. *She's an elf. You're a human. Any feelings you have for her are a useless fantasy. They can never be anything more.*

Instead, he cleared his throat, crossing his arms over his chest.

"Just be careful, that's all."

Without waiting for a reply, he made his way out into the hall, closing the door behind him. His legs felt shakier than he'd expected, but aside from that, he was alright. It was a miracle that he had not been severely injured after what he had attempted to do.

If I had died, it would have all been for nothing. Steel and gunpowder cannot destroy such an evil. Aelrie saved my life, too. All of us. I just wish I understood how.

Pushing the thoughts from his mind, he made his way into the kitchen and rooted around in a cupboard until he found a fresh mug. It was a nice enough house, he thought, simple and comfortable, and it had been very kind of the fisherman to allow him and his friends to use it as a makeshift infirmary. Here, at least, neither foe nor friend would bother them.

Filling the cup with water from the clay pitcher on the table, he opened the cellar door and headed down the narrow stairs, careful to grasp the railing with his free hand.

"Aelrie?" he called out before the room came into view, not wishing to catch her in an immodest position. There was no reply, and he figured that she was probably still asleep.

As he made his way down the final steps, he could see the small cot in the corner, made up neatly with a dark blue blanket. A pair of matching slippers rested on the stone floor next to it, lined up tidily.

And then he saw Aelrie, her back to him, standing on a chair and shoving open a small window.

"What are you doing?" he cried out. She straightened quickly, as though he'd startled her, but Alder dismissed this immediately.

An injured man on clumsy legs does not surprise an elf. And certainly not when I announce my presence ahead of time.

"I'm leaving, Alder," she said, not turning around. He watched as she fiddled with the window, her dainty silver fingers turning screws and prying out a piece of board that had been shoved into the top to keep it shut. "Admittedly, this window is a tad small."

KESSARA

Before Kessara could react, she found herself pressed against her father's burly chest, inhaling the familiar scent of rum, clean wool, and the slightest hint of fish that was somehow pleasant. She smiled, blinking away the tears that sprang to her eyes before he could notice them. Despite all that she and her friends had accomplished, her own war was far from won. She could not afford to appear weak, especially not with Captain Drohma looking on.

She pulled back, giving Drohma a quick nod as she gestured for the men to enter the office. It was simple—nothing like their opulent quarters back home—but comfortable enough. Captain Drohma eased into a chair, his back as straight as the plain wooden walls, and her father followed suit.

Feeling rather foolish, she stepped behind the mayor's large, polished desk and sat down. *The King should be sitting here, not the Princess. But this time, he has failed to lead. I suppose it's fitting.*

She caught an amused smirk on Captain Drohma's face, but she gave him only a sweet smile in return, hoping that she exuded her usual calm confidence. Her reputation would be up in flames soon enough, but she may as well maintain control while she could.

"I should have listened to you, darling," her father said, leaning back in his chair and rubbing his brow with his fingers.

"No," Kessara replied, shaking her head. "You should have listened to your subjects when they told you that danger was near. They tried to warn us. They were afraid for good reason, and you dismissed it as silly superstition."

"It was impossible to verify the truth of what these peasants believed they saw," Captain Drohma cut in. She suppressed the urge to glare. "In any case, the attack could have been much worse. The beast is dead, the elves are dead, and no slavers have come to pick over the town."

"Yet," Kessara muttered, just loud enough for them to hear.

She was surprised by Drohma's reaction. The Red Army had lost many men in the battle—far more than the Galeharbor forces had—and she'd been expecting him to berate her father. She'd planned on being able to defend the King from the Captain's attack, in hopes of getting back into his good graces before she ruined everything again. Now, she could not be sure of what the Aridmoorian's angle was, and it set her on edge.

Still, she found it hard to disagree with the Captain. Even without the aid of their navy, the battle had been won. How it was won, however, still troubled her.

She swallowed, trying to push aside thoughts of Aelrie for the time being. There would be time to second-guess recent events later. She couldn't take back what she'd done, and in the end, she'd saved countless lives. Kessara had to trust the good in that.

"Nevertheless," her father said after a pause, nodding to Drohma. "I wish to request that reinforcements be called back to our coast, and that some of those reinforcements be Galeharbor navy ships. We cannot offer so many troops to the Red Army if it means leaving our people without defenders."

"But, Your Majesty, the Gorok is gone," Drohma protested. "Surely you do not wish to threaten our position of strength in the West Strait to soothe the sleep of fishermen's wives?"

"The elves were part of this attack, Captain," Kessara said.

"The people of Galeharbor will not sit here waiting for a fresh assault as our navy defends those who reside across the continent."

"She's right, Drohma," her father said, looking over at her with a disapproving tilt of his thick brows. "The two of us were present in Windshear when the Blackmasks launched their initial attack. Our own people were carried off."

"Just because no bandits or slavers are here now does not mean that none will arrive," Kessara added with a pang of guilt. She knew that it was disrespectful to speak over the king, but she was glad that her father was on her side for the moment.

Not that it's going to last much longer.

"I will of course pass on the message to King Ursa, Your Majesty," Captain Drohma said, giving her father a slight bow while still remaining in his seat. "But that is no guarantee that he will agree to your terms."

"Then tell him to come to the palace himself to negotiate," Kessara said, unable to keep her voice from shaking. Who was Kylan Ursa to hold the Kingdom of Galeharbor beneath his thumb? Allowing him to gain so much control over Kaveryth was a mistake. It always had been. But for the moment, until their own small force in Auranth constituted a real counterweight to his power, they would have to do the best they could with what they had.

"But Princess, he is—"

"That will be all, Captain," her father said, getting to his feet. "Please inform the King of our concerns, and tell him that I will send another messenger to arrange formal negotiations as soon as possible."

Drohma stood, giving her father a smile that looked more

like a grimace, his lips pinched tightly shut.

"Thank you, Captain," she said, realizing as the words left her lips that she meant it. "You fought bravely, as did your men. Despite our many quarrels, we are undoubtedly in your debt."

Captain Drohma said nothing else, giving only a bow before leaving the room.

Her father pushed the door closed behind him, and for a moment, the two of them sat in awkward silence, listening until the thumping sound of his boots disappeared down the hall.

"Father," she started as he sat back down in his chair, unsure what else to say. The room was quiet again. She found a long mark on the desk in front of her and began to trace it with her fingernail, listening to the sounds of the sea outside, waiting.

"It's time," her father said, leaning over the desk until he was barely a foot away from her. She could see every detail of his tanned face, noticing fresh sunspots that she had never noticed before. He looked even older than he had the last time she'd seen him, as though the stress of a single day could be written in wrinkles upon a man's face. "We can't wait any longer."

She knew that his words should have brought anxiety, but somehow, the feeling did not come. She resisted the urge to turn around and to walk out onto the balcony, wanting nothing more than to stare at the movement of the waves, steady and secure despite all that had happened. Her father used to say that the sea was a mistress immovable in her madness, and now she knew how right he had been.

"I doubt King Ursa is going to be willing to negotiate,

Kessara," he said, shaking his head. "You know that. And we need more soldiers to protect Galeharbor."

"Mmm," she said, feeling the wounded wood of the desk beneath her fingertips as she traced the mark again and again. Nothing he said surprised her. She had known all along that this tide was coming for her, ready to pull her away from the one she loved. She had faced this reality before, more than once. And yet, repetition and time did not quell the pain.

"We need Silverfell's army, Kessara. We need a queen. And I see no other than you who can take up the crown."

Kessara forced air into her lungs.

"My friends could have died last night. Died defending our Kingdom, because our own soldiers were not here to do so. Because you let them go out there to become Kylan's minions."

"Kessara—"

"*I* could have died, father!" she snapped. "And now you come here to tell me that it's time for me to give up my life, my freedom, all to fix your mistakes?"

"That's not fair," he said, his blue eyes flashing with anger. "Galeharbor has been at risk long before this whole mess with the Gorok and the elves."

"Perhaps our Kingdom has been in danger for so long because you have failed to lead as you should."

The words were unfair, and untrue besides, but she couldn't seem to stop them from pouring out. She had endured so much hurt. Perhaps it was time for someone else to bear the same burden.

"I know that a lot has happened," her father said calmly, clenching and unclenching his white-knuckled fists against his lap. "And I know that a lot of responsibility has been placed upon your shoulders. But that is the lot of a princess. To do what is right for your people is your duty. You of all people should be able to remember that."

"I watched the man I love jump from a dragon's back to attempt to kill a sea monster last night," she spat, pressing her fingers into the wood of the desk. The rage was unstoppable now, boiling over like a forgotten kettle, hissing and shrieking. "I thought that he was dead. I felt that pain. And I wasn't there waiting for him, because I had to slit an elf's throat to protect our people."

She gripped the edge of the desk with shaking fingertips. She could still imagine the feeling of the knife in her hand.

"I know that our men should have been there. I know I was wrong–"

"And yet you're here, accusing me of not knowing my duty to my Kingdom and my people," she said. Tears broke free, rolling down her cheeks. She did not wipe them away.

"Kessara–"

"No, father."

She got to her feet and leaned across the desk, her face inches from his, their eyes locked on one another, unblinking.

She wanted him to see her.

She wanted him to hear every cruel word she had to say to him.

"I'm done listening to you. I have my flaws. I live with them every day. But at least I'm not a pathetic old coward like you."

The King opened his mouth to speak, but no words came.

"And in case it wasn't clear," she continued. "My answer is no. I will not marry Wes Cervos."

Her father stared at her for a moment, his face going red, his eyes wild.

She did not flinch beneath his gaze. For a terrible moment, she thought that he would reach across the desk and strike her.

Instead, he spoke, his voice calm.

"Fine. You will get out of this office and you will leave this city. You will no longer use your title. As of now, in the eyes of the House of Manta and all of our subjects, you are nothing but a commoner."

WES

Wes stared at the ceiling as he waited for Alder to return.

Time was passing slowly, and despite his concern over Aelrie, he found himself drifting off, lost in the space between sleep and waking. His thoughts wandered to the autumn feast. It would happen soon, he knew, though he had long since lost track of the exact date.

Captain Drohma was here. Perhaps he still is. Perhaps he will still capture me and drag me away to Umrym. Go against his diplomatic agreement with the King. Force me to fulfill the duties of the Envoy.

His fingers found the scar on his cheek.

Every time he touched it, even now, he felt a jolt of confusion. For so much of his life, it had been a reliable mark, the curving shape of a crescent moon beneath his fingertips. But that was gone now, gone with everything else that had ever felt normal or secure, swept away by the High One's plans for his life.

No. He won't seek me. Everything has changed now. All that remains of Dracodei worship is the greed of foolish men. Even the Septemvirate is gone.

Oria's words echoed in his mind. Elder Gunnan, Elder

Rahma, Elder Derden, Elder Qofi, all dead. Killed. His heart ached at the thought. Whatever evils these men had done, and their sins were many, it was still tragic to know their end. They never got a chance to change their course. And a long strand of history had been cut short with their lives. Only Elder Jate and Elder Bram could carry on now, if they were even still alive.

Was Elder Bram still in Stronghollow, living amid the ruins of his home, preparing for the Feast? Or was there truly more about the cranky old man that he did not see?

I have to know. I have to go to him.

He sat up in bed again, noticing that his head felt a little better. There was still no sign of Alder, and though he couldn't be sure of exactly how much time had passed, he was beginning to get worried. What was taking so long?

He blinked, swallowing the taste of half-sleep as he stretched his arms over his head. He did not want to stand yet, not without someone to aid him if he fell.

He tried not to think of her, tried to push away images of her beautiful face from his mind. She was fine. He knew she was. Even if trouble had somehow found them here, it would take more than a few angry villagers to harm her, anyway.

"As soon as I can get myself up without falling over, we will head to Auranth, stopping in Stronghollow along the way," he said aloud to himself, his voice sounding strange to his own ears after so much quiet. "We will move through the forest in secret. If my city is still besought with mobs and chaos, there will be no diplomatic protection for me now."

He retreated back into his thoughts, his words hanging in the silence.

It was a good enough plan, he supposed, or at least, no better one was springing to mind. He could not put off talking to Elder Bram any longer. He might be dead already, but he had to try. Nothing made sense, and perhaps in Stronghollow they would be able to get some answers.

They would have to be careful. Silverfell was the most religious of the Four Kingdoms, and he knew that his people did not approve of the upheaval that he and Celesyria had caused. There were some who would be more than willing to take him prisoner, eager to return the Envoy to his duties in hopes of putting an end to the chaos that had overtaken their lives.

"High One," he spoke aloud again, waiting for a moment as his words settled in the air of the dimly lit room. "I beg you, fulfill Your prophecy. Restore Your people, and rule over them. I do not know how much more destruction Kaveryth can bear."

Chapter Three

ALDER

"Aelrie, stop this," Alder said, taking a few steps forward and placing a hand on the elf's back. She tensed beneath his touch, but did not turn. For a moment, he feared that she would keep going, pushing through the window and out onto the street. It would be too late, then. He'd never be able to find her out in the open if she did not want to be found.

"You can't leave. It would destroy him," he said, taking a step back. She straightened again, as though she had been struck with a blow.

"You saw what I did."

"What do you mean?"

She said nothing for a moment, until she finally turned to face him, her eyes gleaming with fresh tears. Of course, unlike a human, she still looked perfect. There was no red around her eyes, no snot dribbling from her nose.

Alder thought of Kessara, the way that her whole face went red when she cried, her eyes puffy, her mouth grimacing.

Even so, in his eyes, the Princess was still more beautiful than any elf.

"You saw what happened when I killed the Gorok," she said.

"You used ice from the sea to imprison him," he replied, still unsure what she meant. "It was strange to watch, I'll admit, but it worked. You saved us all. You saved the people of Kingsvier Landing."

A ripple of jealousy coursed through him. He had tried to be the hero, but he had failed, and it had nearly cost him and Celesyria their lives—and that would have been the best case scenario, had the elf not stepped in.

"Exactly," Aelrie said, swiping at her tears with the back of her hand.

"I guess I don't understand why any of that would require you to run. Sure, the people here might be wary of you for a little while, but we can make them understand—"

"Alder," she said, her voice pleading. "What I did should have been impossible. It *is* impossible, by the natural laws of the High One."

"Of course. You used magic," he said, his mouth quirking into a smile before he could stop it. This was hardly a secret.

"Magic is of the Wrathlands, Alder," she snapped. "I had already made a promise to myself never to use it again. Worse, I made a promise to the High One. And last night, I broke it."

His smile fell away.

Though Aelrie had used magic for a good end, he understood why she was so afraid. Magic had always been looked on with deep suspicion in Kaveryth. It was a wicked power reserved to the elves, sought only by witches and other suspicious folk. Not even the powerful Guardians sought to wield it.

"This is no victory," she continued, gesturing toward the window and the city that lay beyond the glass. "Darkness cannot cast out darkness. The Gorok is dead, but we cannot yet know the final cost."

"Will he return?"

She shook her head. "I don't think so. But that doesn't mean that the evil forces of our world will not benefit from what I have done."

"Aelrie—" he started, unsure what comfort he could give.

"I betrayed everything that I have come to believe," she said, wiping away tears. "I am not worthy to stand beside you. I am not worthy to serve beside those who love the High One."

Alder stepped forward, reaching out to hug her before she could shrink away. For a moment, she stiffened at his touch, but then she allowed him to pull her close.

Perhaps it is I who should seek forgiveness. Despite all of the reasons I had to trust you, I chose doubt. I'm sorry.

"The High One will forgive you," he said instead. "You did what you did in a terrifying moment. You were trying to save your friends. We all understand, and the High One will too."

She breathed against his chest for a final moment before pulling away. The tears were coming faster now, the rivulets of saltwater pouring down her cheeks and onto the simple black tunic she wore.

"I hurt Wes," she said, her voice shaking. "I felt it as it happened. Even though I was lost in the darkness, I knew that he was on that ship. I could feel his worry. I couldn't open my eyes, but somehow I could see him. I wanted to tell him to get away, but I couldn't. It was like my body belonged to someone else, and I had no control of what was happening."

"He's alright—"

"I felt it when he touched me. And then I felt his pain, and the pain was coming from me!" she hissed under her breath, her voice thick with sobs. "I thought he was dead. It was like I could see the life fading from his eyes, but I couldn't make myself scream for help. I couldn't make myself move. It was the most horrible thing I have ever experienced."

"Aelrie—"

"I can never risk letting that happen again. I can't do it. I need to get away from here, far away, where I can't bring any more darkness to those I love."

He reached out a hand and rested it upon her shoulder, hoping to steady her. Her legs were shaking.

"He's okay, Aelrie. I promise you. I just spoke to him, and all he cared about was making sure that you're alright. That's why he woke me up to send me down here."

She glanced back at the half-opened window.

"You can't run, Aelrie. Not from your friends. And certainly not from the High One."

She shrugged his hand off her shoulders and moved forward, her fingertips gripping the base of the window as though she might vault herself through the glass.

"Where can you possibly go?"

"Anywhere but here."

"Aelrie. Stop," he pleaded. "You won't do it again. I know that you won't."

It was true. He had told Wes she was dangerous, and he meant it, but not because of this. Her remorse was clear, and he knew the High One would forgive her and give her strength. He just had to make her believe it.

She paused, letting go of the window with one hand and turning to face him. Her face remained impassive, but at least she was hesitating.

High One, give me the words. Please.

"You don't know that," she said finally, her voice breaking with sobs. "None of you know that, least of all Wes. He believed in me long before he had any business doing so, and look where it got him."

"It got him here, with another friend who is loyal to him, in a world where allies are hard to come by," Alder said, shaking his head. He wanted to rush toward her, to try and take hold of her so that she could not run, but it would be like trying to capture a dragonfly. She would slip through his fingers. He had to wait.

"Loyal friends don't hurt one another."

Alder couldn't help but to chuckle at that. "Don't be naive. All of us have hurt one another. Me, Kessara, even Celesyria. Not even to mention Jaconial and Nazzan. Celesyria forgave them even after they kidnapped her. Do you honestly think Wes will not forgive you for something you did by mistake?"

Aelrie leaned against the wall, her face a mask of pain. For a moment, he feared she would slip to the floor. He wanted to reach out to her, to say something that would bring comfort, but instead he waited.

Kessara would wait. And then she would know just what to say when the moment came to speak.

"I've been a part of so much darkness, Alder," she said finally, her voice scarcely above a whisper. "Some of it... I can't even bear to say it out loud. I'm not sure if I can ever leave it all behind. Part of me doesn't want to. Part of me knows where I want to go. Home. Back to the shadows where I was born to stay."

He could not understand how she felt, not really.

He had not known the High One for most of his life, but he had not lived as His enemy, either. Aelrie was different. By the logic of the world, she could not be here. It was impossible. And yet, she was.

"Thankfully, it's not about you," he said gently. He paused, half-expecting her to protest, but she said nothing. "The High One has given you the strength to turn to Him. He has given you the strength to flee evil and to choose good."

"So why don't I do what I should?" she asked, staring at her feet.

"What matters is not that you always do what you should," he said, speaking more quickly now, suddenly afraid that if he did not say his piece she would run again. "That would be great, but that's not a standard you can demand from yourself."

"The rest of you do what's right," she said, blinking away fresh tears. "You're good people. Celesyria isn't even human, and even she knows how to be good."

He found himself unable to argue with that particular point. The dragon really was the best of them, despite every disadvantage she faced. He had to make her see that she could do the same, too, even though she'd been born an elf. No one was beyond the reach of the High One.

"I don't always do what's right," he said, closing his eyes for a moment as though he could block out all of the times that he'd failed. He was far from innocent. Even after finding the High One, he had messed up again and again.

"So how do you keep going?" she asked.

"I say I'm sorry, I ask the High One for forgiveness, and I keep moving forward," he said firmly. "There is no secret to it, Aelrie. Sometimes it hurts. But you know as well as I do that suffering can be love."

She said nothing for a long time. Alder stared out of the window at the sliver of the city he could see, the afternoon sun casting rays of orange light on the cobblestones as it passed between the clouds.

"You have to let Him help you," he said, unable to bear another moment of the oppressive silence. "But if you can't do that right now, you need to at least talk to Wes. Don't leave him like this. Please."

"I was told to stay out of sight."

"I'll take care of it."

He extended a hand, and she took it, her silvery skin warm against his own. Despite the battle that they had just been through, her hands were perfectly clean, a far cry from his own dirt-caked fingers. He smiled as he turned and headed up the staircase, tugging her gently along.

He supposed there were certain kinds of magic that she could not control. She would always be beautiful. She would live longer than any of her friends. She would always move with inhuman grace. But perhaps, in time, she would accept what the High One had chosen for her.

They stopped in the kitchen before heading for the bedroom, fetching another mug of water for Wes. Just as they entered the room, however, Alder realized that they were not alone. Kessara stood next to Wes' bed, a haunted look in her eyes as she watched him come in.

KESSARA

"Thank the High One you're awake," she said softly to Wes, leaning over to give him a quick kiss on the cheek before straightening. "I'll be back soon, alright?"

She turned to Aelrie, knowing that it would be natural to smile, but finding it impossible to do so. Putting on a brave face for Wes had been difficult enough. She had nothing left to give the others.

Ever since she walked away from her father, she'd felt raw, as though her skin had been scoured by the waves of the sea. He was so close, just a few streets away, managing things from the mayor's office, taking her place.

She wanted to go back, to press herself into his sturdy chest, where everything had always been alright. However terrible the things she'd said were, he'd forgive her. But she could not say she was sorry. Not now.

"I need to talk to you," she whispered to Alder as Aelrie took a few careful steps toward Wes. She glanced over at the bed. She felt terrible leaving him now, but if she didn't walk away, she would not be able to contain the tears. Wes had enough to worry about without hearing about her problems.

They're his problems, too. You're supposed to be his wife, remember?

She ignored the nagging guilt.

"Are you alright?" Alder asked, his green eyes filled with concern.

By the Dracodei, he was perfect. Just looking at him was enough to set her heart beating faster, no matter the circumstances.

"Yes. We just... need to speak in private."

Alder gave Wes what she thought was a much-too-hard clap on the shoulder before following her out into the hall. Two Galeharborian royal guards were standing there near the door, no doubt having heard every word spoken within. Her father had presumably sent the men for Wes' benefit, though it seemed that they had not yet been made aware of her new status as a shunned commoner.

As she made for the front door of the little house, they followed, awaiting her royal orders.

"I'll take care of her," Alder said, standing up at his full height and looking rather imposing.

"Please stay here. No one is to disturb the Envoy until the Princess and I return from the beach."

One of the guards caught her eye, and she gave him an approving nod.

"Please do as he says," she said quickly, pushing open the door. "And try to find him something decent to eat."

They walked together in silence, making their way toward the shore. The sun was moving close to the horizon now, leaving the fishing district aglow with soft orange light, but Kessara hardly noticed its beauty. Alder's presence was as intoxicating as ever, his hand swinging as he walked mere inches from her own, but she did not dare to touch him, not with so many heavy words waiting to be spoken.

"I hope the people are alright," she said after a while, glancing over at the stairs that headed up the cliffs. There were several wealthy-looking merchants squabbling near the bottom step, and Alder gestured toward them.

"I would have thought they would all have fled by now," he said, giving her a tight smile. "What happened here can't be good for business."

"Maybe they're more committed to their home city than you think," she suggested, returning his smile. "Or maybe they're just counting their coins now that half of their competitors have been run out of town."

They lapsed into silence again as they made their way onto the beach. The coastline looked different than it had only a day before, and the thought made Kessara's heart ache. Everything in Kaveryth was changing, and deep down she knew that it would never be the same again. Not even cliffs of stone were exempt.

"What did you want to discuss?" Alder said, reaching over as though to touch her hand before drawing his fingertips quickly away again. A gust of cold air blew across the sea as she moved to speak, shushing the words she had intended to say.

"Autumn comes fast in Galeharbor," she said instead, refusing to meet his eyes. "Especially by the sea."

He said nothing, continuing to walk beside her, his boots making a trail of prints in the wet sand. She drew a breath and reached out to touch his arm. He did not pull away, and she managed to hold her chin up, looking into his green eyes as he glanced down at her. Her stomach turned.

I want this moment to be a happy one. I want to kiss you and mean it.

His eyes searched hers, his brows drawn together with worry. "Kessara, something's wrong. I can tell. You need to tell me."

She shook her head, annoyed at the unwelcome sob that was rising in her throat. She knew that this was not going to be a moment for butterflies and happy endings. Not yet. But there was no way that she could turn back now.

She glanced back at the city, imagining her father there in the mayor's office, looking out at the little world that he held in the palm of his hand. Anger coursed through her, propelling her forward. She took Alder's hand, relishing the comfort of his warm skin.

"I talked to my father," she said, the words coming out only a little above a whisper.

"Did he apologize for getting us all into this mess?" Alder asked. His tone was light, but Kessara could see that his smile did not reach his eyes.

"Yes, but that's not..." she trailed off, looking down at the sand beneath her feet, unsure how to put her thoughts into words.

There is no right way to say it.

"I told my father that I cannot marry Wes Cervos," she blurted out, before she could lose her nerve. "I will marry you, whatever the consequences will be."

CELESYRIA

Celesyria dropped another piece of stone into the sea with a satisfying splash as Jaconial did the same at her right. She pumped her wings a few times as she banked to the left, examining the remaining pile of rubble as she moved in to land.

"Do you think we're close?" Nazzan said aloud as she and Jaconial hit the ground, their claws leaving long marks in the dirt as they came to a stop. Celesyria smiled as she glanced at the remaining stone, wood, and pieces of bent metal.

"It will take us only another half hour or so. And I think my estimate is accurate this time."

They had been working in the same spot for hours, and all three of them were growing tired. They had not yet gotten to rest, but Celesyria was thankful that the ships would be able to make it to the safety of port tonight.The people of this town had lost too much already. They would just have to keep going.

All of a sudden, Jaconial stopped what she was doing, letting a long gray board slip from her claws and clatter to the ground. She sniffed the air, looking across the sea and then behind her.

"What's wrong, my love?" Nazzan asked, taking a few steps closer to her and looking in the same direction that she faced.

Jaconial shook her head.

"Nothing, I guess," she said, giving the others a pained smile. "I'm imagining things."

"Trust your instincts," Celesyria said, glancing around the harbor. She saw a few men moving a stack of fishing crates, and a young girl dragging a long rope into a neat coil, but nothing that seemed out of place.

"I just feel off, all of a sudden," Jaconial said. "That's all. There's a strange taste on the wind."

Celesyria reached out to Wes in her mind.

"Are you okay?"

"Fine. I'm feeling much better. Alder and Kessara went outside to talk, and Aelrie is here with me."

She paused, not wanting to tell him what she thought of the two pairs being alone together. Only a fool could miss the attraction that flowed between them, not to mention the small fact that Aelrie had nearly killed him by mistake the last time that they were in close proximity.

"Just tell me if anything changes, ok?"

The dragons returned to their work, moving more quickly now, all three of them eager to be finished. Every few seconds, Jaconial stopped, staring off into the distance, closing her eyes as each breath of chilly air rolled over them. Celesyria eyed the sea periodically, half expecting the Gorok to break free of his prison and attack, but there was no sign of movement.

Finally, Nazzan spoke.

"If you two can finish this up, I'll do a quick pass over the city to make sure everything is well."

Celesyria readily agreed, forcing herself to look back at the remaining detritus rather than out at the sea. A familiar pang of jealousy washed over her as Jaconial and Nazzan touched snouts, whispering gentle goodbyes together before Nazzan leapt into the sky.

He was majestic when he flew, his green scales reminding her of an emerald that Gramnok had once shown her from the mines deep beneath Whitespire.

Gramnok.

The thought of her fallen friend brought a new kind of heartache. He had done a terrible thing to protect her, and she still did not know why. He had left a mystery behind along with her grief, a nagging desire to understand that would probably never be fulfilled.

Only the High One can fill the empty spaces in my heart. I need to learn to be content with Him. Nothing else is permanent. Nothing else is promised.

She glanced over at Jaconial, who had thrown herself back into their task with renewed enthusiasm. Even though the High One was enough, she was thankful to be blessed with friends, especially those who she had never expected.

I will do everything I can to protect them. Even unto death.

Chapter Four

ALDER

Alder gripped Kessara's hand more tightly.

She had spoken, had told him the words that he'd longed to hear for so long, but he couldn't bear to think of what they meant. It hurt too much.

She was here, standing beside him, her blonde hair brushing against his shoulders as the wind caught it. The gentle waves were falling against the shore beside them, gently shushing the approaching dusk, obscuring every other sound but the beating of his heart.

He knew that he was moving, but it was as though someone else was in control of his limbs as he reached out to her, pressing his free hand gently to her cheek, pulling her in. Some sane part of his mind was screaming at him, telling him that someone might see them, telling him that this was all a lie, but he did not listen. He had no discipline left. Finally, after all of the battles he had fought, he could not help but to surrender.

He pressed his lips into hers, feeling her fingertips tangling in his hair, her warm body comforting against the cold breeze that rushed against them. Time stopped, and he felt himself getting lost, falling deeper into the kiss, hungry for all that he had denied himself for so long.

He couldn't bring himself to care who saw them, or the consequences that tomorrow would bring. There was sand, there was space, there was *her*, looking more beautiful than he'd ever imagined that even she could.

Her hands found his chest, and he moved closer, pulling at her hair—

Somewhere inside him a voice was calling, screaming across a vast distance, desperate to get his attention. He let his hands fall and pulled away, glancing over his shoulder, suddenly aware of just how many people roamed the streets nearby.

"Alder?" Kessara was saying. Her face was crumpled with hurt, but he took a few steps back, kicking at a stray seashell with his boot, staring out at the sea.

If he looked at her now, he knew that he wouldn't be able to stop.

He didn't answer, instead taking a moment to draw several slow breaths. His mind was returning to him, but his body was still waiting, expecting things that he had no right to desire.

"What in the Wrathlands is wrong with you?" she spat.

The anger in her voice surprised him. He turned to look at her. She stood with her back to the sea, her blue eyes flashing with anger, but there were no tears in them. She looked like some kind of sea goddess, freed from the prison of the deep, wild and furious.

"Kessara, what are we doing?"

"I told you. We can be together."

He curled his hands into fists before opening them again, noticing for the first time since he'd woken up how painful they still were. His entire body still hurt, and yet, he had almost...He shook his head. This was madness. This was dangerous.

"Another kiss," he said, shaking his head. "Another promise that I cannot keep. Forgive me."

"I told you," Kessara said, stepping forward and tilting her face up to look at him. "I talked to my father. I told him that I'm done. I'm free. *We're* free."

Her words seemed to echo between his ears, pulling him back to the present moment, away from the longings and daydreams that held him adrift.

"This isn't freedom!" he snapped. "We have a duty to our people. You know that better than even I do. You can't just decide that you're not going to uphold your end of the deal."

"You chose to serve your country. I was born with this burden," she replied, raising her voice. He tried to escape her gaze, but she would not step away. "I don't want it. Not anymore. Certainly not more than I want to spend the rest of my life with you."

"Kessara. You know that we can't do this," he said, catching her eye for a moment before quickly looking away. He couldn't bear to see her pain. "It was a dream. That's all it ever was."

He forced himself to remain calm, but inside, he could feel himself breaking.

He knew the words to be true, he always had, but every time that he admitted to himself that there would be no happy ending for the two of them he felt as though his heart would shatter in two.

"It doesn't have to be."

"Yes it does," he said firmly. "Wes needs to keep the House of Cervos alive. You need the ability to rule Silverfell's men. *Galeharbor* needs it. There is no other way."

"Don't you think I know the stakes?" she said, wiping the back of her hand across her eyes. Her cheeks were becoming red and splotchy, but still she did not cry. "I'm not some spoiled child, Alder. Don't you dare accuse me of ignorance. I've spent weeks–months–of my life thinking this over. I'm not some foolish girl who fell for a handsome soldier on a whim."

"I never said that," he said, trying to match her rising anger with calm.

He glanced over his shoulder at the city, glad to see that many of the people seemed to have retreated inside as the sun drew closer to the horizon, the wind hissing faster as though racing to meet the approaching night.

She followed his gaze, saying nothing for several long moments.

There were so many words of comfort that he wanted to offer her, but he knew that they would ring hollow. There was nothing in this world that could take her pain or her burden, and he knew it.

Worse, she knew it.

"I am not strong enough," she said finally, her voice breaking as she swallowed a sob. "I cannot marry a man that I do not love. My father cannot ask me to live this lie for one more day. Neither can you. It's cruel."

"You watched as a sea monster nearly destroyed this town," he reminded her. "You watched as elves swarmed the shores of your Kingdom, ready to kill anyone they saw. Without you and Wes, this will be the reality. This is not what you want."

"Kylan's army is strong. He will resist it. And our men in Auranth will do everything they can."

"It won't be enough, Kessara."

Anger filled her red-rimmed eyes again, but this time, he did not shift his gaze away.

"Do you really think that this is what the High One wants, Alder? Deceit? Deception? A mockery of love?"

He looked down at her, watching the steady rise and fall of her chest as she breathed, imagining her heart racing somewhere within, driving her forward.

She was the most determined woman he had ever met. He wanted to believe her. Wanted to convince himself that everything she said was right. And part of it was.

Love was the highest truth that there could be. He'd understood that ever since the High One first spoke to him in a dream.

But this is not true love. We're the ones who are lying.

"The High One wants us to do the right thing. He wants us to think of others before we think of ourselves."

"You can't do this to me," she pleaded, pressing her head against his chest. Everything in him wanted to wrap his arms around her again, to stop her pain, but he did not move.

High One, give me the strength to truly love her.

"I told my father that I would not marry Wes. It's too late. He told me that I am no longer welcome in Windshear, that I may no longer use my royal title. I'm a commoner in his eyes."

She was crying now, her tears soaking the front of his tunic. He wanted to cry with her. How could she have done something so foolish?

King Manta will take her back. I know he will.

He drew a breath as she continued to sob, his arms hanging uselessly at his sides as he glanced down at the top of her blonde head. He could hold her. He could make everything alright for the moment. But it would destroy her in the end.

It would destroy them both.

She's too stubborn. There is no other way.

"You're right, Kessara," he said, swallowing a sob of his own. "It is too late."

She looked up at him, her brow wrinkling with confusion. "What—"

"I don't love you. Not anymore. Not like I used to."

The words came out in a rush, before he could convince himself to stop.

"That's a lie," she spat. "I thought you were all about wanting to do what the High One asks. Last I checked, he does not appreciate dishonesty."

And I will bear my own sins if it means you are free to live in truth.

"It's the truth, Kessara. You had to have felt it. My feelings for you have shifted lately. You've changed. You're not the woman that I thought you were."

"So why did you kiss me?"

"Because I couldn't be sure of my feelings. I had to kiss you one more time. I had to know. I'm sorry."

She brought her hand to her mouth. Fresh tears were spilling from her eyes, and rolling down her cheeks. She did not brush them away.

Her eyes looked almost as gray as the water.

She stared at him, and in that moment, he knew that he had won.

Somewhere deep down, a part of her believed.

"You almost took everything from me, just to prove to yourself that you didn't want me after all?"

The words came in slow bursts, punctuated by sobs.

He felt sick. Even though he was lying for her own sake, he'd never felt worse about himself in his life. It was just a kiss, and yet, it wasn't. Not in their hearts. They had come far closer to the edge than he ever should have allowed, and it was his fault. His responsibility.

"I'm sorry, Kessara," he said. "I shouldn't have—"

"It doesn't matter," she replied, wiping at her eyes with the back of her hand. "I'm still not marrying Wes. My father can abandon me if he likes. I'm done."

"That's your problem, I guess," he said, forcing himself to sound as dismissive as possible. "I suspect you'll go crying to your dad soon enough."

She narrowed her eyes at him, but the expression of fury did little to mask the depth of her hurt.

He felt all of it, and it made him feel sick, but it was the only way.

I have to keep going.

I have to make her believe it.

"I shouldn't have kissed you. I already knew what I needed to know, as soon as you told me that you weren't marrying Wes. Choosing your own selfishness over what is right for your people? I'm sorry, Kessara. That's the final straw. It tells me everything I need to know about the person you've become."

"Alder—"

"You are spoiled, stubborn, and selfish, just as I feared. And I want nothing else to do with you."

"Wait, don't do this!" she said, trying to move closer to him, to press her body into his chest again, but he stepped out of her way.

Without another word, he turned around and began to walk

up the beach. Near the harbor, he could see the dragons continuing to move their pile of rubble. He did not dare to look over his shoulder, but he did not hear Kessara following behind him.

He reached into the pocket of his trousers and felt the envelope he had hidden there.

There was no time to pity himself, no time to sit around and mourn the death of the love that he had foolishly hoped for until the last desperate kiss.

He had other matters to attend to.

I will go to Boneshire, and I will find Holga.

If Kessara refuses to be Queen of Silverfell, we'll need our lost queen more than ever.

Chapter Five

WES

"Wes," Aelrie said, taking a tentative step toward his bed. He flinched before he could stop himself, expecting the terrible pounding in his head to surge again, but the pain did not come. He searched the elf's blue eyes, hoping that she had not noticed that he had shrunk away from her.

"You're okay," he said, trying in vain to prop himself up comfortably on his pillows. He felt much better, but his body still protested his every movement. Healing would take time, but he doubted he would have the luxury. His life had a way of marching on, even when he desperately wanted a chance to slow down and breathe.

"Of course I'm okay," she said, the corners of her lips turning up in a sad smile. "I wasn't hurt. It was the magic that made me faint, I suppose. Not that I understood it."

She was rambling, and he found this fact oddly comforting. She looked so uncomfortable standing there, twisting her silver fingers around a thick strand of her long black hair. In fact, were it not for the tone of her smooth skin, he might have said she was actually blushing.

You're the beautiful one. I'm the fool who can't take his eyes off of you. What rejection do you have to fear?

When he had been a little younger and a lot pudgier, he'd always imagined that beautiful people did not share his anxieties. He'd assumed that in some distant future where he was fit and handsome, all of the difficulties of his life would fade away.

Things had turned out very differently.

"Anyway," Aelrie said, clearing her throat and giving him another pinched smile. "As I explained to Alder, I'm leaving. I only came to say goodbye."

The pain came all at once, racing through him like a reckless flame, but this time, it was not behind his eyes. His chest felt tight, and he found it difficult to breathe.

"Leave? What—you—you can't leave!" he stammered, forgetting to feel embarrassed by his usual clumsiness with words. "Why would you even say something like that?"

She glanced over at the door as a terrible silence filled the room.

Beyond the window panes, Wes could hear the North Sea whispering to the city as the sun sank away beneath the horizon. Night was near. She couldn't leave now. Surely he'd be able to convince her to wait until morning, at the very least.

For a moment, he thought that she might walk away without another word, but instead she turned, her sad eyes lingering on his own. Even though she still looked immaculate, Wes knew that she had been crying.

A part of him wanted to get out of his bed, to go over to where she stood, and to hold her. He could comfort her. He could make her stay.

But another part of him held him back. Her proximity did not seem to be having any effect now, but that didn't mean he was in the clear. Even if her presence was not a physical threat, he knew that she was dangerous in another way.

He thought of Kessara and Alder, off on their own, speaking words that they would not be able to take back. He could not let the same thing happen to him and Aelrie. He had a marriage and a future to think about.

She took a couple of steps toward him then, until she stood at the foot of the bed, a few inches away, giving him an expectant glance.

He shook his head. He felt no worse than he had a moment ago.

"You've been having headaches a lot, haven't you? I mean, before last night."

Wes sat up straighter, knotting his fingers in the sheets so that he would not rub at his temples. There was no point in denying it. He had been hiding his secret malady for too long, and he realized now that there would never be an easier time to admit to it. Revealing his weakness was going to hurt, no matter what he did.

"Yes. They started a couple of months ago, and they've been getting worse since."

He let out a sigh, feeling a surprising surge of relief. The secret was no longer his to bear alone. Aelrie, however, looked distraught, pacing back and forth at the foot of his bed, a pained expression marring her delicate features.

"I had suspected as much. I wish you'd—"

"The headaches came long before the Gorok. Which is why, among other reasons, that this—" he gestured to the bed "—is not your fault."

I was already weak.

He wanted to say the words, but he could not make them come out. No matter how much he'd been through, no matter how strong he looked on the outside, he knew that deep down he was still the same person he'd always been. Weak. Broken.

For a moment, Aelrie said nothing, her gaze landing on his, unwavering. He imagined what she was thinking. Did she feel the same guilt that he carried with him every day?

Did she fear the same brokenness?

"I almost left once already, before we got to Kingsvier Landing. Back at the palace."

He tried to conceal his surprise.

"Why?"

She glanced at the door again, but at least she had stopped pacing. Her eyes searched his own, and he could sense a question there, though he could not read what it was.

"I just want to understand," he added, shuffling forward in his bed so that he sat only inches from where she stood. "If you're going to leave like this, I need to know why. And I need you to know that I'm not angry about what happened. What's done is done. You made a choice, and we're all alive right now because of it. The rest can be mended."

He felt heat rising to his cheeks as he blathered on. Even as she sat there, glancing at her escape route every few seconds, battling with her own demons, he found himself turning into the same bumbling fool he always became in her presence.

"It's not because of what happened," she said finally, looking down at her feet. "I was listening to you and Kessara. You were talking on her balcony."

Wes felt as though he should have been angry at her for spying on him, but no anger came. Instead, he felt only sadness. He waited for her to continue, dreading what she would say. Dreading what it would mean.

"I knew that you and Kessara are to marry soon, and I

couldn't bear it!" she said, nearly shouting. Wes sucked in a breath. He had never seen her like this before, but he made no attempt at calming her. He wanted to know everything, every painful detail.

"I couldn't stand the thought of losing you," she continued, her eyes pleading. She reached out a hand as though she wanted to touch him, but she drew away before he could meet her fingers with his own. "I couldn't imagine watching you be with another person, even Kessara. Even though I know it's right. The temptation to run from the pain was so strong."

Despite everything else that he knew he should feel, hope coursed through him, wild and stupid and dangerous.

She feels the same way I do.

She cares for me, as something more than a friend.

He extended a hand toward her. This time, she did not pull away. He felt only bliss as their fingers touched, and he moved out of the way so that she could sit beside him, his heart hammering all the while.

"You can't leave," he said again. "There is nothing for you in Nox. You know that."

"And yet, I dream of it," she said, her voice a whisper. "I'm a terrible person. How could anyone be tempted by such a wicked place? By such a life? There is nothing for me there but darkness... just look at you! I could have killed you!"

She was crying now, great sobs wracking her body. Wes wanted desperately to hold her, to tell her that she was not terrible, that everything was going to turn out in the end, but instead he drew his hand away.

Kessara was out there somewhere. Whatever his secret hopes for a different future, her heart was his responsibility. He had already done enough to hurt her and Aelrie both.

"It was an accident. And I'm fine now. I promise, I am not upset with you."

"Don't you understand?" she asked, drawing her knees up toward her chest and hugging them with her slender arms as she choked back another sob. "The things you have seen barely touch the surface. Despite the approaching war, despite the bandits, despite all of it, Kaveryth is still bright. You've never seen Nox. The evil that is being perpetuated by my race..."

She paused, trying to draw air as she cried, tears staining the tops of her knees as she curled up into a ball like a child. Wes placed a hand on her shoulder and lifted her chin, forcing her to meet his eyes.

They paused there, a moment of impossible longing rising within him despite the sorrow. He let his fingers fall away from her face.

"You are not your people," he said firmly. "You have chosen another path."

"And yet, I am tempted to return to them. Even now. It's like there's this thread tying me to them, and no matter how hard I try to break it, I can't get free. And it grows stronger every time I harness the darkness, even in the smallest ways. After I defeated the Gorok, the temptation became more powerful than it has ever been before."

She paused, drawing another ragged breath. The tears were slowing now, as though the hurricane that had raged through her heart had finally passed by.

"Even now, at this very moment, all I want is to surrender. To go to them. And I hate myself for it."

"Aelrie, please, you can't beat yourself up like this," he said, feeling very much like he might begin to cry himself.

Outside, he could hear the wind picking up, and he wondered halfheartedly if the rest of his friends were alright. Time seemed to have stopped for him, but the battle was not over. He had to make her understand.

"I deserve death. How can you deny it?"

"We all deserve death, Aelrie," he said, his words coming out a little more harshly than he meant them, but she did not shrink away. "We all have turned from the High One, in one way or another. Why do we deserve to live at all, if we are not living for our maker?"

"I want to live for Him. But then there's this other part of me that wants to go back. Life in Nox was evil, but at least it didn't hurt so much," she said, her voice breaking on the final words as she looked down at the quilt resting across her lap.

"Everyone is tempted. And some of us are given lives more fraught with temptations than others. The High One never promises that we will not feel that temptation, but He does promise that He will give us the strength we need to overcome it."

For a long while, she did not reply. She stared over at the curtained window, lost in her own wonderings.

Wes could hear the sea growing louder, and the final strands of sunlight that broke into the room along the edges of the curtained windows were scarcely enough to light the space. Still, he did not want to move.

Despite everything, being here with her felt right. And though he had learned long ago that feelings were not often to be trusted, he couldn't bring himself to want anything else. Her very presence was a magic all its own.

"Wes," she started, her voice calmer now, the sobs quieted. "I can't bear the weight of these evils by myself. I need to let them go before they break me. I...I wish I had your strength."

A bitter chuckle escaped his lips. "I've been feeling so sick for weeks that some mornings I can barely stand. And yet I've been too afraid to tell anyone about it because I can't even bear the thought of appearing weak, let alone actually becoming the weak boy I used to be. My strength is pride and stupidity. It's nothing to admire."

"Like I said, I wish you would have told us sooner. We can help you."

Wes shook his head. "I have my suspicions about their cause. I don't think anything can be done."

Aelrie sucked in a breath. "The water."

He nodded. "Not long after the spring Feast. I was in the Dread Ruins, in Boneshire, and I drank. Celesyria and the two children with us drank, too. Celesyria has been fine, but I'm not sure about the little ones."

He felt a pang of guilt. Holga was the lost queen of Boneshire, so it turned out, and he may have been responsible for poisoning her and her brother.

Because Kaveryth just doesn't have enough problems.

"I'm sorry," Aelrie said, rubbing at her temples as though she had just gotten a sudden headache of her own. "Like most of the evils on this continent, you can thank the elves for that."

"So it is a curse?"

He had heard various rumors in Auranth about the water sickness being caused by some kind of curse or dark magic, but most of it had sounded like nothing more than foolish superstition. While Kessara seemed to believe in such things, he dismissed them out of hand. Now, he wondered if he should have used the potion that the herbwoman had given to them long ago.

She nodded. "It was done back during the Boneshire wars, though by now the water has spread throughout the Four Kingdoms."

"And I had the good fortune of drinking right from the fount of darkness," he joked.

"Pretty much," she said, returning his grin. By the Dracodei, it was good to see her smile.

"If this happened over two hundred years ago, why does it only seem to be hurting people now?"

She shook her head. "Humans think in such short stretches of time. Dwarves, too. But for dragons and elves, decisions are made that stretch forward for hundreds of years. A single stone dropped into a pond can change the future, if you look far enough ahead."

"What does the curse do, exactly? Aside from making me feel awful all the time?"

"At the time of the Boneshire war, the elves hoped to win control of the territory. They wanted to bring the darkness of the Wrathlands into Kaveryth. Of course, they were pushed back by the dragon Guardians, but to them, it was not a true defeat. Their plan was still in place. They got their way, really, if you look around Kaveryth. The darkness is here."

Wes turned over her words in his mind, but he could not make sense of it.

"Humans are not as smart as elves. You're gonna have to explain this one to me."

"The elves couldn't take over by force," she said, a sad smile rising to her lips. "So they did something that would weaken the enemy in the future."

"Wait," he said, realization dawning. "The curse makes humans more susceptible to elf magic."

She nodded, her smile falling away.

He leaned back, lost in thought, as he considered the events of the past few months. Some of it made sense, but much of it he still did not understand.

"The water makes humans sensitive to evil, evil of all kinds, but especially the sort of darkness my race draws their strength from. For many who have drank it, they simply die when they are exposed to evil of any kind. For a few though, for those who are strong–I have now come to believe that the protection of the High One plays a large part–the effect of the curse can be resisted," Aelrie said, glancing over at Wes. "It's really a strange curse. In some ways, I suppose, it's doing you all a favor. Perhaps if more humans had despised the sight of evil, we would never have gotten to this point in the first place.

"So, in other words, I am able to bear–with a great deal of pain–much of the evil that is creeping into our world, but you drawing dark power right next to me was enough to…"

He let the words fade away. There was no point in making her feel more guilty than she already did. He could have told her about the headaches long ago. Perhaps now, with the right knowledge, he could find a way to endure them. At least that was something.

Aelrie nodded, tears springing to her eyes once more.

"So do you see now why I wish to leave?"

"I thought it was to soothe your heart."

"That's the selfish reason, and I do not deny it," she said quickly, her eyes meeting his before darting away. "But there is a more noble one. As long as I am in Kaveryth, I am a potential threat to anyone who has tasted of the cursed water. You have been strong enough to resist when I've faltered and turned to magic. But those weaker than you will not be. They will die. And it will be my fault."

"No. If you do not turn to darkness, no one will be hurt. You are not a danger to us."

"But how can I know I won't fall again?" she said, her words a pitiful whisper that drove a knife into his heart. He wished that he could offer her assurance, but there was none. Only the truth.

"None of us can know the future. But you forget that you are not alone to face this temptation. The High One will help you if you ask him. He will give you the strength to do what you must."

"It's still so risky. It will be safer for everyone if I run."

Wes reached out to take her hand again. She did not refuse his touch.

"There are some temptations we can run away from. But this longing for darkness will never be overcome unless you stand against it, no matter how much it hurts."

"But how am I supposed to do that?"

"Just as you have been doing," he started, giving her hand a gentle squeeze. "Every day, one moment at a time, when you choose what is right instead of what is easy. But there is something else you can do. Something else that Celesyria read about once, in a portion of the Codex that was lost back in the fire at Helmm."

She waited for him to continue, drawing a thumb across his knuckles. He tried to ignore the butterflies dancing in the pit of his belly.

"A long time ago, people used to confess to one another. They would open up their hearts and reveal the bad things that they had done. There was a ritual surrounding it back then, but I think it could still help."

She looked horrified.

"You could also talk about the bad things you had seen. You don't have to carry the evils of where you came from alone, Aelrie," he said quickly, giving her what he hoped was a reassuring smile. "And I'm not saying that it's me that you have to speak to, although back then, the Envoy did have something to do with the ritual, but anyway, I think it would still help you. The Codex says it is powerful to—"

Before he could finish his sentence, she had leaned over to him, collapsing into his arms. He held her there, breathing her in, terrified to speak lest he say the wrong thing.

Terrified to draw himself away from her.

Terrified to let her stay.

"Wes, there is a secret I've known about ever since the day we first met," she said, her voice muffled against his tunic. "And I hate to burden you with it, but I can't carry it anymore. It's about... it's about dragon eggs."

He stayed there like that for a long while, stroking her hair, listening to the entire story as night fell. It was dangerous to be so close to her, and painful to hear the words that she had spoken.

But she would no longer bear the memory of such evil on her own.

Not as long as he was there to carry it with her.

Chapter Six

CELESYRIA

"And she's sure? About all of this?" Celesyria said to Wes in her mind as she continued working alongside Jaconial, this time on a collapsed dressmaker's shop further inland. She could scarcely believe what she was hearing. As her race had been dying out, there were elves and dwarves who actively worked to destroy their young. And the dragon mothers had gone along with it.

"She's telling the truth, Celesyria. And it was difficult for her to say it."

She nodded, though Wes of course could not see it. She struggled to find words.

"Is everything okay?" Jaconial asked as she circled past her, a large length of wood gripped in her claws. Celesyria nodded again, unsure where even to begin. She would have to explain it to the others, but she understood at once how Aelrie felt. It was so disgusting that the very thought of repeating the words aloud made her feel sick, as though the shame of it all somehow belonged to her. And yet, there was something familiar about the story, something he'd said before, a memory that she'd half-forgotten...

"Wait," she said as she moved to help Jaconial with the huge beam, each of them taking hold of one side and flying it out over the sea.. It was difficult to focus on her task while having this conversation, but it was the best she could do. *"You said that someone had been arrested before, for stealing the eggs."*

"Yes. A dwarf woman who had been working in the hatchery. Cingra, I think."

Her end of the wood fell from her claws toward the harbor below. Jaconial cried out, flapping her wings desperately as she tried to maintain her grip. Celesyria swept down beneath, managing to rest the heavy beam upon her back for a few seconds until they had cleared the docks and boats. Jaconial released her grip, sending the wood hurtling into the shallow water with an enormous splash.

"Celesyria?"

"By the Dracodei!" Jaconial swore, coming up beside her. "We're going to have to go back for that one tomorrow. It's going to be in the way of the boats if it doesn't land flat. What happened?"

"Nothing. I'm sorry," she said quickly, flexing her shoulder muscles. Everything seemed to be intact. "I'm just speaking to Wes. I'm sorry. It's important."

"Did something happen?"

"No. It's... I'll explain later."

She turned to head back to the rubble, deciding only to carry small items for the time being.

"Celesyria? Are you alright?" Wes asked again, his voice feeling very loud within her head.

"Yes I'm alright! Everyone is fine!" she snapped.

He said nothing for several long seconds, and she pressed

her eyes together for a moment. The exhaustion of the previous night and the current day had hit her all at once.

"I'm sorry, just. Please. I knew the whole thing sounded familiar. There was a girl Gramnok fancied, she worked in the hatchery. And her name was Cingra."

"It must be the same person," Wes said. *"How many Cingras can there be?"*

"More than you'd think, but I think you're right. It was the same one. Gramnok had always treated it like nothing more than a crush, but I sensed something deeper in the way he talked about her. Gramnok wouldn't have been with her if he knew what she was helping the elves to do. He follows the rules, but this? No. He wouldn't. "

"He didn't know, but... perhaps he found out," Wes mused.

Celesyria flew upward, taking a slow circle over the city.

For so long, she had wondered about Gramnok's final day. Wondered how he could possibly have ignited a bomb that destroyed Whitespire, even if he was doing so to set her free. She'd laid awake at night, turning things over in her head, wishing that she'd gotten just one more chance to speak to him.

"She probably was stealing the eggs," she said, the pieces falling into place even as she spoke. *"Gramnok was a good man. He would have had feelings for a good woman, I'm sure of it. She probably realized what was happening, and she tried to stop it, in the best way she knew how."*

"And they threw her—the woman he loved—into prison for it," Wes said.

"They treated her like a criminal, just as they no doubt did to him after I fled to tell you about the High One. He was already resentful. And somehow he learned what they had done. He must

have. It fueled his anger... he knew where the hatchery was. It's not directly above the city, but on a plateau nearby. He knew those eggs would be spared in an explosion."

Celesyria watched as Jaconial flew toward the beach again, carrying yet another load of rubble. She felt a pang of guilt for having left her to do all of the work while she talked. Jaconial was just as tired as she was, but she doubted that she would stop until Nazzan returned.

"I'll be there in a second, I'm sorry!" she called aloud as she pulled up alongside her, finding it easy to catch up without the burden of wood and stone hanging from her claws.

"Whatever it is, I'm sure it's more important," Jaconial said, throwing yet more rubble into the churning sea below. Celesyria nodded her head, feeling a rush of happiness despite the topic of her current conversation. It was hard to believe that just a couple of months ago, Jaconial had been her enemy. The dragon's heart had changed completely, and she was sure that the High One had a lot to do with it.

For a terrible second, she wondered if Jaconial and Nazzan had known about the eggs being smashed, but she dismissed the idea immediately. They couldn't have. Even at her most bitter and unpleasant, Jaconial would never have tolerated the murder of helpless hatchlings.

Then again, others must have. She could scarcely comprehend it.

"None of this justifies what he did," Wes was saying in her mind. *"It was still wrong to put innocents in danger, whatever the cause. But I can understand it. I can see why he'd want to burn the whole thing down. There's no way that the administrators didn't know."*

"All I can hope is that the High One will take the circumstances

into account," she said, fresh grief aching in her heart.

"May His justice be done," Wes replied.

He said nothing more, and she had nothing left to respond with in any case. She was deep in thought as she flew over the harbor, looking at the people below without really seeing them.

Wes had witnessed Gramnok's final moments of life. In a way, he had died to save Wes' life, and to save the Codex, but he had not been sorry for anything else he'd done. Not that Wes could see, anyway. But she took comfort in knowing that the High One knew his heart. Whatever his fate was, she had to trust that He knew better than she did.

She wanted to pray, to tell the High One that she hoped to meet him in the Eternal Lands, but she did not dare speak her hope aloud. She was not welcome there, either. She was destined for the Farplace, and she hoped that by the time she met death, she would be ready to accept that fact.

"Celesyria! Go to the munitions building!" Jaconial's voice called out in her head as she came up beside her.

She did as she was told without hesitation, banking hard to the left. As soon as she did so, she saw that Nazzan had returned, landing in the open patch of space beside the simple structure. Alder was there, too, and she wondered briefly where Kessara was as she landed next to him.

"There are Blackmasks nearby," Nazzan said aloud, waiting barely a second after her claws scraped the sand. "They're approaching the top of the cliffs, from the southwest. They have horses and stags with them."

Celesyria heard a growl rising within Jaconial's chest, and Alder caught her eye. The bandits were ready to pick apart the carcass of the beleaguered city, almost certainly looking for fresh slaves as well as other goods to plunder. "We need to get up there," Jaconial said, flexing her front claws.

Celesyria stretched out her front legs in turn, trying to relieve the constant cramping caused by her manacles. She supposed she would just have to make it a few more hours without sleep.

"We don't have much time," she said, giving her wings a final stretch. "Let's go."

"Wait," Alder said, taking a few steps forward until he was standing in the middle of the three dragons. "We need to make sure that Wes and the others are safe."

Celesyria wondered where Kessara was, and why he had not explained her absence. She had seen the two of them on the beach earlier, but Alder had apparently come to this side of the harbor alone.

"Aelrie is still with Wes," she said. "I'm sure she can handle anyone who tries to come after him, if it comes to that. Where's Kessara, anyway? I thought she was with you."

A sad expression passed over Alder's face like the shadow of a cloud, but within moments it was gone.

"Probably back at the house by now, with the others," he said quickly, not giving her a chance to answer before turning to Nazzan and asking him just how many Blackmasks he'd seen.

Celesyria felt a quiver of trepidation deep within her belly. Something was wrong, but she knew she would have to find the time to ask him about it later. The city was already weakened. If the bandits made it down the cliffs, she doubted that the few soldiers they still had could withstand another assault.

"Are you sure?" Nazzan asked, giving Alder a strange look.

"I didn't watch her every move, Nazzan," Alder snapped. "But yes, it's a reasonable guess. She was on the beach."

Jaconial glanced over at Celesyria, shrugging her scaly shoulders. Celesyria returned the gesture.

"People are going to be dragged from their homes and sold if we don't do something about this."

Alder looked furious, but did not offer to stay behind.

He's worried about her, and yet he didn't take her back to Wes and Aelrie before meeting us here? It made little sense, but then again, when it came to love, not much did. The two of them were complicated, always had been.

She took a few steps forward and thrust out her wings, flapping hard against the currents of air until she was high over the harbor. She tried to convince herself that Alder and the Princess had just had a brief argument, but thoughts of more sinister happenings continued to swirl through her mind.

Several minutes later, the three dragons—with Alder on Nazzan's strong back—were flying across the city's main street. Despite the spitting rain and the cold darkness, gathering crowds cheered and hollered, seemingly oblivious to the threat that lurked scarcely a mile away.

"We won't tell them," Nazzan's voice sounded firm within her mind. *"Not unless we fail. These poor people have tasted enough fear."*

Jaconial let out a loud but good-natured roar as she reached the open space at the foot of the cliff, sending the crowd into a cacophony of fresh enthusiasm. In spite of her worries, Celesyria did the same, looking down in amazement as dozens of fishermen, peasants, nobles, and street children waved up at them.

Her exhaustion evaporated in an instant.

I will fight for you. I promise. With the High One's help, I will never stop fighting until this beautiful land and all Kaveryth is free.

KESSARA

Kessara stood with her feet in the surf, barely noticing as the freezing water soaked through her leather boots. Night had finally fallen, and a fresh wind swept across the North Sea, bringing an autumnal chill with it.

She glanced over at the island of ice where the Gorok was imprisoned, watching as a group of clouds floated toward the shore. The air felt charged with energy despite the cold, as though a storm might break at any moment. It suited her mood.

She had expected Alder to run, or at least to rush, desperate to get away from her pain and her anger, but he hadn't. Instead, he had simply walked away, striding up the beach, his gait just as leisurely as usual.

"I don't need him! I don't need my father, or Wes, or any of you!" she shouted at the sea, her voice lost in the rushing wind. Alder was long gone now, but even if he could have heard her, it was clear that he did not care.

"I gave up everything for you," she whispered to no one, taking a few steps away from the shore and sinking down onto the wet sand. She had given up everything in search of love, and in the end, she had lost. Whether or not Alder was being honest about no longer loving her was irrelevant. Even if he did, she knew it would not be so simple to make him change his mind, even if she wanted to. Which she wasn't sure that she did.

She sat there for several minutes, eyeing the harbor far off in the distance, hoping that Alder would at least have the decency to tell everyone to leave her alone. She couldn't bear the thought of facing them. Her throat ached with waiting sobs, but she had run out of tears.

She tilted her face up toward the sky in hope of finding stars, but the clouds were thicker now, covering over the glimmering lights like a blanket. It would rain soon, and she would be even more wet and cold and uncomfortable than she already was.

The High One was out there, somewhere beyond the night.

"How frustrating it must be to have a world full of children who refuse to love You," she murmured, glancing up and down the beach to ensure that she was still alone. "We don't act the way we should. You could make us do the right thing, make us love you, but You don't. Instead You let us make ourselves miserable. It's madness."

She drew a shuddering breath as a fresh wave of sorrow rushed through her.

He was gone. For real. He had walked away.

She thought of her mother, back home in the palace. Eventually her father would have to return to Windshear, and he would have to tell his wife what he had done. Kessara was certain that the Queen had not known what her husband was going to do. If she had, she would have been here with him, begging with him to change his mind and bring their daughter back at once.

And he would. If I decided to marry Wes after all.

She rested her head in her hands as the rain began to fall, the frigid droplets stinging her neck as they landed. This would be another sea-storm, cold and dangerous. She could feel it.

Soon, she would be forced back into the city. She'd have to face them all.

I will not tell them what they want to hear. I will not do it.

Suddenly, a rush of wind gusted from above her, nearly sending her falling backward. She looked up, watching as Nazzan tore along the coastline, his wings pounding the air as fast as he could.

She felt a chill rushing through her. He was moving fast, faster than he would be if he was just going to help Celesyria and Jaconial clear rubble.

She stumbled to her feet and began to chase after the dragon, already deciding that she had to follow now, whatever promises she'd made to herself. Something was wrong.

Another gust of air slammed into her, this time coming from the direction of the sea, and she stumbled, falling to her knees. Within moments she was up again, her boots sucking against the sand as she made for the harbor.

It was a good distance away, however, and running properly was difficult. To her left lay the sea, and to her right was nothing but a jumble of huge black rocks. She forced herself to keep pressing forward, her legs straining with the effort, her chest tight.

After a few minutes, she sat down on one of the rocks, clutching at the stitch in her side. Her lungs burned, and she couldn't get enough air. She glanced back at the trail of footprints she'd left behind, some close enough to the water that they'd already been erased by the lapping waves.

I've hardly made it a fifth of the way.

She'd always considered herself to be fairly fit, but this was difficult. She got to her feet, trying to lean to one side and stretch out her legs one at a time. She'd seen the trainees do it back in Auranth, both before and after their daily runs. She leaned down, feeling the tension in her muscles, wondering if she was doing it right at all or if she was going to make it hurt even more.

Out of the corner of her eye, she spotted a flash of orange, and then another.

She straightened, taking a few stumbling steps across the beach until her feet touched the water. She heard the sound of beating wings.

Nazzan was following the two females into the sky, his green scales difficult to make out against the gray clouds. Panic gripped her throat. What was going on? Where were they going in such a hurry? Had the elves returned, or something worse?

She broke into a run again, ignoring the cramp in her side and her twitching leg muscles, glancing over at the Gorok's little island again. It was just as still as the last time she looked at it.

She squinted, placing a hand to her brow as though to shield herself from the nonexistent sun, and then she saw him.

Alder was on Nazzan's back.

Chapter Seven

ALDER

"I guess there's no way we're going to sneak up on the Blackmasks now," Alder said to Nazzan as they made their way over the packed courtyard. The cheers continued louder than ever as the three dragons passed above the crowd in turn, flapping their wings as they approached the cliffs so as to gain sufficient altitude to make it over the plateau.

"Good," Nazzan said, giving the crowd the loudest roar yet, his teeth gleaming in a sharp smile. "Let them expect us. Perhaps they will think twice before entering Kingsvier Landing."

Alder found that difficult to argue with. He gave a whoop of his own, exhilaration flooding through his tired body as the people beneath returned his battle cry. He was still tired, of course, but after trying to kill a demon sea monster and a contingent of elf soldiers, he felt confident that the black bandits would present little challenge. His injuries hurt, but the pain was bearable.

Just then, he noticed something.

There on the staircase were two little girls, each carrying a simple canvas bag as they skipped up the now-empty steps. A thin woman who looked far too young to be their mother was coming up behind them, carrying more bags. The children had gotten quite far ahead already.

"Look!" he shouted to Nazzan. "The stairs!"

Before he could react, Jaconial was diving as low as she could go, pulling up mere inches from the cobbled ground as the crowd rushed out of her way.

"Stop! Do not take the stairs!" she thundered at the woman and the two girls, one of whom dropped her pack. "It's not safe!"

Alder's stomach sank like a stone.

Somewhere to his left, he heard Celesyria unleash a rare curse.

Within seconds, there was chaos. The happy crowd swarmed into a mob, pushing and shoving their way down toward the harbor. Alder glanced around, hoping to see Galeharbor and Red Army soldiers pouring out of alleyways and springing into action, but there were no men to be found.

He hoped that Kessara had the good sense to return to the safety of the fisherman's house. He closed his eyes for a moment as he clutched the straps of Nazzan's saddle, and for a second he could see her there, standing alone on the beach, devastation in her eyes. He could scarcely believe that their last conversation had really happened. It was as though someone else had inhabited his body, someone capable of a coldness that he had not until that moment realized he possessed.

He sat back in the saddle as Nazzan gave two hard flaps of his wings, waiting a moment for Celesyria and Jaconial to catch up.

"Keep order!" Celesyria was shouting at the crowd, who continued to push and shove each other as they made their way in the general direction of the sea. Everyone ignored her.

"Come on," Jaconial said, baring her teeth at the mob in disgust as she continued up over the top of the staircase. "They'll have to figure it out. If we don't stop the bandits, they'll be dead or enslaved anyway."

Nazzan said nothing as he followed her, giving a final glance back at the citizens below. Alder shook his head. Moments ago, they had been united. All for nothing. A moment of fear was enough to tear them apart once more.

The night was darker as they reached the flat, locust-eaten grasslands that stood over the city. Alder blinked several times as the dragons circled the area, trying to make out any movement in the shadows.

It didn't take long.

A company of men in black clothing were racing across the plain, weaving between bushes and trees as they made for the city. As his eyes adjusted, he could see them in more detail, picking out both dwarves and men, perhaps seven or eight of each. The black cloth masks on their faces made them look strange and wild, the whites of their eyes flashing in the dim streaks of moonlight that had made it through the clouds.

They were chanting something in a language Alder couldn't make out, sounds of hate and darkness, their voices getting louder and louder as the staircase drew nearer.

"They don't hear us yet," Nazzan said, his deep voice almost lost amid the sounds billowing up from below.

"Let them hear," Jaconial crowed, flying up beside them. A moment later, she was diving toward the ground, letting out a ferocious roar directly over the bandits' heads. The men turned at once, their mouths hanging open as they took in the sight of three massive dragons flying over them.

What did they think they were going to find here? Did they assume that the peasants and fishermen defeated the monster?

Alder didn't bother to dwell on it. The Blackmasks began to run back the way they had come, several of the men tripping and falling to the ground in their desperate attempt to get away. Two of the dwarves crashed into each other, both men careening to the ground and shouting at each other as they tumbled into the stubbly grass. Jaconial flew directly over them and roared again, sending the two men nearly into each others' arms, their hands pressed over their ears as they cowered.

"We have to go after them," Jaconial shouted to the others, circling again as the men rushed away toward the south. "They'll only come back if we let them go."

"I'm coming," Nazzan said, racing to follow her.

Alder did not relish the thought of more bloodshed, but she was right. In any case, it was difficult to garner much sympathy for men who made their living by selling people into slavery.

"Carry me down," Alder called out, taking hold of his sword and preparing to leap off of the dragon's back. "This will be easier on foot."

"Be careful," Celesyria called out, coming up behind them. Her usually girlish voice sounded hoarse and tired. "We'll all stay close. Call if you need us."

"Okay," he said, not wanting to tell her that it would be difficult if not impossible for him to make himself heard over the bandits, who were still shouting periodically. Mindspeaking would have come in handy, but he had not had much time to practice as of late.

"Hold on," Nazzan said. Alder did as he was told, gripping

his sword in one hand and the straps of the saddle in the other. The dragon dove, so steep that for a moment Alder feared he would crash headfirst into the nearest bandit. A second later he was gliding near the ground, and Alder propelled himself out of the saddle, careful not to land on his sword as he tucked his body into a tight roll.

He didn't quite manage to end up on his feet, but it was good enough. As soon as he had his legs properly under him, he began to run toward the nearest bandit, his sword raised. He let out a visceral cry of his own as metal hit armor. It was a dwarf, and fortunately, he was protected only by leather plates rather than metal.

Over to his right, he could see one of the men struggling to nock an arrow as Jaconial dove toward him, her front claws glinting. Most of the thick gray storm clouds had been swept away elsewhere, and the moonlight cast the entire expanse in a blue glow.

The dwarf struck out toward him with his ax, and Alder dashed to the left to avoid it, wishing very much that he had gotten a chance to find his own armor. He raised his sword again as the dwarf snarled at him, twisting to the side, the sword striking his shoulder plate. It was of little help. Alder struck again and again, feeling the leather giving way to the razor-sharp metal of his Aridmoorian longsword. He tried not to hear the man's cries as he bled on the grass, the rage and hate fading from his voice as death wandered nearer to claim him.

A final swing, and it was done.

Alder straightened, looking for his next target. He could see Nazzan and Celesyria to his right, trying to get close enough to strike a tall man who had a bow in his hands. Every few seconds, he was firing, sending an impressive amount of arrows toward the dragons.

Alder could see the delicate spots on their belly armor from where he stood. This sort of open space usually advantaged dragons in a fight, but a good archer tended to complicate things. To make matters worse, Nazzan had already sustained arrow injuries at the beach. He could not afford more arrow wounds.

"I'm coming!" he shouted to them, rushing across the grass as quickly as he could. He watched as several of the other bandits got away, fleeing into a thick patch of trees. Jaconial had landed, giving a final blow with her claws to a man lying on the ground and trying to hack at her with his sword.

He ignored three other passing bandits as he made his way toward his friends, trying not to stumble on his tired legs. He reached the man from behind, but he did not turn. He was focused entirely on his task, drawing his bowstring back again and again, his arrows flying toward the two dragons.

"Get back!" Alder shouted at them, noticing a black substance dripping out along the bottom stitching of his quiver. "They're poisoned!"

Celesyria did as she was told, but Nazzan circled lower, coming back around behind Alder, waiting.

Alder said nothing as he rushed toward the man, his sword held over his head just as the bandit turned, another arrow already drawn. Alder ducked down just in time to avoid being shot, tripping on a hidden rock before getting back to his feet. He tried to strike the man again, but he drew a knife from somewhere within his tunic. It, too, was dripping with the black substance.

"Alder, stop!" Celesyria was screaming. She was right. This

was going to get him killed. He shoved his sword back into his sheath, stepping out of the way of the dagger as the man pressed toward him.

As Nazzan circled around again, he turned sharply, leaping into the air and taking hold of the saddle straps just as the dragon passed. Nazzan could not slow, instead pumping his wings to gain more altitude as Alder's weight sent him tilting to the right.

He gripped the sturdy leather as tight as he could, every muscle straining with effort as he forced his way up into the saddle.

"By the Dracodei, you're a bonehead," Nazzan said, his chest rumbling.

"Leave them, Jaconial!" Celesyria was shouting at her. To Alder's surprise, Jaconial obeyed, coming close and flying beside them as they circled higher and higher toward the clouds.

For a moment, they all caught their breaths. No one seemed to have sustained any serious injuries.

Cold air screamed in his ears, and he longed for the relief of flying lower, where the wind wasn't quite so intense.

They looked down at the plateau, watching as the last of the Blackmasks dodged the bodies of the few bandits they had killed and retreated out of sight. Jaconial tried to speak, but her words were lost in the rushing of the wind.

Nazzan flew downward, coming to land near the cliff. The others followed, and Celesyria strode over to the edge, glancing down at the chaos below.

"Still fighting?" Jaconial asked.

"Better than they were, but yes."

Alder tightened his fists in frustration. He supposed they

would have to deal with that too, even though the thought of any more work made him feel he would keel over and fall asleep where he landed.

"It's not a total loss," Celesyria continued, glancing at the others. "Perhaps they will leave a trail to those who were captured from Windshear already. We could wait a little while, and then follow them, see if we can get a better position, or some help."

Alder felt a pang of sadness. He knew that Celesyria had promised to herself that she would free the captives, not to mention her promise to free her father from imprisonment in Nox. So far, she'd had little time to pursue either goal, and he was sure that she carried the guilt with her constantly.

"That's optimistic," Jaconial was saying, sending a puff of white breath out of her nostrils. Her eyes were flashing with anger. "We might not get another chance. We should go after them right now."

"There's no time," Nazzan said calmly, bumping the side of his mate's neck with his snout and giving Celesyria an apologetic look. "There are other things that we need to do. We cannot chase shadows across the continent."

"But Jaconial's right," Alder protested. "If this city is attacked again, it's not going to survive. Even if it does, it will fall apart. Those who chose to stay after the Gorok attack will flee, and then what will be left?."

"They might flee anyway," Nazzan said, shaking his head and pointing with a claw toward the cliff. A group of a dozen or so people were climbing onto the plateau, dragging packed bags behind them. They could hear the sound of the crowd speaking below, punctuated by an occasional shout.

"If the bandits are waiting in the trees, they'll be killed,"

Jaconial said darkly, looking over at the crowd as though she might roar at them again.

"There's another option," Celesyria said quietly. The others turned to look at her.

"What?" Alder asked, hoping it was something feasible. His exhaustion had already soured his mood, and seeing these foolish people fleeing in the same direction as a group of slavers was apt to send him over the edge.

"We need to report what we saw to the local soldiers. And hope that someone goes after them. Nazzan's right. We have other matters to attend to."

Alder let out a breath between his teeth.

"Go to the Red Army for help?" Jaconial asked, incredulous. "Again?"

"She's right," Nazzan said, stretching his right wing as he spoke. "I have every reason to think our present truce will hold, at least for the time being. Fighting side-by-side has a way of unifying people. They'll listen, even if Drohma doesn't like it."

"That might not hold true for Wes, though," Alder pointed out. "And especially not Aelrie. If they continue to be attacked, they may blame him for leading the darkness here. Even though the people here have never been particularly committed to the Dracodei compared to those in other lands, Kessara has told me of their own superstitions. That aside, I hate to say it, but I think the Red Army is in the best position right now to keep the people safe."

"I suppose if the Red Army won't help, the fishermen will have to step up," Jaconial admitted. "If they were willing to try to kill a sea monster, I doubt that bandits would be enough to scare them off. In any case, I saw that King Manta has arrived. If he hasn't left yet, he'll help to keep order."

"It's settled, then," Celesyria said. "So long as the people don't kill each other in the next ten minutes, I suppose we can figure out our next move."

"We need to get Wes to Stronghollow, then he needs to return to Auranth to watch over our forces, then we need to find the Remnant," Alder said, counting each task on his fingers. "Oh, and don't forget, we need to free a dragon from Nox."

Celesyria gave him a tired smile. It was not a small list, and it was not as though the brewing war would cease while they traveled, but what else could they do?

In the end, nothing would change in Kaveryth until they returned to the High One, and as it stood now, finding the Remnant and talking to Elder Bram seemed to be the best chance they had at figuring out how to restore worship to Him once and for all. He just hoped that it would be worth the risk in the end.

Alder climbed onto Nazzan's back in silence, lost in thought, feeling the envelope containing Raela's letter pressed safely against his chest.

And somehow, in the midst of everything else, I have to get to Boneshire and help a lost queen bring a noble House back to life.

WES

Aelrie had not left his arms. They sat there together on his bed as the night grew deeper, her head pressed against his chest. He knew that he should pull away, remind her of propriety, reach out to Celesyria and ask after his friends, but he couldn't bring himself to move. In fact, he could barely bring himself to think.

The world felt darker than it had mere minutes ago, knowing what he knew now of the depths of evil that plagued Kaveryth, but his own life seemed to glow brighter.

She was here.

They were both breathing, and her raven hair was tickling his nose. It was glorious.

After a long while, she drew a breath as though she was going to speak, but said nothing. After a minute or two had passed, he drew his hand away from where it had been resting against the back of her head. "What's on your mind?"

She leaned back from him at last, one side of her cheek imprinted with red marks after being pressed against the folds of his tunic for so long, and gave him a soft smile.

"Nothing as bad as what I've told you," she said.

He smiled back, but his face felt tense.

All of those innocent hatchlings. Gone.

He could scarcely believe it, and yet, there was no reason for Aelrie to lie about what she had seen.

"Wes," she continued, brushing a messy strand of hair behind her ear. "Do you ever feel like a fraud? When you try to believe?"

"Every day of my life," he said, relieved that she had asked a question he knew how to answer. It was one he had asked himself so often that the answer came as second nature.

"I want to believe. I want to love. But it doesn't always feel like it's supposed to," she continued, stretching her arms as she leaned up against the headboard beside him. "At least, I don't think it does." She was still close enough that he feared he might stammer like an idiot, but he would try his best to make some modicum of sense.

"The love that the Codex talks about is deeper than what

we usually imagine," he told her, reminding himself in the process. He'd told himself this truth many times, but it rarely stuck for very long. Especially when he was constantly around someone like Celesyria, whose love for the High One shone through like a light from within. "It's about allegiance. Loyalty. All of those noble ideals. But more than that, it's about trust."

"I try to trust," Aelrie said, frowning. "I mean it. I try."

"So do I," he said, reaching out a hand to squeeze hers once again. The ripple of pleasure that poured through him was just as intoxicating as it had been a few moments ago. "But part of why we find it so difficult is because we're trying so hard. We're relying on ourselves, thinking that if we can just follow Him with enough zeal, He will love us."

"The High One cares about what we do," Aelrie countered, absentmindedly picking at a piece of loose skin at the edge of his thumbnail, as though she knew his hands as well as her own. "He doesn't just say, 'love me and do what you want', he asks for all of us. Especially the things we do not wish to give. Even I know that much."

"That isn't what I meant," he said, forcing himself not to flinch as she tore out a small piece of a hangnail. "Of course we must obey Him. But sometimes we're not strong enough yet to get everything right. Sometimes, all we can manage is to ask Him to help us to *want* to do what is good. Have you done that?"

The question hung in the air for several long seconds, leaving only the sound of breaking waves out at sea to interrupt the silence.

"I'd never thought of it like that," she said, her fingers going still. "No. I haven't. Not really. I guess I thought that I already wanted to resist the darkness. Figured that if I didn't, why would I feel so guilty?"

"And you do want to resist," he said quickly. "But you're still relying on yourself. You're still expecting that you can please the High One solely by the power of your own will. Even an elf isn't strong enough to do that. I know I'm certainly not."

"I need to lean on his strength, not mine," she said. "Mine is not enough, and never can be."

Before Wes could say more, Celesyria's voice sounded in his mind. He listened as she recounted what had happened in the last hour or so, and explained to Celesyria that Kessara had not yet returned to the little house.

Finally he turned back to Aelrie.

I should be there with them. Not in here like a cripple, torturing myself, dreaming of a girl I am not allowed to love.

The word scared him, even just to think it, as though giving a name and a shape to what he felt might make it irreversible.

She was resting with her chin in her hands, looking very much like she wanted to fall asleep and forget about all of this madness. He had never seen her looking so informal as she had tonight, picking at his dead skin, her always-perfect hair looking almost messy. Somehow this sort of elven beauty was even more frightening.

"I need to leave for Stronghollow, as soon as I'm well enough to get out of this bed," he said finally.

"What happened?"

"The area is not as safe as we'd hoped. Nazzan went to patrol along the top of the cliffs, and he ran into Blackmasks. The other two dragons and Alder went up to the plateau to fight them off, but most of the company got away."

She leapt from the bed, feeling for her dagger and picking her bow up from where she'd left it resting carefully against the door.

"Wait," he said, getting to his own feet with much less grace and coming to stand beside her on unsteady legs. "We're not fighting them."

"We have to. They'll come back."

"They will," he agreed. "And when they do, the Red Army will deal with them. They'll have to. I need to go to Stronghollow."

Aelrie drew a slow breath, her eyes searching his own. "Are you well enough to travel already?"

Wes glanced down at his legs. His knees shook a little as he stretched, and his current headache lingered behind his eyes, but he would be okay.

As long as she doesn't draw darkness.

He would not give voice to that particular fear. Aelrie was strong. Everything she had done already had proven that. She needed only to lean on the High One, and she would become even stronger.

"We will leave as soon as you can be ready," Wes told Celesyria.

He had so many things to ask her about what was going on out there, far above the city, but he supposed he'd see for himself soon enough.

Aelrie looked up at him and asked him what he was saying, but he did not answer. Though the dragons were skilled enough at mindspeaking to carry on multiple conversations at once when the need arose, he was not.

"Are you sure? You're sick. You could take another day's rest," Celesyria suggested.

"No, that would be foolish. I'll make it, so long as I have a

dragon to carry me."

Wes caught Aelrie glancing over at the door, and he stretched out a hand, resting his fingertips on her forearm as though she might bolt.

"Hold on a moment," he told her aloud as Celesyria continued to speak.

"*I should be the one hunting down those slavers. I promised myself that I would go back for them, ever since Windshear.*"

"*What has the High One told you?*"

"*Too little to go on,*" she admitted.

"*Do you want my advice?*"

"*Always.*"

"*You have other duties that are equally important. If you are indeed meant to go after the Blackmasks, you will be led back to them. The High One knows our foolishness. He will give a second sign.*"

There was a long pause.

"*We're flying back toward the city. Be ready to leave.*"

Aelrie waited patiently for several more seconds until he spoke.

"I'm leaving. Now, under cover of night," he said, letting his fingertips fall away from her silvery skin. Immediately, he missed the gentle warmth that seemed to reach straight through to his heart whenever they touched.

"And I'm coming with you," her voice was fierce, almost angry.

He shook his head. "The Gorok is gone. I will ask Kessara to get you both a boat to Auranth. You'll be safe there."

Aelrie frowned. "Safe? Wes, I want you to be safe. That's why I need to be with you."

The end of her words trailed into a whisper.

"I'm not talking about that sort of safety."

"Then what are you talking about?"

"You fear that you will give into temptation, and that you will turn back to the darkness," he said quickly, trying not to falter as he saw the crestfallen look on her face. "And I believe in you. I believe you are strong enough, so long as the High One is with you. But it is foolish to court temptation nonetheless. If you go to Auranth, you will still be able to aid the army. They are in desperate need of a competent trainer, at least until Alder returns. I will return as well, of course. And we can figure things out from there."

She had said nothing for a long while, crossing her arms over her chest as she listened to him speak. Her expression revealed nothing, her prior frustration slipping away from her features leaving only a mask of calm.

He sighed.

If she won't go, Kessara certainly won't.

Wes felt his hands beginning to sweat, but he bit his tongue rather than continuing to babble.

"I understand," she said, tilting her chin up. "But the temptation would only follow me there. There is no running from it, you said it yourself. I need to be near my friends when those moments come. The High One will protect me, but I believe He will do it through you and the others."

He did not have the energy to argue. He would lose.

"We need to pack, then," he said instead, turning toward the trunk at the foot of his bed. He heaved the heavy wooden lid open, pretending that the strain did not bother his sore body, and grabbed hold of his meager belongings.

Aelrie laughed, the tinkling sound of it filling the room. "I have what I need already," she said, gesturing to a small wooden pack that she had sat next to her quiver. "I've already tried to run away twice. I'm well prepared for a quick exit."

Wes smiled back, taking a few steps toward Alder's side of the room. There were three long nails hammered into the wall that served as hooks, and Wes took down a thick cloak that hung on one of them.

He reached for his own cloak, which he had left hanging on the edge of his bed, and handed it to the elf.

"Here. You need to hide your face as best you can, at least while we're in the city. You deserve a hero's welcome, but I doubt you'll get it."

He put Alder's cloak on. It was bulky on him, but at least it was short enough that he would not trip on it.

"Won't Alder need that?" she asked, drawing his cloak over her back. Somehow, she still looked lovely, even beneath the too-large blanket of fabric.

"He'll live. Knowing him, he'll brag about his toughness as he shivers in the wind."

She laughed again as they headed out into the hall, grabbing her quiver, pack, and bow as she passed. Wes could see her knives already sheathed at her waist.

When they pushed open the front door of the house, Wes was surprised to find it unguarded. Aelrie glanced up at him, her brow furrowed. Just then, they heard the sound of a shout coming from somewhere up the hill, followed by another.

Wes drew his sword, feeling a stab of ice in his heart. He hoped that the bandits had not been sighted down here in town, below the cliffs. They stood there for a moment on the little porch, staring as people raced past, headed in the general direction of the water.

"I hope that monster stays put," Wes said.

"He will," Aelrie said, shrinking back from him, her face pained. "But there is always a cost when one tries to defeat darkness with darkness. This is my fault. I could have drawn other evils here, people who are attracted to the darkness are always seeking places where it reigns."

"You don't know that," he said firmly, reaching for her hand. She took it, and he pulled her out onto the street as another group of people rushed by. They quickened their pace, blending in with the crowd.

"Where's Kessara?" she asked, looking around in front of the little house. Wes shook his head. With the guards gone, he had no idea.

"Celesyria doesn't know where she went, but Alder told her that he had left her at the beach."

"Left her?"

Wes shrugged. "It sounds like he didn't want to say more, but yes. He had assumed she would return to the house, but of course, being Kessara, she didn't."

Worry panged in his gut. The Princess was skilled at getting into trouble, especially where Alder was concerned. He hoped that some petty argument would not ruin their plans.

They continued down the winding side streets until they could see the sea, stretching out toward the horizon. The moon was visible between shifting clouds, and the soft light made the rolling peaks of the waves gleam.

Though the people had headed in the direction of the North Sea, they found the long strip of sandy beach almost deserted. Wes eyed the island of ice that floated out beyond the harbor, shaking his head. The people feared the slavers, but they feared the Gorok even more.

"Meet us near the lighthouse," he said to Celesyria. *"We'll*

look for Kessara on the way.”

Chapter Eight

CELESYRIA

"We need to go to the lighthouse," Celesyria called to the others. She glanced down at the steep peaks of the rooflines below, watching as masses of people flitted along streets and between alleyways. "Wes said he is well enough to leave. I see no reason to waste time."

"Is Kessara with them?" Alder called from Nazzan's saddle as the big green dragon flew alongside her.

"No," she said, glad that she did not have to meet his eyes. "He and Aelrie are looking for her."

No one spoke for several seconds as they navigated a patch of strong wind. The night was cold for the season, and Celesyria did not look forward to the winter that was to come.

Just then, without warning, she heard a familiar voice in her head.

"*Please, Celesyria,*" Alder said, his voice just loud enough to be heard over the hushing of the sky. "*Just support me in what I'm about to say. Please. It's important. I need you to trust me with the decision I must make.*"

She was so astonished by his sudden ability to mindspeak that she nearly answered him aloud.

"*Fine,*" she said warily, wondering what on earth he could

possibly be asking of her.

"Jaconial, Nazzan," he called out, his voice audible now that the wind had settled for a moment. "There's something you do not know, and I'll have to explain quickly. Please, just trust me."

Celesyria looked down at the city below as she listened. They were well over the residential area now, approaching the sea. She strained her eyes at the distant beach, hoping to see Kessara there, safe and sound.

"When Kessara and I went to High Keep to send my family to Graveheim, we came into possession of a letter."

"From who?" Jaconial asked, banking her body and gliding to the right so that she was flying even closer on Nazzan's other side.

"Celesyria will explain later," he said. "It's complicated, but it's good news, I can say that. I just need to know that I can trust you both."

"Of course," Nazzan said, his low rumbling voice sounding almost defensive.

"If you couldn't, we wouldn't still be here," Jaconial said firmly.

Celesyria could understand their taking offense, but she could also see why Alder had to ask. Despite all of the good they had done, they had been involved with the actions of the Council. The letter was vitally important. If she was correct in her assumptions, Holga restoring the monarchy of Boneshire was just as essential to the restoration of worship as was Wes giving Silverfell a queen.

Alder paused, and for a moment Celesyria thought that he was going to keep his secrets after all.

High One, grant him clarity, one way or another.

"The House of Noctua is not dead," he said finally, his words tumbling out in a rush. Celesyria did not look over at Jaconial or Nazzan to see their reactions, but she was certain that whatever they were expecting to hear, it was not this. "There is a living heir to the crown of Boneshire, a girl who Wes and Celesyria met long before any of us knew who she was. It is up to me to tell her who she is, and I have already tarried long enough. Her homeland is dangerous already, and it's getting worse. We cannot risk anything bad happening to her."

Celesyria's chest ached with sudden dread.

So this is the part he needs me to support him in. The part where he leaves without telling the woman who loves him where he is going.

"Are you going now?" Jaconial asked.

"Yes."

Celesyria let herself glide for a moment, risking a glance in her direction. There was a pause, and she was sure that she and Nazzan were mindspeaking to one another, the easy, comfortable language of lovers.

A familiar jealousy stung at her heart.

"I will carry you to Boneshire," Nazzan said finally. Celesyria watched as Alder reached down to pat his shoulder scales.

"Thank you."

"And just what exactly am I supposed to say to the Princess?" Celesyria snapped, glad that the others could not hear.

"I'm sorry," Alder said, not bothering to make any excuses.

"You need to tell that to her, not to me," Celesyria said, letting a puff of warm air out of her nostrils. This was a foolish plan, though she doubted there was any point in trying to talk him out of it. *"She's going to be devastated."*

"She already is devastated, Celesyria," he said. *"I left her alone after telling her that I did not love her."*

At that moment, she very much wished that she was human. He needed a slap, or perhaps a nice kick to the rear end.

"You left Kessara alone on a beach, after shattering her heart? Are you mad?"

She dared a glance over at him. His knuckles were white on the leather straps of the saddle, and his face had gone pale as the implications of her words sank in.

It hurt her even to say them, but she knew Kessara. The Princess was smart, capable, and steady–except when it came to the foolish Aridmoorian that she'd fallen in love with.

"She's alright. She's stronger than you think she is," he said firmly, as though trying to convince himself as much as her. *"You'll find her. You have to."*

"Why did you tell her this anyway?" she asked, making no effort to conceal her anger. *"It's obviously a lie. You've loved that girl ever since the moment you stumbled into each other's lives. We all see it."*

"Because she told King Manta that she wasn't going to marry Wes, Celesyria," Alder said, his voice dangerously quiet. *"But you know as well as I do that it was never her choice to make. If I get away from here for a while, she will grieve, but in the end she will do what's right. But I had to turn the knife. I had to make her believe there was no chance that I would ever be with her."*

Celesyria felt like she was going to be sick. She could not justify the lies, but on the whole, she had to admit that Alder was right. Kessara had to fulfill her duty, even if her feelings led her astray. In the end, somehow, she would be thankful for what he had done. But she was not looking forward to picking up the pieces in the meantime.

"Okay," she choked out, looking out at the sea. The light-house was just visible in the distance.

"You must promise me that you will not seek to mollify her anger, or even her sadness," Alder replied. *"I know you will want to, but if you really care about her, you will let her hate me. Hate me with her, if you need to. It's what is right for Kaveryth."*

Celesyria nodded, looking up at the stars. She could see the constellations again, for the first time in what felt like a long while.

A moment later, Nazzan and Alder fell back, turning away toward the south.

Somehow, she would find the strength to do what he asked.

KESSARA

Kessara walked, going nowhere in particular. To one side of the beach, she could see the lighthouse, old and important. She had never seen the great spire in person before, but she could imagine it was somehow the same, standing tall, watching over everything.

Kingsvier Landing lay in the other direction, the buildings jutting into the now-starry sky, the cheerful lights left on in the windows making her nearly forget the violence that had ensued there scarcely a day before. She hoped that all was well, that the people would be safe and happy now that the monster and the elves were gone. Despite what her father might have said to her, she still cared for her people. She still loved them, even if it was a love that she could never really believe was freely given.

She walked along the shoreline, her toes so cold that she no longer felt the sting of the water that soaked into her boots. It felt good to put one foot in front of the other, even though she was going nowhere. At least she didn't have to stand still and feel all of the hurt in one place.

The storm she had expected had not come to pass, and she found the fact displeasing. The stars and the moon were too beautiful to stand vigil over her pain.

At least it is freezing.

The frigid wind screamed across the sea every few minutes, churning up the water into waves. She could imagine his voice in her head, scolding her for being out here alone, and for letting her body get so cold.

For a moment she stopped short, a memory bubbling to the surface before she could stop it. She was there again, in High Keep, feeling the cold stone floor against her back as the men yelled at her, threatened her, tried to... Her chest went tight and she struggled to breathe, the thin air feeling like daggers against the inside of her lungs.

For a moment she glanced out at the sea, pondering oblivion.

I could do it.

I could swim for a while, but I would get tired. My blood would go cold. I would sink away like one more fishing boat, pulled away to the dark and the silence. In a way, I'd be free. The weight would leave my shoulders at last.

The sea continued to roll toward the shore, only to shy away moments later, mocking her.

She continued to stand there, her face chapped, her eyes stinging from the wind.

It was not a real desire. It was foolishness, merely the sick fantasy sprung out of a shattered heart.

Still, guilt coursed through her, a desperate wish to take back the thought and pretend it had never crossed her mind for even a moment. She was stronger than this.

She wrapped her hands firmly around herself, noticing how red and numb her fingertips were as she waited for the anxiety to leave her. She could feel her lungs expanding and shrinking, the rhythm unsteady at first, and then slowing.

The moment stretched out, with only the rhythmic sound of the water to mark the passing of time.

Finally, she stood tall, letting her hands fall to her sides.

"No," she called out to no one in particular, enjoying the sharpness of the word on her tongue. She was smiling, but did not know why.

"They didn't break me then, and no one is going to break me now. No one. Not my father, and certainly not Alder Cadogen."

WES

"*Wes,*" Celesyria said. For a moment, he could not respond. He and Aelrie were clambering over a tangle of wooden pilings that had been pushed onto the beach, blocking their path.

"*There's something else,*" Celesyria said again, her voice sounding more urgent this time.

"Don't wait for me, okay?" he said to Aelrie as they got clear of the debris. She raised an eyebrow.

"Celesyria," he said by way of explanation. She asked nothing else, instead turning away from him and moving toward the distant lighthouse, her boots leaving light prints on the uneven sand.

"*What's wrong?*" he asked, trying his best not to let her get too far ahead.

If she chose to run, there would be no way to catch her anyway, but he felt better when he knew that she was close.

For many reasons.

"Alder's gone. With Nazzan. They went to Boneshire," Celesyria said quickly. He nearly tripped over a piece of driftwood as the words sunk in. *"To find Holga, obviously,"* she added.

"Without saying goodbye to us?" He could scarcely believe what he was hearing.

"Or to Kessara," Celesyria said, her voice so close to a whisper that he almost couldn't make out the words. *"I think that was the point of it."*

He glanced at Aelrie's back as she pressed forward, moving toward the rocks that lined the land side of the beach every so often, watching out for any sign of the Princess. His heart raced, his worry for Kessara cutting through his chest like ice.

"So he just left her? Left her on the beach and decided to fly off across the continent?"

He held his breath as he waited for her response. He hoped that he was wrong, but he knew before she spoke what the truth was.

He listened in numb silence as she explained to him what King Manta had said, and how Alder had chosen to allow Kessara to think he did not love her. He followed Aelrie as she spoke, the lighthouse drawing nearer. The beach remained empty.

Like Celesyria, he could empathize with Alder's solution to the problem, but it did not ease his worries. She had been alone for hours, with no one to check on her.

Maybe she couldn't handle it. Maybe she...

"She's there! Look!" Aelrie was shouting from up ahead, pointing toward the huge black stones that lined the cliffside.

He rushed forward as fast as his legs would carry him as she pointed again.

Her father had pushed her away. Alder had rejected her. She was his responsibility now, more than ever.

Finally, he saw the telltale blue of Kessara's dress, flapping in the wind.

She was moving. She was alright.

"Thank the High One," he said under his breath, blinking away the tears of relief that were threatening to fall.

"Aelrie, wait," he called out. She slowed until they were matching strides, walking quickly over the damp sand. "She's hurting. Because of Alder. I can't explain it right now, but I will, I promise."

Without waiting for a response, he rushed forward again, cupping his hands around his mouth.

"Kessara!"

The Princess stopped still and turned, placing a hand to her forehead as she looked in their direction even though there was no sunlight to obscure her vision. She began moving toward them, her feet moving with no urgency, as Wes heard the sound of flapping wings coming from behind. Jaconial and Celesyria were flying low along the shoreline, trying to rest upon the pockets of cold air. Nazzan and Alder were not with them.

"Where is he?" Kessara called out as she approached him and Aelrie, looking Wes up and down as though examining him for unseen injuries. She did not look sad, as he'd expected. She looked furious. "What happened?"

Before either of them could answer, the dragons were upon them, landing gracefully against the sand. A cold wave rushed up over Jaconial's front claw, and she shrunk back toward the rocky cliffs, letting out a string of curses.

"What's going on?" Kessara pleaded, not offering any sort of hello.

Wes took a few steps toward Celesyria's side, placing the flat of his hand against her orange scales. He could see by the way she stood that one of her manacled ankles was bothering her—probably from her and Alder's fight with the Gorok—but aside from that she appeared to be healthy. Jaconial looked to have made it out of the most recent battle with only minor scrapes and scratches.

"Princess," Celesyria said, dipping her head low until her yellow eyes met Kessara's blue ones. "He's fine. Nazzan carried him off to look for Holga."

Wes shared a glance with Aelrie, waiting for some kind of outburst from the Princess, but none came. She drew a breath as everyone waited expectantly, standing up straight and looking much taller than her average height would imply.

"He didn't say goodbye," she said matter-of-factly. Wes could hear the sob caught in her throat, but she did not allow a single tear to fall. Aelrie opened her mouth as though she might attempt a word of comfort before promptly closing it again.

Wes stepped forward and leaned in to embrace her.

"Don't," she said, stepping back, her voice dangerously quiet.

"I—I just—" he stammered, unsure what to do. His heart was breaking right along with her.

"Don't touch me."

"Kessara, please," he continued, reaching out a hand to touch her arm. She pulled back from him as though she'd been stung.

"Wes, get away from me," she snapped, her eyes flashing

as she turned to walk away. He looked at Aelrie, and then at the dragons. All three of them were standing there in an uncomfortable silence, no one daring to attempt to intervene.

She's embarrassed and devastated. I can't take it personally. She'll come around, and I'll be here when she does.

He forced himself to take a breath as she began to stride away.

Before she was quite out of earshot, he heard her speak.

Though he couldn't make out the full sentence, the words–easy enough to guess–hit him like a punch to the gut.

"Sometimes I wish…"

He marched forward until he stood in front of her, blocking her path.

"Sometimes I wish I'd died instead of Roven, too, Kessara," he spat. "But I'm still here. I'm trying to serve the High One the best I can, and I'm sorry that I've messed up your life in the process."

Kessara's face softened.

"Wes, that isn't what I was going to–"

"Forget it," he said firmly. "It doesn't matter. You need to go back and get your things. We're going to Stronghollow."

Chapter Nine

ORIA

BEFORE

Oria pressed her heels into the stag's side, urging the animal forward. The bandits were closer now, close enough that she could hear their shouting from deep within the trees behind her. She could not make out their words, but she knew that they were vile. She would be robbed and beaten, left for dead in the endless forests of Silverfell, miles from anything.

There are worse things they could do.

A chill rippled down her back.

And at the end of it, they could make me a slave.

She had to get away. Her heart pounded in her ears, and she focused on the sound as she rode, keeping her seat as balanced and light as she could.

"Faster, Belanor," she said to the stag, kicking at his flank again, harder this time. "Faster."

He was already flying, his heavy hooves pounding against the fallen leaves below as he passed between trees and rushed over hills. Her lead seemed to be getting bigger. Their voices were not quite so loud. She had caught a brief glimpse of a camp, and if it belonged to these bandits, they were riding horses. Her stag gave her an advantage.

She kicked the animal again, pressing him to go faster than she'd ever asked him to run. She trusted that he'd forgive her for her use of force. He was one of Elder Bram's animals, and she'd been visiting him at the palace stables for as long as she could remember.

But the stag did not seem able to move any faster. She'd brought him on a long journey already, all the way from Stronghollow to Auranth, and their brief rest in the northern city had not been sufficient to restore his strength entirely before they'd had to head back.

She leaned forward over the stag's neck as they approached a large log that lay across their path. A moment later, the stag was airborne, and she was gripping his sides with her short legs as hard as she could when he hit the ground on the other side.

There was a terrible crunching sound that filled her throat with bile.

The stag let out a furious neigh as his front leg buckled under him, his hoof landing awkwardly against a jagged piece of rock. Oria struggled to get her feet free of the saddle and her hands free of the reins as he collapsed toward the ground. The loyal stag held himself half upright just long enough for her to jump clear before falling onto his side, leaves and sticks cracking beneath his weight.

For a moment, Oria forgot to breathe. The stag let out another terrible sound, one that she had never heard before. He was in agony.

Voices were behind her now. They were close. She looked at Belanor for several long seconds, her chest heaving. Finally she turned to her left, rushing into the thick trees.

She ran, stumbling over roots, her face getting scraped with brambles as she sobbed.

"Pity, he's a beautiful beast," she heard a voice say behind her.

Just kill him. End his suffering. Please.

She wanted to turn back, but she didn't. No animal was worth dying over.

"We'll come back for his tack. Keep moving," another harsh voice said.

She narrowly avoided colliding with a thin pine as she went, moving her legs as fast as they would go. Perhaps if she could find a hollow to hide in, or a large rock that could—

"Just stop, child," a soothing voice said as he stepped out of the trees to her right, both hands raised, as though he was trying to calm a feisty horse. A thin silver blade gleamed in one of them, the tip still red with the blood of his last kill.

She did as he asked. Her legs had already grown wobbly, and her lungs burned with the effort. She sank to the ground, enjoying the feeling of the soft leaves that covered it.

He was going to catch her anyway. She would not give him the satisfaction of snaring his prey.

The two other men joined the first, tramping in along the path she had taken, their heavy footfalls thundering in the whispering forest. The sun had only just begun to set, leaving the landscape bathed in a pink and orange glow.

Your creation is beautiful, High One. Even now.

"I have nothing to steal," she said flatly, forcing herself to look at the men rather than at her lap. The one who had surprised her was clearly a Vilzanian, with dark russet skin and even darker eyes that looked somehow less cruel than the others.

The others were a little paler, though still tan, and she

figured that they were most likely from Boneshire.

How does one arrive here? How does one choose such a life?

She found herself pitying them. They were pathetic. What-ever happened next, she at least knew that her life had meant something.

Even though I failed in the end. You should have come to see Bram, Wes. Or perhaps I should have stayed.

"Liar. You dress like a peasant, but that beautiful deer of yours is of better blood," one of the Boneshire men spat.

She felt like laughing. All her life, she had lived as a peasant in order to stay safe, but in the end, it was no help at all.

She shrugged off her cloak and shoulder pack and threw them in his direction. They held only practical odds and ends, nothing that would be worth it for them to sell.

The three men bent to examine her items, hands fumbling with the leather flap that fell across the front.

She reached into the pocket of her skirt, drawing out her dagger. She was on her feet before the men had a chance to react, lunging toward the man who had accused her of lying. She had his neck against the edge of her blade, years of secret training in swordplay guiding her muscles without need for conscious thought.

And then she hesitated.

She felt her hand shaking, and then the chance was gone. The man spun around, sending her knife clattering to the ground. He had his own dagger in his hand, shorter than hers, viciously sharp.

"Don't!" The Vilzanian was shouting at him, lunging toward his companion, but the man did not hesitate. Oria did not even manage to scream as the blade bit into her thigh, once, twice, a third time. The pain consumed everything, blurring her vision, pounding in her skull like the force of a thousand anvils being struck and set ringing at once.

"She tried to stab me," she heard the man say. She watched through bleary eyes as he shoved the Vilzanian.

"But she didn't!"

"Both of you, shut up," the third man said. "Let's get the saddle and bridle and go. This is a waste of time. Should've taken the stag alive."

She closed her eyes for a moment, trying to focus on continuing to breathe. She felt wetness sliding down to her boots, but she could not feel the warmth of her blood. When she finally opened them, a weak cry escaping her throat, only the Vilzanian remained.

"You shouldn't have attacked him," he said quietly. His brow was furrowed in disapproval.

With a great effort, she managed to shake her head.

"He deserved death. You all do," she said.

The man drew back a little, his eyes widening at her words. He opened his mouth to speak, but she continued.

"But I cannot offer justice this day," she choked out. He was right. "Turn to the High One before the darkness consumes you."

She could see the blood beneath her leg now, a pool of crimson dribbling between the green blades of grass.

One of the other bandits called for the Vilzanian, and for a moment she was sure he would chase after them into the forest without a word. Instead, he knelt down beside her, yanking his belt from the loops of his trousers.

Her eyes opened in horror, but he put a finger to his lips, hushing her as he shifted her leg and pulled the strap beneath her thigh. She bit back the scream that rose to her lips. Every inch of movement was torture, even with the numbing effect of the blood loss.

"I don't know how," the man said, catching her eyes with his own as he pulled the strap tight in one quick motion. She pressed her fingernails into the forest floor, feeling her nails bending against the bits of wood and dirt. Seemingly satisfied, he pulled the metal tongue through its hole and laid it in place.

She risked a glance directly at her wounds. The holes were still there, gaping and impossibly large, but there was no more fresh blood flowing from them. Swallowing her nausea, she closed her eyes for a few seconds, trying to get her thoughts to make sense again.

She felt like the blurring of her vision had extended into her brain, forcing out all reason. She made a noise that she did not recognize as the Vilzanian stepped back, glancing off toward where his friends had run.

"You will find Him if you look," she said, forcing the words out. She tried to gaze into the man's eyes, but she struggled to keep everything still.

The man shook his head, his expression filled with such deep sadness that for a moment she could almost turn from her own pain.

"You didn't have to help me," she continued, but the words sounded strange. Her teeth were chattering, and suddenly she was cold. "Th–th–thank you."

She shuddered against the sudden chill, her entire body shaking now. The grass felt like claws scratching at her back, but somehow the open air above her felt no better.

The man's eyes met hers again, and he did not turn away.

Behind him, she saw one of the others emerging from the woods, stepping over branches with his heavy boots.

"Kamil! What's taking so long? If you wanted–"

He stopped short as he took in the tourniquet around Oria's leg, realization dawning on his bearded face. The Vilzanian turned toward the intruder as the other man drew his knife.

"You won't save her anyway," the man said, waving a hand in her direction as though she was a piece of moldy bread left on the countertop. "If you pity her, put her out of her misery. In fact, I'll do it."

The man was moving closer now, his steps slow and fumbling in the dense foliage.

"Run," Oria croaked to the Vilzanian, blinking quickly as dark patches filled her vision. "You'll outrun him."

"I made things even worse for you," he said, his dark eyes filling with tears as he placed his hands to his cheeks, looking down at her wound as the other man approached. "I'm so sorry. I deserve to die, like you said."

"Go," she said, trying to give him what she hoped was a smile. She wasn't sure if her lips were moving the way that she wanted to, but despite everything, she knew that he would understand. Somehow, the few words she could offer would be enough. "Go and live. Live... for Him."

I deserve to die, too. Perhaps, had I been raised as you and your friends have, I would be a criminal myself. I know better, and yet still I fail. I was my grandfather's only hope, and I failed even him. Perhaps it is I who should seek forgiveness.

There were so many things she wanted to say, but her mouth would not make another sound.

The Vilzanian's eyes met hers for a long moment.

"I'll come back for you."

She knew the words were hollow, but she smiled anyway. It was something to hold on to.

A second later he was gone, running off into the woods. She could hear the other bandit giving chase, but the one with the knife continued to move toward her, each thump of his boots against the ground sounding like thunder in her ears. He was there now, standing over her, rage flashing in his eyes. He scarcely looked human as he brandished the knife at her, a cruel, gleeful sound escaping from his lips.

And then he turned away in disgust and headed off after his companions.

She lay on her back in the grass, looking up at the sky, which had begun to darken into a soft blue dusk. Time passed, and the man did not return to finish her off. He was long gone, off somewhere in the depths of the thick forest. She hoped that the Vilzanian had gotten away from them.

He has a chance, High One. Have mercy on him.

She tried to take deep breaths, but each draw of air hurt. She couldn't turn her head to see what may come out of the woods, which animal may be waiting for her to finally be at her end.

She felt very small.

Mama, I'm sorry.

She felt tears rolling down her cheek as she thought of her, back at home in their little house, waiting for her to return. She hadn't wanted her to leave, but Oria knew that there had been no one else to send, no one that grandfather Bram could trust. She had done her duty. It was up to Wes now to choose if he was going to listen or not.

She felt like she was moving through a thick fog, not quite sure of the real shape of anything until she reached it. But she could see the blue of the sky, and hear the familiar nightly bird songs of Silverfell.

"High One," she said aloud after a very long time, swallowing back saliva that had settled in her throat. "If You would permit it...I would very much like to see the stars one last time."

Without warning, the pain of her injuries began to fade away.

She realized that she was entirely content, laying there bleeding on the grass.

She did not need to close her eyes against the pain. She could still hear her breathing, the air making entirely the wrong sound, but it did not make her chest hurt any more. She could even focus enough to inhale the smell of the forest, right down to the damp soil that lay beneath the grass.

She felt alive. More alive than she had been before, riding through the trees, rushing off to important business that a child should have never had to carry on her shoulders.

I'll take care of everything, my child.

It was something between a thought and a voice, a whisper caught on the soft breeze rippling through the clearing. She tried not to breathe so loud. She didn't want to miss a word of it.

The Envoy will go to Bram when the ordained hour is upon him. Fear not.

"But I am afraid," she said aloud, her voice shaking. There was peace, yes, inexplicable peace... but this did not make sense. This was all wrong. She couldn't be here now, not yet.

"My mother is waiting," she said, sobbing now, fresh tears racing along her cheeks and falling toward the grass. She could imagine them falling to the grass below her, mingling with her blood. She was glad that she could not turn her head to see it, to see the essence of her bodily life poured out like a spilled waterskin. "I'm so young. This is not the way it should be."

No. This is not the world that I made for you. It was never supposed to be this way.

She tried to say more, but the pain had returned, and she found herself coughing every time she opened her mouth.

Do you trust Me, Oria?

She paused for a long moment. Her heart was pounding in her ears. She wanted to scream for help, to try and run from this lonely clearing, to do anything she could to preserve an additional second of her life.

Do you trust Me?

Memories filtered into her mind with no discernible order, both happy and sad.

Her mother, dancing with her in the kitchen as they made the day's bread.

Sitting on her grandfather's knee, learning for the very first time about the mission that had been given to her family to protect the Codex Veritatis.

The stone walls of the fortress in Auranth, where people were preparing to fight for a future that was better.

And then she saw them.

First one little pinprick of light, and then another. The voice did not interrupt her as she watched the stars, blinking into existence as the sky overhead darkened to an inky black. Soon she could see the constellations.

With painful effort, she managed to lift her arm. She extended her forefinger, pointing to the first one that she recognized. *Manta.* It had been her mother who had first shown them to her, laying on blankets in the tiny plot behind their house with mugs of warm tea. She'd been young, but she had always remembered them all. *The Shield. Vavoren.*

She smiled as her finger drifted to her favorite, the great deer. *Cervos.*

Her fears were not so heavy any more. She knew that somehow the House of Cervos would rise again, and that somehow, she'd had the honor in her short life of being a part of it. Her mother would be cared for. The High One would not leave her alone in the world.

"I trust you," she said aloud, letting her arm fall gently onto the grass.

She closed her eyes.

She believed.

Chapter Ten

CELESYRIA

"Silverfell is so beautiful in the fall," Celesyria said aloud to no one in particular, stretching her wings out as far as they could go as she drifted across a cushion of air.

"It would be more beautiful if my back didn't hurt," Jaconial grumbled from beside her, her own orange wingtips nearly brushing Celesyria's own. "No offense, ladies."

Celesyria could hear Wes chuckling from his place on her back.

With Nazzan gone, it had been decided that Aelrie and the Princess would share Jaconial's saddle, and Wes would stay with Celesyria.

"I weighed a lot more back before you all got me involved in this mess," Kessara said, raising her voice slightly to be heard over the gentle rushing of the wind. Below, the trees were beginning to turn orange and yellow, and every now and then Celesyria saw one that had already lost its leaves altogether. Autumn was upon them. "I should tell the lesser House noblewomen back home that scant rations of bread and dry meat make a fantastic diet."

"Don't forget the rigorous dragon-riding routine," Aelrie said, giving her tinkling laugh.

Celesyria felt a rush of warmth filling her chest at Kessara's small joke.

The Princess had been quiet ever since they'd left Windshear, largely keeping to herself as they made the long journey. The others had joked around by the fire each night, but the Princess had slept early, waking only when it was nearly time to leave for the next leg of the trip.

Celesyria longed to comfort her, to give her hope that things between her and Alder might work out in the end, but she knew that she could not.

"Are you okay?" she asked Wes, cringing at the memory of what the Princess had nearly said to him back on the beach.

"Sure," he said in her mind, not sounding particularly confident. *"It's not about me. She's hurt."*

"Has she apologized? Properly, I mean?"

She could feel Wes shifting his weight in her saddle and wondered if he was shaking his head out of habit, though of course she could not see it.

"No. But I keep insisting to myself that I've already forgiven her. I suppose eventually I will feel it."

"Have you broached the topic of your marriage?" Celesyria cringed even to ask. She could scarcely imagine the difficulty that the situation presented for Wes.

"I will be loyal to her," he said after a long pause. *"The rest is up to the High One."*

Celesyria cast a glance at Aelrie, who was clinging to Kessara's back. She was glad that reading minds was not among the elf's skills.

The poor girl would be hurt, too. There was no way around it. Fulfilling one's duty was not often easy.

"I assure you both that flying is a lot more difficult on our end," Jaconial was saying as she continued to argue with the women, though she did not sound quite so annoyed anymore. Even Kessara was smiling. "Carrying two riders is man's work."

"I thought you were fearsome beasts, afraid of nothing," Wes put in. Celesyria caught Kessara giving him a quick glance before looking forward again.

"We are," Jaconial said. "But I still miss Nazzan."

Celesyria was pleased to notice that her usual pang of jealousy did not surface. If Jaconial could find a good mate like Nazzan, perhaps she would as well. At least she was not in the position that Wes was, forced to marry someone that he had no romantic feelings for.

"I can take one of the ladies for a little while, the next time we land," Celesyria suggested.

"No," Kessara said. Jaconial's wing brushed the end of her wing against her own as she caught a fresh gust of air. Celesyria followed her upward, the trees shrinking beneath them as they glided along. The ground below had been rather deserted for quite awhile, but she knew that they were approaching Stronghollow. They needed to exercise caution. "You were hurt by the Gorok, and you need to rest."

Celesyria let out a plume of warm breath into the chilly fall air.

"This is hardly a warm nest."

"She's right," Jaconial said glumly. "You shouldn't be flying at all. Neither should Nazzan, for that matter."

She paused for a moment, no doubt thinking about the green dragon and wondering if he was alright. They were much too far away to mindspeak now.

"Besides, I'm stronger," she added. Celesyria glanced over

at her, unsurprised to see her lips curling up into a grin.

"I'm not going to argue," Celesyria said with a chuckle, flapping her wings as she felt the air becoming thin.

"Wait. Look there, in that little valley."

She had noticed a little clearing resting beside a rockfall that would be a perfect place to camp for the night.

"We're stopping now?" Aelrie asked.

"We're nearly in Stronghollow, so it's now or never," Wes said. "I'd rather face all of this in the morning, if it's alright with you."

Jaconial quickly agreed. Kessara said nothing one way or the other, seeming to have retreated back into her solitude already.

Within another half-hour, they had landed in the clearing and the humans had set up their simple tents.

An even simpler dinner was eaten afterward—Celesyria and Jaconial managed to snare a couple of nearby rabbits, which was not nearly enough—and then Wes made a small fire, largely hidden in the shadow of a large overhanging rock. They could not know who might be lurking between the trees.

Kessara had gone to bed as soon as her bread was finished, giving only a brief goodnight before heading off to her little tent.

The others sat for a while as the dusk deepened into darkness, telling pleasant stories of their pasts to one another. Celesyria was content, her scales warmed by the emberlight until Wes told her that it was time to stifle the flames. They could not risk the light drawing anyone to their camp.

She was too tired to mind the ensuing cold. Kessara was right—she was still in need of rest, and the long journey had begun to add heavily to the toll on her body. She got to her feet, stretching out her wings as far as she could. Jaconial did the same.

"I'm going to sit up a little while and pray," Wes said, gesturing in the general direction of the open side of the clearing. "I'll take the first watch."

"Wake me as soon as you're tired," Aelrie said, getting up from her place beside him and stretching her silvery arms over her head. Celesyria watched them, feeling nervous that they would meet again, alone, in the silence of the autumn night. A strange energy seemed to simmer in the air between them, and she wondered if they realized how dangerous that energy was, especially considering what Kessara had done.

"Let me," Celesyria said to the elf. "I'm hardly tired. You should rest."

Aelrie hesitated, but a moment later she yawned, the sound of it almost comically loud. "Thank you," she said, smiling and looking down at her feet.

"Goodnight," Wes said as they walked away, Jaconial and Celesyria to their makeshift nests, Aelrie to the tent she shared with Kessara.

Celesyria felt her eyes closing as soon as she curled up in the soft leaves, the lingering heat from the fire keeping her blood warm and her body comfortable.

With a final prayer for their protection, she fell asleep, certain that she would find only happy dreams.

KESSARA

Kessara had always assumed that elves were too perfect to snore, especially an elf as lovely as Aelrie. She had been sorely mistaken.

Aelrie had entered the tent with her usual quiet steps,

stripping to her underclothes and getting beneath her blanket with only a few sounds, but it was of no use. As soon as she'd fallen asleep, the snoring had begun, filling the tent with its impressive loudness.

Kessara tossed and turned beneath her own quilt—borrowed from the kind fisherman who had taken them in back in Windshear—but she could not sleep, snoring or not. She had gone to bed far too early, and now she had little tiredness left to push her back into dreaming.

Are you alright, Alder? Are you awake somewhere thinking of me, too?

He didn't even know if Holga was still alive. The whole thing was a huge risk, and he'd chosen to take that risk without a word to her, even though she'd been privy to the letter's contents from the beginning. The man was infuriating. The passing days of travel had dulled the pain, but it was still there, waiting beneath everything, ready to send her back into despair at a moment's notice.

She set her jaw, wishing very much that she could beat her straw pillow with her fists without waking Aelrie. She was tired of it, tired of pretending to hold it together. All she wanted to do was to wallow in her own misery and loneliness, but she had made a promise to herself on the beach, and she intended to keep it.

She climbed off of her bedroll, the sound of her rustling blanket loud enough that she was certain Aelrie would open her eyes, but she lay still, snoring just as loudly as ever. She couldn't stand it anymore. She couldn't hold all of this inside of her any more. She had tried to talk to the High One, of course, but He was not inclined to answer out loud.

Shaking her head, she moved through the door flap of the

tent, careful not to trip as she picked her way toward the remains of their fire.

The air outside of the tent had grown much colder since the sun had set, and she drew her arms tightly around herself, wishing she'd thought to grab her cloak. Wind was rushing through the valley, bringing a chill from the east, and she bent to face the ground as she picked her way toward where Wes was sitting.

She drew a breath, pushing between two trees, debating whether or not she should go back inside of her warm tent to try to sleep until the sun rose.

You can't talk to him. Not after everything you've done to hurt him. He doesn't show it, but he must hate you by now. All of this back and forth has not been easy for him, either.

The accusations rose in her mind, but she ignored them, brushing against branches as she stepped into the open space between them. Wes turned at the sound, and she raised a hand in an awkward greeting.

"Sit," he said after a brief pause, gesturing to the ground next to him, where a fallen log served as a convenient backrest. The fire still had a few glowing orange coals, but they gave off little light and even less heat. She shivered as she sat down at his side, wishing she had not only her cloak, but her quilt as well.

"The fire is no use, but I made some tea earlier. I kept it warm in the embers," he said, handing her a strange-looking metal mug that had a lid attached on the top.

"I recognize this," she said, turning the vessel over in her hands. The warmth glowed against her fingertips. "The sailors use these back home to keep their coffee hot. And their ale cold, more importantly."

She gave a little chuckle, but her mouth felt as though it was stuffed with sawdust. To her relief, Wes gave her one of his usual warm smiles.

He waited as she twisted the lid off and drank the steaming liquid.

"Good, right?" he asked when she came up for air.

She nodded, her tongue feeling a little burnt.

"Aelrie found a few old summer raspberries. Apparently, the leaves make an excellent drink."

At the sound of the elf's name, Kessara felt her breath catch in her chest. There were so many things she wanted to say. So many hurts that she longed to heal. But when it came to his feelings for Aelrie, she knew that no hope existed. She was an elf, and he was a man.

She took another sip of tea, trying to figure out what else to say. Despite everything, it was still so comfortable to be with him. She was glad she'd come.

He's my family. Family always forgives.

"Wes," she started, trying to force herself to look at his eyes rather than the ground.

He took the mug from her outstretched hands and took a sip of the tea, raising an eyebrow.

"I'm sorry. I did almost say what you thought," she said quickly, pressing her eyes closed as though she could hide from him while sitting less than a foot away. "Sometimes I do wish Roven was still here, but I never mean it. It's a fleeting, nasty thought. It's never been more than that, I promise you."

He looked at her for a couple of seconds, and she could not figure out what he was about to say.

"I know that sounds horrible. Maybe I could have given a better excuse, tried to make myself sound better," she said, the words tumbling out before he could open his mouth. "But I can't hold my sins inside any more. I need someone, someone who knows all of me, even the ugly pieces."

She paused, thinking of Alder.

All this time, she thought he knew. Thought he understood her. Thought that of all men, he could love her best.

Maybe he could.

But she couldn't make him try.

"Kessara—"

"You've always told me that I can come to you. That whatever happens with us, you're my friend and I can trust you. I hope that's still true."

Wes leaned over and wrapped his arm around her, pulling her close and wrapping his cloak around them both. They stayed like that for a long while, listening to the sounds of the forest as the wind rushed through the trees. Kessara felt safer than she had in a long, long time.

"Sometimes I think of other awful things," she said finally, adjusting her head beneath his chin. "I imagine a world where Roven lived, and I was his wife, Queen of Silverfell after all."

"And that's terrible?" Wes asked with a gentle chuckle.

"Not that part, but the rest. The part where it means I never would have met Alder. It would have saved me so much pain."

Her throat felt tight. She swallowed the sob that threatened to break loose. She couldn't keep crying over him. It brought no relief, only more hurt.

"I can understand that wish," Wes said, his voice barely above a whisper. "I certainly don't blame you for it."

He paused, and she felt him taking a long, deep breath. She didn't dare to speak or to move, wanting him to finish his thought, even though her arm was beginning to ache.

"It won't be a surprise to you that I've wished for much darker things."

She knew he had. Everyone who was close to him did.

But he did not know just how close she had come to wishing for the same.

"I used to long for death," he continued, looking off into the darkness of the forest around them. "More recently and more often than I care to admit."

"I'm glad you're still here," she reminded him. "We all are."

"Being with Aelrie on that boat, feeling the darkness for myself...I tasted what life without the High One's goodness felt like. It was so terrifying and so painful that I can't adequately describe it."

He paused, shaking his head.

"I guess you would think that after having experienced that, thoughts of giving up would just go away. They didn't. I'm still the same broken person. I still dream of the same broken things. But I'm thankful for that fear and that hurt, all the same. I know that I'm becoming stronger through it, even if I wish that I could reach the end of my path tomorrow."

She pulled back for a moment until she could look at him, searching his face. He had gone through things that would have destroyed weaker men, but instead, he'd continued to change for the better.

"And Kessara?"

She waited, looking up at the night sky. Celesyria would be here for the next watch soon. Finally, she was beginning to get tired.

"I just want you to know something. You're getting stronger, too, even when it doesn't feel like it. I hope that you don't forget that. I love you, and I always will, no matter what happens."

Her throat felt tight, and sudden tears stung her eyes. She tried to blink them away, but more quickly took their place. She did not know what she'd been expecting him to say, but this was not it. He was too good. He was too kind, and she knew that she didn't deserve it, not any of it.

"The High One loves you too, Kessara. He knows you're trying," Wes continued.

A wounded cry escaped her throat in place of words. She wasn't sure what she had even been trying to say.

"It's okay to cry, by the way," he added, giving her a half-smile as she began to sob, leaning back against his chest in surrender. "I still do. Sometimes."

Once she started, she couldn't bring herself to stop.

It felt good to let go, to feel her chest ache, to taste the salt against her lips. All of the numbness fell away.

She felt the autumn wind brushing tendrils of blonde hair against her face as crickets sang to one another in the shadows.

She smelled the lingering smoke from the fire.

Her heart ached, and somehow, it was glorious.

Wes said nothing, offering no words of comfort and asking no questions. She kept opening her mouth to speak, but she couldn't bring herself to say a word.

She wasn't ready to tell him that she'd changed her mind, and she didn't know if she ever would be.

I turned away from my family. I turned against the will of the High One. I lost the man I love.

She wanted to put her hands to her ears, to silence the accusing voice in her head, but she knew that it was pointless.

The words were her own.

Worse, they were true.

"I don't know if I can believe you," she said aloud. Her voice sounded very small.

"About what?" Wes said gently, stroking her hair. To her surprise, the gesture reminded her not of Alder, but of her mother, of a time long ago when lost dolls and split lips were her biggest worries.

"You love me," she said, swallowing the lump in her throat. "You're stupid for it, and I don't deserve it, but I believe you."

"But?"

"The High One wants us to do what He asks. He wants us to turn from the darkness, to choose what is good over what is easy."

"Yes, and?"

"I haven't done that, Wes. And I'm still not doing that," she said, drawing a breath.

She hoped he wouldn't make her say it out loud. To say the words was to admit defeat, to confess weakness. Everything inside of her was screaming.

She felt the rise and fall of Wes' chest beneath her cheek.

He did not say a word.

"I'm still not going to marry you, alright? I know that's what I should do, and it's what the High One wants me to do, but I can't. And I'm sorry. I'm sorry for the damage I'm causing to my Kingdom and to yours. I'm sorry for everything, but I'm not strong enough. I told that to my father, and I told it to Alder, and nothing has changed. Even though he told me he doesn't want me, I'm still carrying on like there's hope, because I'm a fool," she said, the words tumbling out in a rush. "So no, Wes, I don't believe you. I don't believe that I've gotten stronger, and I don't believe that the High One still loves me."

He continued to stroke her hair, the steady rise and fall of his chest reminding her how to breathe. He did not say anything, not even as the moon rose higher in the sky, not even as she let forth a fresh wave of sobbing cries against the tear-soaked front of his cloak.

"Celesyria will be here soon," he said finally, still stroking her hair.

"Okay," she said quickly, trying to pull away. She did not want anyone else to see her this way. She dreaded the thought of returning to a shared tent. All she wanted was to be alone.

"Wait," Wes said, placing his hand under her chin and tilting her face up until her eyes met his. In some other world, perhaps a world where she was an elf instead of a princess, the gesture would have been romantic. But now, it was a different kind of love she could see in his eyes.

Different, but just as real.

Just as strong, and just as important.

He released her and she sat beside him, twisting her fingers together.

"I'm sorry," she said again, not sure what else there was to say.

To her surprise, he laughed. It was loud enough that for a moment she thought he might wake the entire camp. Somewhere overhead, she could hear a starbird scolding him, firing off his chirping song in rapid succession.

"Kessara," he said, pausing for breath. "No, I'm sorry for laughing. It isn't funny. I know exactly how you feel. I'll probably believe the same stupid thing a week from now, even though I know better. We're all stupid. It's just the way it is."

She crossed her arms over her chest, raising her eyebrows at him.

"Kessara," he said again, the smile falling from his face. "If we had to already be perfect for the High One to love us, there would be no hope at all. Of course He wants us to do the right thing. Of course He wants us to follow His plan for our lives. And of course the Wrathlands are real, for those who persist in refusing Him."

She swallowed. That fact was not lost on her.

"But He also knows us. He knows you and loves you more perfectly than I or anyone else ever could. He knew that right now, you wouldn't be ready to do what He is asking. None of that is a surprise to him. But you have to choose. Are you going to ask Him to help you find the strength to follow His will, or are you going to give up and hate yourself for where you are right now instead of nurturing the person that you can become by accepting His help?"

She turned his words over in her mind.

Somewhere deep within her bones, she knew that this was a lesson that the High One had taught her before, more than once, without using words.

They sang of truth, as clear and piercing as a chorus of birdsong.

"I don't know," she said finally, deciding that the honest answer was the best option.

Wes stood up beside her and planted a kiss on the top of her blonde head.

"When in doubt, my dear friend, you should always choose love."

Without another word, he strode off to wake Celesyria.

Chapter Eleven

ALDER

The village of Rill was even smaller and shabbier than Alder had imagined. As he made his way down what he assumed was the main street, he debated whether or not he should remove the hood that covered his telltale Aridmoorian hair. Everyone he passed was already looking at him with suspicion, leaning out through glassless windows and ducking from behind fenceposts.

There could not have been more than a few hundred people in the entire village, and he had no doubt that most of them knew each other by sight, if not by name. He saw others who drew the same whispers, though, and he figured that in this case it might be better to be mistaken for an average criminal rather than what he actually was.

Nazzan had stayed safely out of sight, having to hide three miles away where the red-stone cliffs and hills were tall enough to conceal his body. Even though Alder had gotten much better at mindspeaking, he knew that doing so at this distance lay well beyond his abilities. He was on his own.

After getting his bearings for a few minutes, he found the local inn and pushed his way through the door. Over his head, a rusty bell sounded, announcing his arrival to the pleasant-looking woman behind the bar.

"Hello, dear," she trilled, beckoning him over. He crossed the room, passing a few patrons that had settled in for a very early dinner of some kind of soup. The inn looked a bit worse for wear, but he had to admit that the food smelled decent enough. Perhaps he could return later on. He was growing very tired of his travel rations.

"Room or soup?" the barkeeper prompted cheerily as he leaned against the worn wooden countertop. She was wearing a simple gray dress and had her hair up in a kerchief. She was smiling as she dried a heavy metal mug, her soft cheeks flushing red. She looked to be anywhere between nineteen and thirty-four.

"I will hopefully be back to eat, ma'am. That soup smells wonderful, and I am growing tired of bread," Alder said, flashing her his best smile. Much of his face was concealed in the shadows of his hood, and he figured it was wise to offer whatever charm and good looks he could without giving himself away. "For the moment, though, I need help finding someone."

She set the mug on a shelf behind her. Far above her head, just beneath the ceiling, he could see another shelf where a black-and-white cat lay. The creature had one paw dangling over the edge, and it gave a loud yowl as the woman turned back to give her attention to Alder.

"Quiet!" the woman called good-naturedly to her pet, swatting at the cat with a flick of the cloth in her hand. The animal only meowed again, looking down at Alder with wide green eyes.

"Sorry about her," she said, smiling. "Most obnoxious animal in all of Rill. Showed up at our door one day, and of course my children just had to feed her. Eventually, I managed to pawn her off on an older farmer who wanted a nice mouser. But she found her way back. Four miles! Can you believe that?"

Alder grinned, feeling his shoulders relax. No one else in the inn was paying them the slightest attention, and he had a few hours of light left. The only annoyance was the too-heavy wool of his hood. It was making the back of his neck itch.

"We had a dog like that once, back home," he said, hoping she would not inquire as to where home was. "A mutt, but he was a good soul. Lived to be fourteen."

She beamed at him. "Well, if you come back, I'm sure Nibbler would love to come down and meet you. In the meantime, I know everyone. Who is it that you're trying to find?"

"An herbwoman," he said, lowering his voice. "I believe she's called Malka."

"We only have one of those, dear," she said lightly. "Malka is indeed her name. She lives just two streets away, past the butcher."

"Thank you," Alder said, not wanting to pull away from the bar. He could see bottles lined up along shelves, the place surprisingly well-stocked for its size.

"You'll know the house, trust me," the woman said, rolling her eyes. "She's got bits of herbs strung up in ribbons, old bones on the windowsills, the usual. She's one of a certain kind."

Alder wondered if the woman was more witch than healer, and for a moment, he considered just asking the barkeeper where Holga was. He was certain she would know. But as he glanced behind him at the other patrons, he knew it wasn't worth the risk. He was a strange man asking after a little girl, and it would draw unwanted attention, no matter how discreet he tried to be.

"Thank you," he said again, reaching into the pocket of his trousers and laying a few silver coins down. "I trust you'll hold an ale for me."

The woman swept the coins out of sight. "Certainly. You're welcome any time," she promised.

As he made his way back out into the street, he noticed that the shadows had already begun to change. The afternoon sun had begun its descent toward the horizon, making the reddish stone and sand gleam even more brightly against the blue sky. He walked past a couple of shops until he found the butcher, and then turned down a side street.

The houses here were even more decrepit than those that lined the main street, with canvas roofs that would never hold up against the sort of rain that was common in most of the Four Kingdoms. Many of them had old bits of rusted fence and other rubbish on their front lawns, and of course there was no real grass to speak of. He could hear a vibrating sound coming from between the strange dry plants and scattered stones, the song of some strange desert insect that he had never heard before.

He spotted Malka's house easily. There were indeed dried plants strung up, and strange little animal skeletons used as morbid decorations, but there was also a strange feeling about the place that made him uneasy. He thought back to Raela's letter and shuddered. She had trusted this woman, but he knew that he could not, not if she still continued to deal in death as well as healing.

Still, she was his best chance at finding Holga.

He looked around as he stepped up to her blue door. The street surrounding him was empty, though he could hear the scuttling and clucking sounds of chickens coming from somewhere nearby. He raised his hand and rapped twice on the old wood, pulling his hood more tightly around his face.

Almost too quickly, the door swung inward, and he was met face to face with a middle-aged woman nearly short enough to be mistaken for a dwarf. She had wispy hair—brown, streaked with gray—that frizzed about her tanned face. Her sharp brown eyes looked nearly red in the beam of afternoon light that slipped past him through the doorway.

"I can't see anyone else today," she said before he could open his mouth to speak, wiping her hands on her once-white apron as poofs of yellow dust billowed to the floor. "Least of all a stranger. The Zam boy broke his arm, and I have three babes coming any day now."

Relief rushed through him at the mention of the births, even though he doubted she'd tell him of her other services, if they still existed.

"I'm looking for someone. Her name is Holga. Holga Zahrezain," he said quickly, taking a step forward so that the tip of his boot rested on the threshold of her little shack. She stared at him, her eyes searching him up and down.

"She has a brother. She lives here in Rill—"

"I know," she said, turning to smash a spider that had crawled up the side of the doorframe, not bothering to use anything but her bare, worn hand. "What I don't know is what business you have looking for her. We don't get many Aridmoorians here, and certainly not those of your kind of blood."

He gaped at her, and in one fluid motion she had reached up

to her full height and knocked the hood off of his head. "Ha!" she crowed, steadying herself on her feet again. "I knew it. You plains folks have a certain walk. But you're more than that. You're a soldier. I can see it in your shoulders."

He slumped a little before he could stop himself, as though a momentary slouch could conceal years of military training. "I was," he admitted, glancing over his shoulder at the street behind him.

"No one will see you," she said, waving a hand impatiently. "Half the men on this road will be at the inn already. The other half aren't yet finished sleeping off last night's drink."

He straightened, trying not to appear as nervous as he felt. *Is she very perceptive, or is this some kind of witch-trick?*

"Anyway, I'm Malka. An herbwoman, just as I appear," she continued, giving him a bright smile that revealed a couple of missing teeth. Though he could guess at her approximate age, she looked much older than he'd imagined. "You're an ex-soldier from King Ursa's army. Can't say I blame you. King Radagar was a decent man, but that son of his is trouble."

He nodded, not wishing to offer his own name unless she asked for it. He got the feeling that she knew a great deal about what was going on in the broader world, and he doubted that the rebellion of Wes Cervos and his friends had escaped her notice.

"Can you please tell me about Holga?" he asked again, hating the pleading sound of his voice.

The sun was moving closer to the horizon with every passing minute, and unless the herbwoman wanted to offer a spare bedroll, he would have to make it back to Nazzan that night. Wes had once escaped a pack of ironwolves, out there in the desert. Alder had no interest in repeating his adventure.

Malka gave a long sigh.

"There were other strange men here not too long ago. Not soldiers, but not peaceful, either," she said, raising an eyebrow at him. He felt suddenly very small beneath her accusing gaze, but she gave him no time to protest his innocence. "They took the boy. Gohr, Holga's little brother. Said they were taking him straight to Vaevar Academy."

She waited, eyebrow still raised.

His heart pounded in his chest. "That's awful."

"The poor girl has been trying to go after him ever since. Her parents are dead. He was all she had, aside from those of us in the town who try to look out for them. And they took him away. So if you plan on bringing her more sorrow, you can get out of here right now–" she paused, glaring at him with those fire-filled eyes again. "–or I will make sure you don't get to leave this village at all."

Alder took a step back, stumbling on the little stone walkway. He placed a hand out to catch his fall, recoiling as he realized that he had leaned on some dried-out lizard that hung on a nail along the doorway.

"Goodness, boy," Malka said, crossing her arms over your chest. He could see a gleam in her dark eyes. "I wouldn't have told you so much if I thought you were going to hurt her. But glad to see that you can recognize a legitimate threat when you hear one."

"Why did they take Gohr to Vaevar?" he asked, swallowing his annoyance.

"He survived the bad water that's been plaguing these lands. Supposedly, the Elders are looking for a cure," she said with a shrug. "Or maybe just the one or two that are left. I heard that there was an attack in Stronghollow, but I'm not exactly sure which came first."

Alder nodded. "Most of the Elders were assassinated. So far as anyone can tell, it was elves that did it."

Malka made a clicking sound with her tongue. "I guess their Dracodei weren't interested in protecting them, after all."

She did not look particularly sympathetic, and Alder found it difficult to fault her for it. The burden of the Feast of Offering was felt especially heavily in poor areas like Rill, where treasure was hard to come by and even harder to keep.

Boneshire had been without a ruling monarch for two centuries, and the bureaucrats who held de facto control of the wounded Kingdom were known more for their corruption than anything else.

"One Guardian came, but she was too late."

"Wouldn't have been enough, anyway," Malka said. "But it's good to know that some of the dragons are still willing to help us little humans, even if it's just a few.

She gestured in the vague direction of where Umrym lay, hundreds of miles to the west.

"Anyway, Holga has been planning to go after him just as soon as she's saved up enough money for transport and a guide."

Alder felt a pang of pity for the child. Joining the army at fourteen had been a difficult burden, and she was even younger than that. "Where does she work?"

"All over Rill. At the laundry, or doing mending, or cleaning horse tack. When I have work for her, she helps me out. I'm trying to teach her all that I can of my trade so that she can replace me one day. It's not much money, of course, but at least it's a living."

He stole a glance through the door and into Malka's home

but saw nothing of interest, at least from where he stood. He hoped that Holga had not helped with any of her immoral services, but he doubted the little girl could afford to be choosy. Anything was better than working the street.

"So where is she now?"

Malka looked him up and down again, as though his cloaked body and shadowed face might reveal new answers. "Follow me."

She closed the door behind her and headed along the side of her house, kicking aside a round tangle of weeds that had rolled up against a wall. Behind her hut, Alder could see nothing but cacti, red sand, and rocks. Malka made her way forward, picking along a path he couldn't make out, and he followed, finding it surprisingly difficult to keep up with her.

They walked for only a couple of minutes before a patch of purple flowers came into view, tucked between two ridges of red stone. Sitting there was a little girl, her fingertips yellow with pollen. She wore her brown hair in braids, and her skin was dark. She looked up as they drew closer, her green eyes going wide with alarm when she caught sight of Alder.

"It's alright, love," Malka said, gesturing for him to remove his hood. He obeyed, savoring the cool breeze as it rushed against his sweaty neck.

"I'm Alder. Alder Cadogen, of Aridmoor," he said, leaning down and extending a hand. She did not take it.

"Isn't taking my brother away enough, my *good sir*?" she snapped. "Are you here to take me away, too?"

"No," he said quickly, giving Malka a quick glance. She stood there with her arms crossed, not saying a word. "It's nothing like that. I'm not from—I just need to speak to you."

"Malka," the girl said, refusing to look at him. "Please, tell this gentleman to leave."

"For what it's worth, love," the herbwoman said, giving her a knowing smile. "I think I trust him."

Holga looked cross, and for a long moment, he thought she was going to go striding off into the desert without a final word.

"I'm a friend of Wes Cervos. The Envoy."

Holga green eyes went wide. "Really? You know him?"

She glanced over at Malka who offered only a shrug.

"He and the dragon Celesyria are dear friends of mine. And I know all about the time that he rescued you and your brother from bandits."

He hoped that she believed him.

"I was just with him not too long ago, in a city called Kingsvier Landing."

The little girl paused, and then to his great relief, a smile spread across her face.

"Kingsvier Landing. Along the coast of Galeharbor," she said, getting up from her seat amid the flowers and dusting off her skirt. "One of the biggest fishing towns in all Kaveryth. There's a rich merchant in Redvale—he specializes in gemstones, especially Aethlainetite, the kind that's mined only in Mardeer—who has dried squid imported from one of their fishermen. It has to be a specific kind, though. Most species of squid lose flavor if salted too much. Importing squid, in a desert! Can you imagine? Oh, isn't Kingsvier Landing not too far from Vilzan? As you could probably guess, I have quite a lot of Vilzanian ancestors, going back—"

"Perhaps you could come and speak to him inside," Malka cut in quickly, shooting Alder a tight smile and shrugging her shoulders. He blinked, unsure what to say to any of it.

Perhaps making this child a queen was not so impossible. He could only imagine the knowledge she could gain if poverty did not hold her back.

They made their way back toward the house, Holga chatting all the while. He should have mentioned Wes straightaway, but he was glad for the moment that he had not brought up the recent defeat of the Gorok. The girl probably knew all of the legends of the beast even better than Aelrie did, and would share them at exhausting length.

Alder glanced around again before stepping into the house, again seeing no one, but the town was beginning to sound more lively as sunset drew nearer. He hoped that Nazzan was doing alright. He knew that hunting food in the desert wasn't always an easy task.

Malka ushered them into a small living room, with such small chairs that Alder feared the one he was offered might break under his weight. Fortunately, it held, and as Malka stoked the dying fire, it began to feel rather cozy in the little shack.

"It gets cold at night," Holga explained, filling a brief moment of silence. "People think it's always warm, because in the daytime it's hot all year. But the air is so dry that the heat escapes overnight. We often need to light fires, like right now, for instance. Oh, but I suppose you know all of that. You're from Aridmoor. You had to travel to get here. Probably not the most luxurious trip, judging by your attire—oh, how rude, forgive me!"

He smiled in spite of himself. "Yes. I've traveled all over Kaveryth," he said, taking a cup of warm tea that Malka offered him. "I came by dragon, actually."

No point in hiding it now, I suppose.

Holga's face lit up with excitement, but Malka only shook her head and made a tut-tutting noise under her breath, as though he'd just announced that he'd arrived on some newfangled cart that did not need to be pulled by a horse.

"Anyway," he said quickly, before she got a chance to launch into a monologue on herpetology. "There is something rather sensitive that I need to discuss with you."

Holga looked suddenly nervous.

"Is Gohr alright? Did something else happen?"

He shook his head apologetically. "I don't know anything about your brother, I'm afraid, aside from what Malka explained to me. It's something else."

The girl glanced over at the herbwoman. Malka nodded, giving her a reassuring smile. "As I told our guest earlier, I have three women waiting to deliver, ready any day now. I promised the Crockett girl that I'd check on her before day's end."

"You must tell me if any babies come," Holga insisted, beaming back at her. "I can't miss it."

She turned to Alder. "Malka is going to let me assist! I love babies. It's such a joy."

"That's right," she said. "Holga has been watching and learning for almost a year. She's ready."

Malka looked so happy that Alder felt a renewed flash of anger. How could someone who loved bringing new life in the world be willing to snuff it out for a few coins?

Malka gathered up a few supplies and made her way out into the dusky evening, leaving him alone with the girl in the shabby, but comfortable, room.

Holga looked over at him from her own chair, her mug of tea still steaming in her hands. Finally, she was quiet.

"Holga," he started, setting his own drink down on a rickety wooden table near the stove. "There's something I came to tell you, and it's important."

"Yes, I know," she said, giving him a puzzled look. "I think that has been established."

"Right," he said, feeling suddenly nervous. He was here, after all this time, fulfilling Raela's dying wish. So much depended on her reaction to it, but he supposed that there was little he could do about that. He just had to trust.

He reached into his cloak and unbuttoned the top of his tunic, drawing out the letter from its hiding place. She wrinkled her nose at him. "You came all this way to give me your sweat? Really, against the chest is not the best place to hide a paper document. In battle, it's actually more common to–"

"Holga," he said, thrusting the letter into her hands. "Please. It's important. Just read the whole thing, even if it doesn't make sense right away."

Holga took the paper between her fingers, but did not move. It occurred to Alder that despite her apparent knowledge, the child might still be illiterate. Many of the poorer kids back home in High Keep did not learn to read, let alone those in the underbelly of Boneshire.

"I could read it aloud, if you like," he offered.

She rolled her eyes. "My parents taught me to read, Alder Cadogen. Better than most of the men here in the village, even the merchants. I'm always trying to convince Malka to let me teach her, but she says she's too set in her ways for such things, even though it would–"

He released a breath. "Holga, my dragon—my friend—Nazzan is waiting for me. Can you please read?"

"Oh, of course," she said, her face flushing red beneath her brown skin. "Forgive me. I'm always like this, I'm not quite sure how to stop the words."

He smiled at her. "I don't mind. Not ordinarily. But thank you."

Biting her lip, she unfolded the rectangle of paper and began to read.

WES

Rain had begun in the night, pattering against the roof of Wes' little tent as he waited for dawn. He had found himself unable to sleep after his conversation with Kessara, and it was with some relief that he emerged from his tent at the first sign of sunlight.

Kessara and Aelrie had followed not long after, the Princess complaining of water seeping into the side of their tent. Aelrie was quiet as the two women packed up the camp, leaving Wes to attempt to make a fire. Even with Jaconial's help, he was unsuccessful, and in the end they had eaten a quick and rather miserable breakfast, half-sheltered beneath a nearby outcropping of rock.

The dragons had flown ahead toward Stronghollow, leaving the three humans to follow as best they could through the thick trees. Soon enough, Wes reached a clearing he recognized, and he urged his companions to be still.

They hid behind the trees and waited, Kessara and Aelrie shrugging at each other. Sure enough, within only a few minutes, a doe and her fawn wandered onto the patch of grass and began nibbling at it with their soft lips.

"A late fawn," Wes said in a whisper, his hands pressed into the thick bark of an oak tree. "An old Silverfell legend says that autumn fawns bring tidings of good fortune."

Aelrie smiled softly, watching as the little creature nuzzled up to its mother and began to nurse. Kessara gave a low snort.

"Sounds like something I would say."

"Never said I believed it," he said, putting a finger to his lips.

"I can see why one would," Aelrie chimed in. "She's so lovely."

So are you.

The thought rose to his mind before he could stop it. It was the truth. Even after a night spent sleeping in a leaking tent–apparently while snoring, as Kessara would tell it–she looked as delicate and pretty as the suckling deer.

"Maybe it's a boy," Kessara whispered, a little too loud. The creatures raised their heads for a moment, their ears flicking to and fro as they listened to the forest. No one breathed. The only sound was the gentle trickling of rain pouring off of leaves.

"It's amazing that they begin life so small," Aelrie whispered back, more quietly. "They look so ordinary, until they grow into these huge, majestic creatures."

"Do you have animals in Nox?" Kessara asked.

Before Aelrie could answer, there was a rushing sound overhead. The two deer darted off into the forest at once, their hooves leaving nary a path in their wake. Wes blinked, and found it easy to forget where they had stood.

Jaconial and Celesyria made a tight circle over the ring of treetops before coming to rest on the grass, their claws leaving jagged strips of torn grass and upturned dirt.

"You scared away two deer," Wes scolded.

Jaconial groaned, the sound rumbling through the air. "I

was hungry, too."

Kessara opened her mouth in horror. "Jaconial, it was a little fawn and her mother!"

"So?"

"So, it's barbaric!"

"So is death by starvation!"

"Please," Celesyria said timidly. Wes could tell by the sad look in her eyes that they did not come bearing good news.

Wes put up a hand, silencing any further bickering.

"There's bad news," the dragon continued, giving Jaconial a sidelong glance.

"What? What happened?" Wes asked.

"I think it's better if you see for yourself, Wes," Jaconial said.

Panic gripped his chest. "Let's go, then," he said, the words coming out more crossly than he'd intended.

A few minutes later, they were flying toward the city, large droplets of rain striking their faces and soaking into their clothes. Wes leaned forward against Celesyria's back, his cloak pulled over his head as far as it would go, retreating deep into his own thoughts as he attempted to hide from the rain. He did not know what they would find, and the dragons would not explain.

Is Elder Bram dead? Am I too late?

A second later, he heard a gasp.

He looked up to see Kessara, her hand gripped over her mouth, her eyes wide.

They had reached the remains of Stronghollow.

The pleasant smell of autumn rain mingled with the taste of ashes. Every building he could see was burned black, most of them reduced to nothing more than thick support beams that continued to send rivulets of smoke into the air as the raindrops struck them.

Perhaps a city of stone like all the others would have been wise, after all.

The palace had been burned like the rest of the city, though certain sections of it had fared a little better than the shops and homes that belonged to the peasants.

Wes gripped the leather strap of his saddle as Celesyria turned, flying low over the wreckage. He felt his throat tightening, and he swallowed, determined not to allow a single sob to escape his lips.

He would not cry, not over this.

Every person who had made this palace home—his father, his mother, Roven, even Elder Dorold before he'd found out the truth about him—were long dead.

He would not weep over a pile of wood and nails.

Chapter Twelve

KESSARA

Kessara wanted to close her eyes, but she couldn't bring herself to look away.

"At least we probably won't have to worry about being attacked," Wes said after a long moment, glancing over at where she and Aelrie sat on Jaconial's back.

The dragons flew side by side, unconcerned about being spotted. So far, they had not seen a single soul. Still, the forest surrounded the city on every side, concealing everything that hid between the thick trees.

"Perhaps you should keep watch, anyway," she suggested as Jaconial came to a landing in the vast courtyard in front of the palace. Kessara's heart tightened at the site of the huge decorative trees, reduced to blackened skeletons in their massive pots.

She glanced over at Wes, but his face was unreadable.

It was a completely different world than it was the last time they had seen it. Her friend had already lost so much, and even if he put on a brave face, she was certain that his heart was being broken once again. It was people who made a home, but even floors and walls held memories that could not so easily be replaced.

"We'll stay," Celesyria said after a moment. Jaconial nodded, and the two women climbed down from her back as Wes followed.

"Will there be anything to find?" Aelrie asked.

Kessara cast a glance in the direction of the palace. The main door stood nearby, still intact, the thick old wood singed but not completely burned.

"I hope so," Wes said, moving toward the door as Kessara and Aelrie rushed to follow him. A moment later, she spotted movement in the shadows of a nearby street.

"Hello?" she called out.

A woman emerged, her dark brown curls turned nearly gray with clinging ash.

"Are there any survivors? I'm a healer, perhaps I can help—"

Before Kessara could finish, the woman strode toward them, finger extended, until she stood barely a foot in front of Wes.

"You," she whispered, her eyes flashing with hate. "You have caused all of this. You have angered the Dracodei, and brought death and destruction upon us all!"

Before anyone could move, the woman spat, her spittle mingling with the rain on the front of Wes' tunic.

"How dare you," Aelrie said, stepping in front of him. Kessara could see that her silver fingertips were resting on the the hilt of her dagger, the movement almost imperceptible.

"Aelrie," Wes warned, shaking his head.

"You should have done your duty. I've lost everything. My husband is dead. My home has been destroyed!"

The woman dropped her hand to her side as though all of

her energy had suddenly faded. She began to cry, the rain sending rivulets of ash-gray water to mingle with the tears on her cheeks.

Kessara felt a pang in her chest.

High One, how do you allow such pain? Wes tries so hard to obey you. Why must his people pay the price?

"I'm sorry," Wes said, taking a step toward the woman. "But you don't understand—"

"How dare you tell me that I don't understand!" the woman said, her voice rising. Kessara glanced behind her, hoping that she did not alert any more bitter townspeople.

"I mean no offense—"

"You have destroyed our lives. Everything that your parents and your brother defended for so many years, you have broken," she said, stepping forward to meet him, her face inches from his. Her eyes looked wild, darting over his face as she spoke, her hands balled into fists at her sides.

"I'm sorry," Wes said again. His voice shook.

"I'm sorry that you were the one who lived. But I suppose it's only natural for the scraps to be left behind."

Kessara rushed forward before Aelrie's fingers found her dagger.

"Get away from him," she said, mustering up every ounce of calm authority that she possessed, punctuating each word.

"Why should I care what you say?" the woman said, spitting again. Kessara stepped back just in time. Aelrie reached for Wes' hand and pulled him away, his face flushing red as he blinked away tears. "Word spreads fast, even here. You're nothing but a commoner now, *Kessara Manta.*"

She spoke her name like a curse.

The words felt like a punch to the gut. She shifted on her

feet, struggling to maintain her composure, as Wes sucked in a breath.

"You will listen to her because she's right," he said. "Hurting me will not take away your pain. I am sorry for what you have lost, but I am not sorry for refusing to offer the sacrifices. The Dracodei are imposters. Only the High One can restore Silverfell."

The woman glared at Wes, brow furrowed. For a moment, Kessara thought she noticed a softening in her jawline, but a second later it was gone, her mouth a grim line. She spat a final time before turning and walking away, her soot-covered skirt flapping behind her.

"Are you okay?" Aelrie said as soon as she was out of earshot. Her eyes gleamed with tears, but she made no attempt to wipe them away.

"I'm fine. She was just hurt."

"And everything she said was disgusting nonsense," Kessara said firmly.

She caught his eye, hoping that he had not taken the words to heart.

Of course he did. I said almost the same thing. And he says the same thing to himself.

"Thank you for defending him," Aelrie said, her voice quiet as the rain began to fall more quickly. The courtyard was quickly filling with a thin layer of water, each droplet sending circles rippling out in all directions.

"He's my friend," Kessara said, shaking her head. "Just because I don't want to marry him doesn't mean I don't love him. Even if I've said awful things, that love has never changed, not in my heart."

"Of course," the elf said quickly, giving her a gentle smile.

"I can relate to that. That sort of love."

Wes looked at his toes, and Kessara could see the pinkness that rose to his cheeks.

They reached the front door at last, Wes tugging it open and taking up the lead.

Kessara stole another glance at Aelrie as she followed Wes into the shadows of the damaged palace.

We all see it, you know. I'm sorry that you have to bear the agony of impossible love. I wouldn't wish that pain on anyone.

She hoped that Aelrie would not hurt him again like she did back in Kingsvier Landing, but despite her nagging worries, she was glad that the elf was here.

She liked her.

"Who's there?" a deep voice called from somewhere down the hall. Kessara blinked, trying to force her eyes to adjust to the sudden darkness as they continued forward.

They all went silent for a moment, until finally Wes spoke.

"Wes Cervos."

She considered scolding him, but thought better of it. Lies would do them no good here. Everyone knew his face.

Torches sprang to light ahead of them, casting the burnt hall in a warm orange glow.

There were three soldiers standing there, all wearing green Silverfell uniforms with varying levels of burn damage. For a moment, Kessara felt a pang of anxiety.

Silverfell men had followed the orders of King Ursa. They had thrown Wes in prison. They had taken hold of her like she was a common criminal. She knew that there were still posters of Wes' face pasted up throughout the Four Kingdoms, and even though they seemed mostly forgotten in the light of brewing war, she did not think he was safe.

A second later, all three of the men rushed forward, taking turns to tap Wes on the shoulder and engulf him in an armored embrace. Kessara glanced at Aelrie, a smile of relief tugging at her lips.

"Is Elder Bram still alive?" Wes asked, forgoing any further pleasantries.

"If he is, he'll be in here somewhere," one of the men said with a shrug of his shoulders. "We have been trying to search for survivors since we got the fire under control, but it's been slow going."

It seemed that no one was in a particular hurry to find the miserable old man, and Kessara found it difficult to blame them. If what Oria said was true, Elder Bram was a master of patient deception. He had done very well at making himself hated.

"What happened here?" Aelrie asked, stepping into the torchlight.

The men looked at Wes, puzzled.

"She's my friend, and an ally of Silverfell," he said firmly, gesturing to the elf.

"I'm sure none of you will be surprised to know that it was elves," one of the soldiers said, shooting Aelrie another glance. "They came through a couple of days ago, on horses and stags. They carried glass vessels filled with some kind of oil. Once they got it onto as many of the buildings as they could, they lit torches. The fire was like nothing I've ever seen. Most of the citizens fled for Briarcroft, or took shelter with families farther out into the woods."

"Where are the rest of the soldiers?" Kessara asked.

The man glanced at his companions.

"Most of them are gone, Princess," he said, noticing his

mistake immediately. "Or, erm, my Lady. Whatever it is."

"Kessara is fine."

"Anyway, there weren't very many of them to start with, and most of them went with the civilians. We're mostly just here to keep looking for survivors and to keep the—forgive me, madam—dogs away, at least until our messengers reach King Ursa's men. We need help with the burials. Still, we will ramp up our search for the Elder immediately."

Kessara's stomach churned.

"I understand," she said after an awkward pause, thinking of nothing else that could be said. As much as she did not want King Ursa to rule over the Four Kingdoms, she knew that the Red Army was the only option they had for aid.

She thought back to her trip to High Keep, where she had intended to speak with him, to try and get him to see that they were ultimately on the same side.

She had never gotten the chance, but perhaps she would have to try again, if the opportunity presented itself.

If anyone had a shot at getting through to him, it was the former Princess Kessara Manta of Galeharbor.

WES

The familiar rooms and passageways of Stronghollow palace had become incomprehensible.

Leaving the soldiers to their work, Wes and his friends had borrowed torches and continued on their own, making their way deeper into the damaged structure. He led the way, trying to visit the places that the Elders frequented in better days, but little he saw made sense.

Finally, after opening doors to several ruined servants' quarters, he found the palace gallery. He waited at the door, terrified to open it, terrified of the desolation he might find within.

"Did Elder Bram come here?" Aelrie asked, lifting her torch and glancing down the hall in both directions.

Every so often, they heard the sound of footsteps as soldiers traveled through the long passages and up stairwells, but mostly they heard nothing but the rain pattering on the roof.

Wes shook his head. "From time to time."

He did not turn to look at the women behind him. Neither of them spoke, so he continued.

"My mother practically lived in this room. She was a painter," he said, surprised that he was able to recount this fact without tears prickling at his eyes. "I used to help her. I was always terrible at art, and I still am, but she let me chime in on her work anyway. She'd have me washing brushes and giving her advice."

He chuckled.

"I hope we can see some of her work," Kessara said, leaning around him and taking hold of the doorknob. "We won't know unless we look."

Wes drew a breath as she pushed the door open.

The fire had badly damaged the space. All around them stood blackened easels, their once-sturdy wooden frames thin and cracking. The carpets that had covered the wooden floor were singed, their once beautiful patterns obscured by dark soot. The acrid smell of burnt paint filled his nostrils, and he pressed the edge of his tunic to his face.

None of it mattered.

He walked forward toward the back wall, his footfalls muffled by the thick rugs. He could hear the footsteps of his friends behind him, but he did not turn.

Finally, he came to a stop, looking up at a painting in a heavy gold frame. It was an image of Stronghollow from the perspective of the sky, the green forest stretching to each edge of the canvas. The city was nestled in the middle, and even the towers of the palace looked small and insignificant when compared with the nature that surrounded it.

"She got to ride on a dragon once," he explained as his friends admired the painting. "A long time ago, back when I was too young to remember it. She told me that she never wanted to forget how the world looked from the sky."

What would she think of me now, seeing the world from a dragon's back?

A knock at the door split the reverent silence.

"My Lord," came a voice. "Please come quickly."

Wes' breath caught in his chest as he turned away from the painting and headed back toward the hall. He hated to leave yet another memory behind, the paint and fabric defenseless against the ravages of vandals, but he had no choice. There was no practical way to deliver it safely to Auranth, at least not now. In another life, he would have been able to ask a servant to handle the whole matter, but that world was gone, long-buried beneath the ashes.

As he and his friends ducked out of the gallery, they were met with a grim-faced soldier he did not recognize. He was breathing heavily, as though he had been running.

"We found him. He's in the conservatory," he said quickly between gulps of air. "The ceiling collapsed. He's not in good shape."

Wes muttered a few words of thanks, pushing past the man and rushing down a narrow passage that opened to his left. He had begun to get his bearings now, despite the twisted shapes of burnt wall-supports and buckling ceilings.

"Come on," he urged Kessara and Aelrie as he raced between the narrow walls. His torch illuminated the dark path ahead of him, the orange light flickering against the wood, until the hallway came to an abrupt end. Piled in front of them was a great tangle of splintered wood and crumbled stone, still simmering as rain trickled in through a hole in the ceiling above.

Suppressing a curse, he turned back the way they had come without another word. He could hear Kessara and Aelrie scurrying behind him, but he did not slow.

It is already becoming cold outside, especially at night. If the ceiling has fallen in, and he's laying there exposed...

Elder Bram was old. There was no time to fool around if they had any hope of speaking to him.

He found the narrow archway he'd been looking for, a gaping mouth of shadows as his torchlight hovered at the entrance.

"Right here," he said, his words muffled in the tight space as he entered.

"Watch your head," he heard Kessara calling to Aelrie behind her as she ducked into the hall after him.

It was really more of a tunnel, and it had been much easier to run through back when he was a child, but it was the fastest way to the south side of the palace. Within a few moments of stumbling along in the dark, they emerged at the other side into a sitting room he could barely recognize.

The ceiling bowed toward them, the wood panels of the walls were cracking and flaking away, and the furniture had been reduced to ashy rubble.

"I'm not sure what kind of oil they used," Aelrie said from

behind him. "But look. They must have used quite a lot of it here."

Most of the rugs beneath their feet had been entirely burned, but on a few of them he could see great reddish stains soaking into the fabric. No wonder this room had been so badly damaged. It smelled of something foul that he could not recognize.

"I hope the conservatory fared a little better," he said as he crossed the room, reaching a small metal door that was set into the wall near a small fireplace. As soon as Kessara and Aelrie had caught up, he turned the metal knob and pushed.

The conservatory was made of metal and glass.

Part of him had hoped that it would remain relatively untouched, with no wooden walls for the flames to devour, but that had been a fool's wish.

Kessara burst into a coughing fit behind him as he blinked away the acrid smoke and particles of dust that filled the air. Aelrie stepped closer to his back, and he felt her shivering in the sudden cold.

The metal support beams stretched toward the ceiling, though he could not see how far they reached or how damaged they were. The floor was covered with thousands of shards, but they did not glimmer beneath the thick gray cloud that filled the room. Between the glass and the cold air that buffeted them, he imagined most of the windows must have been shattered.

"He's over here," called a man's voice from somewhere on the far side. Wes couldn't see him. Between the smoke and the overcast sky outside, it was difficult to make anything out further than a few feet away, but at least the rain seemed to have stopped for the time being.

He wanted to rush forward across the glass, but instead he reached for Kessara and Aelrie, taking one of their hands in each of his.

"Be careful," he said, feeling foolish as soon as the words had left his mouth. The women could obviously see with their own eyes how treacherous the floor was, but he didn't want anybody to be separated.

They made their way along, picking over the glass. Once, he almost tripped, but his friends caught him before he could land amid the razor-sharp pieces.

Despite everything, he could not help but to notice the warmth of Aelrie's hand in his own. It sent shivers down his back that had nothing to do with the autumn cold seeping in through the broken windows.

But Kessara was there too, steady and strong. Stronger than even she understood. Somehow, he would have to make her see that the High One would give them the strength they needed to marry.

He only wished that he was more confident in that fact himself.

Chapter Thirteen

CELESYRIA

The deer thrashed in Celesyria's claws for a few seconds before going still.

She hated that part. Hated seeing life snuffed out, even when it was necessary.

"You have one already?" Jaconial called out in her mind.

She could see the other dragon passing above her, her orange body dipping so close to the trees that Celesyria imagined leaves had to be brushing against her belly.

Some of the trees were already changing color, bright greens fading into oranges and yellows and reds. The change of seasons was coming fast this year, and part of her wondered if it was entirely natural, or if the intrusion of darkness into Kaveryth was bringing cold as well as hate.

"Yeah. Come eat," she said, dragging the creature and resting it against the edge of the clearing where she stood. It was a large buck, with soft fur and magnificent horns, but his eyes had already gone glassy. He would feel no more pain. She took no enjoyment in that part of the process, but she was eager to eat. The others had been gone for a couple of hours, and they had no idea when they would return. They may not

get another chance to hunt.

Jaconial landed, pulling her wings up to slow her speed as her legs touched the grassy floor of the clearing.

"Sorry," she said, padding over on clawed toes and admiring the buck. "You'd think after all of this time, I'd finally get used to hunting for my own meat."

"It took me a while," Celesyria said, nudging the creature toward Jaconial with her snout so that she could take the first bite.

For a few minutes, neither said anything, enjoying the taste of fresh meat. After a while, Jaconial pulled back, wiping blood from her mouth on the grass below.

"Do you ever miss home?" she asked.

Celesyria needed no time to consider her answer.

"All the time. I miss the cafeterias, that's a big one," she said, cracking a smile, but Jaconial's expression remained pensive. "I miss the dwarves. I miss the libraries. I miss a life where I wasn't constantly avoiding arrows or swords."

When Jaconial did not say more, she continued.

"It's not home, though. At least not for me. Now that my parents are gone..."

She trailed off for a moment, terrible thoughts of what her father may be facing in Nox swirling through her mind.

"Anyway, my home is in Auranth now, with my mother. I hope she's doing okay. And I hope my dad is alive, somehow."

She stumbled over the last few words. It was strange to be opening her heart in this way, to Jaconial of all creatures. They had all been so busy in Kingsvier Landing, and now finding Elder Bram. It had been easy for her to push her worries beneath the surface. Now, though, she couldn't run from them, even if Jaconial was the only one she could confide in.

"We're going to find him," Jaconial said at last, her voice firm. "We haven't forgotten. At least I haven't. I promise you that."

Celesyria's heart warmed. Though Jaconial was still not ready to accept the High One entirely, it was clear that she had grown in recent weeks. There was hope.

"What about you?" Celesyria asked after a long pause.

"What do you mean?"

"Your family. I don't know anything about the life you left behind."

Jaconial didn't say anything for a few moments as she picked up the remains of the deer in her claws, throwing the carcass deeper into the woods. It would be a treat for the various scavenging animals that resided in the forests of Silverfell.

"My mother was my family," she insisted, not meeting Celesyria's eyes. "She's dead. I don't really know my father. Their marriage was arranged, but it didn't work out very well for them. He left us and went to Helmm."

"I'm so sorry," Celesyria said, an aching feeling rising in her chest. "I had no idea."

She couldn't imagine such a life. Her parents had been arranged to marry as well, but they'd always been happy. She had simply taken it for granted that Jaconial had grown up the same way.

"It's not something I go around talking about," Jaconial said, giving a snort. "Instead I lashed out at anyone and everyone. Including you. I'm sorry."

"It's okay," Celesyria said, a little too quickly, guilt rising like a lump in her throat.

"No. It's not an excuse," Jaconial said. "I was jealous of

you. I was jealous of your family, and I was jealous that you were a legacy candidate for the Guardians, especially when I knew you didn't care about the job. It was foolish."

"Jaconial—"

She shook her head, continuing. "So many have died that any able-bodied dragon can now volunteer. It's the only way I got in, but it's not the same. I always told myself that I wanted to be a Guardian so I could help people, but now I know that was a lie. I wanted it because I wanted the prestige. I wanted to be like you."

She paused finally, drawing a breath and catching Celesyria's eye.

"It's not an excuse," Celesyria agreed, trying to choose her words carefully. "But it does help me to understand. I'm sorry that I made light of something that meant so much to you and to so many others. It was immature and foolish."

Jaconial smiled at her, dipping her head in a bow. They stood there for a moment in a pleasant silence, the tension that had passed between them for years finally fading away in the autumn chill.

"So," Celesyria asked. "How did you meet Nazzan? Did he join the Guardians recently, too?"

Jaconial chuckled. "No, like you, Nazzan was being groomed for that job ever since he was still in his egg. We met when we were hatchlings, at a training exercise. My mom died when I was young. Nazzan became my family."

Celesyria waited for a pang of jealousy, but instead she felt peace. Jaconial deserved someone like that, someone to make her feel like she belonged. She was thankful that she'd found someone to love.

"Anyway, we plan to marry, just as soon as..." she gestured

vaguely with a front claw. "As soon as things go back to normal, which doesn't seem like it's going to happen any time soon, if ever."

"I know what you mean."

"Sometimes I wake up at night and I just can't believe it's real. The bandits, the elves, the sacrifices, it's like I've woken up in a nightmare version of a world that once made sense."

Celesyria knew that feeling all too well, but she'd struggled to put it into words.

"That's exactly it. It's this chaos that goes deeper than what we see on the surface, poisoning everything."

"Like a battle between good and evil?" Jaconial prompted, giving Celesyria a half smile.

"I believe it is one," Celesyria said, letting out a plume of breath. "And I believe that the High One will be victorious, even though that day of triumph seems so far away."

Jaconial went quiet, her expression unreadable, and for a long moment, Celesyria worried that she'd said the wrong thing.

She played with a dry flower that was pressing into her toe claw, glad that the rain had finally stopped, leaving only a dull chill behind. Somewhere beyond the trees, their friends would either find Bram, or they would not. And if they didn't, she had no idea where the answers they needed would come from.

Jaconial cleared her throat.

"I'm starting to believe He will win," she said, her voice quiet against the backdrop of the rustling trees. "And I think I need Him, too."

ALDER

Alder watched Holga's face as her eyes slid back and forth across the lines of the letter, trying to figure out what she was about to read before she got to it. She leaned back in her chair, shivering slightly as the fire began to falter, but he could not bring himself to get up and add more wood.

He'd read the letter so many times that he had it nearly memorized. Raela had been dear to him, practically a second mother, and he still did not understand exactly what had led to her death. He foolishly hoped that if he kept searching the words, he could find an answer that made sense, but the black ink continued to stubbornly spell out the same words.

When I was sixteen years old, I met a somewhat older young man. I fell for him. We were stupid and reckless. We did what those who are not married should not do.

He glanced over at Holga, who was reading quickly, her expression unchanged.

I met Victor at the market in Rill, a little town in the south of Boneshire.

His heart ached for what she would come to understand, but for the moment, Raela was still a stranger.

I told him things that I should never have said, that I never would have dared to say if I hadn't been so enchanted by him.
I told him that I knew that owl, knew that it was the ancient, forbidden symbol of the House of Noctua.
I told him that I was one of the last two members of that noble House, along with my father, that we were masquerading as a

wealthy merchant family.

Alder had tried to find the same symbol, anywhere in Rill, but there was nothing. The town was devoid of art, as far as he could tell. No pictures, no paintings, no statues.

He made me promise to marry and to bear as many children as I could.

We had to wait. We had to find me a respectable man to marry.

Instead, I told our darkest secrets to a stranger. I fell in love with him.

The irreversible deed was done.

I said nothing of Victor to my father until my belly grew too large to hide.

Holga's brow furrowed as she continued to read, turning to the second piece of paper and setting the other one on the arm of her chair. Alder felt as though he could barely breathe.

He told me to see a young herbwoman called Malka, barely a teenager herself then, who he knew would keep things quiet. Of course, she assumed that she was dealing with a child that threatened our wealth and status, not a child who bore noble blood.

He told me that I must take a potion and get rid of our child. He feared that I had destroyed any chance of restoring the House of Noctua.

Holga's eyes widened, but she said nothing, her eyes flitting faster over the words, eagerly devouring them.

I refused to kill my child.

I told him that I was going to marry Victor the tapestry maker.

They killed him in his bed.

Victor taught me all he knew about the High One. I knew that his sister, Lysha, and her husband Dallan believed as well.

Holga placed a hand to her mouth. "Lysha and Dallan. Lysha and Dallan were my parents. And Malka..."

"I'm sorry," Alder said, not knowing what else to say. He leaned over in his chair and rested a hand on the girl's shoulder. "Keep reading. Please."

I went to Malka just as my father had suggested, and instead of helping me to kill my child, I asked her for help.

I hid in Lysha's home for a couple of months, I had my daughter with the aid of Malka, and I gave her to Lysha and Dallan to raise as their own.

We all agreed to name her Holga.

Holga was crying now, tears flowing freely down her cheeks and onto the paper. She did not brush them away.

My grief over Victor's death was washed away in the tears of joy that I wept for my daughter.

Letting go of her was the most painful thing I have ever experienced.

I never told Lysha or Dallan that Holga had noble blood.

"Noble blood," she whispered between sobs. "Noble blood?"

He could think of nothing adequate to say.

I could not have given my daughter better parents. They would raise her to know the truth about God.

I heard, years later, that despite their infertility they'd been able to have a son of their own, a little brother for Holga. I know that the High One must have rewarded them for what they had done.

"Gohr," she said, a smile lighting up her face, despite the tears.

I was afraid that if I accepted her status as an illegitimate child that the House of Noctua would never be restored.

I did not want her to carry the burdens that I spent my life carrying.

I wanted more for Holga.

I wanted her to live life on her terms, to fall in love with whoever she wanted, to be raised by people who not only knew of the High One, but actually followed Him with everything they had.

"He's going to be alright," Alder said after a moment, glancing out the small window of Malka's hut. The sun had set, and he could see nothing but the dark blue of the desert sky.

I do not have time to explain why I am dying. It was not a tumble down a staircase nor an accident at the kiln. It was my own fault, but I have asked the High One for forgiveness, and I must content myself with His mercy.

Alder, you must find Holga. You must tell her who she is.

She deserves a choice, and she is strong enough now to know the cost of making the right one.

Please tell her how much I love her, and please ask her to forgive me.

Holga set the letter down, wiping her eyes as she got to her feet. To his surprise, she threw herself into his arms, sobbing as he held her against his warm cloak. "Shh," he said, stroking her braided hair. Memories of Kessara curling up against his chest flitted into his mind. Even here, miles and miles away, he could never quite manage to forget about her.

"She's gone. I can't believe she's gone, and I didn't even know about her," Holga said, her voice muffled against the fabric until she raised her face to look at him. Her eyes were red. "But you knew her."

"She was a wonderful person," he said, tears pricking at his own eyes as he thought of her back in her little house, laying there on the edge of death, he and Kessara keeping watch. At least he'd gotten the chance to say goodbye. "I will tell you stories about her, all that you want."

"But..." Holga paused, swallowing a sob. "I don't know how to feel. It's like my life was a lie. My parents even lied. Malka lied. Everyone did."

"They told the truth about the most important thing," Alder said, feeling the bumps of her braid beneath his fingertips. She felt so small, so much younger than she had first seemed. "You were raised to know the High One. And your parents loved you. You were their daughter. That doesn't change because of this letter. I promise."

He swallowed, surprised at the fierceness of his words. He thought of Kessara, and of the little lie he had told her in hopes of preserving a greater truth.

He loved her, and he knew that he would never be able to stop, but like Raela, he had to give the person that he loved up. He had been given no other choice.

Holga was crying again, fresh sobs wracking her tiny frame.

"Understanding why someone does something doesn't make it hurt any less," she choked out.

He shushed her again, rocking her back and forth as though she was still a little baby, soaking in her final moments with her birth mother.

His heart broke for her.

His heart broke for Kessara.

His heart broke for himself.

"Holga," he said, trying to choose his words carefully. "This letter changes things. Your life is going to be different now."

She pulled back and gazed up at him, her eyes filled with steel. He had no doubt that she was clever enough to understand the implications of every word that Raela had written.

"You don't have much time to process this," he continued. "There are dark forces at work in Kaveryth, and they will not wait. Boneshire is suffering. They need a queen."

She shook her head.

"They've waited two hundred years. My people will survive a little longer."

"You can see that the situation is dire," he protested. "I know this is overwhelming. You're not prepared to be queen. But we can help you–"

"Alder," she said firmly. He paused. Something about her tone conveyed an unexpected authority.

"If you want me to be queen, you need to help me. I am not going anywhere or doing anything until you take me to Vaevar to rescue my brother."

Chapter Fourteen

WES

The conservatory had been another one of his mother's favorite places. She had brought him here to teach him about the various plants of Silverfell, which had never been his favorite activity, but now he would have given anything to play another one of her flower guessing games.

The plants were no doubt gone now, burned up or crushed, but he could not see their husks. The sky overhead remained stubbornly gloomy, and there was not enough of a breeze to clear the room of smoke and dust.

"We can't move him," the man's voice was saying from up ahead, closer now. Wes gripped Kessara and Aelrie's hands more tightly as they stepped over a few fallen metal beams. He tried to look up at the ceiling to see if they were in any danger of being struck from above, but he could not see well enough through the haze.

Finally, a soldier melted into view, and Kessara and Aelrie let go of his hands.

The man—a boy, really—was kneeling beside what looked at first to be a pile of metal and glass, but when Wes looked closer, he could see Elder Bram's grizzled face peering out. His eyes were open, roving around the collapsed ceiling overhead, not settling on anything.

"He's under quite a lot of metal, and he's bleeding," the young soldier said, his voice wavering as he spoke. "I'm worried that if I pull him out, it'll make it worse."

"Leave me," Elder Bram choked out, still looking off into nothing. His voice sounded as though he'd swallowed broken glass.

The soldier paused, his hand holding a piece of cotton cloth to the man's chest. "Let me talk to them alone," he gasped, more insistently. The soldier straightened, dusting off pieces of glass that had stuck to his trousers.

"Thank you," Wes said, giving the boy a clap on the shoulder. "You did what you could. Be careful."

With a final glance up at the dark sky overhead, the soldier made his way back into the fog, disappearing like he'd never been there at all.

"Elder?" Kessara said, kneeling down at his side, using the calm voice she reserved for diplomacy and healing. "I'm going to check your wounds, is that okay?"

He grunted in response, and Wes wasn't sure if he was annoyed with her or merely in pain.

He and Aelrie stood back as Kessara checked him over, the old man groaning as she prodded at certain parts of his body that were hidden beneath the debris.

"Why does a Princess have healing skills?" Aelrie whispered as she worked.

Wes couldn't help but to smile. "She's always gone above and beyond what is required of her. She speaks multiple languages, she's brilliant in mathematics, and when she was barely a teenager she insisted that she apprentice with the palace healer. Her father tried to slow her down, at first, insisting that a Princess needed to focus more on decorum, but even he came around."

Wes felt a pang in his heart as he remembered what King Manta had said to his friend. Despite her at times unconventional way of doing things, being Princess of Galeharbor was Kessara's life.

And she'd been willing to give it away, all for the love of an Aridmoorian soldier.

A love that he cannot accept. A love that I cannot approve of, either.

Kessara stood, her fingers dotted with blood. She shook her head.

"I'm sorry, Elder," she said to him, his eyes never managing to quite meet hers. "The soldier is right. We can't pull you out."

"I know I'm going to die," he said, coughing so hard that Wes could see his chest shuddering. "We can't waste any more time."

Kessara stepped back, blinking away tears.

"But thank you, Princess," Elder Bram said. Wes thought he could see a slight smile on the old man's lips. "I didn't deserve your help, but you gave it. Your infamous virtue, proven once more."

With a final squeeze of the man's hand, Kessara moved to stand beside Aelrie, ushering Wes forward. He knelt at the man's side, trying to ignore the metallic scent of blood that filled the air.

"I'm sorry I didn't come. I had hoped you would come to Auranth."

"I never got the message," the Elder said, his voice so quiet now that Wes struggled to hear it. He leaned closer, trying not to breathe in the ominous smells of death. "My Oria has not yet returned."

Bram's eyes continued to move, but Wes wondered if he could actually see out of them. He wanted to ask more about Oria, but he knew that Bram could draw his last breath at any moment. He needed the information he came for.

"I'm sorry," he said again. "I trusted Oria, but I was afraid to trust you. Maybe I still am."

"After all I've done?" Bram choked out. "You would be a fool to trust without verifying."

Wes drew a slow breath, glancing back at Kessara and Aelrie. The two women had moved several feet away toward the edge of the room, where they could breathe the cleaner air from outside.

"I want to understand."

"It was the only way," Bram said, the wild-eyed expression on his face revealing no emotion. "I had to make everyone think I hated you. Including you. It was the only way I could protect you."

Questions swirled in Wes' mind as he tried to make sense of the events of the last few months.

Protect me from what?

"You imprisoned me," he reminded the old man.

"Yes. I was trying to ensure that you were safe until the time was right, and the safest place I could think of was under lock and key."

"Did the other Elders know about this?" Wes asked, the words escaping his lips with some force. After all that he had been put through—not to mention Elder Dorold's betrayal—his patience with the Septemvirate had grown rather thin.

Bram shook his head for a moment before stopping, a

grimace furrowing his brow.

"No. They knew nothing. Jate still knows nothing, assuming he's still alive. I wanted them to think that I was on their side, that I was plotting against you in order to continue to serve the Dracodei. It had been my plan all along to take Dorold's place as leader."

"How does Oria fit into this? How does she know so much?"

A sad smile spread over Elder Bram's face. For a moment, Wes saw another man laying there, a person who he did not recognize. He couldn't think of a time he'd ever seen Elder Bram smile.

"She is my granddaughter."

"I had never heard of you having children."

"You were never meant to. It was vital that my daughter and her child had no public connection to me. My wife is dead, but no one ever knew of her, either. Only the High One."

Wes' breath caught in his throat at the sound of the High One's name. It sounded alien on the Elder's lips.

"So Oria worked as a servant so that no one would suspect her true heritage?"

Bram nodded, and as he moved, Wes noticed fresh blood pooling beneath him on the floor. "You can't move," he said quickly, trying not to let the red liquid touch the tips of his boots.

The Elder gave a quiet cough, and then continued.

"My daughter and granddaughter lived a life of poverty in order to serve the High One," the Elder said. "Oh, I can't see the look on your face, but I know it's there. You wonder how I could live in luxury while my own family suffered want."

Wes didn't deny it.

"I felt guilty about it every day, but it was Oria who kept

me and my daughter strong. She served without complaining. Her love for the High One and for the people of Kaveryth was absolute. "

Wes had so many questions to ask, but the Elder continued to speak. The mention of his granddaughter seemed to have filled him with renewed energy.

"She saw that this was the only way to fulfill our duty, and she considered her humble state to be an honor. I miss her terribly. I wish that I had the chance to say goodbye."

Without quite knowing what he was doing, Wes reached out and placed his hand atop Bram's own. His flesh felt soft and wrinkled. He did not pull away.

There was no other comfort that he could offer. What he said was the truth. He was going to die long before Oria ever made it home, assuming that nothing evil had befallen her on the way.

"I still don't understand," Wes said instead, trying not to think of the child, riding alone across the vastness of Kaveryth.

He watched as the man's chest rose and fell, his breathing growing less steady as the minutes ticked by. Every so often, his breath would hitch inward, making his thin ribs jut out.

"There are long stories I could tell," Bram said. "But the truth does not need so many words."

Wes waited as the out-of-place breath came again, followed by a string of coughs. There was not much time left. His own lungs burned with the acrid smoke, but he wouldn't leave a sick man alone while he sought fresh air.

"For generations, my family has been charged with protecting the Codex Veritatis. I'm nothing special, none of us were, but the High One used us, ever since the early days when the elves began driving the truth out of Kaveryth.”

Hope surged in Wes' chest. He'd been so sure that the final known copy of the Codex was gone, buried beneath the wreckage of Whitespire. Could it really still be here in Stronghollow?

“Where is the Codex now?”

Bram said nothing for a long moment, fresh coughs wracking his body.

There was blood on Wes' shoes now, but he could not find the energy to wipe it away. Finally, after so many months of stumbling around in the shadows, trying to figure out what the High One wanted him to do, the answer felt so very near.

“Kessara and Aelrie can get it,” Wes added quickly, taking the man's hand again and grasping it more tightly. “I won't leave you alone. I promise.”

The silence was terrible.

For a moment, neither man drew breath.

Wes felt panic clutching at him, warmth rising up his collar even in the chill of the room.

No, High One. He can't die. No!

There was another shuddering cough, another inhale that drew Bram's sunken chest in.

“You must forgive me, Wes,” Bram was saying, gripping Wes' hand with surprising strength as his eyes continued to shift.

“I should have acted sooner. I had opportunities that I could have taken long ago, even before the loss of your family.”

Wes swallowed. Words screamed in his head. He wanted to scream at the dying man, to demand every ounce of truth.

Could you have saved them? Would they still be alive were it not for you?

He wrenched his hand away.

"Wes," Bram pleaded. "I was waiting for a time when revealing the truth of the Codex would be easier. I thought that if I was lead Elder, it would be easier to get the people to listen. But I was a fool. I should have trusted the High One, not myself. Finally, I realized that that time would never come, and I sent Oria to Auranth to make things right.

"But that's not the worst of it. Despite knowing that my daughter and granddaughter were living in poverty, a part of me enjoyed the luxuries of palace life. I had servants at my beck and call. I ate the best food. Most of all, people respected me, even though many hated and feared me, it was a power that I craved. I am a wicked man, and now I see that all of those things were worth less than nothing. They are a weight I will carry with me into the depths of my grave."

Wes forced mouthfuls of filthy air into his lungs. He was too exhausted to maintain his anger. He looked at Elder Bram again, studying his features. A sad, hated man, crushed beneath the weight of his failures and regrets.

He found himself unable to keep on hating him. At least he was finally learning the truth, no matter how much it hurt.

"Elder," Wes said, trying to keep his voice gentle. "Where is the Codex?"

He knew the answer, but it still struck him in the gut when it came.

"It's gone, Wesley," the Elder said, his full name startling in Wes' ears, a reminder of Elder Dorold, of a time when he didn't understand his true friends and foes. "Buried in the scorched rubble of the old building where it had been kept safe for hundreds of years. Right where I left it."

Tears were filling the man's eyes now, rolling freely down

his cheeks. The pools of blood had grown much larger, and his skin had begun to lose color.

He's fading.

"I–I'm–" the man stammered, working his jaw, unable to make the words come out. "Forgive me. Please. I beg you."

Wes leaned toward him, brushing away his tears with his tunic's sleeve.

"Elder," he started. "I know you're in pain, but I need to know more. The autumn feast is upon us, and I still don't know what the High One wants from me. If the Codex is gone–"

"There are others like me," he said, his words coming out as a gasp. "The remnant. They will know."

"What if I can't find them? There must be more you can tell me," Wes said, his desperation growing. "Something. Something that will put me on the right path."

Elder Bram did not respond for a long while.

His eyes were half-closed, the whites peeking out from between his papery eyelids.

"I'm sorry you have only known my hate and my cowardice."

Each word was punctuated with slow, rattling breaths.

Wes thought of the dying elf in Galeharbor. He had given him the bread of hope, or at least tried. Now, he was in the middle of a crumbling palace, surrounded by ash. Even if he could call to Kessara and Aelrie, it was unlikely they'd find anything edible.

No. He would have to trust the High One, even more than he had the last time.

Every other option had been stripped away.

He reached for the man's hand again. He could feel no

warmth left in it, but the man continued to breathe, his chest rising and falling stubbornly, sucking in the noxious air that surrounded them.

I'm sorry you have to die here in the cold. I'm sorry we couldn't offer you greater dignity in your final minutes of life.

He drew a breath, trying to think of the right words to say. The Elder gripped his hand, his thumbnail digging into Wes' wrist as though he was drowning, trying to pull himself out of the water that was dragging him down.

"Bram," he started, thinking it more fitting to use his first name. He'd never been an Elder, never been a servant of the Dracodei and the current order, not really. He was just Bram. An ordinary man, thrust into fulfilling duties that he'd never asked for. Wes could understand that better than most.

"You did right in the end. You did everything you could, even if you were late in doing it. And the High One brought me here, just in time, so that you could make amends and go to your maker at peace. If that doesn't prove He still loves you, whatever the mistakes you've made, I don't know what would."

Bram smiled, his fingers relaxing their grip on Wes' skin. His breaths were coming more slowly now. His chest was still moving, but only barely.

"I have two requests," the man said, his voice so quiet that Wes nearly missed it.

"Anything."

"Please tell Oria how proud I am of her. Please pray for me."

His eyes closed for the last time.

He will open them again. He will behold the glory of the Eternal Lands.

Chapter Fifteen

FALLOREN

The Black Beach was visible on the horizon, but only just.

Falloren squinted at the ripple of dark sand, obscured every few minutes by the tremulous waves of the West Strait. There were human boats dotting the water's surface, navy ships with masts that struck out at the clouds overhead, but most of them were leaving. He had watched them for a week now, moving one by one toward the North Sea, their men hiding belowdecks unless they had to adjust a sail. They were terrified of the elves, terrified of an attack that they were certain could come any moment.

Falloren smiled.

They should be afraid, especially after the Gorok had gone to Kingsvier Landing. Sure, the traitor had defeated the beast, but the damage had been done.

"The time to invade is near," he said, turning to one of his men. "The men are becoming too weak to resist us."

The other elf—a man, young for the army by elf standards—smiled at him, fingering the thin sword that hung at his belt.

"And better, they're afraid."

Before Falloren could say more, he thought he heard a voice.

He glanced over at Jishon and the man shrugged. They had assumed that the cliff where they stood was empty.

The citizens of Nox did not live so close to the water. Most of them wanted to be far away from men, free to live as they liked, not wishing to be spied upon. He had only ventured here to do a bit of reconnaissance, and already after an hour he was eager to leave.

He longed for his comfortable home in the middle of the capital, his warm bed waiting for him to climb into it for many hours of blissful rest.

"Falloren," came a voice on the wind, clearer this time. He turned, puzzled.

Regent Meira Daeleth stood on the cliff, striding toward them. Her long blonde hair flowed out behind her, icy pale beneath the gray sky. She was so beautiful that his breath hitched in his chest, in spite of his terror.

"My—my Lady," he stammered, bowing low. Jishon joined him, a few seconds behind.

"We need to speak," she said airily. "Alone."

Jishon bowed again, moving off inland without a word, walking so fast that he nearly broke into a run. Falloren couldn't blame him for his haste. Meeting with the Regent was always intimidating, but meeting her unexpectedly was far worse.

"What of the dragon and the Envoy?" she asked, striding up in front of him, the wind whipping at her hair from behind. The waves behind her seemed to grow in an instant, as though her imposing presence had called up wind from below.

Perhaps it had.

"Will they pose a problem for us? I'm concerned. Especially after your stupid stunt in the Whitespire caverns."

She said the words calmly. An almost-smile rested upon her red lips. But he knew better than to let down his guard.

"It–it was a regrettable error, and I again must beg forgiveness," he said, forcing his voice to remain steady.

An understatement. I told the dragon of our secrets. I told her that our races had once been allies. Fool! Worm!

"Yes, the whole matter was so foolish, I could scarcely believe the telling," she said, her tone so light and unconcerned that he could believe she was talking about something of no importance whatsoever.

"So foolish," he echoed stupidly, unsure what else she would want him to say.

"But to run away for the surface without being certain the dragon was dead? That is another level of foolishness entirely."

A smile tugged at her mouth, her silvery cheeks moving without a single dimple or wrinkle. She took a couple of steps closer to him, chin raised, and though she was still nearly a foot shorter than him, he found himself cowering beneath her gaze.

"I'm sorry, my Lady, '' he repeated again, unable to bow with her standing so close. There was nowhere to turn. He'd seen her suck the life out of other elves for far pettier offenses.

"I know, Falloren."

"Everything was chaotic. I couldn't even see where the dragon was. For all I knew at the time, she'd tumbled off of the platform with the obelisk. The dwarven mines are deep. I thought she was probably dead."

Meira laughed, a tinkling sound that filled his throat with dread. "But you weren't sure, Falloren. You weren't sure. And now, all of Nox is at risk due to your incompetence."

Her eyes met his, dark and burning, blinking up at him with glistening black lashes. He shivered, but he forced himself to hold her gaze. The only thing she hated more than stupidity was weakness.

"General Falloren," she said, adding his official title this time. "Listen well."

She raised a perfect fingernail to his face, pressing it into his own smooth cheek. He wouldn't flinch. He wouldn't give her the satisfaction.

He swallowed, waiting, his knees trembling.

"Oh, stop it," she said, laughing again, throwing her head back, her white teeth gleaming. "Relax. If I wanted you killed—and believe me, for a while, I did—I would have killed you long before now."

A rush of relief poured through him. He let out a breath, but his body would not stop quivering.

"But then I thought about this war, and the challenges that come with it. You have failed me, but only once. You may be incompetent, but the others are worse."

She waved a hand in the general direction of where Jishon had walked off.

"Anyway, I hope you will get the chance to redeem yourself," she continued, giving him another gentle smile. "I truly do, Falloren."

His heart hammered in his chest.

The Regent rarely deigned to offer second chances, and he was absolutely certain that he would not be given a third.

KESSARA

Wes was quiet as they made their way out of Stronghollow palace, and Kessara did not wish to be the one to break the gloomy silence. Aelrie trailed behind them, glancing back at shadows. Wes moved as though in a daze, turning corners, speaking to a few more Silverfell soldiers as he passed.

After he had watched Elder Bram die, holding his hand all the while, he had beckoned Kessara and Aelrie over to aid him.

The three friends had been able to move some of the rubble that had trapped the old man, freeing his torso and most of his legs. It was clear as soon as they'd gotten him loose that he had been beyond saving, his body mangled and pierced in several urgent places, the blood bubbling from gaping wounds.

Wes had offered prayers for safe passage into the Eternal Lands, though none of them managed to stay in reverent silence for very long without bursting into fits of coughing.

Finally, Aelrie had found a piece of dark green curtain that had not been completely burned, and with the help of her sword had managed to turn it into a passable shroud. Kessara had laid it gently over the Elder's face and body as Wes said goodbye, letting go of the man's hand for a final time.

Kessara had begun to cry as soon as they'd left the conservatory, and every time she thought that she'd be able to stop, fresh tears had rushed to her eyes. She'd hated Elder Bram, ever since she was a child, and the cruel comments she had made about him when he wasn't around rang in her ears.

There was so much that I did not see. So much I did not understand.

The others hadn't questioned her tears. They were lost in

their own thoughts. Aelrie hadn't known the man, of course, but seeing death up close had a way of bringing on melancholy.

"I hope Celesyria and Jaconial are okay," Wes said after a long while as they strode across the palace courtyard. The angry woman they had seen earlier was gone, but they were not entirely alone. A few men in shabby clothes wore hard expressions as they ducked furtively down side streets, their faces obscured in the shadows.

A chill made Kessara's neck prickle. She was wary of men like that, especially now.

She knew what they were capable of.

"They're still safe," Aelrie assured him. "It's quiet now. I'd know if my people were near."

Kessara could think of nothing else to say, and apparently the others couldn't, either. They lapsed into another tense silence as they made their way back the way they had come.

They couldn't see exactly where the sun was, but Kessara was sure that noon had to have passed. She could feel a pang in her stomach, and she hoped that the dragons would share some of whatever they'd caught. A real meal next to a warm fire was tempting after such a morning.

"At least there's still no rain," she said finally, just as a gust of wind rushed past the burned buildings, shushing her into silence again.

And then she heard a scream.

It sounded distant, but the terror in the woman's voice was unmistakable.

The three friends stopped in their tracks, straining their ears against the rushing air.

"Did you hear—?" Wes asked.

Aelrie nodded, placing a finger to her lips and darting over to a nearby building. There was an old ladder resting against its blackened wall, and she darted up it until she reached the roof. She scanned the horizon as a few pale tendrils of smoke from below licked at her boots.

Wes and Aelrie heard the scream again, louder this time. There was no mistaking it.

Aelrie was free of the ladder in an instant, pulling her cloak over her head and darting into a nearby alleyway. Wes and Kessara rushed after her, their boots leaving deep marks in the thick mud as they went.

This had been a poor part of Stronghollow, long before the fire, and Kessara couldn't seem to calm the racing of her heart as they pressed forward.

You're safe. Wes is here, Aelrie is here. Nothing is going to happen.

The voice in her head did not sound like her own, nor did it resemble the voice of the High One. But it was familiar, all the same.

She shook her head, forcing her legs to move faster. She couldn't think of him. He wasn't here to protect her this time, and she couldn't bear the thought of never feeling the safe embrace of his arms again.

"There!"

Aelrie was shouting from up ahead. Kessara saw her rushing off to the left, out into a larger side street. Wes followed, huffing away as he dodged the remains of the neighborhood rubbish as well as debris from the inferno. Kessara was relieved when her feet hit cobblestone again, but her lungs still burned.

And then Aelrie stopped.

Wes and Kessara caught up to her, falling in at her side,

trying to catch their breaths.

Blood pounded in Kessara's ears, the thumping of her heart drowning out the cries of the wind. A chill rippled through her sweaty body as the cold autumn breeze ruffled her clothes.

There was a woman, but she was no longer screaming.

Her legs and arms had been bound, the thick ropes biting into her and edging her flesh with red marks. A filthy rag was stuck in her mouth. She had the pale skin, dark hair, and dark eyes common to Silverfell.

A peasant, most likely, in the wrong place at the wrong time.

Five men dressed in black stood between them and the woman, their backs turned.

The captive's eyes were brown, and they went wide as she noticed Kessara and the others. Without thinking, Kessara began to walk forward, her boots sending a splash of water up out of a nearby puddle.

She felt a hand grabbing her arm, and then another. She tried to scream at them to get off of her, but Wes clapped his hand over her mouth, pulling her backward.

With the help of Aelrie's strength, she knew she would not escape their grasp. Kessara watched the woman's haunting eyes as she was pulled backward, into the shadows of a nearby alley.

"Don't talk," Aelrie said, their eyes meeting. "Promise you will be quiet."

Kessara pressed her eyes shut for a moment, considering the elf's words, until finally she nodded.

Wes let his hand fall off of her face, and she licked at her lips, tasting his sweat.

"Sorry," he whispered, leaning out from behind the wall to peer out at the woman.

"What in the Wrathlands are you doing?" Kessara hissed, looking between her two friends in disbelief. "She needs help."

"There are five Blackmasks, and I don't see any soldiers anywhere," Wes replied. "You can't help her. You'll die, and before that—"

He cut his sentence short, snapping his mouth closed.

"Before that, they'll do to her what those savages almost did to me in High Keep," she finished, her voice shaking. "I'm not going to leave her to such a fate. I don't care what happens to me."

Perhaps it was the adrenaline, or perhaps she was going mad, but she meant every word. She felt no fear. Her blood pulsed through her veins, every nerve on alert, her feet itching to move. She'd been helpless before, but things were different now.

She'd felt the terror of knowing that something horrific was coming and being unable to stop it.

She'd felt it in High Keep, laying there at the mercy of a group of men, helpless to resist their shameful violence.

She'd felt it in Kingsvier Landing, watching as Alder fell from the sky toward the mouth of a beast, believing that the man she loved was dead.

She'd panicked. She'd begged. She'd mourned.

And in the end, the High One had protected her and the person she loved.

This time would be the same.

"Kessara," Wes pleaded as she tried to head back onto the street, her eyes roving over the alley entrance in hopes of spotting another glimpse of the woman. He had taken hold of her again, gripping her thin forearm with his hands. "You can't do this."

Cruel insults rose to her lips, but she bit them back.

"Let me go."

"No," Aelrie hissed into her ear, pressing her arm into Kessara's neck. Despite Aelrie's delicate appearance, Kessara could feel the solidity of her muscles. She'd never get away from her. But she had to try.

She lashed out with her feet as she heard a peal of laughter coming from the street. Some small part of her hoped that the men would have accidentally alerted the city's remaining soldiers, or that one of the townspeople would raise the alarm, but she knew it was foolish. She and the others were the only hope of rescue this poor woman had.

"Don't you get it?" Aelrie snapped, sounding as angry as Kessara had ever heard her. For a moment, she stopped struggling, trying to force air into her lungs despite the obstruction at her neck. "If you try to help her, you will die, and she will still be enslaved. If we wait and go after them, avoiding detection, we have a shot at freeing her and their other prisoners as well."

"She's right," Wes chimed in, letting go of Kessara's arm. She rubbed at it with her free hand, unable to make the small red marks left by his fingertips go away.

She let her body go limp, and after a moment, Aelrie released her. She couldn't think of a reason to disagree with her friends. They were right. The woman would have to wait.

Another round of laughter rang out, dulled against the sodden walls of the damaged alleyway.

Kessara drew a deep breath as the memories flooded into her mind.

She wanted to put her hands over her ears, or for a gust of

wind to drown out the sound, but she knew it wouldn't help.

The monsters were already there inside her head.

CELESYRIA

Celesyria listened as Wes, Kessara, and Aelrie explained what they'd seen. Jaconial sat beside her, scraping at a stone with her sharp claws, her eyes fierce.

"We can't let these slavers get away," Jaconial said firmly. "Not for a second time. We need to put an end to this, or it's never going to stop. I know none of you desire violence, but..."

She let her words trail away. Celesyria took a breath, trying not to let her annoyance show in her voice.

"I'm willing to use violence when it is necessary, but there are other considerations we need to take into account," she pointed out.

"Elder Bram said that the remnant would have the answers I need," Wes said, his face falling slightly at the mention of the dead man's name.

They had told the dragons what had happened, but there hadn't been much time to talk about the implications, not with a woman being dragged off into slavery as they spoke.

"He's right," Aelrie chimed in. "And we don't know what's happening back in Auranth. Bargren has basically been left to lead an army. What if King Ursa decides to put a stop to it after all? Or worse, what if the elves decide to attack them? They're close to the West Strait, and to Nox."

Celesyria cast a glance at Kessara, who was fiddling with the fabric of her dirty blue dress. Alder was off somewhere in Boneshire. They had no idea if Holga was even alive, let alone willing to take up the crown of her Kingdom. The best chance they had of finding out was to return to Auranth.

But she couldn't do that, either.

"My father has been imprisoned in Nox for months now," she said as soon as there was a pause, trying to keep her voice calm despite her annoyance. No one else had even thought to mention it.

Perhaps they have already accepted that he's dead. Maybe I need to do the same.

She pushed the dark thoughts away as soon as they'd come. No. She wouldn't accept it, not until she knew for sure. There was always hope.

For a moment, none of the others spoke, casting uncertain glances between one another.

"We haven't given up," Jaconial said finally, as the others began to nod. "I can't speak for everyone else, but I am willing to follow you into that dark land when the time comes. Nazzan would, too."

Celesyria was touched, but she knew what the others wanted to say.

And they were right.

She stretched out a wing, careful not to send a gust of air over the small fire they'd built to cook their quick supper.

"I am determined to rescue my father," she said. "But the High One has brought these Blackmasks into our path twice now."

Everyone seemed to let out a held breath at once.

"I think it's a sign," Kessara said.

"Me, too," said Wes. Aelrie nodded, running her fingers through the ends of her long black hair.

Jaconial gave a half-grin that looked more like a grimace, showing her sharp teeth.

"There's no time to waste, then," she said. "We can't let

them get away, but we won't be able to follow them until nightfall. We can't risk detection. If they sense that they're being watched, they're hardly going to lead us to their other merchandise."

Celesyria flinched at the word, but she got Jaconial's point.

"They're going to be difficult to see," Aelrie warned. "Especially from the sky. They dress in black for a reason."

"I know this forest better than they do, I'm certain of it," Wes said, standing up to his full height as though daring someone to disagree.

Celesyria smiled. He was so different from the chubby, doubting boy she'd met not so long ago.

"I'll follow them on foot until nightfall. The rest of you can fly behind me, keeping a very good distance. I'll mindspeak with Celesyria or Jaconial and keep us all on the same route."

Kessara stuck out her chin. "I'm going with you. I saw the woman's eyes meeting mine. I know how afraid she is. I want to be there."

Celesyria watched as a look passed between Aelrie and Wes.

"You can't go, Kessara," Aelrie said gently. "You're too valuable. If these men capture you–."

"I already told you all that I'm not marrying Wes," she said, an edge to her voice. "You don't need to treat me like I'm made of glass."

"You don't know the future," Celesyria ventured, leaning over and touching Kessara's shoulder with her snout. Kessara flinched slightly, but didn't pull away.

"You need to be safe. We're still going to rescue the woman," Wes said, his face flickering orange in the firelight.

Celesyria could see the hurt in his eyes. Even though she knew that he had no romantic interest in marrying the

Princess, she was certain that the rejection still stung.

Kessara let out a humorless laugh. "Well, if *you* die out there in the woods, my political value drops to zero anyway. I'm a commoner now. You may as well let me help."

Celesyria considered mentioning Alder, but decided against it, remembering her promise. She couldn't give her anything that resembled hope. The best she could do was protect the woman he loved, no matter what happened between them in the end.

For several seconds, no one spoke. Kessara's blue eyes were fierce.

Finally, Aelrie raised a hand, as though she was in a human school waiting to be called upon. Jaconial let out a little snort that may have been a suppressed chuckle.

"I'll go with him," the elf said, glancing between the dragons and Kessara.

It made the most sense. Aelrie was the strongest of any of them, and quiet, too. Wes knew the way, but Aelrie could make sure they weren't spotted. Still, a pang of worry clutched at Celesyria's chest.

What if she hurts him again? What if she gets scared, and calls upon the darkness, even by accident?

As if reading her mind, Aelrie spoke again.

"If Wes becomes ill, I'll get far away from him, I promise," she said, her mouth a grim line. "I'm stronger now. I'm not going to give in."

She watched Kessara expectantly until the princess finally nodded, her expression softening.

It was decided.

Finally, after all this time, they would set the captives free.

Chapter Sixteen

ALDER

Night had come quickly to Rill.

The darkness rushed across the desert as Alder and Holga made their way to his camp, the warm colors fading away into purples and blues. The air was cool, too, and Alder found himself sticking his hands into the pocket of his cloak to keep warm. Holga seemed not to notice, moving between the scrubby bushes and over rocky hills without looking back.

When they'd reached Nazzan, the dragon had been delighted with the child, and the feeling seemed to be mutual. Funny stories about Wes, Celesyria, and the others were shared over a blazing fire. Alder tried to enjoy himself, but worries pricked at his mind like annoying cactus needles.

He couldn't help but to think of Kessara, the freezing air whipping over the North Sea, pulling her hair in all directions as she stood there on the beach.

Alone.

Alone, because he'd left her that way.

As Nazzan and Holga laughed, the orange firelight flickering on the dragon's green scales and the girl's brown skin, Alder balled his hands into fists.

A deep, desperate part of him wanted to go to Auranth straight away, where with any luck Kessara and the others would be waiting for him. As much as it was nice to relax for a couple of hours before taking off on yet another journey, he couldn't get his heart to stop racing. He was wasting time. Every moment they spent here in this Dracodei-forsaken desert was another moment Kessara was without his protection.

He stared into the flames, forcing himself to laugh along with the others at the appropriate moments, but he was sure Nazzan knew him well enough by now to see right through his act.

If anything happens to her, I will never forgive myself. And I hope the High One won't forgive me, either.

After more laughter and a welcome meal of roasted sand pheasant, the three of them had finally gone to bed, with Nazzan keeping watch for ironwolves.

Holga had managed to borrow a tent from someone she knew in Rill before they left, though it was so threadbare that it was hard to tell which sections were the patches and which were the original canvas. Alder had offered her to trade with him, but she insisted on taking care of herself.

After he retreated to his own tent, he lay awake for a long while, every cricket-call and rustle of running mice setting his teeth on edge.

Although it was probably a good thing for Boneshire that Holga was so smart and strong-willed, it still made him nervous. Kessara's stubbornness had nearly gotten her killed more than once, but at least she was an adult. Despite her maturity and intelligence, Holga was still a child, and Alder feared that manipulative traitors would be drawn to her side because of it.

Finally, after a couple more hours of tossing and turning, Alder had fallen asleep, only to be woken up what seemed like only minutes later by Nazzan's snout pressing against the side of his tent.

As soon as tents had been put away and breakfast had been eaten, they were off, soaring through a blue meadow of fluffy clouds. The sky was so beautiful that it was hard to imagine anything bad happening beneath it, but Alder knew better.

Holga was a natural at flying, even though it had been several months since she'd flown on Celesyria's back. Alder was pleased that she did not share Wes' penchant for motion sickness, and he found he hardly noticed her small frame perched behind him, clinging to the sides of the saddle as Nazzan's wings flapped up and down.

Maybe I'll sit up here with my own children one day.

He could almost see them then, little red-haired wildlings, running across the wide open spaces of the Aridmoor plains. With his luck, they'd be just like him, getting into trouble as naturally as breathing.

He looked toward the horizon, trying to focus on the un-changing, barren landscape below.

The children of his dreams had Kessara's blue eyes.

They always did.

WES

The headache had returned, worse than it had been in days.

Wes forced his hands into the pockets of his cloak, resisting the urge to rub at his temples. Aelrie carried enough guilt already. He wouldn't be the cause of any more.

He looked up at the patch of gray cloud that he could see between the trees, trying to figure out where the sun was. The shadows had grown thicker as they walked, and he was sure that the sun had to be setting very soon, perhaps within the hour.

Somewhere in the sky behind them, Celesyria, Jaconial, and Kessara flew, following at a safe distance. Up ahead, Wes could no longer hear the barking laughs and inane conversation of the slavers, but he knew that Aelrie could.

Every few minutes, she would stop, resting her fingertips against a tree as she listened to the forest, and to those that defiled it with their wicked deeds.

She did so now, pressing a hand to her lips as Wes stepped down hard on a twig, the cracking sound impossibly loud in the stillness. He wasn't worried. So far, the Blackmasks had given no indication that they knew they were being followed. They would assume that the occasional scuffling noises in the distance were caused by deer or rabbits, not a silent elf and her less-silent companion.

Wes shivered in his cloak as he waited for Aelrie to finish listening, a chilly breeze passing through and making the leaves shudder on their branches. Some of them had begun to fall, and he was sure that the autumn Feast had to have come by now, if anyone was still attempting to organize it.

It was strange. Not so long ago, it seemed the whole world revolved around the sacrifices. His world did, at any rate. As much as he was thankful to have been given the truth by the High One, it was still unsettling, just as change always was.

"Sorry," Aelrie said, giving him a gentle smile and stepping back onto the path, standing mere inches away from him. "No change in direction. Seems this deer path is good enough for them, for the time being."

They continued along the seemingly never ending path, not

daring to step more than a couple of feet into the shadowy trees. They could hear birds chirping from somewhere deeper within, the new songs indicating that night was very near. Soon, they would be plunged into darkness, relying on circles of torchlight to find their way.

"Let's hope they stay on it until morning," he said, glancing at the packed dirt and crushed leaves beneath their feet. It was not a big trail, but it was distinct enough that Celesyria could make it out from the sky, if she flew low.

Though he knew the forests surrounding Stronghollow better than almost anyone else he knew—save perhaps Roven and some of the soldiers they'd grown up with—they were venturing into unfamiliar territory. He was not interested in taking any chances, not without the benefit of sunlight.

Aelrie shuddered. "Agreed."

They continued in companionable silence for a few minutes as Wes checked in with Celesyria, who assured him that they were still following their position.

The gray light filtering in through the trees overhead grew darker and darker, finally fading away completely. They stopped again, Aelrie listening as Wes gathered their torches and lit them, handing one to the elf as she fell in beside him.

"The dragons will meet us when we can find a clearing for them to land in," he said, wrinkling his nose. "Hopefully it's not more than a couple of miles."

"Are you tired?" she asked, holding her torch out ahead of her. They could see nothing but trees, just as before, but the shadows behind them had grown far more menacing.

"Not really," he said, trying to keep up with her without tripping on some unseen root or fallen log in the dark. "Mostly, I'm weary. As much as I enjoy your company, this afternoon has felt incredibly long."

"I don't understand that," she said, shaking her head.

"What do you mean?"

"Time, I guess," she said. He glanced over and saw that she was smiling, the firelight flickering against her smooth skin. "Back in Nox, time was unimportant. We live so long. Our children grow so slowly. Events come to pass over centuries. We don't think of hours and days as you do. Not even weeks or months. I think in years, even now."

Wes considered this, finding it difficult to comprehend. He was only eighteen, and yet even his short life had felt like a long time. He couldn't imagine a world where his entire existence, all of his memories, passed in the blink of an eye.

"Anyway, not to dismiss your weariness over what I'm sure is a long day for you. I guess I find the human world easy to get my head around, compared to what I'm used to," she added quickly.

"Now that you've offended me," he said, grinning so that she knew he was joking, "I have a question for you that's considered very, very rude for human women. How old are you?"

She grinned back.

"Nearly 200. I was born right around the end of the Boneshire wars, but I'm actually not sure of the exact date. Again, elves are not as concerned with such details."

Although he should have expected such an answer, he couldn't stop his mouth from falling open. Had she been human, he would have guessed that she was even younger than he was, perhaps sixteen or seventeen.

"Goodness," he said finally, fearing that if he said anything else, he might end up accidentally hurting her feelings. She smiled, letting the matter pass.

"You know, in a way, I kind of understand what you mean, about the weariness," she said, plucking a straggly purple flower from a nearby tree limb and crushing it between her fingertips. "Though perhaps in the opposite way. Life in Nox is very safe. It's strict, and brutal, but it was secure. It was easy to fall into it, and to let months and years pass without giving much thought to the idea that life could be different. Now, everything has changed for me. Every day, I'm faced with some decision that could change the course of my life. It's very exhausting when one isn't used to it."

He wasn't sure what to say. It was so far removed from his own experience that he could offer little commiseration and even less advice. He supposed his life had been more secure before his parents died, but he was always aware of the sudden events that could shift everything in a moment.

"So," she said, breaking the increasingly awkward silence. "Do you think it's strange how old I am?"

"Yes," he said honestly, giving a small chuckle. "But only if I think about it for too long."

He stole another glance at her pretty face. He thought of what it would be like to kiss her, despite what had happened the last time he touched her skin.

She was smiling, but her eyes were sad.

For a second, he thought she would say something else, but she only quickened her pace, letting him fall behind her.

He followed in silence, lost in his own thoughts.

If we could be together, the age difference would be a problem. You would go on living, I would die, and it would be tragic. But it doesn't matter anyway. Kessara will come around.

She has to.

"Look!" she called out after a few more minutes, coming to a stop and raising her torch.

Relief rushed through him as he did the same.

The orange circles of light revealed only shadow. They had found a meadow.

Within a few more minutes, they were climbing onto Celesyria and Jaconial's backs and taking off into the night.

Somewhere far below, an ironwolf gave a lonely howl, and Wes settled into a comfortable position on Celesyria's saddle. He suspected that the night would be long, and the days to come would be even longer.

Aridmoor would rise up beneath them soon enough, and then the deserts of Boneshire would follow.

There was nothing else to do but to fly, and to wait for the days to pass.

Justice for the imprisoned slaves would come soon enough, and it would sound like the beating of dragon's wings.

Chapter Seventeen

ALDER

Vaevar Academy rose up in the distance, an imposing collection of stone buildings jutting out from the flat ground beneath. To the west, Alder could see the final runoff of the Waymere River, stretching all the way from the north of Silverfell before coming to rest here in Aridmoor.

They had flown through the night, and the sun was finally beginning to peer over the horizon, bathing the stone structures in soft orange light. Though the Academy was primarily a school of learning, it was also a small, self-sufficient city with several hundred residents.

"They grow all of their own food here," Holga was saying behind him, pointing excitedly at the buildings. "This part of Aridmoor is rather desolate, and it can take weeks to have things delivered from High Keep. Sometimes, in the winter, it's actually easier to purchase goods from all the way up in Stronghollow! Yes. It's true. The Waymere River rarely freezes, and sometimes boats can travel down it even when the banks are covered in snow."

"Very interesting," Alder said, only half-listening as he scanned the surrounding area, looking for a place where they could camp out of sight.

"About fifty years ago, there was a terrible blizzard. The wind was so fierce that the ice cut people's faces and made them bleed!" Holga added, sounding rather too pleased with this fact.

"Anyway, there was an outbreak of plague, and the three healers died—they were all very old—before they could create new medicine. So they had to get it from High Keep, but they couldn't. The men they sent out died on the plains, frozen to the ground with their horses. And then many of the people back in Vaevar died, too."

"Well, that's horrible," Alder said as soon as she paused for breath.

"How do you know all of these things?" Nazzan asked, his body rumbling beneath them as he spoke.

Holga gave a little giggle, as though pleased to have impressed them with her miserable tales. "My parents taught Gohr and I to read well, and I suppose I really took to it. There's a nice man in Rill, he's a barrister, and he always lets me sit in his library for as long as I'd like. Even after all this time, he still has books I haven't read, though I'm not sure I want to. They sound far less interesting than 'Green's Dendrochronology', or 'Dracological Reptilian Morphology', or 'A Complete History of the East Aridmoor Trade Company'. They're mostly about commerce law, which could be alright, but they don't even include any amusing case studies!"

She made a face, and Alder couldn't help but to laugh.

"Something tells me that you will do just fine with the academic side of a noble education," Nazzan said, shaking his head.

"There," Alder said suddenly, noticing a stand of a few trees about a quarter mile away. It would not provide the most privacy, but it would have to do. Few soldiers came through here, anyway. "We can camp by those trees."

Even Holga went silent as Nazzan began his descent, catching a cushion of air and riding it slowly toward the ground. Alder eyed the Academy buildings, but he doubted a person could see them from here, if anyone was even bothering to look out of some of the taller towers.

Alder helped the child off of Nazzan's back, and for a moment the three of them simply sat and drank from their watersacks, enjoying the feeling of solid ground.

"So," Alder said after a while, to no one in particular. "We've made it to Vaevar. I'm sure you both assumed I had stirred up a brilliant plan, but I haven't quite gotten it figured out."

As a point of fact, he'd spent most of the last few days trying to figure out the best way to rescue the boy, to no avail. The place was not well guarded in terms of manpower, but it was still a little fortress in terms of its construction. There was a stone wall surrounding all of the buildings, and he doubted there were any entrances other than the huge metal gate he'd seen on the way over.

Nazzan blew a puff of warm air at him through his nostrils.

"Dragons have terrible breath," he said, wrinkling his nose as he turned to Holga.

"I know, I read about it in Balderson's Study of—"

Alder raised a hand. "Tell me later. We need to figure this out."

Holga's face fell, as though she had finally realized just how near they were to Gohr, and how far they were from freeing him.

"Forgive me," she whispered, her eyes pooling with tears.

Alder clapped a hand over her shoulder and squeezed gently. She was so small and delicate. When she spoke, it was so easy to forget just how young she was. "We're going to find him. I promise."

He swallowed. He tried not to make promises if he could help it. He couldn't bear it when he failed to fulfill them.

"I had an idea on the way," Holga said after a couple of moments, glancing shyly between Alder and the dragon. "Papa always used to say that the simplest solution is often best."

Nazzan nodded. "Your father was a wise man."

"I can march up to that gate and request a meeting to visit my brother."

Alder sucked in a breath. "Does such a place allow visitors?"

"Well, according to the Journal of–" she paused for a moment. "–according to my research, this place is actually quite open to outsiders. Lectures are hosted here, and courses are offered to the general public. Nobles, anyway. I don't think the person at the gate will bat an eye at my asking. They probably won't even know who Gohr is or why he's here."

"She has a point," Nazzan said, his deep voice rumbling through Alder's skull.

Holga beamed at them. "Alder, you can pretend to be my hired protection. You're Aridmoorian, I doubt you'll draw attention."

"I'm also known across Kaveryth for my military exploits," he reminded her. "And that was before I became a traitor to the Kingdom by following the Envoy."

Holga shook her head. "Vaevar is isolated, as I told you. People come and go, but they're all very specific *sorts* of people.

They will know of what Wes has done, but I'd be willing to bet they don't know any of the details. And the eggheads here won't know or care about the exploits of some ex-soldier."

His ego had been stung a little, but he hoped that she was right.

"Unless we run into a military historian, or something," she added.

"Well, it's worth a shot," he said finally, unable to think of any better ideas. He wanted to do all he could to resolve this situation without actual violence, but he would use his sword if he had to.

They ate a quick breakfast of dried meat, firm cheese, and salty crackers, taking a few more minutes to get their story straight. Alder was more worried about himself than he was about Holga. He had little doubt that the child could talk her way out of almost anything, especially in a place like this. She'd fit right in.

Nazzan curled up beneath the trees for a nap as Alder and Holga set off across the waving grasses, glancing back every few minutes to make sure that the huge dragon was decently well-hidden. By the time they drew up to the gate, they could no longer see the sun flashing on his green scales.

Alder moved to pull his hood over his head, wishing to hide his face in shadows as usual, but Holga stuck out a small hand and stopped him.

"It's nice out today. You'll look way too suspicious."

She gestured to the sky overhead, where they could not see a single cloud. Birds chirped merrily as they bobbed on long stalks of grass, and there was a pleasant scent of damp leaves carrying on the breeze. It was cool, but certainly not so cold that a grown man would feel the need for a cloak.

"Fair enough," he said, pulling off the cloak entirely and shoving it into his pack. Beneath it, he wore a beige tunic tucked into a pair of plain brown trousers. He'd gotten the chance to wash the outfit back in Rill, and he had fortunately been able to keep it mostly clean during their travels. He looked like an ordinary citizen of Aridmoor.

"Ready?" Holga asked, her eyes flicking across the huge metal gate.

He reached out and gave her hand a squeeze. Despite her obvious nerves, there was a steely determination in her eyes.

She reminded him so much of Kessara that it sent a pang through his heart.

Without another word, they marched up to the little stone gatehouse, Holga stepping ahead to raise the iron door knocker. She was dressed much better than Alder was, with fresh braids she had put in her hair this morning and a neat purple dress. She could have almost passed for a lesser House noble, and Alder wondered if pretending he was her bodyguard had been her plan all along.

"Greetings, my Lady," the short man at the door said, stepping onto the threshold and looking Holga up and down. "Sir," he amended, spotting Alder.

"A beautiful morning, isn't it?" Holga said breezily, giving the man a quick smile. "I'm here to visit someone who is staying here."

"Excellent," the man said, dipping back into the little room behind him. "Please come through."

Alder watched open-mouthed as the guard raised the gate without any trouble at all. Holga stepped through, her chin raised, and he followed, unsure whether it was better for him to look like a noble or a bum. He settled on something in the middle, standing straight, but without the confident thrust of the jaw he was used to as a soldier.

"Money," Holga hissed at him, sticking out a hand close at his side.

For a second, he was confused, but quickly recovered, reaching into his pocket and plunking a few silver coins into her palm.

"My good sir?"

Holga turned to the gateman, extending a hand until the man held out his own. She took the coins and dropped them into his callused fingers.

He thanked her, giving a little bow as he stumbled back into the gatehouse and closed the door.

"Okay. That's step one," Holga said, already making her way down the cobblestone street. "We need to find where they would be holding him."

Alder stood in stunned silence for a moment before falling in beside her, making sure to stay a beat behind her confident steps.

Nobody will doubt that she is the rightful queen of Boneshire. Nobody.

WES

The river cut through the grasslands below, shimmering beneath the dawning sun as the calm water meandered toward its destination. Wes looked down at the gleaming surface from Celesyria's back, not sure whether to admire its beauty or to turn away in sorrow.

He recognized this place. He had approached from a different angle before, but still, he knew it, somewhere deep within his bones.

A few seconds later, his intuition was proven correct.

"We need to stop!" he called out to Jaconial, Kessara, and Aelrie, who were flying nearby. "I'll explain when we land."

No one argued. After days spent chasing bandits across half of Kaveryth, everyone was eager for any excuse to make camp. He only hoped that the bandits would be stopping soon, too, as they usually did at this time of day.

Unsurprisingly, the Blackmasks preferred to travel from late evening through the night. It was easier for them to evade detection from forces below when they could retreat to the shadows.

As they landed on the bank, Wes glanced downriver, an uneasy, sick feeling rolling in his gut. The Dread Ruins were only just visible on the southern horizon.

"I noticed them too," Celesyria said inside his head as he climbed off of her back. *"At least we've almost reached Boneshire. I'm ready to end this."*

The other women were getting out of their saddle as well, stretching out arms and legs as they settled onto solid ground. Jaconial promptly curled into a tight ball with only one eye peeking out. Wes smirked. She'd be asleep within seconds.

"Nobody drink the water," Wes said, making sure all of the others acknowledged him, even waiting for Jaconial to give a sleepy grunt of agreement.

"Even using the weird potion stuff that herbwoman gave us no longer puts me at ease," Kessara said, frowning. "Better than nothing, I suppose.

"We should be extra careful here," Aelrie said, gesturing to the ruined buildings in the distance. "This was where the curse was first brought to Kaveryth."

She caught his eye, and for a moment, he felt the urge to tell the others everything.

I drank the water long before we met the herbwoman.

The headaches are getting worse.

I'm afraid I'm going to die.

He looked away. He couldn't think about that right now. Soon, the bandits would fall asleep, and they would need to act.

"Anyway," he said, pointing downriver, "the Blackmasks will camp in the Dread Ruins today. Celesyria and I know the layout. This may be the last chance we have to rescue the captives before they meet with their elven buyers."

"How do you know they're going to stop?" Kessara asked. "It's still early."

"I just do," he said firmly.

The truth was that he had no better explanation for his certainty. He thought that maybe the High One was leading him.

Perhaps He had not left Wes without direction after all. Perhaps a whisper in his heart was just enough to keep him moving.

"We trust you," Celesyria said. Aelrie nodded. Jaconial was asleep, but he knew that she would do what was asked of her, even if it meant waking up and striding into a hive of Blackmasks. If anything, Wes thought she would enjoy some action after so many boring days in the sky.

"Fine, I'll take your word for it," Kessara said, fidgeting with the dirty hem of her blue dress and eyeing the river. Wes rolled his eyes.

"You're not actually thinking of washing that, are you?"

She gave an exaggerated sigh, punching him gently on the

arm. "I suppose not. Not worth the risk. I guess I'll just have to get used to being dirty."

"Works well enough for me," Wes said with a shrug.

"Suit yourselves," Aelrie said, wrinkling her nose. "I would wash mine if we weren't in a hurry. Elves are immune to the effects of the water, anyway."

"I'm jealous," Kessara said, sighing again. "But there's no time. We need a plan."

Everyone looked at Wes expectantly. He shrugged again.

"I said Celesyria and I knew the layout. That's a far cry from having a plan. I'm open to ideas."

Aelrie caught his eye again as she strode across the haphazard camp, winding her way past their small pile of saddlebags and packs. She put a hand to her forehead, watching, though Wes couldn't imagine she could see very much from where she stood, even though the sky was almost perfectly clear.

They were standing almost precisely on the border of the two Kingdoms, the Aridmoorian grassland fading into Boneshire desert within only a mile or two. The view was striking, despite the circumstances.

"Reconnaissance," she said finally, striding back to the others.

"What?" Kessara asked, crinkling her nose as though she'd smelled something foul. Wes rolled his eyes again.

"The word was on the military strategy test, so I shouldn't be surprised you have no idea what it means," he quipped, narrowly avoiding her hand as she attempted to swat him.

"At least I know arithmetic and languages, unlike some of us," she replied.

"Fair enough," Wes said, grinning. He couldn't refute it. He had been a hardworking student, but his marks on exams had always been average at best. Unlike the Princess, he had never been expected to rule, and had been exempted from high-level courses once it became clear that academics were not where his talents lay.

Kessara was insufferably good in school, and even better at taking exams. Military strategy was the only exam she'd ever failed, and Wes and Roven had made fun of her for it at every possible opportunity. The fact that Roven had done terribly on the same exam made no difference.

"We need more information on what they're doing," Aelrie explained, her gentle voice patient.

"Right," Kessara said, shooting Wes another glare.

"I'll go," the elf added, grabbing a ribbon from the pocket of her trousers and tying her black hair out of her face. "It won't take me long."

"No," Wes said, a little too quickly, stepping forward and placing a restraining hand on the arm of her tunic. "Not by yourself. It's too risky."

Aelrie shook herself free, and Wes noticed a flash of anger in her eyes that he was not used to.

"Wes, please. I can handle myself."

"That's—that's not the point," he stammered.

"There is safety in numbers—" Kessara chimed in.

"But not when conducting reconnaissance," Celesyria finished, nudging Wes with the tip of her snout. "Aelrie's right. It makes no sense for anyone else to go with her. She will be able to hide more easily on her own."

Wes rubbed at his temples, another headache threatening to boil over.

"These Blackmasks are not doing this by themselves," Aelrie said, gathering a waterskin and a few hunks of cheese from one of their packs. "They are selling these innocent people to elves. This is the fault of my people. I am going to do all that I can to help all of you put an end to it. And right now, I'm the only one who can get close enough to them to see what they're doing."

No one spoke. Wes could hear nothing but the autumn wind rushing over grass and sand.

"Promise you'll be careful," Celesyria said finally.

"Get some rest. We should have plenty of daylight left when I get back."

Wes moved toward her, wanting to embrace her, or to take her hand, or to do anything at all to say goodbye. Instead, he stayed where he was, their eyes meeting as he crossed his arms over his chest.

The anger in her eyes was gone, replaced by something else entirely.

Longing.

A minute later, she was gone, her slim frame disappearing into the scrub bushes like she was never there at all.

Wes stared after her for a while, trying to quell the rapid beating of his heart. He had no doubt that these wicked men would see an elf woman as a particularly delectable and forbidden prize.

Kessara cleared her throat.

"Wes," she said when he did not turn.

"Yes?"

"Take a walk with me. I need to talk to you. In private."

Celesyria turned toward Jaconial and moved to lie down, brushing away a small pile of dried greenery with the end of her tail before settling onto the ground. She seemed to be closing her eyes, but Wes could see a small slit poking out between her eyelids.

"I know there's no real privacy when some of us can mindspeak, but I thought I'd try," Kessara added, rolling her eyes as the two humans strode away from the dragons.

The silence between them quickly grew uncomfortable as they made their way along the curve of the river, facing away from the Dread Ruins. There was still grass here, but the ground beneath was reddish and sandy, as though the desert had snuck its way in between the thin, waving stalks of green.

"I know how you feel about her," Kessara said at last, coming to a stop near a pile of gray stones. She sat, beckoning for Wes to join, but he stayed on his feet, cheeks flaming.

All his life, his face had a way of betraying how he felt. He had hoped that for once he could keep his secrets to himself, but as usual, his friends could see right through him.

His head ached behind his eyes, as though reminding him that there was at least one secret that remained largely his own. The fact brought him little comfort.

"My feelings don't matter," he said flatly, seeing no point in denying the truth of her words. "I'm a human. She's an elf. It's impossible."

Kessara crossed her arms over her chest, but her expression remained serene.

"Feelings do matter, Wes. Feelings are what's stopping me from marrying you."

Wes knotted his fists into the fabric of his tunic, willing himself not to walk away.

"Temptations will always be our lot in this life," he said, trying not to let his annoyance show, though he doubted he'd have much success. "What matters is that we resist them."

"I agree, I guess," she said, giving him a sad smile. "But

that's not always how things work out in the real world, is it?"

"No."

"I know better than to proclaim my weakness as strength," she said, looking down at her lap. "But I guess I still hope that the High One will help me, even though I've admitted defeat. Maybe that's naive, but I can't bring myself to accept any other option."

Her voice shook on the final few words, and Wes reached over and rested a hand on her shoulder. She stiffened a little, but did not push him away, instead continuing to speak.

"Do you ever feel like that about you and Aelrie?"

"What do you mean?"

"Hope. Like, maybe the High One will work a miracle, and you'll end up together in the end?"

Ever since I met her, including the day where she almost killed me.

He set his jaw. He would not say such words. He would not surrender any more than he already had.

"What I hope and what I pray," he said instead, forcing himself to keep his hand on her shoulder, "is that Alder will remain steadfast in his refusal to marry you. And I hope that you will eventually do the right thing and consent to marrying me, for the good of our people."

Kessara did not flinch. She did not move at all. The light of the early morning sun made her blonde hair look like it was struck through with gold filigree.

"I'm sorry," he added, his voice barely above a whisper.

Without waiting for a response, he began to walk back to where Jaconial and Celesyria were waiting. A moment later, he heard her graceful steps behind him.

The two of them continued up the river in silence, picking their way between sand and grass, meadow and desert, surrender and courage.

Chapter Eighteen

ALDER

Alder stood by feeling rather useless as Holga sought information from several people on the street. Most of them were male, of varying ages, but every so often they'd run into a group of younger women in matching dresses and headscarves. He wondered briefly if Vaevar housed some sort of religious sisterhood, something like the Cenobites in Graveheim.

A couple of months back, with the help of Kessara's connections, he had sent his mother, his sisters Violet and Marya, and Marya's beau, Kristoff, to stay with the women's order. At the time, he had advised that his sister marry the man she loved straightaway. Perhaps she was married now. She could even be carrying his niece or nephew.

He felt a pang in his heart. He had no idea when he would be able to see them again. He could only hope that the High One was watching over them, even as they hid among some of the most devout worshipers of the Dracodei.

"Yes, sir, we are looking for a laboratory. Or perhaps a hospital?" Holga was asking an elderly gentleman walking up the street in the opposite direction, a heavy leather-bound book clutched under his skinny arm.

Alder was only half listening. He'd heard Holga ask the same question several times. A few people had given vague directions, but most had simply shook their heads at her and told her to carry on with her other business. This time, though, something different happened.

The man took hold of the child's arm, half-dragging her behind a nearby statue. Alder followed, his hand moving instinctively to one of the daggers he kept strapped to his trousers.

"My Lady," the old man was saying, shaking his head, tufts of thin gray hair flapping this way and that. "You cannot ask such things on the streets, do you understand?"

"I fail to see where else I am to procure the information I need," Holga said, raising her chin slightly, though she was still much shorter than the stooped old man. "Perhaps you would be so kind as to direct me."

The man shook his head again, his mouth pinched tight as though he was in pain.

"Listen," he said under his breath, smiling and raising his hat at a couple of men as they passed by, both with similar books under their arms. "I don't know many details–" he paused, giving them a warning sort of look "–but there are whispers that even my old ears can hear."

Holga waited, her eyes never straying from the man's face. Alder tried to tuck himself more deeply into the shadow of the statue as a group of women walked by, but they kept looking straight ahead, paying little attention to the people that strode near them.

"What sort of whispers?" Holga said finally.

"The water. The water sickness has gotten very bad."

"I know," she said curtly. " I've seen the results with my own eyes."

Alder expected her to launch into a boring monologue on the subject, but she said no more, preserving her charade as a wealthy, well-connected, and likely rather dim little girl.

His respect for the child grew even deeper than it already was. It was one thing to be naturally clever. It was quite another to possess wisdom, especially at such a young age.

"Forgive me, my Lady. Of course," the man said quickly, giving his hat an almost imperceptible tilt with his wrinkled fingers. He looked over his shoulder as another man walked by, leading a freshly-groomed gray horse behind him, its hooves clacking on the cobblestone. He lowered his voice to a conspiratorial whisper. "There's talk of a boy who survived it."

"Many have survived it," Holga said, shrugging her shoulders. Alder felt relief rush through him. At least they knew for sure now that Gohr had indeed been brought to Vaevar as Holga had been told.

"Not like this," he said, shaking his head. "This boy got very ill. He was near death, but in the end, he came through. The Septemvirate caught wind of it it a while ago—before the assassinations in Stronghollow—and they wanted him to be studied."

"This sounds like more than whispers," Alder said, drawing a disapproving look from Holga, which he ignored. He drew himself up to his full height, noticing that the old man took a couple of steps backward. "It sounds to me like you know a great deal."

"Shh!" the man hissed at him as another group of women strode by. "As I said before, this is not the sort of thing to be asking after on the street. But yes. I know more than I've admitted to. I am on the council board of the hospital, and they keep me abreast of such goings-on. But I didn't lie. I don't know the details."

Holga spoke before Alder could say anything else.

"Sir," she said, looking at her feet. "I know more than I've admitted to as well. I'm not a lesser House noble, or the daughter of a rich merchant, or anything else you might have assumed. I'm Holga Zahrezain, from Rill. This boy you speak of is my little brother, Gohr."

Alder clenched his hands into tight fists, ready to pick up the child and flee, if necessary.

For a moment, no one spoke, the old man glancing from behind the statue at the street beyond.

"Come," he said, shaking his head, his eyes filled with pity. He stepped out onto the cobblestones, Holga following a couple of feet behind, her head held high once more. Alder followed, feeling as though every wandering pair of eyes that landed on them knew exactly who they were.

The walk was short. Alder recognized the door that they stopped in front of as one that he'd seen before in their wandering, perhaps more than once. It was nondescript and lonely, small and half-hidden behind a tall potted plant with flat green leaves.

The man knocked once, twice, waited several seconds, and then gave two more faster raps.

"Mr. Braddock," a woman said as she pulled the door open, ushering him inside. Her eyes had widened in surprise upon seeing him, but she recovered quickly, smoothing out an invisible wrinkle from her white apron. "A pleasant surprise. What can I do for you?"

The man gestured to Alder and Holga to follow. The door closed behind them with scarcely a sound, the bright autumn sun outside replaced with a sudden gloom, their eyes not yet adjusted to the lack of light.

"Gohr Zahrenzain's sister is here to see him," he said.

"We have not been allowing visitors–"

"She is his only living relative. She will see him for a brief visit."

The man's voice was smooth and confident, making him sound much younger than his wrinkled skin and stooped stature would suggest.

"Right this way, sir," the woman said, waving a hand toward a nearby hallway.

"I have a meeting with the Botany Guild. But I expect that no trouble will be made for the child."

"And I wish for my escort to remain at my side," Holga added, gesturing to Alder. The man nodded.

"Of course," the woman agreed at once. "The boy is in the courtyard, taking his morning constitutional. Right this way."

Holga followed the woman as she made her way down a dim hallway. Alder took one final glance at the old man before he followed as well, but the strange Mr. Braddock said nothing else. They didn't even get the chance to thank him for his unexpected kindness.

The woman opened a door at the end of the passage, and all at once they were surrounded by sunlight. They were outside again, between four walls that seemed nearly to touch the clouds, and sitting on a bench nearby was a little boy.

His eyes lit up when he saw his sister, and before he could say a word in greeting, she was throwing her arms around him.

The two of them began to laugh, happy tears rolling down their cheeks as the woman who had escorted them looked on.

Alder smiled, glad to witness their joy, but he couldn't seem to quell the pangs of trepidation in his gut. Holga would have to tell the boy the truth, that they were not blood relatives after all. And worse, Gohr could still be in immediate danger. Alder did not trust the Septemvirate to conduct ethical medical research, and he had not yet been able to form an opinion about the doctors here who were carrying it out.

"It's nice to meet you," he said finally, as Gohr and Holga stepped back from one another. "I'm Ald–"

"A friend," Holga said, giving him a sharp look.

Fair point. Probably best not to spread my name around more than I need to.

The boy shook his hand with surprising firmness, but Alder caught him giving his sister a puzzled look.

She shook her head, quickly glancing over at the woman. She continued to watch them, hands on her hips, though she did not seem very interested in what they were saying. Still, Alder was glad that Holga had picked up on the same feeling of unease that he had. Mr. Braddock seemed kind enough, but he wasn't going to let his guard down for anyone. There could be eyes and ears of all kinds in such a place.

"So," Holga said instead, sitting next to her brother on a nearby stone bench. Alder did the same, taking up a space next to a huge pot of sweet-smelling purple flowers. "What's it like here in Vaevar?"

"Oh, you'd love it," Gohr said quickly, his smile not quite meeting his eyes. "There are more books here than you've ever seen, though I hear there's even more in the libraries outside of the hospital. Miss Leafley told me that if I continue to do well on my tests, I will get a chance to see them."

"That's right," the woman said, the firm line of her mouth softening into a half-smile. "We'd just like to see you put a little more weight on. Shouldn't be much longer, if you keep getting your porridge in. There's a risk of infection if you're around too many people too soon."

Alder could feel her staring at him, but he did not meet her eyes, instead taking in her tidy gray uniform dress and the white apron that covered it. He wondered what sort of job she had here. Was she truly concerned about Gohr's health, or was it all a ruse?

Before he could think about it further, however, there was the sound of a metal gate swinging open from across the expanse.

"Elder Jate," the woman called Miss Leafley said, placing her hands behind her back and giving him a bow at the waist. "We have visitors."

"So I've been told," the man said as he crossed the courtyard, the leather soles of his boots quiet against the cobblestones. He looked even older than Mr. Braddock. Sprigs of white hair seemed to grow out of his ears, and his thick eyebrows dipped over eyes obscured with milky-white cataracts. The rest of his hair was long and silvery, reaching nearly to his shoulders.

"You may return to the ward, Miss Leafley," he added.

Alder felt a pinch of panic in his chest, unsure if the Elder would recognize him. Alder had seen the old man in Stronghollow a while back, while Wes and Celesyria were imprisoned, and he certainly recognized the old man. Fortunately for Alder, between the man's poor eyesight and his shorter haircut, he did not seem to remember who he was. He glanced over him with little interest, his gaze settling instead on Holga.

"So, you must be Holga," he said, extending a liver-spotted hand, which she took. "Gohr speaks of you often. But we did not expect for you to make it here, all the way from Rill!"

"It would have saved me the trouble, had your men allowed me to come with him in the first place," she said, her voice filled with steel.

"As Miss Leafley says, it was for his own protection," Elder Jate said easily. "In any case, Mr. Braddock is not a man I would refuse, certainly not while here in Vaevar as a visitor. What's done is done. Though I'm quite curious as to how."

Alder wondered who exactly Mr. Braddock was, but there were far more important questions he planned to ask.

"I had money saved from my work, Elder. I hired an escort," Holga said, gesturing toward Alder without taking her eyes off of Elder Jate.

"And then you walked here?" he asked, his eyes gleaming, reminding Alder of a hawk waiting to alight on his prey.

Alder knotted his fists in the fabric of his tunic.

"What sorts of experiments are being conducted on my brother?" Holga asked, ignoring his question entirely. Alder thought of Nazzan, most likely sleeping soundly at their camp at this very moment. He was glad that Holga had not mentioned his role in their journey.

"Perhaps we should speak in private," the Elder suggested, glancing over at Gohr, who was pretending not to be paying attention.

"Fine. But my escort will join us," Holga said, getting up from the bench where she had been sitting. Alder did the same, falling in behind the child without a word. He didn't want to leave Gohr, but he saw no other choice at the moment.

Elder Jate let out a slow breath, saying nothing as he strode across the courtyard. They followed him through another door on the far side, and then down several narrow corridors. The man walked quickly for his age, and did not seem bothered by the sudden lack of light.

"My office," Elder Jate said after a long silence, reaching for one of the many unassuming doors that lined the hall. Alder drew a breath, forcing himself to wait until all three of them were inside and the door was closed firmly behind them.

"Now, your brother—"

Before the man could say another word, Alder was upon him, knife drawn and pressed up against the man's throat.

Holga stood as still as a statue, a hand clasped to her open mouth, as Alder led the Elder to take a seat at his large oak desk.

"I'll talk. You listen."

KESSARA

"She's back."

Kessara felt a hand jostling her shoulder, and she found herself wide awake at once. It was still light out, and she barely remembered falling asleep.

"Aelrie?" she asked, rubbing her dry eyes and getting to her feet. She had passed out against a stone that sat near their fire, but now only a pile of ashes remained.

Wes nodded, extending a finger toward the horizon. Kessara squinted against the light, the sun high overhead. She saw a dark figure moving toward them, rippling in the heat like a lost shadow.

The two of them stood there watching for a few more minutes, and then woke Celesyria and Jaconial, who seemed to be enjoying their daily naps in the sun ever since they'd crossed into the southern end of Aridmoor.

Kessara rubbed at her sweaty forehead as Aelrie greeted her friends. Despite the heat and the lack of sleep, she did not look the least bit exhausted.

"The slavers are still sleeping in the daylight hours, as we hoped," she said, reaching for a waterskin that had been left near the firepit and taking a long drink.

Wes glanced up at the sky. "Still, we don't have much time. Evening will come fast."

Aelrie swallowed, wiping a few stray droplets of water from the edges of her mouth.

"As far as I could see, all of the captives—including the woman from Stronghollow—are being held in one tent. Some were already here."

She paused for a moment, taking another drink of her water.

"There's more of them?" Jaconial asked, sniffing at the air.

Aelrie nodded. "Dozens more, and dozens more Blackmasks to guard them."

"The High One was looking out for us, after all," Celesyria chimed in. "They led us right to their camp."

"Just as we hoped," Wes echoed.

"So what do we do now?" Kessara asked, glancing in the direction of the Dread Ruins. She couldn't bear the thought of so many innocent people, including Galeharborians, being kept in this desolate place. Even if it was a little better than being sent immediately to Nox.

"The captives are all in one area, which is good," Aelrie said.

"But?" Jaconial asked.

"I was able to watch a couple of the women being brought back in. Their arms were tied behind their backs. I suspect the other prisoners are being treated the same way."

Kessara winced at the thought of being expected to spend every day with her hands bound, as if being sold and imprisoned wasn't degrading enough. It would also make it much more difficult for her and her friends to get them out.

"Tell me the good news," Wes said.

Aelrie gave him a quick smile, nearly imperceptible, but Kessara caught it. Their feelings for one another were dangerous. Wes was right about that. Whether or not he would stick to his lofty ideals, however, remained to be seen.

"They only have two guards posted outside of the captives' tent."

"They probably don't think anyone would dare approach so many of them, even on the off chance that someone is traveling near the Dread Ruins," Celesyria mused.

"Exactly," Aelrie said. "I was able to get way closer than I'd expected to be able to. They're overconfident. I'm hoping that will work in our favor."

"That's the only chance we have," Wes said. "There's too many of them."

Jaconial chuckled, the sound rumbling in her chest. "Celesyria and I could take down their whole camp. We need not fear them."

"If we attack openly, we risk harming the slaves," Kessara said.

"They're all in one place. We can avoid them!" the dragon argued.

Aelrie shook her head. "I got close, but it's not like I was walking through the camp and ducking into tents. There could be others."

There was a pause as everyone considered the implications.

Kessara twisted her fingers into the hem of her blue dress, sending bits of sand fluttering to the ground.

"So we're not going to try and rescue them all?" Celesyria said after several seconds.

"We will do what we can," Wes said firmly, looking from face to face. "The dragons will circle overhead, out of sight–shouldn't be too difficult with the sun so bright today–in case the other men wake up and we're forced to attack directly."

Kessara heard a grumble coming from Jaconial's direction, but to her surprise, she said nothing. Wes was a natural leader on the rare occasions where he tried to be.

"But I'm hoping it won't come to that," he continued. "Even if we knew the camp was clear of innocents, it would still be foolish to try and kill them all. We are not vigilantes. Their day of justice will come."

Kessara felt his eyes burning into her face, but she did meet them with her own.

As Queen of Silverfell, I could bring them to trial, hang the leaders properly, and imprison the rest. And that would be after I found out everything I needed to know to bring their whole operation to the ground.

She didn't want to think about that possibility.

"There's a large waterfall at the eastern edge of the city," Wes was saying. "We should stick to the river, and get out on that side. Hopefully, it'll buy us some time to get the people away."

"Okay," Kessara said, the plan falling into place in her mind. She hoped that they would not have to get too close to the water, even though she knew that she need not fear it so long as no one drank. "But how are we going to get the captives out of their tent in the first place?"

"The simple way," Wes said. "Two of us are going to sneak in there and cut them loose."

"And the other will deal with the guards beforehand," Celesyria said, her voice sad.

A memory surfaced in Kessara's mind without warning, so vivid that for a second she feared she might start crying.

Another overconfident enemy, certain of his right to continue maiming and killing. An elf. Bow strung, arrow nocked, the crowd waiting, helpless...

Kessara could still feel the weight of the dagger in her hand, still smell the iron in his blood as he crumpled to the ground.

She would not volunteer. She hoped never to have to kill a man again.

"I'll do it," Wes said.

"No," Aelrie said before the words had fully escaped him. "I will."

"No, Aelrie. I will," Wes snapped. "I've been through battle, too. I don't need women rescuing me all the time."

Kessara caught Celesyria's eye. The dragon lowered her head a little, a silent nod of understanding. Wes was stubborn, but his words didn't surprise her. Alder would probably have reacted in the same way, even though no one would ever doubt the soldier's ability to take care of himself. Men were strange that way.

"It's nothing to do with you needing to be rescued," Aelrie said, her voice quiet, shrinking away from his harsh words. Kessara could see the look of regret on his face, but he said nothing more. "If I go into that tent, those people are going to be terrified of me. It has to be you and Kessara. I'm going to do all I can to knock them out instead of killing them, but if it comes to that..."

No one stepped in to finish her sentence.

Wes was strong. They all knew that.

But Aelrie was an elf, and elves were made for killing.

Kessara thought of the woman taken from Stronghollow, hauled off away from everyone and everything she knew, terrified and alone. She thought of the men, women, and children she'd seen taken from Galeharbor, carried off on steeds rigged with explosives.

She hoped that by some miracle they were still here. She couldn't bear the thought of letting this go on.

"It's settled, then," Jaconial said after a pause, standing up to her full height and surveying the faces of her friends.

"Aelrie will go up ahead," Wes said, the fire gone from his voice. "Kessara and I will follow, and head for the tent as soon as the way is clear. Dragons, you'll guard from the skies."

"Let's do this," Kessara added, reaching for the hilt of the dagger hidden between her skirts.

She never wanted to use it to slit someone's throat again, but she would if she had to.

Chapter Nineteen

"What are you doing? Let him go! Alder!"

He was vaguely aware of Holga shouting at him, batting at his other arm with her fists. He wanted to ignore her, but she was becoming louder by the second.

He had to remain in control, at least for the moment.

Elder Jate sank into the chair without putting up the least bit of resistance, but Alder did not let the knife move an inch. He could feel the soft folds of the old man's neck, touching the sharp blade every time he inhaled.

"Holga," he hissed, the words passing between gritted teeth. "If you don't shut up, they're going to kill us both."

The child stopped hitting him and went quiet, as if suddenly realizing where they were and how much danger she was in. "Don't hurt him," she croaked out, her voice reduced to a whisper.

"Please," Elder Jate said, his neck touching the blade again as he swallowed hard. "I'm old. I can't possibly be a threat to you. Let me go."

Alder's anger coursed through his veins as he thought of Gohr being led through the desert by a bunch of Septemvirate goons, not knowing if he'd ever see his sister again. It was despicable.

You took a child away from his home and family, all so that you could run medical experiments on him. You deserve the worst of fates.

He kept the knife completely still, not retreating an inch.

He had no intention of hurting the old man, let alone killing him, but he needed him to be sufficiently terrified. He couldn't risk him calling on some unseen group of Vaevar guards.

Holga said nothing else. The confident future queen had faded away in an instant, leaving only a simple orphan girl behind.

"You—you must understand!" Elder Jate stammered. Alder could see the indent of the knife on his skin as he spoke. "I have—I have my reasons."

Alder waited, saying nothing. What reason could possibly justify what he had done?

"I can't talk with this—" the Elder said, pointing a shaking finger at his neck. "It—it hurts. I promise, I won't move."

Alder considered this.

"Let him talk," Holga said in a whisper, glancing over at the door.

She was right. He didn't know how much time they had to get answers. If anyone caught wind of what they were doing, Gohr would be swept off to who knows where.

"Don't even dream of running," Alder said fiercely, letting the blade fall away from the man's neck. He did not return it to its sheath.

The man rubbed at his skin, though Alder had left no marks.

Unpleasant, is it? Like being kidnapped and subjected to medical experimentation against your will?

"I'm from Boneshire, you know," he said finally, wincing as his thin fingers assessed the nonexistent damage. "The only member of the Septemvirate ever to be born in the desert Kingdom."

"Yes, very thrilling," he said when the man did not continue.

"Most of my ancestors died in the war," he continued. "My family line was nearly wiped out, but a few survived."

"I understand what that's like," Holga chimed in. Alder allowed himself a small smile. If only the Elder knew just how important the child's bloodline really was.

"Yes, your family tree," Alder said, waving a hand. "Can we approach the point?"

The Elder eyed the knife that Alder still held in his hands, turning it slowly between his fingers.

"I have a nephew, an orphan. A young child, perhaps a year or two younger than Holga here."

Alder tapped at the blade with his fingertips.

"He lives near Redvale, where he's apprenticing with a blacksmith. There's safe water in the city, but he wandered off into the wilderlands with some older boys. Chasing lizards, or some such nonsense," the Elder paused, grimacing as though he'd tasted something unpleasant. "The others swear that they tried to stop him from drinking in time, but it was too late. I don't know if I believe them. He was a child! Just a stupid child!"

The man's calm control slipped away at once. He was nearly yelling now, arms waving as he told his tale.

"They should have warned him. They should have known better! And now it's too late to do anything. I've tried. I brought him here, to Vaevar. I've hired the best herbwomen in the Kingdom. I would have sent our palace healer from Stronghollow, but she's missing. Probably dead."

He was shaking his head.

"Please speak quietly," Holga said before Alder could chide the man. To his relief, Elder Jate lowered his voice. So far, no one seemed to have noticed their presence.

"Anyway, I went so far as to petition King Manta in Galeharbor. I don't think he ever got my letter. If he had, he would have sent one of his best. I know he would have."

Alder felt a pang in his heart at the mention of Kessara's father. Elder Jate was right. Whatever tension was felt between Galeharbor's monarchy and the Septemvirate, the King and Queen would have done whatever they could to help this child.

Elder Jate was quiet now, rubbing a few tears from the corners of his eyes.

"Nothing helped, did it?" Holga asked softly, extending a hand as though to comfort the man before drawing it back to her side.

He shook his head.

"I assume most people back home think that I am here only to hide from the violence that has befallen my friends. But that isn't true. I do not fear the elves. I'm here because my nephew is here. He has no one else. I won't leave him. Not until the end."

Alder searched the man's face. He could see no hint of deception. Only sorrow.

Holga was blinking away tears of her own.

"You thought that studying Gohr was your last chance," she said.

"It was Elder Dorold's doing, actually," Elder Jate said. He did not sound as though he was placing blame. In fact, Alder thought that he sounded almost proud. "He was my friend for many years. When I went to Vaevar to be with my nephew, he wanted to help. When he heard of a child in Rill who might provide a cure, he contacted me. The scientists here were reluctant to act, but Dorold had the ear of King Ursa. He got the royal permission needed to study the boy."

"His name is Gohr," Holga said, her voice shaking as her tears fell.

Alder clenched his fist around the knife.

Morality aside, King Ursa had no jurisdiction over Boneshire. As usual, the law mattered little, so long as one had power. Elder Jate was used to snapping his fingers and having his demands met. Even if a little boy's life was caught in the balance.

"I'm sorry," Elder Jate said, looking down at the desk in front of him, refusing to meet their eyes. "It was not just about my nephew. You have to believe that. I am not so heartless. Elder Dorold and I knew that if a cure could be found, hundreds or even thousands of lives could be saved."

"So it would be worth it to sacrifice my little brother's life?" Holga demanded, her voice rising. Alder reached out and rested a hand on her shoulder.

"We didn't know if it would come to that," Elder Jate said, his voice pleading. "We still don't know. We will do what is necessary, no more."

"You're talking about a human being."

"I'm talking about hundreds of human beings. Thousands! Innocent people who are sick and dying. Is one life worth more than many?" Elder Jate snapped.

Alder fingered the knife in his hands, trying to think of the right words. There was a time when he thought in the same way that the Elder did, but things had changed. The High One had changed him.

"I understand your fear for your nephew," he started, trying to keep his voice calm. "I'm sorry he's sick. So is Holga. We really are."

Holga nodded in agreement. He had no doubt that she was sincere, perhaps even more sincere than he himself was.

"And what of the others?" the Elder reminded them, his gnarled fingers gripping the edge of the desk. "Am I supposed to let him go, sealing the fate of all of those who bear this illness?"

Alder let out a slow breath. He did not need the Elder's approval to free Gohr. They were going to do it regardless of what he said. But his cooperation would make things much easier.

Holga was shaking her head.

"I don't think the water causes the sort of sickness that can be cured," she said quietly.

"I agree," Alder added. "I'm not one to put much stock in witchcraft and magic, but it seems to be a curse."

"And what if it isn't? There's a chance. We have a chance, right now, to put an end to this terror. There is no time for foolish sentimentality. We must think of the greater good," the Elder said, his eyes flashing. "But I am sorry that the life of your brother is the price that must be paid."

Holga withdrew as though he had slapped her.

Alder was on his feet in an instant, the knife in his hand, pressing against the old man's throat with even greater pressure than before.

You deserve death, you rotten old snake.

"Alder, stop this," Holga said, standing up from where she sat. Something in her voice made him pause.

"We cannot commit evil to fight evil," she said to both of the men, her gaze moving between them. "Bad things happen in this life. We all know that. It can be painful. It can be unfair. Usually, we never get an answer as to why, and it eats us up inside. But even when we do understand, it still hurts. I know this from experience, however short my life has been."

She paused for a moment to catch her breath. Elder Jate said nothing. He sat limp in his chair, his breathing shallow as he tried to avoid the edge of Alder's knife.

Alder felt tears springing to his eyes. He wanted to hurt this man. He really did.

And yet the child who he had wronged desired mercy.

"My nephew is innocent," Elder Jate said, his eyes growing red as he tried to blink away the tears. "He's such a good little boy. His smile brings light to everyone who meets him. I can't just watch him fade away and die. He has no one else to fight for him."

"I'm sure he's wonderful," Holga said softly, placing her small, smooth hand on top of the Elder's wrinkled one. "But you cannot end suffering by causing more of it. You cannot do evil in hopes of finding good. You have to let go. You have to trust that someone greater than you are is in control."

He felt his anger slipping away as the man began to sob.

His chest heaved as he rested against the desk, his fingers gripping the edge as though he was adrift in some great sea, desperate to stay afloat.

Alder returned the knife to its sheath. There would be no trouble from this broken old man.

Holga placed a gentle hand on Elder Jate's shoulder. "With

the help of the High One, our suffering is given meaning. Nothing is pointless, so long as we offer it to Him. He can take our brokenness and bring forth joy."

For a long while, he did not speak.

Holga kept her hand where it was, consoling the older man until his sobs finally began to ebb away.

Alder wanted to flee, to go and find Gohr, feeling almost ashamed that he was here to witness this man's grief.

Instead, he waited in silence as well, admiring the little Queen of Boneshire.

He had planned to come in here and get what they wanted by force if necessary, but Holga had chosen a better path.

"We can't always run from suffering, Elder," Holga whispered. "Sometimes it is necessary. But sometimes, we are given the opportunity to ease the pain of another. I ask that of you now. Please, let Gohr leave this place. Let him go home."

Elder Jate got to his feet so abruptly that Alder's hand instinctively found his knife.

"Wait here," he said.

Without another word, he left the office, closing the door behind him.

Alder and Holga could do nothing but wait, and hope.

WES

"This is it," Wes said, gesturing toward the river. Kessara took a few quick steps and fell in beside him, her boots making a shuffling sound against the dirt. "Aelrie told me that it all started here, during the Boneshire wars. They cursed the water, and over the years, the sickness made its way across

Kaveryth."

"It doesn't seem like anything special," Kessara said, bending down to look at the rippling water. The level of the river was low, rising to what looked like only a few feet, though the swirling muck made it difficult to see where the bottom was.

They saw no fish, no signs of life, but then again, that wasn't unusual. Most of the land animals were hidden away, too, waiting for the cool shadows of night. The only thing that broke the silence was the buzzing of insects, humming and chirping in the hot sun.

"No," Wes agreed. "But that is."

He gestured toward one of the buildings.

"The owl," Kessara said, her voice dropping to a reverent whisper. "The symbol of the House of Noctua. I don't think I've ever seen one before. Not even in books."

"And yet, you recognized it," Wes said, smiling, his eyes narrowed against the harsh early-afternoon sunlight.

She smiled back. "The elves wanted to destroy the art of the people they sought to conquer, but they failed. Despite everything, there are people who remember, even if many of them are not in Boneshire. I hope their queen will one day be able to bring the motifs of her House back to the people."

Wes thought of Holga, somewhere out there. He hoped that Alder had found her by now, safe and sound. But even if he did, how was a little orphan girl going to learn to rule this broken land? The bureaucrats who were currently in charge were not going to hand over control lightly.

Kessara had kept reminding him that the High One was with her, and that she did not need the whole Kingdom to follow her, not right away. Just like with their own army in Auranth, change would begin with a few loyal people who saw the truth.

He had to hope that it would be enough.

"Wes, get ready," Celesyria's voice sounded in his mind, cutting short his thoughts. *"She's coming up on the guards. You won't have much time."*

"Okay."

He stood up straight, pulling the straps of his pack until it was tight against his body, out of his way in case they had to run.

"What?" Kessara asked, her eyes wide.

"It's time."

Kessara slipped her cloak over her head, and Wes did the same, stepping ahead of her and leading the way up the river. As they got closer, he could hear the waterfall on the opposite side of the city, to the east.

"No matter what happens, get up there and follow the river back," he said, pointing toward the cliffs. There were a couple of small stone staircases nearby, as well as an area where the rocks had crumbled into more of a jagged hill.

They would be able to make it. They didn't have any other choice.

As they made their way past the broken buildings and various tents, they heard and saw no one, save for a few horses and stags that watched them with wide-eyed interest. Wes felt exposed in the afternoon sun, wishing that there were more shadows to hide behind.

Finally, they saw Aelrie, gesturing toward the largest tent they'd seen yet.

"Are they gone?" Kessara whispered. Aelrie nodded quickly. *Probably dead. So be it.*

Wes passed through the tent flap, Kessara close at his heels. Aelrie waited outside.

The smell hit him all at once. Bile rose in his throat as he began to cough, putting a hand over his face, desperate to keep the contents of his stomach down as he examined the scene before them.

There were so many people, far more than he ever thought would fit inside a single tent. Men and women of all ages stood gaping at them, their hands tied at their backs, reeking of sweat and filth. Most of the crowd was made up of Vilzanians, though Wes saw a few people who might have been taken from Galeharbor. The people were so dirty that it was difficult to tell.

One face, however, was familiar. In the front corner of the tent was the woman from Stronghollow. Her eyes looked haunted, but aside from that, she seemed to be better off than most of the others.

The majority of the captives were thin enough that their ribs stuck out like tree roots in shallow dirt. Several were wounded that they could see from the entrance, but he knew that there were probably more.

Without warning, a child began to cry, a lone sobbing voice in the middle of the cluster of bodies.

Wes and Kessara froze, glancing behind them, but of course they would not see if anyone was coming until it was too late.

"Shh!" a woman's voice rose over the crowd, who had begun to whisper amongst themselves. "Listen to them."

To their relief, the noise abated, silence rushing through the cramped space like a wave. For whatever reason, the woman's simple words conveyed authority.

"We cannot explain ourselves now," Wes said, trying to be heard without alerting anyone outside of their presence. "But this may be your only chance to get you and your children out of here. You need to trust us."

"No," a man spoke up, his whisper rumbling with depth. "We cannot leave."

Other voices of affirmation rose around them, followed by more shushing from the crowd.

"I'm Wes Cervos, Envoy of Silverfell," Wes said. "And this is Kessara Manta, Princess of Galeharbor. We are on your side."

More chatter broke out, louder this time.

Perhaps they've heard of our escapades, even here.

"Shh," Kessara pleaded. "You can trust us." The crowd ignored her, their whispers rising, filling the space.

"We need to leave. Now."

"Let's go," the woman who had spoken earlier said, her voice low but fierce as she pushed her way to the front. "Anyone who wishes to leave, follow me. All of the children are leaving."

The crowd went quiet again as people embraced one another, tears streaming down faces as the crowd separated into two. A little less than half of the group remained near the back of the tent. The rest pushed forward toward the entrance, children clasping the hands of their mothers.

"You need to leave," Wes said to the others, stepping closer. He forced himself to breathe through his mouth, unable to acclimatize to the stench. "Most of your captors are asleep. This is the best chance–"

He felt a hand on his shoulder. The woman who had spoken leaned toward his ear. Wes could see a dark bruise across the woman's forehead and right eye socket.

"They won't go. I'll explain later," the woman said.

Wes stared at her for several moments before finally nodding. They were out of time. They would save as many as were willing to run.

He drew his knife, and noticed that Kessara was already clasping her dagger in her hand. gesturing to the people to turn around. They obeyed. Long minutes passed as they cut the captives loose. Wes could hear nothing but breathing.

"Stay quiet. We will follow the river, toward the waterfall," Wes said when the last person was free, stepping forward and pressing a hand against the flap of the tent.

He turned back to face the others who were staying behind. Some were old and decrepit, with hunched backs and walking sticks, but most looked perfectly healthy. They had tears on their cheeks, but most were smiling.

He shared a puzzled look with Kessara, but as the woman said, they would not be able to stop and discuss it now.

Wes headed out into the morning light, Kessara and the others following behind in a tidy procession as he made his way into the sunlight. Even the hot desert air felt cool on his tongue after the cramped, reeking tent. He sucked in breath after breath as they began to walk, trying to clear the stink from his nostrils. He could hear Kessara doing the same behind him, though the prisoners seemed to have grown used to the stink.

A few feet away from the tent, they saw the two guards laying on the ground. Their chests were rising and falling in a gentle rhythm. Aelrie was nowhere to be seen, but they knew she was close. Wes had wanted her to travel with the group. If things went badly, they would need her help protecting the people on the ground.

"There's an elf with us," Kessara said as the people continued on. The crowd began to whisper to one another, fear rising on each face. She spoke again, more firmly.

"No. She helped to free you. She is with us."

The chattering quieted, but only a little. Wes stood on a rock at the tail of the crowd, hand to his forehead, searching for movement in the ruins.

"You can trust them, or you can stay behind," the woman—the apparent leader—spoke up again, elbowing her way through the people until she stood beside Kessara. "Stop making noise."

The crowd hushed instantly and began moving forward again, glancing warily back and forth at the tents and stone buildings that lined their path.

The woman fell in beside Wes. She was much younger than he had first assumed, perhaps in her mid thirties.

"I'm Luna," she whispered, not slowing her pace. Like the other slaves who had been left behind, she was smiling.

Before he could reply, Celesyria's voice sounded in his mind.

Kessara was at his side in an instant, knowing by the vacant look on his face that he was speaking to one of the dragons.

"What's—"

"They're coming," he said, nodding to Luna. She turned to the others, urging them to follow as quickly as they could. His boots pounded against the dirt, sending up puffs of dust as he forced his way up the river, hoping he was right about where the waterfall was located.

He had no idea how they had been alerted, but there was nothing else they could do.

It was time to run.

Chapter Twenty

ALDER

There was a knock at the door of the study.

Alder got to his feet in an instant, stepping in front of Holga, yanking his sword from his belt.

There was silence, followed by a second knock.

There were no windows in the room, so he could not mark the passage of the sun, but he was sure that they had been sitting there in silence for at least an hour, perhaps more.

They had spoken little, both of them lost in their own anxieties. He had urged Holga to nap, but she insisted that she couldn't, and he did not doubt her. Gohr was out there, at the mercy of Elder Jate. He couldn't rest, either.

Finally, the door swung open.

Elder Jate stood there, looking even smaller and weaker than he had before. He stared at the sword, his eyes widening, and for a moment Alder was sure the man was going to faint.

He slipped the weapon back into its sheath.

"Where is my brother?" Holga demanded, striding forward until she was nearly touching the old man.

He wouldn't meet her eyes, looking instead at Alder.

The soldier clenched his fists together at his sides, wishing that he still had the comforting weight of his sword in his hand.

"They–they told me that it's not my decision," he said, sounding surprised by his own words. He shook his head. "They said that we needed permission from King Ursa to study him, and that same rule applies to ending said study."

Holga went pale. Elder Jate looked as though he was going to start crying again.

Alder drew his sword.

The old man raised his hands, protecting his face.

"Is Gohr still in the courtyard?" he asked, ignoring the man's whimpers.

"Yes," Elder Jate nodded. "Yes. He likes to stay out there much of the day, often until tea."

Holga was already moving for the door. Alder turned to follow her, but stopped, looking back at Elder Jate, who was now cowering in his chair.

"A word of advice," he said, looking at the man up and down, pity swelling within his chest. "If you live a good life, death becomes much less terrifying."

"What–"

"Thank you for your help," he said.

Without another word, he pushed past Holga and out into the hall, shielding her small body with his own.

To his relief, they didn't run into any wayward students or servants as they made their way through the winding halls. They took several wrong turns, but finally they reached what Holga was certain was the right door. He decided to trust that she was right.

"What if they don't let him go?" she whispered as he moved to turn the knob.

"I already know that they won't," he said, smiling in spite of himself. Their time in Rill had been quiet. He was beginning to long for a little action.

He burst into the courtyard, Holga rushing out behind him, and rushed over to where Gohr sat nearby, reading a large book with a painting of mountains on the cover.

Miss Leafley, who had apparently returned from the ward, rushed over to them, a shocked expression on her pleasant face.

"What do you think you're—"

"I'm taking the boy home to his family," Alder said firmly. Holga took hold of Gohr's hand, pulling him in behind Alder. The book clattered as it fell to the stone floor.

"What's going on?" Gohr asked.

"Just obey me, please," Holga said, grasping the boy's fingers more tightly.

"Guards!" Miss Leafley shouted. Alder could hear the sound of movement a few seconds later. Holga looked alarmed, but he stayed where he was, a few feet from the nurse.

"You're not taking him anywhere," the woman said, hands planted on her hips.

Before she could say more, three young men in white tunics rushed in. They had no weapons.

"Sir, we must ask you to leave this facility," one of them said, his voice ringing with calm authority.

Miss Leafley was nodding. "Mr. Braddock will have—"

"Take it up with the Botany Guild," Alder said, unable to stop a chuckle from escaping. "We're leaving."

The men took a couple of steps forward, arms raised, as though they were trying to calm an unruly stallion.

Alder raised his sword.

"Or, I suppose, you could try to stop me."

The men stopped short, glancing at one another.

Mere seconds passed before they headed back the way they had come, picking up speed as they raced across the courtyard before slamming the door behind them.

With a final glance at Gohr, Miss Leafley retreated as well, marching off toward one of the other rooms without a word.

"Bye, Miss!" Gohr called out as she slipped away. "Thank you for your kindness during my stay. I hope we don't get you into trouble."

Alder smiled at the children, leading them in the direction that he hoped would take them to the main entrance.

At the end of the day, power had little to do with brilliant tactics or great intelligence.

More often than not, the path forward was found at the end of a sword.

And if that sword was wielded in service of the High One, so much the better.

Chapter Twenty-One

"What tipped them off?" Jaconial asked, the tip of her wing nearly touching Celesyria's own.

"Who knows," she replied, her eyes trained firmly on the ground below. Black-clad soldiers rushed through the streets, reminding the dragon of skittering roaches. Tents opened, one after another, reinforcements pouring out as word spread of the attempted escape. *"Maybe they saw us. The sky is a lot clearer than it was earlier."*

She knew that Jaconial was itching for destruction, but she had to keep her in check. They had to get a handle on the situation before they rushed into action. Even dragons were not invincible, not against the swarm of enemies that lurked in the Dread Ruins below.

"Look! There are more men by the waterfall!" Jaconial said, her head held low as she watched the scene unfolding on the ground. Celesyria followed her gaze up the river. Her heart sank as she saw what her friend was looking at.

Men were pouring in from outside the ruined city, following the river toward their companions, and cutting off Wes' planned escape route.

"Wes," she called to him in his mind, praying that he would be able to hear and focus on what she was saying amid the chaos. *"You need to go the other way. They have reinforcements coming in from that direction."*

Wes cursed, and considering the circumstances she thought it best not to scold him.

"Where are they coming from? How did they hear us?" he asked.

"They may have seen me and Jaconial," she admitted. Guilt coursed through her. It was the most likely answer. Perhaps it would have been better if she and Jaconial had stayed behind entirely, but there was nothing she could do about it now.

"It's difficult for dragons to hide in the sunlight," he said. *"You guys pretty much sparkle."*

His attempt at an excuse made her feel even worse. There were human lives at stake. They should have been more careful.

For a moment, neither of them said more, listening as the cruel chanting of the Blackmasks began below. She had heard that sound twice before, and each time, it made her blood run hot. They barely sounded human, and for a moment, she could see why Jaconial longed to fly down there and start tearing these monsters limb from limb.

Before the temptation could take hold any further, however, she spotted Kessara taking the lead of the group of captives below, rushing through one of the wider streets as slavers poured out of ruined buildings and nearby tents. Wes had taken up the rear, shouting, urging the group forward.

"If we go in now, we might hurt the captives," Celesyria warned as Jaconial flew ahead of her.

"I know," Jaconial said, her voice edged with frustration.

"What do we do?"

Celesyria didn't get a chance to answer.

Time seemed to slow as a woman fell at the edge of the group, tripping over a long piece of rock that jutted out into the street. She was old, a Vilzanian, with tight curls of white hair pressed to her skull.

Within seconds, three of the Blackmasks descended upon her, their knives raised. Celesyria felt her blood pounding in her ears as the other captives screamed. Only Wes and Kessara were armed. They would have to leave her.

High One, please watch over–

She did not finish her prayer. Aelrie was there, appearing as if out of nowhere, her sword slicing through the air with impossible speed. Her blue eyes were filled with rage, her long black hair flying out behind her as she fought the three men at once. Celesyria and Jaconial circled as low as they dared, listening to the sound of metal clashing against metal.

"Move!" Kessara was shouting at the dumbstruck crowd. Wes screamed for them to run, shoving at two of the men standing near the back of the company.

Celesyria watched as the group picked up speed again, little children stumbling over broken cobbles, their bare feet leaving streaks of blood.

One of the men near the back of the group stopped, reaching out a hand and helping the old Vilzanian woman to her feet.

"Archers! Come around!"

Jaconial's voice sounded in her head just in time for an arrow to fly past her face, and then another. She pulled her wings in, turning to the left as quickly as she could. There were more and more of the men now, all dressed in the same soulless black clothing, dozens of them raising their bows and nocking arrows.

When she came back around, Celesyria flew low, trying to get a better look at Aelrie in case she needed assistance.

High One, help her. Help her to hold them off. Wes and Kessara need more time.

The others were running as fast as they could, making their way down the length of the river. Wes held his curved sword in his hand, and Kessara grasped a short knife, both of them shouting at the captives to keep moving.

The clanging of metal continued, making her ears ring. Some of the other Blackmasks stood behind the three men that Aelrie was fighting. They looked nervous about moving forward, not wanting to get into close combat with an elf.

Celesyria rolled to the side as a fresh volley of arrows shot toward her. Jaconial flapped her wings, rising above her and narrowly missing a direct hit to her chest.

Aelrie was almost directly beneath them now as Celesyria rose higher, trying to catch her breath as arrows continued to fly through the air.

One of the men had fallen, his sword laying uselessly against the ground. Aelrie's sword was moving so fast that Celesyria struggled to see it, but a moment later, a second man cried out before collapsing to the ground.

Celesyria heard Aelrie scream, a cry that seemed loud enough to shake the sky around her. She was jumping now, sword raised. A moment later, the third man fell, his blood trickling through the gravel beneath him.

Several of the men who had been watching turned to flee, their swords left hanging at their belts.

Aelrie bolted after them.

Celesyria could hear the shouts of Wes and Kessara from

somewhere downriver.

She and Jaconial had to get to them, had to make sure that they got free of the ruins. If they were on the open plains, the dragons would be able to fight the Blackmasks off, flying low and swiping the men out of the way.

But they couldn't leave Aelrie. Not like this.

Panic seized Celesyria's chest as she turned back to the elf, who was chasing down the slowest bandit. He had not even attempted to draw his sword before he stumbled and fell to the dirt, pulling his hands up over his head, waiting for a killing blow. Aelrie was close, her nimble feet sure against the rocky terrain.

"Can you see her eyes?" Celesyria asked, watching as Jaconial came around, flying low. The arrows were still coming, but they were more sporadic now as quivers began to run empty.

"What?"

"Aelrie! Can you see her eyes?" she repeated urgently, trying to fly lower herself as a few stray arrows shot toward her. She felt a slight pang as one of them struck her front foot, just below the metal manacle that encircled her ankle, but it didn't stick between her hard scales.

She turned, trying to get a better look as Aelrie reached the man, her sword raised, her hair gleaming in the sunshine. She looked beautiful, a dangerous goddess ready to unleash fury upon the world itself.

High One, please, I beg you. Do not let her do this. Call out to her with Your voice. Help her to hear You. Do not let her turn to the darkness again.

Celesyria watched as Jaconial dove, her body whipping past Aelrie, so close that she only narrowly avoided being sliced by the elf's sword.

"They're blue," Jaconial said as she pulled up, unleashing a roar at the fleeing soldiers as she went.

Relief flooded Celesyria's chest as she circled again, another arrow plinking against her tail.

The elf stood there for a long moment, watching the man on the ground cowering before her.

You are made for more than this, Aelrie. None of us are beyond the High One's love. Not me, and certainly not you.

Resist.

Aelrie slid her sword back into its sheath and took off running in the direction of their friends.

"Let's go," Celesyria said, pulling out ahead of Jaconial and racing along the river. The sunlight reflected off of the surface of the water, which was growing rather choppy again as they neared the edge of the city.

They flew over a row of swordsmen who were running in the same direction, shouting their terrible chant at the sky.

Jaconial roared at them as she passed, her hot breath enough to stop them in their tracks for several seconds before they continued rushing forward.

Celesyria considered knocking them over with her front claws, but decided quickly that it was too dangerous. The riverbank was narrow here, with only a few feet of space between the edge of the water and a crumbling old city wall. If she tore a wing, she'd be in trouble.

"We could light them on fire," Jaconial suggested, as though reading her mind. The other orange dragon craned her neck as she flew, watching as two of the slower men fell behind the others, the whole group continuing to yell. *"They deserve it."*

"It's not so simple," Celesyria said, shaking her head as the two dragons flew beside one another, high above the top of

the wall.

The river was rushing downhill again, and what had been a gentle embankment was quickly steepening into a cliff. Celesyria dared a quick glance at the others up ahead, hoping that everyone would be able to keep their footing despite their terror at being chased.

"This again! We're not attacking the Four Kingdoms," Jaconial protested. *"The oath will not bind us. We can use fire against Kaveryth's enemies. Why does it matter if they're humans?"*

Celesyria shook her head. *"We will not risk exile. Don't be foolish."*

Jaconial grumbled, dipping low again as they cleared the city wall, trying to get a better look at the men. They were still moving fast, but fortunately, the captives had a decent head start.

"It would be easier if we knew the rules of the oath that controls our lives," she added, pausing to roar at the man below once more.

A few arrows flew past them from somewhere upriver. Celesyria could see the fletching wavering back and forth as the arrows passed, too slow to maintain balance in the air, let alone to puncture dragon scales.

"I know," Celesyria agreed, unsure of what else to say.

She could understand Jaconial's frustration.

For as far back in history as she knew, dragon hatchlings had been warned against using their fire to attack men in battle, even if it seemed clear that they were an enemy of Kaveryth. By the time of the Boneshire wars, this aversion to their own flame was so deeply ingrained that the dragon Guardians refused to use fire even against the elves.

Celesyria had used her fire only once, to burn down a

forest in order to help Wes, and even that had scared her. These barbarians were certainly not worth being sent to the Wrathlands over.

A few seconds later, however, an alternative presented itself.

"Look!" she called to Jaconial, but she was sure that her friend already noticed the same thing.

Most of the riverbank was narrow, nothing more than a strip of gravel beside a cliff, with thick brush and piles of impassable stone lining the other side. But there was a small plateau up ahead, perhaps a hundred feet across.

Wes, Kessara, and the others had already passed it, with Aelrie following at a safe distance to watch the rear of the column.

The Blackmasks were still approaching, swords raised as they sang their guttural song.

"I've got this," Jaconial said, giving Celesyria a pointed grin as she flew in a tight circle above.

"Don't kill them unless you have to," Celesyria said quickly, watching as her friend raced toward the captives, turning around when she had passed the flat space.

Memories pressed at her mind again. She could still imagine herself shoving the ladder in Windshear aside with her claws, still hear the sound of the bandit's body hitting the ground.

Death.

She pressed her eyes shut for a second, enjoying the feeling of the warm sun on her body, the light glowing red behind her eyelids.

She hated killing, even when it was necessary.

Jaconial had an easier time with the realities of war, which made Celesyria especially nervous. The darkness would find any weakness, any vice, and use it to bring destruction. They had to be vigilant.

To Celesyria's relief, Jaconial's voice sounded in her mind once more before she reached the bandits.

"I have a better idea."

Celesyria circled again, crossing the shimmering river and coming back around just in time to see Jaconial dive.

In a single motion, she took hold of two of the men in her claws and pulled back up. The chant was gone, replaced by shrieks of terror as the dragon lifted them higher and higher. She gave them a few moments to enjoy the view, and for a second, Celesyria was worried that she was going to drop them to their deaths on the sharp rocks.

Before she could urge mercy, however, Jaconial was on her way down again. This time she flew farther to the left, past the stones, until she had reached an area containing only brush. When she was only a few feet from the tops of the spiny ground plants and late-flowering bushes, she let the men fall.

They landed without injury, aside from the hundreds of tiny needles supplied by the plants. Jaconial let out a cheerful roar, and Celesyria found herself joining in. That much they certainly deserved.

By the time Jaconial flew back to the clearing, the remaining men were gone, racing back up the path toward the city as fast as their legs could carry them. The others were trapped in the brush, trying desperately to cut themselves free with their knives.

"Brilliant," she said as Jaconial came back around, the two of them flying side by side along the swirling river below.

Their friends were still making their way up the path. They were moving quickly, but for the moment, their enemies were far behind them. Celesyria flew in a slow circle, and then another, trying to catch her breath.

Jaconial smiled over at her as she did the same, but Celesyria could see something else in her eyes.

"Everything okay?"

"I'm fine. I just—it's just that—it's nothing," Jaconial said, glancing down at the river. Celesyria was sure that she would be blushing now, if she had been human.

"You sound like Wes," Celesyria joked, knowing that her friend wouldn't really mind even if he had heard. Wes' stammering had gotten a lot better as of late, but it still happened from time to time when he got nervous.

"I know," Jaconial said, shaking her head. *"Anyway, I just—I wanted to thank you."*

"For what?"

Celesyria was taken aback. Though the two of them had put most of their petty differences behind a while back, Jaconial was not exactly the type to be generous with apologies.

"I miss Nazzan," she continued. *"He always looks out for me, but more than that, he always tries to bring out the good that I have to offer."*

"He's one of the good ones," Celesyria said carefully. It was true, of course, but she was always nervous that her silly infatuation with the handsome green dragon would be brought to light. She'd never do anything to damage their relationship, but the lingering spark of jealousy and longing was hard to do away with entirely.

"He is," Jaconial said, letting out a slow breath. *"And you are a good friend. You always look out for me, even when I make myself my own worst enemy. Thank you."*

Celesyria was touched. No matter what had happened in the

past, it was good to be able to trust that the High One could bring people together for His plan.

"You're—"

An explosion shook the sky, stealing the words from Celesyria's mouth.

ALDER

Their camp was merry.

The sun had fallen beneath the horizon, leaving a black canvas behind for tens of thousands of stars. Their fire snapped and crackled cheerfully as Alder tossed another log onto it, sending a cascade of sparks into the air.

Alder had managed to catch four fat rabbits nearby, and he, Holga, and Gohr had enjoyed the best meal he'd had since leaving Auranth and Mella's cooking. Nazzan had been able to snag a large stag for himself, and had gone off to eat it away from the fire, so as not to alarm the children.

By the time he had returned, licking the blood from his lips, the little boy was already fast asleep, his head resting on one of their packs. Alder would move him to Holga's tent soon enough, but for the moment he saw no reason not to let the child sleep beneath the constellations.

Somewhere in the distance a pack of ironwolves howled. Alder could picture them out there on the plains somewhere, sitting in a circle, their huge snouts pointed up at the moon.

Holga pulled her blanket closer around herself, moving a few inches closer to the log where Alder sat every time she heard a fresh howl.

"I'll take care of any wolves that come our way, I promise,"

Nazzan assured her from across the fire, the orange light flickering against his emerald-green scales. "In fact, I'd be happy to. I'm still hungry."

Holga smiled at him.

"I'm not scared," she insisted, casting a glance off into the shadows. "But thank you."

Gohr stirred for a moment, a bead of drool dripping out of the side of his half-open mouth. Though he had gotten plenty of rest while imprisoned at the Academy, the day had been long, and Alder supposed it would be good for him to get a few hours sleep before they set off for their much longer flight tomorrow. Not that Gohr nor Holga knew where they were going.

Like his sister, Gohr had been immediately at ease with the huge dragon, not even hesitating for a moment when he was told that he would have to climb on his back and fly hundreds of feet above Aridmoor. He had settled in at the front of the saddle—Alder in the middle and Holga at the back—and held on for the ride, giving an occasional whoop of joy as they went.

Alder clasped his metal mug with his hands and took a sip of steaming tea, glancing over the rim of the cup at Holga. The calls of the wolves had quieted, and she was sipping her own tea, the beverage made, of course, from some obscure flower she had found that Alder had never heard of in his life.

Though he was eager to get his own saddle space back, he had to admit that he enjoyed being with the children, even with Holga's penchant for impromptu educational lectures.

Thoughts of Kessara rose in his mind before he could push them away.

He stared into the flames, watching as the wood burned away into embers, the sound of the hungry flame loud beneath the silent night sky. She was out there, somewhere, with the same moon and stars looking down at her.

Was she safe? Was she still with their friends? He had no way of knowing.

He thought of what their children would look like, running through the grass, shouting and laughing together as their parents watched over them.

He dreamed of not only a family, but a home, a permanent place where he could bring his mother and sisters, where he wouldn't have to leave all the time to earn his keep by way of his sword.

It would be beautiful, with a thatched roof and stone walls, hidden somewhere on the plains, somewhere King Ursa would never have a reason to look for him. They'd keep Aridmoorian warhorses, letting them roam free over the grasses, their flanks gleaming in the sun.

Marya and Kristoff could have children, too. He and Kessara's children would have cousins. He'd always wanted cousins growing up.

He was tired, and for a few precious minutes, his worries faded, replaced with happy imaginings.

Kessara will be dancing, her blue eyes lit up by cheerful firelight, smiling at me. That's after we marry, of course. A beautiful ceremony, in Windshear, I imagine.

The High One will approve, and so will our friends, and all of Kessara's subjects.

My subjects, I suppose.

I'd be King.

How am I supposed to be King?

I suppose I'll figure it out, if I have to...

All will be well...

His eyes shot open, lukewarm tea pouring from his cup and landing directly on his lap.

Nazzan chuckled at him. *"Time for bed, I think."*

"Guess so," he muttered, rubbing his eyes and trying to blink away the dryness from the fire.

"I'll keep watch," Nazzan offered. Holga had moved to sit near the dragon already, her tea mug long since emptied. She was using his tail as a backrest.

Alder stretched out his arms over his head, feeling suddenly very much awake.

"I'm fine," he insisted, getting to his feet and moving toward where Gohr lay.

The fire was still going strong, and though Alder found the smell of smoke pleasant, he doubted it was particularly healthy for the child to sleep near so much of it.

He picked up Gohr with ease and carried him to Holga's tent, pulling a wool blanket up under his neck. His eyes fluttered behind his lids for a moment before going still.

Back at the fire, Holga had found a long stick, and was sticking the end of it into the hot coals until it gleamed red.

He drew a breath. There would be no better time for this conversation.

"As much as I'm enjoying this reunion with your brother, decisions have to be made before dawn arrives," he said.

To his surprise, Holga did not launch into any sort of monologue or lecture. Instead, she stayed quiet, plucking the stick from the fire and examining the burnt end, saying nothing.

"I need to head to Auranth, to reunite with my friends," he said, running a hand over his dirty hair. He was thinking mainly of Kessara, but he knew that was foolish. Even if he was assured she was indeed alive and well, it wouldn't change anything. As much as he wanted to heal some of the hurt that he had caused her, there was only so much he could do without causing fresh problems.

"Do you know where that is?"

The child nodded. "I've heard of it. It's where the Envoy is building his army."

He expected her to say more, but she didn't. She looked sad, and he wondered if she knew what he was going to say next before he even opened his mouth.

"You and Gohr would be welcomed there. Wes and Celesyria should be there soon, if they haven't yet returned. There is also an elf there called Aelrie. A good elf, who is a believer in the High One."

"My betrothed, Jaconial, is there as well," Nazzan chimed in, flicking the end of his tail against the grass. He didn't talk about her very often, but Alder could tell how much he loved her when he did. Perhaps, like him, he avoided mentioning his beloved because missing her hurt too much.

"Yes," Alder said, licking the dryness from his lips. "And Kessara Manta of Galeharbor."

He spoke quickly, not wanting to linger on her name. He could hardly believe that speaking a single word could cause so much pain.

"The Princess," Nazzan added, narrowing his eyes at Alder.

"Yes," Alder said, looking at his feet. He was not sure whether or not he should obey King Manta and omit her title or not. It pained him to think of her as a commoner, but on the other hand, he wanted her to give up on her dreams of marrying him. He didn't want her to give up her family and her birthright.

Before Nazzan could argue further, however, Holga put up a hand, silencing them both.

"No," she said, her eyes blazing in the firelight. "I cannot go to Auranth. You should do what you must, but I ask that you first bring us home to Rill."

The dragon lifted his head, looking over at Alder and shrugging his massive shoulders.

"Holga," Alder said gently, trying to choose the right words. "Rill is already dangerous. I figured out as much when I found you there. And as this war with the elves continues to escalate, it's going to get worse. You need to go where you can be safe. In Auranth, you will have allies, and people who can teach you how to rule as queen. It's not something you're going to be able to just stumble into. Powerful people are going to do everything they can to oppose restoring the House of Noctua."

Holga listened quietly, tucking her knees up under her chin and pulling the warm blanket more tightly around her body. A slight breeze had picked up, making the loose ends of her unwashed braids flutter. It was getting colder with each passing day. Soon enough, the snows would begin, transforming the grasslands of Aridmoor into an endless sea of white.

"I understand," she said finally. "But there is more that you have not considered."

She paused, waiting.

Nazzan cleared his throat. "It is as Alder says. Your Kingdom has been broken since the wars. The dragon skeletons dotting the desert should be enough to testify to that."

Alder watched his eyes as he spoke, sadness reflected in their cat-like depths. For a moment, he thought he saw something more, but he did not wish to ask after it.

"I don't deny it," Holga said, pressing her chin against her bent knees. She looked even younger than her years, curled up in the thick blanket, hiding from the chill. "But if I go to Auranth, if I try to legitimize my power from across Kaveryth, the people will see me as nothing better than King Kylan Ursa. If I am to be Queen, I need to do it with the help of my people. No matter the risks."

She paused and took a breath, as though she was going to say more, but instead lapsed into silence.

Alder extended his cold hands closer to the fire, enjoying the slight tingle as his fingertips began to warm. He had to admit that the child had a point. Kylan Ursa's stewardship over Silverfell was seemingly tolerated for the time being, but Alder wondered how long even that would last with the loss of the Septemvirate's power.

"I see your point," he conceded. "But where does that leave you for the time being? No matter how mature and brilliant you are–" he glanced at Nazzan, who nodded in agreement "–you work as a midwife's apprentice and in a laundry. You do not know how to rule a country."

Holga smiled softly, looking up at the constellations over their heads. Alder followed her gaze, his eyes instinctively settling on a large circle made up of five stars, with another brighter one for a tail.

Manta.

He pressed his eyes closed, feeling the warmth of the fire on his skin. He could not think of her now. He wouldn't let himself.

"My parents always told me that our family was descended from the greatest tapestry-makers in the whole continent. There was a story about a distant uncle who fell in love with a

House noble and was entrusted with her secrets, preserving them in his art. I... I guess maybe they were trying to tell me the truth, or at least allow me to see a shadow of it."

She did not take her eyes off of the stars. Alder waited patiently for her to continue, his eyes flitting between several more of the collections of stars that he recognized. Celesyria had taught him well.

"If my parents were still alive, I wonder if any of this would have happened. I think I would have ended up like them, making geometric tapestries for rich merchants and lesser House nobles."

Alder pressed his fingers to his temples. He was growing tired, and he had no idea what the child was getting at.

"I learned to work in a laundry, to heal the sick, and to assist the birthing women because I had to. That was just as much my destiny as anything else chosen by blood. Don't you see?"

He certainly did not, and he told her so.

"It is the blood of the House of Noctua that flows in my veins, to be sure," she said, sitting up straight and letting the blanket fall back onto the ground. "The blood of my mother. Raela. But that is not what will make me queen, not really. It's essential, yes, but it's not enough."

She got to her feet, and Nazzan stretched out his tail, which she had been resting on for quite some time. Alder shivered as a breeze rippled through the camp, making sparks jump from the waning fire.

"I don't understand," he admitted finally, drawing his cloak around his shoulders as he moved for a bucket of sand to douse the fire.

"It is by the will of the High One that I am to be queen. He chose the members of the House of Noctua who came before, and now he's choosing me. And if He is calling me to lead this broken kingdom, I have to believe that He is going to give me what I need in order to do it."

"I admire your faith, Holga," Nazzan said after a moment, stretching out his wings as he got up from his place at the fire.

"As do I," Alder added. "But the High One can also work through other people. How do you know that He doesn't want you to be trained in Auranth?"

Alder felt a hollowness in his chest even as he said it. He already knew the answer, in the same way that Holga did.

"I just do."

No one spoke as Alder dumped sand on the fire, the light fading away, replaced by the gentle glow of stubborn embers. The moonlight looked brighter now, sending a blue cast over the waving grasses and making Nazzan's green scales look even more emerald-like than usual.

"I understand," Alder said finally, blinking away the after-images of the flames. "I've certainly followed a voice I have heard only in dreams. But you need to be careful. It's easy to let your own imperfect heart deceive you."

Holga nodded, staring off at the stars again, her pensive expression betraying a deep maturity that he found himself unable to doubt. She would be okay. She had been following the High One for far longer than he had, despite her young age. She would understand how to discern the whispers of His voice.

"I won't be alone in Rill," she said finally, slipping her hands into the pockets of her trousers. "My parents were loved. I have friends there, and even some from Redvale who might help me to make the right connections. I doubt I'll have much time for apprenticing with Malka, but she will help me all the same."

Alder thought of the herbwoman, confusion twisting in his gut. He hoped that she was finished with the business of killing. He could tell by the look in Holga's eyes that she was probably considering the same thing, but he decided to keep his mouth shut. For the time being, the child needed someone she could trust, and Malka already knew the secret of her lineage. It was the best option she had.

"I will tell Gohr to follow you to Auranth," Holga said, her voice catching in her throat. "He'll be safer there, as you say. But I think he will refuse. I do not wish to force him, but you are bigger and stronger than I."

"I will not take him against his will," Alder said with only a moment's hesitation. "We will carry you to Rill at first light."

Nazzan did not argue.

Gohr would indeed be safer in Auranth, but the threat of war loomed in every inch of the continent. They could not outrun it, not really. There would always be a risk.

If the worst happens, they shouldn't have to die alone.

They were all that each other had.

Chapter Twenty-Two

CELESYRIA

Celesyria couldn't move.

Her wings felt frozen in place, as though her brain was suddenly unable to control her muscles. Somewhere to her right, she could hear Jaconial calling out to her, but she could not see anything.

Black smoke rushed up from below, filling her lungs, burning her eyes, and blocking her view of the path. She closed her eyes just in time for her wings to begin working again, and for several seconds she flew blind. All she could think about was getting away from the smoke. She wanted to outrun the ringing in her ears. She couldn't focus. She couldn't think.

Finally, a voice in her head made its way through the noise.

"They're on the path!" Jaconial was shouting, over and over, desperate to get her attention. Celesyria forced her eyes open, coughing against the smoke, trying to get her bearings. She could hear Jaconial, but the words did not seem to register.

For a moment, she thought of how ridiculous it was that smoke bothered a dragon who could breathe fire, but she didn't exactly have time to dwell on it.

She was over the river now, closer to where Jaconial had been flying, but her friend was nowhere to be seen.

The smoke was less thick here, and she sucked in several small breaths as she flew higher into clearer air, struggling to think. She must have been right near the bomb when it went off. Jaconial couldn't have been more than twenty feet away from her.

Where was she? Where was Wes? Where were the captives?

She craned her neck behind her, trying to see where the bandits were, but she could see nothing but a black cloud of smoke shrouding the source of the explosion.

Still, she understood what she could not see.

She drew her front claws in so tightly that she almost made herself bleed.

They had used a calesca bomb, just as they had threatened to do back in Windshear. Celesyria recognized the deep blackness of the smoke they produced, and she understood at once what the Blackmasks had done. The explosives were capable of blowing through stone and felling trees.

She understood.

"Jaconial!" she shrieked aloud, ignoring the ringing in her ears. To her relief, her friend flew up from the smoke below, her claws streaked with fresh blood.

A breeze blew across the river, and for a moment, the smoke was thin enough for her to see what Jaconial had.

What had minutes before been a natural fortress of stone and tight scrub bushes had disappeared along a long stretch of the bank, replaced with nothing but soot. Men were pouring through the gap, their black outfits blending them into the scorched earth beneath their feet.

There were dozens of them.

"We have to try and pick some of them off," Jaconial was saying, diving toward the bank. *"But I've only managed to stop two."*

She pulled up just feet away from the men, unable to avoid her wings being caught on the jagged cliffside. Celesyria could hear a string of curses, shouted aloud as Jaconial tried to reach the men again and failed to do so.

They were chanting again, their vicious cries sounding even more exuberant than before. She wasn't sure if they had come from within the Dread Ruins, or perhaps had been traveling toward it, but none of that mattered. They weren't going to be able to stop so many, not even in an open field.

"Wes!" Celesyria called to her friend, flying low along the cliff, trying to see if Jaconial's plan was even remotely possible.

She watched as she snagged one more of the men, her claw catching on the hood of his tunic and sending him flying into the fallen rocks that lined the riverbank. She looked away as his body landed, but she couldn't help but to imagine the sound it must have made.

Wes wasn't answering. The smoke had settled into a grayish fog, and she could not see very far down the path. The bandits were moving fast, off into the haze where she could not see.

She told Jaconial to keep trying to slow them down before taking off after them, as fast as her wings would carry her. She forced her smoke-burned eyes to remain open, ignoring that the sunlight was now directly in her face. Behind her, the rushing men continued to yell and to chant, the sound excruciating as it hammered in her damaged ears.

It didn't matter.

She had to hurry.

High One, please. Do not let anyone fall behind.

At least she could be certain that they would have heard the explosion. They would know that they had to run faster. Perhaps they could get to open space.

They can split up. At least a few of them might have a chance at running off into the brush.

Her heart seemed to catch in her throat.

All of a sudden, she could see them.

"Wes!" she called again. She saw him standing there, but he did not turn. They were standing still, the line turned to face the edge of the cliff. Kessara and Aelrie stood nearby, saying something she could not hear to the group of strangers.

The men were still coming fast. They couldn't stop for rest. They had to go as fast as they could, if they wanted even the slightest chance–

She watched in horror as the captives began jumping into the raging river below, one after another.

KESSARA

"Are you sure?" Kessara asked, staring at the churning water, the toes of her boots resting against the edge of the cliff. A wave of dizziness gripped her, and for a terrible moment, she felt herself wobbling on her feet.

Aelrie took hold of her wrist, steadying her.

" Yes," Aelrie said firmly, turning to Wes as she spoke. "It's the only way. The water is moving fast because it's going downhill, but there are few rocks. We'll make it. It will slow eventually."

Kessara stared at the black-haired woman, wondering whether Aelrie knew this river somehow or if she was sending them to a potentially deadly fate on nothing but instinct.

She glanced behind her. She could hear the shouting of the bandits, but she could not see them yet. Somewhere along the river, there had been an explosion, and the smoke had blurred everything in sight.

They were getting closer. They didn't have very much time to decide.

"Okay," Wes said finally. Kessara looked along the row of captives, their faces pale as they stared down at the ravine below. They were already scared of Aelrie, who had appeared out of nowhere, and now the elf was telling them to jump off a cliff.

She could see a few of the children clutching at their mothers' legs and hands, their sobs filling the air, punctuated with the hollering of the approaching bandits.

"There's no other way. Be strong," the young woman called Luna said, nodding to the man beside her. The rest of them nodded their own approval. It was a simple decision. They could choose certain death here, or they could take a wild chance at living.

One by one, the captives began to jump.

They fell impossibly slowly, their bodies seeming to linger in mid-air before plunging into the white water below. Some of them jumped together, hands clasped tightly, not letting go as they sank beneath the water and bobbed up again. A couple of the people thrashed in the water as they landed, and others took hold of them, keeping their heads above the deluge.

She saw the woman from Stronghollow take a running start, getting free of the cliff wall as much as she could before plummeting to the water. To Kessara's relief, she was a good swimmer.

Kessara heard the roars of Jaconial and Celesyria, and looked up to see the dragons flying over the river, following the captives from above. The ravine looked wider up ahead, and Kessara hoped that they could get close enough to help those who could not swim onto their backs if they had to, but she knew that they couldn't take them all. They would have to swim for their lives to survive the rough current.

Soon, only the three friends remained on the platform. Aelrie had not let go of Kessara's wrist.

Kessara stood there, paralyzed, realizing that they expected her to go next. She could hear the bandits even more loudly now. If she dared to turn around, she was sure that she would see them, black demons rising out of the smoke on the horizon.

"Jump, Princess," Wes said, gesturing toward the ledge.

She stepped back, yanking her wrist free, and sat down on the rocky path.

It was a simple decision, but she couldn't make herself move, couldn't force her legs to carry her off into the sky.

She knew the death that was coming for her at the hand of the bandits.

She had almost faced it already, the helplessness of being pinned down, knowing that someone bigger and stronger than you was in control.

And she had survived it.

But the water...

She had almost died there, too, sucked under by a tidal wave.

This was worse. This water was poisoned, cursed. Even if the captives and her friends lived, what if it made them sick?

Neither choice was a good one. She feared both.

But at least sitting here, she was not chasing death. It was chasing her.

"Go, Aelrie," Wes urged, taking a step toward the elf, who shook her head.

"I will, just as soon as Kessara does. Don't worry. Stay with the captives."

She watched as the two of them paused for a moment, their hands touching, their eyes meeting.

And then it was over. Wes leapt into the air, disappearing over the cliff's edge and out of sight, following the people who needed him.

"I can't," Kessara said, fighting back a sudden rush of tears. "I can't. Just go. Please."

Aelrie said nothing for a moment, and Kessara watched as the dragons disappeared out of sight, lost in the afternoon sunshine and the lingering smoke.

"Only drinking the water can harm you," Aelrie said, reaching out her hand. Kessara ignored it.

"I know."

She looked at the elf, hoping she was right. Fears and what-ifs swirled through her mind. The height felt dizzying. She would be pulled under, at least for a moment. The water would find the inside of her mouth if not the inside of her lungs. How could Aelrie be so sure they'd be okay?

She could see the bandits now, making their way out of the haze and along the bank.

"Go, Aelrie." she said, trying to keep her voice from shaking. "Please."

She wouldn't get the elf killed. This was her problem. She would face the consequences alone.

Up the bank, she could see several of the men glancing over the cliffside, watching as the last of the captives floated off along the water.

Their chants fell apart, leaving only chaotic shouts of rage as they realized that their quarry had gotten away.

"They will not follow us into the river," the elf said, watching as the men rushed closer, their swords raised as they noticed the two women, alone on the bank. "Don't you trust me, Kessara? After all this time?"

She said nothing. She felt numb, the warmth of the sun doing little to quell the chill that slithered up her spine.

She had been here before, back in Kingsvier landing.

On the beach, after he had left her. After he had told her that he didn't love her. Alone. So utterly alone.

She had wanted to be consumed by the waves. She had wanted death, even if only for a moment.

But something in her had told her to be stubborn.

She could hear that voice again, a whisper, louder than the raging mob swelling behind her.

She reached for Aelrie's hand, and allowed the elf to pull her to her feet.

It felt solid, safe.

It felt like friendship.

Someone who was willing to stand here with her to the very last second, and perhaps beyond it. Perhaps even unto death.

Even though she had done nothing to deserve such friendship, Aelrie had offered it without a second thought.

And that was something worth holding on to. She wasn't alone.

"Don't let go," she gasped as they rushed forward, their boots shushing against the gravel of the path.

The view was beautiful. She could see that now.

They didn't slow down.

The ground fell away, Aelrie's hand gripped hers, and she waited, the screams of those who hated them ringing in her ears.

Chapter Twenty-Three

The water was colder than Kessara had expected.

It pulled her under for what felt like a long time, the waves moving her body as though she was nothing more substantial than a thrown twig. She held her breath, her eyes firmly closed, half expecting her face to collide with the rocky riverbed, even though she had seen the others bob safely to the surface.

A part of her wanted to give up, to open her mouth and let the freezing water fill her lungs. She was tired. Her entire body ached, her leg smarting from some wound she didn't know she'd attained.

But Aelrie's hand was in hers, and the elf did not let go.

Finally, the water shoved them back toward the surface. They emerged, shivering and coughing, taking in as many gulps of air as they could as they were pulled along the ravine. Kessara fought to keep her eyes open as she watched the cliff walls rushing by on either side. They were moving impossibly fast. One rock outcropping out of place, one wave sending them too far to either side–

"Look!" Aelrie cried out before a torrent of white water

struck her, forcing her back under. Kessara had a moment to take a final breath before she reached the same spot, the force of the current pulling her down alongside her friend.

She closed her eyes again, forcing herself to remain calm, counting the seconds.

She could still feel Aelrie's hand grasping her own. So long as she kept holding on, they were going to be okay. She couldn't bear to consider any other possibility.

The water didn't spit them out this time, not like before.

Instead, they bobbed above the surface several times, just long enough to take a half breath. They were blind, waiting, holding on to each other with as much force as they could manage.

And then it was different.

They found themselves at the surface more and more, with plenty of time to breathe. Up ahead, Kessara could see what Aelrie had spotted.

The water changed. It was no longer white, but an impossibly clear blue, the sun sparkling on its surface.

Up ahead, they saw Jaconial and Celesyria standing along a sandy bank, their tails extended out into the river. Wes and the others were there waiting for them, ringing out their hair, most of them looking like they wanted to kiss the sandy ground.

Kessara and Aelrie floated in their direction, their bodies moving gently along, caressed by the water.

They let go of each other only when they had taken hold of Celesyria's tail, floating on their backs as she pulled them to safety.

Kessara half-walked, half-crawled up the gently sloping embankment. The adrenaline was gone, and she felt the full brunt of the chill. Even the hot desert sun was not enough to quell the shivers that coursed through her body.

"Are you okay?"

She felt Wes' arms wrapping around her as he eased her down onto the sand. She rested against him for a moment. He was already dry, his body warm from the sun.

"Y–y–yes," she stammered, trying to get her fingers around the end of her braid so she could get more of the water out. She said a silent prayer of thanks that they would get a few more hours of daylight. The desert was cold at night, especially now that they were well into autumn, and it was not as though they had brought enough blankets for all of these people.

Wes pulled back a little, looking at her.

"I'm fine," she said, giving him a weak smile.

He smiled, but she could see that his gaze had already moved past her, the longing plain in his eyes.

Thankfully, Aelrie appeared to be in much better shape than she herself was, already hard at work pulling their few blankets and cloaks from the dragons' saddlebags and wrapping them around a couple of the older women's shoulders.

"She saved my life," she whispered, the words feeling heavy on her heart, as though she had been offered a loan that she would never have any way to repay. Wes gave her hand a squeeze and let go, moving to help the others.

Jaconial was staring upriver, sniffing the air.

"Are we safe?" Kessara asked no one in particular. She could still hear the chant of the bandits lingering in her ears, even though she knew that they must have gotten far ahead of them by now.

It was Aelrie who answered, standing up and striding into

the center of the motley group.

"They wouldn't dare enter the river after us," she said quietly, pausing for a moment to clear her throat. When she continued, her voice was stronger, carrying across the expanse of sand and red stone. "The bandits have a visceral terror of the cursed water. They wouldn't dare to enter it."

"Care to enlighten us?" a man chimed in from somewhere in the crowd. Kessara couldn't place the voice.

"It's a long story," Aelrie said, glancing off toward the eastern horizon, keeping watch. "But I can say this: they fear the water because they deal in darkness. They know that they are not innocent. Deep down, they fear that one day, somehow, they will get what is owed to them."

Kessara shivered, though whether it was at Aelrie's words or due merely to the lingering dampness of her body and clothes, she could not be certain.

"But just because they will not follow us into the river doesn't mean we're safe," Aelrie said quickly. "They will follow on foot. Others will return to the Dread Ruins and bring their horses. There will be more bowmen, and sharpened swords. We mustn't linger here."

The crowd shifted, mumbling to one another, their damp faces clouded with fear and worry. Kessara could see the woman from Stronghollow near the back of the crowd, helping a young boy to clean a wound on his ankle.

Kessara wanted to talk to her, but she didn't know what to say. Her friends had been right. In the end, they saved her. But she hated that she'd had to endure more terror in the meantime.

Instead of trying to find the words, Kessara caught her eye, smiling until the woman smiled back.

She remembered them. She knew.

Kessara's heart felt full. It was enough.

She turned, searching the crowd for anyone in need of a healer's assistance.

Somehow, no one seemed to have sustained any new injuries more serious than a bruise. They were still starving and weak, but at least they wouldn't be carrying anyone with broken limbs.

Kessara glanced at the river. Here, it was gentle; even beautiful. But a thousand things could have gone wrong amid the rocks and falls upriver.

A miracle. There is no more reasonable explanation than that.

When Aelrie did not continue, Kessara made her way toward where she stood, standing a few steps behind the elf. She had so much to say to her, so much to thank her for, but it would have to wait.

"We need to head out, as soon as your feet are steady enough to walk. It will be easier for us to dry out the rest of the way before sunset. I don't want the young and old among us to be sleeping damp," she said, holding her chin high, settling into the practiced posture of her noble class.

"Wait," Wes said, stepping forward.

The crowd watched him, their chattering beginning anew. Kessara could see Luna standing there, just ahead of the others, and wondered if she was going to share her opinion as well.

Kessara glanced back upriver, expecting to see dark figures heading toward them, but the cliffs were empty. Despite the chill that lingered in her bones, she was ready to move. She wanted to be far, far away from here.

"Why did the others stay behind?" Wes asked, his brows

furrowing as he looked at the crowd. "Why wouldn't they at least try to escape?"

Kessara sucked in a breath. She didn't want anyone to suggest that they attempt to go back for them. It was too dangerous. They had made their choice, as much as it pained her, and they couldn't do anything about it now. The bandits would be on their guard this time.

Luna stepped forward, and Jaconial and Celesyria moved a few steps out of the way to give her more space.

The crowd went quiet immediately.

Kessara couldn't help but to stare at the bruise that covered the woman's face. What horrors had she endured? How often had she been in the position that Kessara feared above all else—pinned to the ground, waiting for the pain, helpless?

"Our friends stayed behind because they were not captives," she said, a sad smile spreading across her face. The rest of the group joined her, the entire mass of faces transformed in an instant, as though radiating light from within. "They are redeemers."

"Some of us were captured in our home lands, especially the children," one of the men chimed in from the crowd. "But when we were brought here, we learned that Luna and the others came on purpose. They ransomed themselves to free those who had been taken, including a large group taken from Galeharbor's capital a couple of months back."

Kessara felt her breath catching in her chest.

They traded places with my people? They chose this?

Luna nodded. "That is why some chose to stay behind. They want to be brought to Nox, if possible, because they know that there are other slaves there. They want to serve them in whatever way they can, even if it is too late to free them. As for us, we decided that your arrival was a sign from the High One that we had done what He asked, and that it was time to accept His gift.”

Kessara felt tears prickling at her eyes, wondering just how good a person would have to be to be willing to choose such a terrible fate. It was far beyond her own virtue, that much was certain.

Celesyria lowered her head until she was eye-level with Luna. “Who are you? All of you?”

“Some of us are normal folks, taken by evil people. But some us, myself included, do not hail from this land,” she said, meeting the dragon’s eyes. “I believe that you refer to us as the remnant. Our home is in the east, beyond the sea, but some of us saw what was happening in Kaveryth and decided that we had to return.”

Kessara could hardly believe what they were hearing.

After all this time, all of these questions that they had to ask, they had found the remnant by accident.

The High One brought us here, without needing to even utter a word.

“As much as I want to learn more,” Aelrie said as soon as there was a break in the conversation, “It will have to wait. We have to keep moving.”

Several of the others in the crowd called out their approval, and Luna stepped back from the center of the group, falling in with the others.

“Where will we go?” Jaconial asked.

Aelrie looked over to Wes for a moment, and then continued.

“We wish to bring you all to the city of Auranth, in the north. It has become a refuge for those who are loyal to the cause of the Envoy. We have been working to build up an armed force, independent of King Ursa's men, and you should be safe there."

She paused, and Kessara pondered her words. She missed Auranth, but whenever she thought of it, she couldn't help but to wonder if some terrible fate might have befallen their friends while they were gone. They had heard no news, but news from Auranth moved slowly at the best of times.

Still, it was the only option.

"We need more men," Wes added, clearing his throat. "If anyone wishes to join our army, they will be more than welcomed. But we also have people there who can help to get you home. You will not be pressured to stay."

Kessara looked for Luna in the crowd, as did the others who surrounded her. When she nodded her approval, the people began to talk all at once, asking questions she could not hear.

"Wait," Aelrie said, raising a hand. "We cannot head to Auranth directly. Not until we are sure that the bandits are no longer following us. My plan is to cut south, and then head east, following the Boneshire desert along the mountains as long as we can before cutting back north across the plains."

Kessara tried to imagine a map of Kaveryth in her mind. The river that cut through the Dread Ruins cut back and forth several times, and she struggled to get her bearings on exactly where they were. Fortunately, the elf and the two dragons were much more skilled at navigation.

"Wouldn't it be safer to go more directly through Arid-moor?" Celesyria asked, looking off to the north. "I doubt even the Red Army will get in the way of a company of freed slaves."

"Yes," Aelrie agreed. The crowd began talking amongst each other again, eyeing the elf with renewed suspicion. "The desert is dangerous. But we don't know where the bandits are. There could be more of them, coming to bring others to the Dread Ruins. Sure, we could run into some more heading to Nox, but they won't be actively looking for us in the north."

"That makes sense to me," Jaconial chimed in, tracing lines in the dirt with one of her front claws. "They'll be guarding the area surrounding the ruins, expecting us to pass. We'll be well on our way through Aridmoor before they realize their mistake."

Soon enough, they were on their way, the dragons flying ahead to scout the area.

Kessara had asked Wes to take up the lead of the column, and he had, leaving her to follow along behind.

Aelrie was moving alongside the crowd near the center, her sharp eyes roving across the landscape as they went.

The remaining grass thinned out with every hour they walked, giving way to an endless expanse of sand. There was no discernible path to speak of—the frequent windstorms in Boneshire had a way of shifting the landscape overnight—but there were enough landmarks to keep them moving in the right direction.

The dragon skeletons were frequent here, dotting the desert every few miles. Kessara couldn't decide if she found them creepy, or fascinating.

In the distance to their left, they could see the Severed Summits, marking the border of Umrym and making it nearly impossible to get lost. The Dread Ruins was somewhere behind them, far away, along miles and miles of rushing river.

They carried on for the rest of the afternoon without incident, stopping only to drink from their meager water stores and to let the youngest and oldest rest their feet.

Still, as night finally fell, Kessara's nerves were on edge. There were few trees here, and she felt exposed. If the bandits were close, the dragons would provide their only chance at a warning.

Finally, after the moon had risen nearly overhead, Wes called out that it was time to stop for the night.

Kessara had not realized just how tired she was until they stopped walking. They had found a large rock formation to rest beside, where they would at least be somewhat protected from the wind, but she knew it was going to be a long, cold night.

When they were moving, the chill was tolerable, but as soon as she had caught her breath, the cold wind swept it away again.

She walked over to Celesyria and began removing her saddlebags, taking out the few blankets and cloaks that they had. There was nowhere near enough to go around, and worse, they were still damp from earlier in the day.

She shook her head. They would have to make do. When the sun rose in a few hours, it would be hot again. She ignored the fact that they would face the same problem tomorrow night.

"Are there any more tents?" Aelrie asked from somewhere beside her, making her jump.

"Sorry," the elf added. "Didn't mean to startle you."

"No, it's fine," Kessara said, grabbing one of the tents and passing it to Aelrie, who tossed it to one of the Vilzanian men nearby. Several of them were already setting up the few tents they had, trying to weigh them down with chunks of rocks so that unexpected gusts of wind couldn't pull them away.

Aelrie turned to join them, but Kessara caught her arm.

"Wait. I—just—thank you. Thank you for saving my life,"

she said, cringing at the way she was stammering.

She was ashamed. Even if it was only for a few seconds, she had wanted to give up. Again. It had taken the love of a friend to remind her that there was so much that she still had to live for.

But that was not something she could admit out loud.

"I'm proud of you," Aelrie said, giving her hand a squeeze, Kessara watching as the moonlight glinted on her silvery flesh. "You were scared, but in the end, you jumped. You trusted. I'm blessed to have been a part of it."

Kessara plastered a smile on her face, but it fell just as soon as Aelrie walked off to join the others. She was so tired that she swore her bones hurt. More than that, she just wanted to be alone.

"Here," a voice said from behind her. A flash of annoyance coursed through her, but this time, she did not jump. It was Wes, handing her a bunched up piece of brown fabric. He was shirtless, and she felt herself blushing. He looked so different than he had a year before, his soft body turned to hardened muscle, gleaming in the blue starlight. Not that she was trying to stare.

She took the fabric mutely, forcing herself to meet his eyes.

"Not the warmest thing here, I know," he said, giving her a quick smile. "But the children and the older ones have the cloaks and blankets. It might help a little."

Realization dawned, and immediately she tried to press the shirt back into his hands.

"No, Wes, I'm fine, don't–"

He pulled his hands back, raising them in mock surrender. "Take it. Please."

Before she could argue further, he was walking away, back

toward where the dragons stood sentinel on the open expanse in front of the rock formation. They didn't want to risk starting a fire tonight, not while the bandits could still be close, but at least the night was clear.

She slipped the tunic over her dress and made her way toward a secluded corner between two rocks, settling down into the cold sand. She let the soft grains fall between her fingers for a long while, staring up at the stars and listening to the sounds of the camp.

Soon enough, it was quiet, save for the sound of Celesyria's snoring and the occasional cry of an ironwolf. She could see Jaconial and Aelrie keeping watch.

She was safe, but her mind wouldn't slow down enough to let her sleep.

She leaned her back up against the stone, trying to get comfortable. Wes' shirt helped with the cold, but still, every time a breeze rushed past, kicking up puffs of sand, she struggled to keep her teeth from shaking.

You'll get used to it, Princess. Those captives—half of which decided to become captives of their own accord, mind you—got used to a whole lot worse.

She shook her head to herself. The thoughts in her head often sounded a lot like Alder. Even now, miles and miles away from wherever he was, she couldn't escape the hold he had on her. She wasn't sure that she wanted to.

They were willing to give up everything to serve the High One and their fellow man. They were willing to risk torture, hard labor, even death in order to show their love. Their love was a love willing to be hurt.

She still struggled to get her mind around it.

She wanted to talk to them all, wanted to understand where

they found such strength. It was more noble than anything she had ever witnessed in her life, and she had been blessed to have grown up surrounded with goodness.

I think you are going to love like that, Kessara. I know you may not believe that, but it's true. You're so much stronger than you give yourself credit for.

She stared up at the stars overhead, trying to find something to focus on so that she could stop herself from crying.

This was worse than usual. These words were so unlike anything she would ever say to herself that she thought she must be going insane.

She preferred that to the alternative. She would rather be insane, so long as it meant she could shut Alder up. Every time she felt her heart beginning to heal the slightest bit, the wound was torn open again. She couldn't beat it.

Just breathe, Princess. I promise it's going to be alright.

But it wasn't alright. It hadn't been alright, not ever, not since the moment that he walked away and told her that he didn't want her.

The tears were falling now. She had given up trying to stop them, instead clamping a hand over her mouth to quiet her sobs. Wes and Aelrie were worried enough about her as it was.

She thought of Alder's perfect green eyes, the feeling of his lips on hers, his strong arms pulling her close.

She thought of their little redheaded children, making swords out of twigs, laughing as their father pretended to tackle them.

It was a future so real she could nearly taste it. She wanted it desperately, deeply, more than she had ever wanted anything in her life.

But it was not her future.

CHAPTER TWENTY-THREE

It was not what the High One had chosen for her life.

You're okay. Just keep breathing.

The wind whipped through the rocks again, but she scarcely felt it.

The pain was coursing through her now, crashing over her like the waves of the river, forcing every last bit of air from her lungs, sucking the blood from her veins. She couldn't breathe. She felt like she was being torn apart from the inside, every joint of her bones snapping in two.

For a moment, she let the grief consume her.

She did not try to soften it, or to run away. She had to feel it, feel all of it.

She knew that now.

There was no other way.

The love hurt already, there was no escaping that.

But she had a choice. She could suffer the pain, or she could offer it, give it to the High One to transform it into something better.

For a long time, she cried, her tears soaking the front of Wes' tunic.

Her future husband, the man who had always been there for her, no matter what she did or how broken she was.

The man who would sleep shirtless in the desert if it meant giving the woman who had rejected him a little more warmth.

The tears were no longer coming. Her head had a dull ache, and her throat felt numb, but the tidal wave of grief was pulling away.

Part of her wanted to hold on to it, to be dragged out to sea with it, but for whatever reason, she couldn't.

She dried her tears with the back of her hand, blinking up at the stars. A feeling of peace was settling on her. She could not help but to feel it.

Alder still loved her.

You know that. You've always known that.

He had only told her otherwise because he wanted her to let go. Because he wanted what was best for her, even though he knew that she was nowhere near ready to accept it.

She loved him, more now than she ever had. There was no denying it, not even to herself.

She loved him enough to feel the pain.

This time, she would offer it willingly.

She slid down the rock face and laid on the ground, the soft sand feeling almost like a pillow even as it stuck into her hair.

She should have felt shattered, but she didn't.

She felt only tired.

With a final smile at the stars, she closed her eyes, listening to the gentle sound of her own breathing. The gentle voice remained, but it changed. It was someone else who spoke into her heart now, His words as clear as the desert night.

I am with you.

I will carry you, no matter what.

Ask Me, and I will move mountains for you.

I will fill the empty spaces in your heart.

That is My promise to you.

Chapter Twenty-Four

WES

Wes opened his eyes, the red light of dawn piercing and warm.

His first thought, as it often was these days, was of Aelrie.

Usually, the only exception were those days where he woke up with a particularly horrible headache. He was glad that this was not one of them. Today, there was only a dull ache. He could handle that easily.

He sat up from where he had been curled against a stone, the soft sand beneath serving as a surprisingly tolerable sleep surface. He looked out at the red expanse of the Boneshire desert as he stretched out his tight limbs.

He could hear the sound of voices, and when he made his way to the open space where the dragons rested, he saw that Kessara, Aelrie, and the others had already lit a small fire.

"Morning," he said, clearing his dry throat.

One of the men standing nearby handed him a waterskin, and he gulped from it gratefully before handing it back.

Kessara had used her strange tincture on the river water yesterday, filling all of their empty waterskins again, but still, many of the captives had not been willing to drink it.

They had been told by their captors that they were being

given safe water from elsewhere while in captivity, but Wes doubted it. Even with their horses, it would have been a lot of work for the bandits to haul water to the Dread Ruins, assuming there was a safe source nearby.

On the other hand, he supposed the bandits could have been telling the truth. Perhaps the elves wanted their slaves to be in good health, and didn't want to risk them being exposed to illness. There was no way of knowing, and he decided to keep his musings on the topic to himself instead of raising doubt and worrying the others.

"Good morning," Celesyria said aloud, ducking her head and giving him a tap on the chest with her snout. "You'd best find a shirt. You'll be red as a tomato in this sun."

He felt a blush creeping to his cheeks. He had grown up very pudgy, and consequently had taken great pains to avoid ever being shirtless in front of others if he could help it. Now his muscled form was beginning to rival Alder's.

"Oh, right," Kessara said, yanking his tunic over her head and handing it to him. He caught her eye for a moment, and to his surprise, she was blushing, as well.

He stood there stupidly for a second, holding the crumpled fabric, before finally realizing that he should in fact put it on at once.

He took an extra second to put his arms through the sleeves, hiding behind the warm fabric before facing the others again, hoping that the flush had fallen away from his face.

"I thought a fire would be safe. Considering how bright and clear it is," Aelrie was saying, her slender arms filled with a load of dried twigs and bits of other plants. She deposited them near the fire, where one of the Vilzanian men sat, tending the rather pathetic flames with a pointed stick.

"You're probably right. I'm still a little cold," Wes said, taking a few steps closer and sinking into the sand. He felt the tiny fire's heat beginning to warm his insides.

"No sign of the bandits, sir," one of the other men chimed in, gesturing back the way they'd come. Wes followed the river with his gaze, but saw nothing on the horizon. Even the tallest towers of the Dread Ruins were too far away to see.

Any bandit who dared to catch up to them now would find the dragons were quite formidable when they could fight out in the open. Not even to mention Aelrie.

He stole a glance at her as the others began to sit, her back turned to him as she helped Kessara and several of the others to prepare breakfast.

She had saved their lives by urging them to jump into the river.

No. The High One saved us. He's the only one who could have made a group of slaves put their lives in the hand of an elf.

He had sought her out the night before, hoping to get a few moments on their own so he could thank her, but the opportunity never came.

Then again, he might have tried harder, but part of him had been afraid of what he might say or do if she got too close. Perhaps it was for the best that she'd kept her distance.

"Here you go," Kessara said, handing him a small hunk of bread and an even smaller piece of dry cheese. She sounded cheerier than she had in days, and he could not think why. They were guiding nearly two dozen people through the most dangerous lands in Kaveryth, and they were already nearly out of food. Not to mention the fact that she was clearly still upset about Alder.

He accepted his breakfast without comment, watching as

the rest of the group sat down as close to the fire as they could, their bare legs bumping into one another as they chewed on their bread.

"I can't believe it gets so cold here at night," a girl was saying, tucking a lock of dark red hair behind an ear. She looked to be a teenager, but only barely. "Aridmoor gets cold winds, but this was much worse. The chill reaches right down your throat."

She shuddered for emphasis before tucking her knees beneath the fabric of her torn gray dress.

"You're from the plains?" Wes asked, taking a break between bites of bread. His stomach felt hollow, and he wanted to make the feeling of filling it last. Lunch was going to be even more paltry than breakfast, if they had it at all.

"Yes. From the capital."

The women had finished gathering breakfast, and no one spoke for a moment as they took their places in the messy circle around the fire. Someone had thrown a few bigger sticks onto it, and finally it had begun to crackle respectably, giving off enough warmth that Wes knew he would dread to leave it. The others continued to eat, passing around waterskins and sipping from them between bites of dry bread.

"We have a good friend from High Keep," Wes said, daring a glance at Kessara, who did not look up from her cheese. "He was with us at the battle in Kingsvier Landing, but he had business to attend to. You'll meet him in Auranth."

"Perhaps I know him. My family has been in High Keep for generations."

"His name is Alder Cadogen," Kessara said, not looking up.

Aelrie caught Wes' eye for a second before she turned away, hiding her face behind a waterskin as she drank.

The girl clasped her hands together, precious crumbs of bread falling down into the sand. "Even in my town, we all know his name. He joined the army at fourteen. Fourteen! And then he made it into the Protectorate, back when Radagar Ursa was king. He took part in all kinds of adventures and military successes. He's kind of a legend."

"That he is," Celesyria said, her hearty chuckle filling the camp. "And he doesn't tend to let us forget it, at least, not most of the time."

"He's a good man," Jaconial said, nodding in agreement. "My betrothed, Nazzan, is with him now."

Soon, the rest of the group was deep in cheerful conversation, names of long-lost friends and distant relatives swirling through the early morning air.

Kessara was quiet as she finished eating. Wes watched as she began picking up handfuls of red sand, letting the tiny grains fall through her fingers.

She was putting on a brave face, but the sadness in her pretty blue eyes whenever Alder's name was spoken always gave her away.

I'm sorry, my Princess.

I'm sorry that it has to be me after all.

CELESYRIA

Celesyria sat back on her haunches next to Jaconial, wishing very much that she had space to lay down.

She glanced up at the sky, hoping that it would stay clear for the rest of the day. The sun was still too low to provide much heat, and the humans were taking up all of the room near the fire. Her blood felt cool and thick within her veins, and all she wanted to do was to go back to sleep, preferably until the next morning.

As if reading her mind, Jaconial let out a yawn so loud that it made several of the younger children jump. She had taken a longer watch the night before than Celesyria had, so she knew she had no right to complain, but it was little comfort at the moment.

"I have a million questions before we move out again," Wes said in her mind, looking up at her from where he sat, the orange flames of the fire flickering in between them.

"Me too."

"I suppose they do, too, but I don't exactly look forward to the moment when they finally ask them."

"The High One will provide," she told him firmly.

She glanced over at the river, running a hundred feet or so behind where they had made camp. They would have enough water for everyone for another couple of days, but after that, they would reach the truly desolate section of Boneshire. Even if they did find water, she knew that Kessara's little vial could not last forever.

They had only a couple more days worth of food in their packs, but she hoped that she and Jaconial would be able to hunt the rest. There were few deer in the desert, but the people would eat ironwolf meat or anything else if they had no other choice.

"I just don't see how we're going to survive this," Wes was saying. The rest of the crowd continued to talk amongst each other, and not so long ago, he would have struggled to focus on a conversation in his mind with so much commotion around him. *"I've had this guilt lingering in the back of my mind ever since we ran out of that tent. What if we brought them out of captivity and into something worse?"*

"I've thought the same," she admitted, catching his eye again. *"But you know the answer to that question as well as I do. The High One brought us to them, and He's going to take care of them. I know it."*

The words felt almost like a lie as she spoke them. The fear tightening her gut did not let up.

But she knew that her heart often lied even when her mind did not. Sometimes it helped just to speak the truth out loud.

She watched as the others finished up their meager breakfast. The sun was getting higher with each passing minute, the soft blue glow of dawn giving way to bright light and long shadows.

She felt safer here where there were huge rocks to hide behind if need be. The Dread Ruins were still too close for comfort, but once they left their camp, there was a good chance they'd find nothing but open sand.

They had to talk, and it had to be now.

She caught Wes' eye, and he nodded. Sometimes, she and Wes didn't need to mindspeak. They just knew without words.

She raised her head as high as she could, and called out for a moment of their attention.

The chattering crowd quieted instantly at the booming voice.

Kessara and Aelrie sat near each other now, their faces trained on Wes.

The small crowd parted as Luna walked through it, her ochre skin seeming to blend in with the ground beneath her as she sat down near Wes, Kessara, and Aelrie.

Celesyria thought she was very pretty, with a regal nose, a slender neck, and black hair braided in an intricate style. Only the dusting of sand and the bruise on her cheek marred her beauty.

"It would be an honor to answer the questions of the Envoy and his friends," she said, giving them a half bow where she sat.

Celesyria wanted to ask why the young woman was in charge at all, with so many elders present, but there were more pressing concerns. If the people accepted Luna as their leader, she didn't need to question it, anyway.

"If I may," she said, clearing her throat.

"Of course," Wes said quickly.

"I was captured back in Umrym, and I witnessed a strange council of elves, men, and dragons. They met in a strange room deep below the earth, with a black obelisk in the center," she began, glancing over at Jaconial and giving what she hoped was a reassuring smile. Though she and Nazzan had been the ones to drag her into the Whitespire caverns, they had done it under some duress, and she didn't hold it against them now.

A few people in the crowd began to whisper to their neighbors as she continued.

"One of the elves—a fellow called Falloren, if I remember right—told me that the dragons and the elves had once been allies. It's been bothering me since I heard it, but I was never able to find out anything more to confirm if he was telling the truth."

She paused, glancing over at her friends, their eyes wide with curiosity as they waited for Luna or one of the others to answer.

The mystery had troubled her sleep for far too long. She had to know that this was nonsense, a lie by a delusional and dangerous man, intent only on hurting her as much as he could before he had her executed. But as the moments passed, she began to worry that there would be no relief to her fears. Luna opened her mouth as though about to speak, and promptly closed it again. Whispers began, the shushing of voices barely audible over the sound of the fire.

"We need to know," Jaconial snapped, flicking her tail against a nearby rock in annoyance. "Whatever is going on in Kaveryth, we need to know the truth. I'm sick of risking my life for nothing but suspicions and shadows."

Celesyria could see pain behind Luna's eyes, hiding somewhere within their dark brown depths. She drew a slow breath, glancing at the other captives who were sitting nearest to her.

"It's true," she said, her voice so low that Celesyria strained to hear it. She cleared her throat and spoke louder. "What Falloren told you was the truth."

Celesyria forced air into her lungs. She stared past the fire, past Luna and Wes and the others. She could see the river, blue and pretty and gently heading on its way, leading anyone foolish enough to follow it deep into the barren wasteland.

She thought of Falloren.

He had been hideous, the skin of his face barely clinging to his bones, his glamor pushed aside by the magic of the black obelisk. The very thought of him terrified her.

But she decided then and there that she preferred terrifying ugliness to deceptive beauty.

At least the dry rocks, the inedible plants, and the scoured bones of the fallen dragons told the truth about what Boneshire was.

So much of the beautiful, praiseworthy things that she had admired all of her life had turned out to be a lie. How could she have expected the history of her race to be any different?

"I don't understand," she said, truthfully, not sure what else she could possibly say. Jaconial was shaking her head back and forth, muttering to herself.

Half of the crowd of captives–members of the remnant, she guessed–were looking at the ground, their faces painted with grief. The others listened intently, waiting for Luna to explain.

Wes, Kessara, and Aelrie all looked sick.

She wished that Wes was near her, curled up against her flank. She didn't want to face this alone.

Luna shook her head. "I'm so sorry, Celesyria."

"It's not your fault," she said. "I just want to know. I want to know all of it, everything that you can tell us. Jaconial's right. I'm so tired of being surrounded by lies."

She saw Aelrie getting to her feet and moving to the outside of the circle, hand to her forehead as she glanced off in the distance. They would have some warning if they had to leave in a hurry.

At the moment, she struggled to care about being caught at all.

Answers that she had been seeking for so long were here, now, and she knew that they couldn't risk letting the opportunity to know the truth slip away.

"Part of your history is correct," Luna said. "Part of it is not."

She glanced over at Wes, and he nodded, his mouth set in a grim line. The whispers had finally ceased, the entire crowd training their attention on their apparent leader.

"A long time ago, the race of dragons was called forth from the Farplace. But it was not to protect the people as you have been told. It was to aid the Elf-queens in maintaining control."

The words didn't register.

Not at first.

Luna paused, waiting, but no one spoke.

When her words at last began to sink in, Celesyria found herself staring down into the sand, feeling suddenly dizzy. Falloren had been telling the truth, and she suspected that the dragon with him, Dajin, had been as well.

Another lie, a lie that cut to the heart of who she was, who her parents were, who her race was.

A lie that the High One had allowed to spread for hundreds of years, until the whole world lost sight of the truth.

"As I assume you accept by now–" she gestured first to the dragons, then to Wes, Kessara, and Aelrie, and then to the rest of the assembled crowd "–it is the High One who created our world and everything in it. The Eternal Lands. The Farplace. Even the Wrathlands. All of these domains are His."

Wes said something in Celesyria's mind, but she couldn't make herself comprehend his words. She was spellbound, watching the crashing wave before it hit the shore, unable to turn away.

She was so close to the answers. She knew it. She would finally understand–who she was, why she had been created, why she had been chosen to deliver the truth to the Envoy, all of it.

It hurt, but it was necessary. She had to understand.

"The dragons were created for a purpose, as well, one that has been lost for millennia," Luna continued, her dark eyes gleaming in the morning sunlight. She was standing now, looking at her audience, who hung on her every word.

Somehow, Celesyria knew deep within her bones that she

could trust that what the woman said was true. There was a sincerity to her that could not easily be feigned.

"They were settled in the Farplace to guard the gates of the Eternal Lands. It was their purpose, from the very beginning of creation. The dragons were granted beauty, intelligence, and wisdom, all so that they could ensure that nothing impure ever reached the homeland of all joy and glory."

Celesyria relaxed a little, imagining the Eternal Lands as Luna spoke.

It was a mysterious place, a fortress that could only be entered through death, with walls that dragons would never see beyond. No one knew what it was like there, unless, of course, that information had been a lie as well.

"But the dragons were not content to defend the gates. They wanted to go in, to taste of everything that, in their minds, the humans were being offered unjustly."

"But they couldn't, right?" Celesyria blurted out, overcome with a shred of fierce and unrelenting hope that perhaps she'd been wrong all along. "*'The fire-breathers have come to us out of the Farplace, and to the Farplace again they must return. The worst among them and the best alike have no place in this world the High One has made. A soul is necessary for all who belong here, and a soul that race will never possess.'*"

She noticed Luna staring at her wide-eyed as she recited the portion of the Codex, but she did not stop. The quote had haunted her ever since she had learned of it, written deep within her memories, impossible to forget.

"No. You're correct. They could not enter the Eternal Lands," Luna said, shaking her head.

Celesyria had known it was true, had trusted the words of the Codex, but the words still hurt. Her final spark of hope blinked out, leaving a hollow darkness behind.

"The Elf-queens were powerful, even then. We may never fully understand why the High One permitted them to possess such strength, but He did. Kaveryth was in shambles, with men and elves fighting for control. They decided to seek allies from beyond the bounds of space and time. They shored up all of their strength, drawing upon the darkness instead of the power of goodness and truth, and they were able to offer the dragons a choice. They could stay and serve the High One, fulfilling the purpose that He had created them for, or they could serve the elves."

"Why would anyone seek to serve those monsters?" Jaconial hissed, her forked tongue slipping out between pointed teeth. "Sorry," she added, glancing at Aelrie, who only shook her head, eyes trained firmly on Luna.

"Because the elves offered them something that the High One would not," Luna answered calmly. "The Farplace is not like our own world. The dragons who live there are spiritual beings. The elves offered them a chance to possess bodies of their own, a chance to be in control of their own destinies. It was an illusion—there is nothing that the High One does not have dominion over, even in our world—but it was a compelling one. Many chose to turn away from their purpose."

"But some remained?" Celesyria asked.

Luna nodded. "Yes. There are faithful dragons in the Farplace still, but their number is not many. The majority of them came here to Kaveryth, which precipitated the battle of the Severed Summits."

She paused again, waiting for a moment to see if there were any more questions before continuing on.

"The dwarves had a similar purpose, once upon a time. They were tasked with guarding the initial door to the Eternal Lands, sort of a first line of defense against the darkness."

"The great spire," Wes said, his voice filled with awe.

"Yes. It was the place of sacrifice and offering from the beginning. The dwarves were tasked with protecting the Envoy's mission in those days, ensuring that no one else dared even to approach the base of the stairs."

But what did the Envoy do then? How did the Feast of Offering take place? Did he simply carry pieces of bread to the sacred cave, or was there more to it?

Each answer led to more questions, but she bit her tongue, forcing herself to keep listening. The sun was rising higher in the sky, and she knew that eventually they would be forced to move on. In the meantime, she wanted to imbibe every bit of knowledge that the remnant could offer them.

"Like the dragons, the dwarves began to tire of their mission. They wanted to mine deeper than the High One had permitted them thus far, to find beautiful treasures beneath the surface of Umrym. They wanted control. When the dragons came, they clashed over territory. After that, things are closer to the history books. The two races realized that they each had strengths that the other lacked, and an alliance was formed."

"But I thought you said that the dragons and the elves were allies," Kessara broke in as soon as Luna paused for breath. "Were they all on the same side? I don't understand."

Celesyria didn't understand, either.

She longed for a book to read, so that she could trace a timeline with the tip of her claw, understanding how every event related to each other. But Luna's telling of history would have to do.

"Yes, and no," she replied, one side of her mouth drawing up into a small smile. "Kaveryth was in turmoil in those days, and the Elf-queens were desperate to maintain their grip on the continent. The oath that the dragons took was a promise that they would never attack the Four Kingdoms, on pain of exile to the Wrathlands, just as you have been taught. But you must understand that at that time, it was the elves who ruled here, for reasons that I will explain when I can. The oath protected the monarchy, which was elven at that time. The human kings had already lost control."

She paused again, letting her words sink in for the crowd.

Celesyria tried to ignore the hushed whispers. She could remember her conversation with Dajin, back at the strange council, where he had insisted that it was the human kings of Kaveryth, not the Elf-queens, who were evil. That was false, of course, but it seemed that he had told her a fair bit of truth along with the lies.

"So yes, to answer Kessara's question, they were all on the same side, despite their squabbling. They had forged a vast rebellion against the High One's order."

"Would we really be sent to the Wrathlands for going against the oath?" Jaconial cut in, not bothering to wait for a pause in Luna's words. "How could the elves bind us to such a thing? What about the generations who came after?"

Celesyria thought of at least three more questions she could add, but she did not voice them. She could see by the look on Kessara's face that the Princess was probably thinking the same.

Luna shook her head. "The High One permitted the elves to do a lot of evil. We may never understand why, especially not in this life. He has allowed them to enforce physical death on those who break the oath, but He maintains full dominion over the spiritual state of all creatures. The elves think that they can send others to the Wrathlands, but we do not believe that to be true. The High One will choose for all of us where we will spend our eternities, oath or no oath."

"But does it apply to us in the first place?" Jaconial pressed. "Celesyria and I never agreed to any of this. We were born into it."

Luna's dark eyes filled with sadness.

"We have become foolish in our modern age. We think that the world is all about us, that the things we do have no impact on other people. We think that we can make decisions in isolation from one another. But that was never true. Your ancestors made a choice, but you still must live with the ramifications."

Jaconial snorted. "That's unfair."

In the crowd, others nodded, outrage clouding their features.

Celesyria said nothing.

Ever since she'd learned that she had been made for the Farplace, she had rebelled against it, wanting something better, something higher.

Even though she should have trusted the words of the Codex Veritatis, she had stood here hoping that Luna was going to tell her something different, something sweet that would take away the bitterness of the truth.

She deserved to carry the weight of this oath, just as much as the dragons who had placed it on her shoulders.

Her pride wanted her to believe otherwise, but she knew.

She would have made the same choice they had.

Chapter Twenty-Five

ALDER

Alder knew that the streets of Rill had not changed, but somehow, everything looked different.

The fate of Boneshire had shifted, and he could see it even here, beneath the surface of this little town.

He walked with the two children, one on either side.

Despite their pleading for him to go to Auranth, Gohr had refused to leave his sister's side, just as they had known he would. It would be difficult to leave the boy here, but Holga was right. The High One had chosen her for something important, something world changing. Alder had to believe that her creator would not neglect the care of the person dearest to her.

Night had fallen, and down a side street he could see a group of men gathered, their barking laughs loud against the silence of the main road.

He had wanted to wait until morning to return, but Holga had insisted that it would be safe enough, so he'd agreed to come at night. The child paid no attention to the men, nor to the several starving dogs that roamed past them as they reached the town square. Perhaps she was so used to the marks of poverty and instability that she did not see them at all, but Alder knew better.

Still, he would be able to keep them safe easily enough, his sword strapped to his belt, hidden away beneath his gray cloak.

Holga and Gohr had not made any effort to conceal their identities. The people would see soon enough that the little boy had returned, though Alder wondered what Holga could possibly say to explain how they had freed him from the Academy.

"Where are we sleeping?" Gohr asked from beside him, a yawn escaping his mouth. Alder ruffled the child's hair with his gloved fingers. Traveling on dragonback had been exciting for the boy, but he knew from experience just how exhausting it could be. Not to mention how cold it was outside, the remnants of autumn warmth erased with the setting of the sun. All he wanted was to set up the little tent he had brought and rest under several wool blankets, but there would be time for that at dawn.

"I'm bringing you to Malka's," Alder said.

"Oh," Gohr replied, his voice unmistakably sad.

Holga said nothing.

The day before, he had finally agreed to allow Holga to read her younger brother the letter in its entirety. Despite the fact that they shared only a little blood, the boy was nearly as quick-witted as his sister, and had comprehended far more than his age had implied he would.

Like Alder, he had been especially troubled by the letter's admission that Malka had been willing to poison Holga to death while she was still in Raela's womb. It was not surprising that he was reluctant to seek refuge in her home.

Still, there was no one else Holga could think of who she trusted more, at least as far as showing up in the middle of the night seeking a warm bed went.

"So," Holga said after a few minutes had passed, their footsteps shushing quietly against the sand at the edge of the road. "I guess this means that my real name is Holga Noctua."

She made a face as she said it, as though the word tasted strange.

"I suppose it does," Alder agreed.

No one spoke for a moment, lost in their own thoughts.

He couldn't imagine what it would be like to wake up one day and find out that he was no longer Alder Cadogen, no longer the person that he had spent his entire life being. Everything had changed for Holga already. There was no turning back. And even though Gohr did not have royal blood in his veins, his life would never be the same, either.

Finally, they reached the street that led to Malka's little hut. As they turned the corner, it grew even darker, and Alder was thankful for the natural light of the moon and stars.

The autumn feast had surely passed by now, and the positions of the constellations indicated that the first days of winter were drawing near.

A new season, and yet here I am still, away from her.

He couldn't help but to wonder if Kessara found herself under the same stars tonight, her slender fingers pressed in a circle around her eye, scoping out the celestial arrangements that Celesyria had taught her.

She could be anywhere. She could be across the world. He hoped she was. He hoped that she was far to the east, in Galeharbor, safe within the walls of Windshear palace, in the house of her parents where she belonged.

But he knew that she was too stubborn for that. It would take longer for the reality of his rejection to sink in, and even then, he doubted that she would leave Wes, Aelrie, and the others. She had chosen who she wanted to be, and she would be true to it. Even if he could have done anything in the world to change her, he knew it was impossible.

She was the sea and the mountains, wild and immovable at the same time.

He felt his fists tightening at his sides.

Even if a thousand miles lay between them, she still had a way of making him want to scream, to cry, and to kiss her, all at once.

"I suppose you should head back to Nazzan," Gohr said as they reached Malka's door, Holga moving forward to knock. Alder glanced behind them, certain that he had seen a person hiding in the shadows, but the street remained deserted.

"He's right," Holga chimed in, rapping her fist against the wood. "We'll be okay. And I will send a messenger to Auranth with news, as soon as I can."

Alder shook his head, crossing his arms over his chest.

"I'm not leaving."

He could see a candle flickering to life from behind the front window as Malka moved around inside. "Not yet," he added. "Not until I'm confident you're going to be safe here."

"We've lived in this village long before you came along," Holga pointed out.

"Not as the lost queen of Boneshire," he said firmly. "Things are different now. You need to understand that."

"I do," she insisted, tugging at the end of one of her braids. "I've already had to grow up faster than most. I know this city like I know my own brother. I know who is harmless, and who to pass on the other side of the road."

A memory surfaced, unwelcome.

Alder thought of that terrible night in High Keep, seeing Kessara there on the floor, fearing that she was dead...

"I grew up fast, too, Holga," he said, forcing the memories of that dark night aside. "I was a soldier at fourteen, and I was taking care of my family before then."

"But you don't know how to be a queen," she said, the hint of a smile on her lips.

"Fair enough," he said, unable to help himself from smiling back. "Neither do you–"

She opened her mouth to retort.

"–But admittedly, you've read a lot more books," he finished, just as Malka opened the door.

The woman stood there for a moment, the shock on her face transforming into joy in an instant.

She rushed forward, pulling Gohr into her arms and kissing the top of his head, tears streaming down her face. Holga joined their embrace, smiling as she cried.

Alder turned to leave without another word, taking a final glance at the shadows as he strode back toward the main street. He'd keep watch until the sun rose.

Chapter Twenty-Six

Wes looked at Celesyria's pained face, squinting as the sun reflected off of her orange scales.

She had always been the best of them, always so confident in the High One's strength, but even she was only a creature. Even she had fears, and doubts. And he knew that there was nothing that worried her more than the thought of being sent to the Farplace when she died.

He had hoped right along with her for a different outcome.

That hope was gone now, borne away on the cool morning breeze.

Fresh worries sprung to his mind just as quickly.

"There's something else," he said, giving a little cough as he broke the silence, the eyes of the crowd looking to the dragons with unmistakable pity. "I need to know. Does the remnant possess a copy of the Codex Veritatis? One that is complete?"

Luna shook her head.

"No. Only fragments remain."

"Not even in the east? Not even in your home?" Wes asked, grasping for some possibility, some place they may have forgotten about where the direct words of the High One could be found.

Whitespire was no more, buried beneath rubble.

Helmm's library had been burned to nothing.

Elder Bram's family had kept their copy secret for genera-tions, but in the end, it was gone, as well.

Wes felt his jaw tightening as Luna shook her head once more.

"We wrote down the words of the High One before we fled Kaveryth, centuries and centuries ago. For obvious reasons, there were never very many copies."

"So it's lost," Kessara said quietly, looking as dejected as Wes had ever seen her. "After all of this, in the end, it doesn't matter."

Her words set off a murmur within the crowd. Within seconds, the whole mass of people were caught up in it, hushed words mingling over their heads like invisible smoke.

"It still matters," Aelrie was saying, placing an arm on Kessara's shoulder. "It was all within His plan."

Jaconial swore.

Celesyria made a wounded sound somewhere deep within her throat. "Years of my life, hundreds of books, all in hope that—"

"That's enough!"

Luna pointed an accusing finger at Wes, even though he had not spoken.

Her shout was so surprising that everyone had gone silent, the crescendo of whispers almost immediately hushed.

He opened his mouth to defend himself, but she did not wait.

"Do you not see it? Do you not understand? You are here! *We* are here! After what felt like a thousand nights in that camp, waiting for pain and death, we saw you at the door."

She let her hand fall to her side, and Wes could see her chest rising and falling rapidly, as though she was out of breath.

"That's a miracle, Envoy. And you and your friends are going to worry because we can't find the Codex Veritatis?"

"Forgive me," Kessara said, not sounding the least bit contrite. "You're right. I don't understand."

There was a tight smile on Luna's face, her dark curls bouncing as she lowered her hand.

"I'm sorry," she said after a moment. "It's just—I see things differently. I grew up within the remnant. The High One has been real to me for as long as I can remember. I don't know everything, of course—none of us do, at least not in this life—but the teachings of that book have been impressed upon me every day, dawn to dusk."

Kessara's brow furrowed. "People have died to protect *that book.*"

"No, no, I—I worded that poorly," Luna said, slouching a little, her confidence withering away beneath Kessara's stately gaze. "I know people who have died for it. My aunt did, actually. So did my grandfather. Not to mention my ancestors who died for those words before all of them were even written down."

"I'm sorry," Aelrie put in.

Kessara nodded, her face betraying nothing.

"I would have died for it if it came to that," Luna said, her dark eyes flashing. "Just as I was willing to die to set others free. I guess that's what I am trying—poorly, I'll admit—to explain. It's all connected. The High One, the Codex, all of us who believe in Him—He has not left us orphans. Even if all of Kaveryth possessed copies of the Codex—if it was legal, if the Dracodei were not worshiped in these lands—do you think that would be enough?"

Wes bit his lip. He was not sure how to answer that.

Perhaps he could say that it had been enough for Celesyria.

She had been given nothing else to go on but those words, divine treasures cast in ink, drawn from all over Umrym.

But for him, for Kessara, Alder, Holga, and their other friends... there had been those words, but they had been offered with so much more. The High One had spoken to them in the way that they needed to hear Him. He had broken through their walls, Codex or no Codex.

With Aelrie, the High One had pulled her from the darkness of Nox, without her ever having a reason to love Him at all.

"No," Celesyria said after a long while, bowing her huge head low, the firelight flickering within the depths of her eyes. "Discovering fragments of the Codex was what brought me here. It was an accident, but it set me on a course that changed my entire life."

"It set you on a course that changed the entire world," Jaconial amended.

Celesyria nodded, and Wes was sure that she would be blushing, if dragons were able.

"I guess—after all this time, it's clear to me that none of it was an accident. I was searching for knowledge, but how did I know where to look? How did I know how to *see* when I finally stumbled onto the truth?"

Luna smiled gently, waiting for her to finish her thought.

"I don't know if things would be different if the truth was given to everyone, written in black and white," the dragon said, shaking her head. "It's not that simple. Without the light of the High One to illuminate the path before us, the

Codex would indeed be nothing but a book."

"Exactly," Luna said gently. "His immortal words can never be torn, or burnt, or lost, however much His enemies might try. He is alive, and we do not need to be afraid."

There was a pause as everyone considered this, lost in their own thoughts.

Birds were calling out as the sun rose higher, but still, Wes could see no one coming along the river.

Some of the captives in the crowd–those who were not a part of the remnant, he suspected–looked nervous, shuffling from foot to foot. He couldn't blame them for wishing to continue on their way. However safe they seemed to be now, he knew it probably would not last.

It was Aelrie who broke the silence.

"So, the dragons and the elves were allies."

She paused, waiting for Luna to nod.

"What made them stop? Why did they begin to fight?"

The woman glanced up at the sky. It was just as clear as it had been all morning, a cloudless ocean of pale blue.

"Perhaps I should begin at the beginning," she suggested.

"Perhaps," Jaconial said, raising a scaly brow. "So long as you can speak quickly. The quiet out here makes me nervous."

"I agree," a man said from somewhere in the crowd.

"Please," a blonde woman added. "My children are hungry and exhausted. As am I."

There were a few murmurs of approval.

Others nodded, and Wes found himself doing the same. The desire to understand still burned within him, but he wouldn't permit curiosity to lead them all to ruin.

"The Four Kingdoms were given to Kaveryth by the High One from the very beginning. Silverfell was the possession of the King of Earth. Aridmoor was given to the King of Air, Galeharbor the King of Water, and Boneshire the King of Fire."

Luna paused, but Kessara waved a hand impatiently, and she immediately continued speaking.

"The names of those Kings are interesting, and do not translate as one would expect, but I suppose we could get into that bit of history later. In any case, the names of the Kingdoms and the later names of the greater Houses—which I will explain presently—were modified into common tongue usages. The ancient names of these kings have been lost."

Wes glanced over at Celesyria, who looked somewhat disappointed that they would not be digging into the matter any further, but she did not comment.

"The dwarves were given the land of Umrym. They created vast underground systems of caverns, cities, and mines. Their calling was to guard the great spire, and so long as they did so, the High One offered them freedom to do whatever else they would like. They became famous for their precious gems and skill with shaping stone, just as the histories say.

"The elves were not given territory of their own. Instead, they were charged with care of the fledgling human race, and sent to the Four Kingdoms to act as counselors to the kings. Their true habitation was in the Eternal Lands, to keep company with the High One. He created them with a beauty, grace, and wisdom that is beyond this world. They were immortal, free from the fear of natural death, meant only to remain until humans could steward the High One's creation without their aid."

Luna paused, and Wes watched as every face turned toward Aelrie.

She blushed, and he expected her to stare at the ground, but she managed to keep her head held high.

The other elves had lost their gifts, condemned to ugliness and decay, but not her.

At that very moment, he understood just how lonely it must be for her to exist anywhere, in Nox or in Kaveryth, in time itself.

Aelrie was the last of her kind.

She sat nearly close enough to touch, but he refrained from reaching out his hand, instead watching as Kessara placed a protective arm over her shoulders.

"In any case," Luna continued, breaking the spell "it was the male elves who did most of the advising, but the High One did not wish to send them into our world alone. He sent their wives with them, expecting them to have children and create families, with the ever-present thought at the back of their minds that one day they would return to their true home.

"From the beginning, the High One was to be worshiped in all of Kaveryth, by every person, young and old, dwarf and human and elf alike. This worship was brought to its fullness in one person, the man who bore the moonscar on his face."

Wes felt his fingers tracing over his cheek, the shape of the moonscar obscured by a burn mark, long since healed.

He wasn't sure if he was still the Envoy, or if he had become someone else.

Across Kaveryth, two Feasts of Offering had gone on without him, and soon enough there would be a third.

How long could this go on?

He had grown used to the current state of things, but he knew it was not to last.

Eventually, sooner or later, someone would kill him if they could not force him to perform his duties. Whether it would be a believer in the Dracodei, or someone seeking to hold onto their political power, he didn't know.

But unless the High One intervened, he knew that the time was racing until his end.

He felt a coldness spreading through him at the thought.

"Only one person at a time was given the role of Envoy. It was always to be a male, and he could be from any of the Kingdoms, but he was always raised in Silverfell and educated by the Septemvirate."

Wes stiffened at the mention of the elders, his memories dragging him back to the ruined palace in Stronghollow, where Elder Bram took his final breaths.

Was Elder Jate still alive? Or had the Septemvirate been wiped out entirely?

"The Septemvirate was not content with what they had been given, of course. As the years wore on, discontent began to spread. Elders, dwarves, kings—all of them began to question what the High One had asked of them. They wanted more. The Elders wished for more power. The dwarves wished to dig deeper..."

She trailed off, glancing at Aelrie and then at Wes, as though trying to say something without knowing the right words.

"And the elves? The kings?" Jaconial prompted.

"The kings fell prey to the snare common to men of every age," Luna said, sighing. "And it was the elves—well, the elf-women—who set the trap."

She paused, and Wes could see Aelrie's silvery brow furrowing in confusion.

"The elf-women were impossibly beautiful, and many of them grew tired of the lot they had been given, refusing to raise children and care for their husbands. They knew that they were just as wise—and perhaps even more cunning—as their men were. At first, they wished only to advise the rulers of the Four Kingdoms, and they did, but that was not enough for them."

"What about their husbands?" Celesyria asked.

Luna shrugged. "Some were killed. Others were afraid they would be, and fled to the wilderlands. Some were married to good women, and did not realize just how deep the problem was becoming. It was like a sickness, spreading slowly at first, and then all at once."

Wes looked at Aelrie, but she would not meet his eyes. She looked like she wanted nothing more than to run away, shame burning red on her cheeks.

He reached out a hand and touched her fingers with his own, only a moment, but it was enough to send heat through his belly.

He pulled away.

"The human kings were fools. They could have married any of the women that the High One had created, forming noble families to last for centuries, but they could not look away from the elves, blinded by their own lust. Back then, the beauty of the elves was real. They did not deceive with glamors as they do now."

Some of the captives in the crowd glanced at one another in confusion, but others who understood turned to Aelrie, staring openly as tears sprung to her eyes.

Wes felt his hands curling into fists as he moved toward her, placing his arm around his shoulder and pulling her to his chest, shielding her face from their unfriendly glares.

"Neither does she," he snapped. "She is not disfigured like they are, because her heart isn't filled with darkness."

And she would still be the most beautiful woman in this entire world, whatever she looked like.

He wanted to whisper those words to her, but instead, he pulled away, not bothering to shy from Kessara's knowing stare.

"Need I remind you all that she risked her life to free you?" Kessara added, her blue eyes pale in the sunshine. "Have a little respect."

Luna, to her credit, looked horrified at the hurt she had caused.

"I'm sorry," she said. "I didn't mean–"

Jaconial opened her mouth to speak, but Celesyria jabbed her with the edge of her wing.

"I'm fine," Aelrie said quickly, eyeing the dragons warily. "I appreciate you both defending me–" she gave Wes a smile so small it was barely perceptible, but it was still enough to shatter his heart "–but I know the evils of my race better than anyone. None of it comes as a surprise. Just as the dragons are left with the consequences of their ancestors' actions, I must bear the sins of every other elf. I understand."

She sounded cheerful, like she was making a joke, but he recognized the hurt within her eyes.

"Shall I continue?" Luna said after an awkward pause, her deep skin covered in a sheen of perspiration.

Aelrie nodded.

"Anyway, there were many elf-women who wanted to become queens, but in the end, the choice was made. Their names were Manta, Cervos, Ursa, and Noctua. The kings enjoyed their new wives, thinking that little would change, but they were wrong.

"Little by little, it became clear that a terrible mistake

had been made. Their subjects could see it, could see the wickedness of the queens who ruled over them. For a time, there were good elves who remained, trying to counsel the foolish kings and their wives to do what was right for their people, but the Elf-queens could not allow it. They were still immortal in those days. They knew everything that had happened from the beginning. They would always be a risk to the queens' power, so they were killed.

"The Elf-queens began to bear mixed-blood heirs, and eventually, their husbands died off. But they were still immortal, and saw no reason that their ruling power should be passed on to their descendents. Still, as time went on, their Houses grew, and the races of man and elf became deeply intertwined. Their blood was spread all across the Four Kingdoms over several centuries, but still, they remained on their thrones.

"The High One had intended from the beginning for men to rule the land, for kings and queens to pass into dust, for wicked rulers to be replaced within the natural order of things. The citizens grew tired of the Elf-queens, who were becoming more corrupt with each passing decade. This included many of their own blood relatives, though some were loyal to their Houses, satiated with power and coin even though their places in the line of succession had long been ignored.

"The High One was still worshiped to some degree, but the Elf-queens knew that He was a threat to their power, and they had already begun to devise a plan to make the people forget Him.

"Hundreds of men—by this time, almost all of them had at least some elf blood—began to be exiled to the east, and they became the group that we now call the remnant."

Luna paused for breath, and Wes caught her eye. Hundreds and hundreds of years of history, years where those loyal to the High One could have been wiped out; and yet here they were.

"Many of these men and women saw how bad things were becoming in Kaveryth in those days. They saw the wickedness and cruelty, saw how easily people could forget the teachings of the High One, and they knew that anyone who followed Him would eventually be punished. And so, many years before the great exile began, they began to write a book, filling it with the truth about the High One and about history."

"The Codex Veritatis," Kessara said softly, listening with rapt attention to Luna's account.

Wes had never given much thought to exactly how the Codex had come to be, but now that he knew, it all made sense. The history of Kaveryth—the true history—was coming together, one piece at a time.

"Yes. They knew that the persecutions would only grow worse, and they wanted to be sure that somewhere within the continent, truth could still be found, even if it took centuries. As the ships were filled and elves and men were exiled across the sea, those who awaited their time did everything that they could to spread copies of the Codex across Kaveryth. It wasn't easy—the Elf-queens and their lackeys were watching—but they did the best that they could.

"Soon enough, only loyal mixed-blood men and elves remained. But even that was not enough. No matter how they tried to cull dissenters, the race of men was stubborn. New insurgencies were always taking shape, threatening to upset their control. Men could not be trusted. They had to do something."

Luna paused for effect.

"Is this when the dragons were called?" Jaconial prompted, glancing at Celesyria. Her former bluster had faded away, and she looked exhausted by everything that they had heard. Kessara and Aelrie wore similar expressions.

"I'm getting to that. Around the year one thousand, things grew dire from the perspective of the Elf-queens. Every week a different city or village was being taken over by some new faction. Every month, new alliances of men were being formed, armies big enough to take control of large sections of territory.

"Worse still, the High One began to punish them directly. They had long since abandoned their inborn grace and wisdom, choosing instead to lust endlessly after power. Their natural immortality was lost, and they were barred from ever entering the Eternal Lands. But this was not the worst thing, not for those vain creatures…"

She trailed off, looking over her audience. The entire crowd was silent, with only the occasional glance in the direction from which they had come interrupting their focus.

"Please," Kessara said, "We do not have much more time to sit around. Tell us what we must know."

She was polite, but Wes could hear the edge in her voice.

Luna nodded, speaking a little more quickly now, all business.

"The High One took away their otherworldly beauty. They were a thousand years old now, decaying and terrible, but unwilling to die. Instead, they sought to replace the High One's gifts with the power of darkness, using magic to keep them alive and to hide their disfigurement. But they knew that even with magic, they would not be able to remain in their bodies forever. They began to train a Regent, Meira, one of their many mixed-race elf descendents, imbuing her with much of their power with the knowledge that one day she would act in their stead.

"Anyway, at this time, the final vestiges of worship still remained in Kaveryth. The Elf-queens had permitted the people to continue to offer sacrifices at the top of the great spire. Most of the people continued out of custom rather than genuine faith and, in their pride, the elves had begun to see this act as no more than silly superstition, without any real effect. But when the High One decided to punish them, that all changed.

"They could have chosen to return to Him, to accept that they were lowly in comparison, to renounce their unlawful rule, but of course, they did not. They realized that so long as anyone in Kaveryth still worshiped the High One, He would continue to act on their behalf. They felt as though they were pinned into a corner, with stubborn men on one side and an otherworldly power on the other. And so, they came up with a cunning solution.

"They called forth the dragons from the Farplace, knowing that they could offer them a deal that they would not refuse. Soon enough, they had them under oath, bound to protect their illicit monarchy. In return, the dragons demanded their own territory, clashing with the dwarves for control of Umrym until an alliance was finally forged. With the material aid of the dwarves, the dragons helped the Elf-queens to put down rebellions, killing thousands in the process, which in turn frightened much of the population into submission.

"But something happened that the elves did not intend. Hundreds of years passed, and still the men of Kaveryth continued to fight back. No matter how many they killed with the aid of the Guardians, no matter how hopeless they tried to make the fate of rebels seem, the spirit of resistance simply refused to die. Strong women gave birth to strong sons. Alliances continued to be made. Warriors continued to train as hard as they could. The people of the Four Kingdoms refused to give up, even though they had long since forgotten so much of what their true birthright was."

"The High One was fighting for us," Wes said, hearing the awe in his own voice. Even through the exiles, the persecutions, the wars... He had not abandoned them.

Luna nodded again. "He did. Even though worship had been reduced to a shadow of what it had been, even though few men even understood who He was—the Codex was already very much hidden in those days—He was faithful. Eventually, after a centuries-long struggle, the race of men was victorious. They defeated hundreds of Guardians, and they managed to drive the Elf-queens and their loyal followers out of Kaveryth.

"They were exiled in the opposite direction of the remnant, to the west, where the desolate continent of Nox stood waiting. New human kings and queens were crowned in Kaveryth, keeping the names of the elven Houses, a reminder of what they had overcome."

The entire crowd stared at Luna, their eyes shining as they listened to the tale of struggle and victory. Wes felt hope swelling in his chest, as though in some alternate world the story could still have a happy ending, the fate of Kaveryth not yet set.

He glanced over at Aelrie, but her expression remained somber. His heart clenched. He couldn't imagine how painful it must be to hear such a tale. When he looked at his ancestors, he could at least search for heroes, take comfort in their deeds. For her, there was only pain.

When Luna spoke again, the glint in her eyes had gone dull.

"The peoples of Kaveryth had been given another chance to turn to the High One, to restore the old ways, to worship Him with their whole hearts. They were safe. The elves were gone. The dragons were now bound to protect their new kings and queens. The hidden believer families, keepers of the Codex Veritatis, tried to get them to see. But they failed.

"The restoration was not to be. The arrival of the dragons, hundreds of years back, had brought new legends to Kaveryth. The people began to worship the first Guardians, the ancestors of the dragons. It was they that came to be known as the Dracodei."

Luna paused, and for several moments, no one spoke.

Wes glanced at Celesyria, trying to catch her eye, but she only looked at the ground. It was what they had all suspected, and yet to hear it confirmed still hurt.

"So they don't exist, then," Jaconial said flatly. "And they never did."

Luna shook her head.

"The Elf-queens had lost access to the Eternal Lands, they had lost their beauty, and they had lost their wisdom. But they did not lose their intelligence. From the day that they called forth the dragons, this was part of their plan."

Aelrie looked up, realization dawning in her eyes.

"The elves knew that the people would not simply give up worship of the High One," the elf said. "They knew that they had to offer them something else, a false god to take His place, a usurper to accept their offerings. The mysterious, otherworldly dragons fit the role perfectly."

Luna only nodded.

"But what about the treasures?" Kessara asked. "Wouldn't the elves want the wealth of the people for themselves?"

"In an ideal world, they would have preferred to be seen as gods themselves," Luna said. "Their own hubris blinded them. Some say that they really began to think that the High One had no power over them, believing their own lies. They certainly didn't think that they would be exiled, or that the oath they had made with the dragons would be used against them. It was scarcely a possibility in their minds."

"They had manipulated history so that even if they were somehow defeated by men, the reign of the High One would still be destroyed," Wes mused aloud, trying to make sense of it all. "They wanted to destroy the faith of men, even if it was the only thing they could do. And they succeeded."

He paused, letting his words sink in.

The thought made him sick to his stomach. So many hundreds of years, so many lives lived in darkness. It was hard to fathom such pride, but he did not doubt the elves possessed it. Hundreds of years of rebellion against the truth would do that to any race, but especially such a powerful one.

"No," Kessara said, glaring at Wes, her blue eyes as hard as steel. "They didn't succeed. We're here, and we're not giving up."

Aelrie nodded, as did several of the others in the crowd, many of whom were already part of the remnant.

As for the other captives, he would not blame them if they were ready to simply go home and allow others to fight for the High One's glory. The price they had already paid was more than enough.

Celesyria took a step forward. "How much do the dragons

know of this now? The Guardians, the commanders? Have they all just been lying to us?"

"Probably," Jaconial said, her eyes fierce. "Everyone else on this continent–"

"No," Luna cut in, her brows knitting across her brow. "As I told you, the Dracodei are an idea. That's all they've ever been. It was easy enough for the Septemvirate to spread a new story, especially to a population that had begun to waver in their faith already."

"But the Elders knew?" Wes asked, his stomach tightening, certain that he already knew the answer. Even after all that they had done, a part of him was unwilling to let go, unwilling to believe that such a sacred office had been just as corrupt as all the others.

"Only one," Luna said. "The head of the Septemvirate was the one charged with keeping the secret. When he was near death or retirement, he told his successor the truth about the Dracodei, and it carried on like that until the present day. The elders of the Septemvirate had many flaws of their own, but most–barring some exceptions that even I do not know about–were as ignorant as their subjects."

For a moment, Wes considered correcting her words to the past tense, but decided against it. Maybe Elder Jate was still alive, but even if he was, he was not the head Elder. He did not understand what he was a part of, not entirely.

"When Elder Dorold burned, the truth about the Dracodei burned with him," Wes said, feeling a chill coursing through him as he relived the memory.

"Yes," Luna said. "That secret is no longer theirs to keep. It rests with us now."

Wes stared off into the distance, still half expecting bandits to come rushing over the red sand.

He wanted to cower, to be silent, to pray for some way that he could go back to a normal life, but he knew it was nothing but a fantasy.

The truth was coming out, in small whispers and in shouts, all across the world.

All he could do was allow the High One to use his voice. He would not be like Elder Bram.

He would not let fear rule him until it was too late.

Not this time.

Chapter Twenty-Seven

DOROLD

BEFORE

Elder Dorold eyed the staircase with suspicion as he waited.

He had been inside the base of the great spire dozens of times throughout his long life, but however familiar it had become, the place always made him nervous.

He knew that it was only superstition that kept him from climbing to the top himself and replacing the Claim, but still, he did not move.

The Dracodei were not real. They would not curse him for stepping out of line. And yet, legends and myths about the High One swirled in his mind, shadows of a time that had not existed for thousands of years. He was not one for disrespecting tradition.

At least, that was what he told himself. It was better than admitting that he was afraid.

Footsteps sounded, and he saw that one of the dwarf women was approaching. He listened to the lonely sound, her bootfalls echoing in the silence as she made her way over to him and bowed low.

"Elder," she said, waiting, getting to her feet only when he gestured that she do so.

He reached into the pocket of his cloak, drawing out a small metal object and turning it over in his hands. It was beautiful, with tiny flowers and trees molded upon its surface, the marks chosen to denote the spring Feast of Offering.

He handed the Claim to the woman, who tucked it away into a small velvet bag she wore at her belt.

"Any words today, sir?" she asked.

Dorold looked at her blankly for a moment before remembering that he did, in fact, have a message for her to deliver. He reached into his cloak again, drawing out a piece of parchment tied with black ribbon.

How strange to forget the very words of the gods in your pocket.

He chuckled to himself as she made her way up the staircase and out of sight.

When he was a younger man, back when Elder Tadysh died and he became head of the Septemvirate, he used to worry about the dwarf womens' loyalty. Each time the secret was passed on, they had told a few of the dwarf women, requiring their assistance in logistical matters. It made him nervous. After all, he doubted that women in Umrym gossiped any less than those back in Silverfell.

He always feared that the women he'd been forced to trust would bring forth a piece of parchment with his handwriting, declaring to dwarf and to dragon that the words of the Dracodei had been scribbled by an old man in the wagon on the way from Stronghollow. Telling them all that the divine messages that they thought they were receiving were nothing but the silliest deception.

After a few years as head Elder, however, he realized that his fears had been in vain, just as Elder Tadysh always told him.

Even if the dwarf women were to tell someone, no one would believe them. It would be their word against the word of the Septemvirate, and the Septemvirate would win.

He made his way out of the base spire and into the brisk spring air, looking out over the cluttered expanse of White-spire as he crossed back toward the nearest entrance to the underground city.

He thought of the spring Witness, a Galeharborian sailor who went by the name of Odrigh. He seemed a sturdy enough fellow, despite Elder Rahma's yammering. It was Deermaster Lev that Dorold was worried about.

He'd known the man a good many years, but like Elder Dorold himself, Lev was growing old. Before long, he'd be too weak to lead Wesley on his journeys across Kaveryth.

A flicker of worry rushed through him at the thought of the boy.

The Envoy had always been his responsibility, a task for the Septemvirate left over from the ancient days of the High One's reign, but Wesley Cervos was special. He had lost his parents at the age of twelve, and Dorold was the closest thing to a father that he still had.

It pained him to see the difficulties that the boy endured to fulfill his duty, and more than once he had found himself wishing that the leadership of the Septemvirate had fallen to someone else, perhaps Elder Bram. It would have been much easier to encourage Wesley if he was as blind as the others were.

In their eyes, the treasures the Envoy carried were offered to the Dracodei in exchange for safety. In a way, he supposed, that was still true. The dwarves and the dragons relied upon that money, and the Septemvirate saw a fair bit of it as well. But ultimately, the oath of the Guardians had nothing to do with the sacrifice of copper and silver. The High One had never demanded such trinkets, and certainly not in the manner they were offered now.

Still, Dorold knew that there was nothing to be done about it.

Wesley had his duty, and so did he.

Whatever happened to him, the rest of the Elders would make sure that he was able to carry the treasures to Whitespire.

All would be well.

Chapter Twenty-Eight

KESSARA

Kessara watched as Wes stared off into the distance, his mouth set in a firm line. She hated everything that she was hearing, but she was glad to finally understand.

She was used to corruption, used to the way that the promise of power and money could destroy the hearts of men. But this was a world of lies beyond anything that she could have imagined.

"If Elder Dorold knew, why was he so desperate to get his hands on the fragments of the Codex that Wes and Gramnok Beastbane carried?" she asked.

"Because he feared what would happen if the people of Kaveryth began to believe," Luna said, giving them a smile that did not reach her eyes. "The elves did everything they could to destroy the Codex. They found secret believer families that the remnant trusted, torturing them to find out their secrets and then killing them when the copies of the book were in their possession. This went on for hundreds of years, but still, the words of the High One remained."

She paused, swallowing and looking at the ground.

"What else?" Jaconial said, the words escaping in a hiss.

"The raid on Stronghollow that killed King and Queen Cervos, and Prince Roven...that was only a secondary goal for the elves. Their first goal was to secure the remaining copies that they believed to be hidden in Silverfell. But they failed."

Kessara leaned toward Wes, pulling him toward her. To her surprise, he permitted it, leaning his head on her shoulder, staring at the ground. He did not cry, but she could hear the way that his breathing hitched in his chest.

Be strong, dear one. You have borne this pain so many times before. At least now you know the entire truth.

"Elder Bram," Aelrie said in a whisper, lifting a hand as though to comfort Wes before letting it fall into her lap once more. "It was all true."

"So he's dead, then," Luna said flatly. Aelrie nodded. "We had hoped he would be different. We had hoped that with his position, with how far he had gotten, that he might have been the one person who could share the truth of the High One's words. But I guess that we were wrong."

"No," Wes said, sitting up so quickly that his head nearly collided with Kessara's jaw. "He tried to tell me the truth. He sent his granddaughter to Auranth to find me, but I was afraid. I saw no reason to trust him, and I refused to listen. By the time I finally made it to Stronghollow to hear him out, the elves had finished what they started. Elder Bram had hidden his copy of the Codex, but it didn't matter. They burned the city to the ground. It's gone."

Kessara's heart ached at the memory.

She couldn't imagine what it would be like if Windshear were to meet such an end. Seeing her home city swarming with bandits had been bad enough.

It was your home, Wes. Another thing you have lost. It's okay to mourn it.

And yet, she did not see a single tear in his eyes. He was so much stronger now than he had been not so very long ago. But his was a quiet strength, the ability to carry burdens upon his shoulders, even when he stumbled.

For a moment, looking at him then, she could imagine a different future unfolding before them, a future that usually filled her with dread.

She loved him already, but this was something more.

Few men had earned her respect and admiration.

She could name them on one hand.

Her father, Roven, and Alder.

She felt the edge of his tunic brushing against her fingertips.

And Wes.

"I see," Luna was saying. "A terrible loss."

Kessara forced her thoughts back to the present. Her heart had waited so long to find peace. She could keep waiting.

"Most of Bram's family still lives in the east, safe and free. But his grandparents chose a different life. They all served faithfully in their own ways, but when Bram was young, they saw potential for something even greater, the chance to protect the Envoy with the hope of revealing the truth to him one day. It is a blessing to know that he died a faithful death."

The people in the crowd nodded their heads as a respectful silence washed over them. Kessara did the same, closing her eyes, enjoying the brisk wind as it swept over her face.

"Did many others within the remnant know that he was on the side of the High One?" Celesyria asked.

"It was too risky. Until today, I doubt anyone here aside from myself knew that he was anything other than an elder of the Septemvirate. Only a handful of people back east knew the truth."

Many of the freed captives nodded their heads in agreement.

"For those of us within the remnant, especially those who travel to Kaveryth, being tortured is always a risk. We usually share only what is necessary," Luna paused, giving a little chuckle. "Today is an exception."

Kessara caught Aelrie's eye, and she imagined that the elf's stunned expression mirrored her own.

I cannot fathom such faith. I can't imagine being willing to give up my freedom to become a slave, or to offer to carry information that could get me tortured or killed.

Shame mingled with the guilt swirling in her belly, and she hoped that her cheeks had not gone scarlet.

These people would do anything for the High One, whatever the cost.

And yet here she was, pouting to her father like a child, unwilling to marry a good man because there was another man that she cared for even more.

"There's something else I'd like to understand," Celesyria ventured. "What do you know about the prophecy of a thousand years?"

"Probably not much more than you," Luna said. "Though the High One communicated His plans to my ancestors, they were rarely very detailed."

Kessara glanced at Wes, looking away before he could notice her gaze.

Giving us obvious answers doesn't seem to be His way.

Celesyria waited for Luna to elaborate.

"When the elves were exiled, the remnant had hoped that it was the beginning of a great change in Kaveryth. We thought that the side of good had finally won, and that worship would be restored, but it was not to be. Even though life had gotten better without the elves, greed and corruption persisted.

"The High One knew it all, of course—it wasn't as though the unfaithfulness of his subjects was a surprise to Him—but He allowed us to hope. He made a promise to us. He told my ancestors that for a thousand more years, He would permit all races to do as they liked. But after that time, He would bring His people to Himself and restore true worship across the continent."

Celesyria nodded her huge head. "I read as much in the Codex."

"You look disappointed," Luna said, a genuine smile tugging at her lips.

"I guess I just thought that when we found you, we would know what it is we have to do," Celesyria said. "Obviously, we want this prophecy to come to pass."

Wes and Aelrie nodded, and Kessara found herself doing the same.

"I want to do what He asks of me," Wes added, running his fingers through his dark curls, "but I feel like I'm chasing shadows. I'm never sure that I'm on the right path. Honestly, I'm not even sure if I'm the right person to handle what I've been given."

Luna's amused expression remained. "Well, who else would be chosen? You bear the moonscar."

"Not anymore," he said.

Kessara felt her fingertips brushing her own cheek as she glanced at Wes' scar. It was no longer the neat half-moon that she'd gotten used to seeing in childhood. It was rougher, uglier, the result of real pain, as though one of his many interior wounds had spilled out onto the surface of his skin.

"No," Luna agreed, reaching out a finger as though she could examine the burn mark from where she stood. "What you have is something greater. You talk of following shadows, but the High One has lit up the path ahead of you time and time again. You really think that this new scar means nothing?"

Wes paused, and Kessara could see him thinking, doubt and faith battling somewhere deep within his heart. She knew what that was like.

Did it ever go away?

Would any of them ever rest again?

"I suppose not," Wes admitted. "I suspected even then that it was a sign. But then–"

"–But then you move forward, and nothing goes exactly as you hope it will, and you begin to doubt," Luna finished.

Wes nodded.

"Yes. And that makes me second-guess everything even more. Why would the High One choose someone who doesn't even trust Him?"

Kessara noticed Aelrie shifting where she sat, her eyes filled with sadness as she gazed at Wes.

"You do trust him," the elf cut in quietly. "If you didn't, you wouldn't still be here."

Luna's brown eyes seemed to twinkle. "She's right, Wes. Sometimes the High One does give us shadows to follow. It's frustrating. We wish He would just come down from the Eternal Lands and shout at us, but instead, he chooses to whisper in riddles."

Wes opened his mouth to speak, but Luna continued, her hands moving animatedly as she talked.

"But the important thing is that you keep listening. Keep

running in His direction, even if you take some wrong turns. Keep trusting Him when you feel like every bit of your strength is gone."

Luna paused, letting her words settle over the crowd.

Kessara felt a stirring in her chest that she had not felt in a long time.

She glanced at the desert, astonished at the size of it, the vastness of the blue sky over their heads, the billions of particles that made up the red sand. This world that the High One had created was beautiful, but everything in it pointed to something even greater.

There would never be rest for them, not here.

Not until they reached home.

"Wes Cervos, your role as Envoy is just as important as it was at the beginning of the world," Luna continued, her eyes fierce. "There is no one greater, not even a king. Never forget that. Never doubt your calling, even when you're tempted to forget everything else."

Kessara watched as Wes seemed to sit up taller, air filling his chest.

You were always a good man, Wes. You were always worth being proud of.

She was glad that he seemed to believe Luna, even if he struggled to believe those who had always loved him the most.

For the first time in a long while, she thought of Roven.

Wes looked so much like him now, especially his eyes. He would be amazed at what his little brother had grown up to be.

"So what is it he's actually supposed to do now?" Jaconial asked.

Kessara smiled. The dragon was trying to hide it, but she

could hear the impatience in her voice. Jaconial wasn't the sentimental type, and she doubted any amount of beautiful words from Luna or anyone else could make her into something she wasn't.

"For centuries, humans and dwarves and dragons have trusted in themselves," Luna answered. "They are so sure that they can shape the world as they like, remake it in their own image. What Wes—what all of us—must do is to continue to trust in the High One. We need to stop leaning on ourselves. We need to stop worrying about where the path ahead may become shrouded in fog, and think only about putting one foot in front of the other."

Jaconial seemed to accept this answer and said nothing more, but Kessara could hear the hint of a frustrated growl emanating from her orange chest. She could understand the sentiment.

After all this time, had the High One brought them to the remnant only to hear a history lesson?

"Things are changing," Luna continued. "We can all feel it, and the passing of years confirms that the time of the prophecy's fulfillment is at hand."

"So why are things getting so much worse?" Celesyria asked, her girlish voice a contrast to Luna's serious tone. "The Guardians do not seem strong enough to protect Kaveryth anymore, oath or no oath. We have very few hatchlings. We're dying out."

Kessara saw a look that she could not read passing between Wes and Aelrie at Celesyria's words, but she hardly had time to ask about it now.

"Yes," Luna said. "And worse, it is only a matter of time before a full elven invasion takes place. As of now, they are trying to bring most of their slaves to their settlements in Umrym. The dwarves and dragons continue to turn a blind eye, though of course I am only reporting gossip I've heard on the road. Still, none of this bodes well."

Kessara felt a chill running down her spine as she glanced at the other captives, her eyes settling on the woman from Stronghollow. Even if Luna told them nothing else, she knew that this had all been worth it. At least these people had a chance now.

Celesyria swallowed, her eyes troubled, but it was Jaconial who spoke.

"Curse those cowards," she spat. "Nazzan and I included. We should have seen all of this, long ago. We should never have appeased the elves for a single day. How dare they settle on our mountains? How dare we let them!"

Aelrie nodded, her voice gentle as she spoke. "Don't blame yourself, Jaconial. There are few in this world who have never been deceived by the machinations of the darkness."

"If all of this is true..."

Celesyria spoke, her words trailing off as she glanced at Wes. He nodded to her, and she pressed on.

"If all of this is true, it may be too late to rescue my father. I had hoped there would be an opportunity for stealth, but if elven armies are amassing on the Nox borders, I don't see a way into their territory without incredible force. Where does that leave us?"

She spoke fast, the words tumbling over one another. Kessara could see the hurt in her huge eyes, and she felt a pang of guilt. All of them had wanted to attempt to save him, but there had always been a more immediate concern that presented itself.

Could we have done more? Would it have mattered?

She knew that her questions had no answers.

"Every faction in Kaveryth is tainted with corruption," Luna said carefully, not quite meeting the dragon's eyes. "They all want to keep the lie of the Dracodei alive. The dragons and the dwarves want money and comfort most of all. The humans seek protection. Selfishness reigns. But they at least have the excuse of ignorance. The elves know the truth–even if many have forgotten it–and they willfully choose the lie instead."

She paused for a moment, and Kessara noticed that everyone present save Wes and the dragons had their eyes trained on Aelrie, who looked as though she wanted to disappear.

"It is only by the grace of the High One that I was brought to the truth," the elf said, her voice strong and clear. "I know of at least one other elf who died a good man. Wes and Alder helped him. Most of my race will be lost to the Wrathlands, in the end, but I beg you to remember that hope shines brightest in the darkest of places."

"She's right," Luna said, her eyes meeting Aelrie's and the others let their accusing glances fall to their feet. "We may still be able to bring some of our enemies to the truth, but that does not preclude us from fighting them with all we have. Their land has been overrun with evil. The four Elf-queens–whatever is left of them–remain even to this day, though they have lost their physical bodies. They are filled with the sort of false life that can only come from the darkness. It is Meira Daeleth who rules Nox now, and she frightens me even more than they."

"I agree," Aelrie chimed in. "She is far worse than a wicked queen. Meira is a bureaucrat, hungry for a crown that she can never wear. Her lust for power has made her especially bitter and cruel."

"I hope our army is still growing back in Auranth," Jaconial said, shaking her head. "It seems like the fight may be coming to us sooner than we'd hoped."

For a long moment, no one spoke.

Kessara glanced up at the sky, noticing that the sun was nearing its zenith, and still no one had caught up to them. Perhaps the bandits were not coming after all.

So why am I so afraid?

She knotted her fingers in the fabric of her dress, not wanting to look at her friends, or Luna, or the others.

She knew the answer, but the very thought of making her lips form the words filled her with dread.

High One, help me.

She let the words rest in her mind, hoping against hope that she would hear something back.

The wind whispered through her blonde hair, tossing it into her eyes.

She imagined the moment where she stood on the ledge, Aelrie at her side, urging her to take a leap of faith.

She had done it. She had stepped out into the emptiness, and in the end, the High One had saved her from her fears.

Luna and the other members of the remnant had done the same, but they had not held back anything. They had been willing to choose death, and they had been given a second chance to live.

She glanced over at Wes, who was looking up as a flock of birds flew overhead, singing their happy song, unaware of the turmoil that filled the land beneath them.

I don't know how He will bring me through this, but I know He will.

High One, I trust you.

She got to her feet, sand falling from her dress. Everyone stared at her in surprise as she stood in front of Luna, but she did not shrink back from their gaze. She had to do this now.

If she waited, she knew that she'd keep waiting, standing there on the cliff over a rushing river, afraid to even try to live.

"Are you alright?" Aelrie said, looking up at her from where she sat, her brow furrowed with concern.

Kessara managed a smile.

"I'm—I'm okay," she said, drawing another breath, not wanting her voice to waver. "But Jaconial is right. We don't have enough men in Auranth. Not even close. If we try to fight them now, they'll burn Kaveryth to the ground."

She saw Aelrie opening her mouth to speak, but she did not stop.

"I know it's bleak, but that's the reality. We need to face it," she said, swallowing. "*I* need to face it."

She forced herself to catch Wes' eye, beckoning to him to stand with her.

He got to his feet without a word.

"If—if we combine the forces of Silverfell and Galeharbor, we might have a chance. We could still lose in the end, but at least we'll have done everything we could."

"Kessara," Wes started, taking her hands in his, his eyes searching her face. "Are you sure?"

She forced herself to meet his gaze and nodded. She couldn't look at Aelrie, couldn't see the hurt and the disappointment in her eyes.

Letting go of Alder was bad enough.

She couldn't bear to cause someone else even a fraction of her pain, but she knew that there was no way to avoid it.

"Wes and I will marry, and I will be Queen of Silverfell," she said, forcing the words out as quickly as she could. "We will be able to take back Silverfell's men from King Ursa's Red Army, and my father will do the same in Galeharbor. The Septemvirate is gone. I'll be able to do what's right for our people."

"I'm willing," Wes said simply, giving her hand a squeeze.

She felt no attraction, but there was no shortage of love. He was a good man, more than she deserved, and they would do what was right.

Together.

Luna cleared her throat, and Kessara felt Wes letting go of her hand.

The Vilzanian woman wore a pained expression.

"I'm sorry," she said, shaking her head. "Your plan may work in the short term. You may be able to gather more men. You may even win this war. But your marriage will not aid in fulfilling the prophecy of the thousand years."

Kessara blinked at her, certain that she must be mishearing the woman's words.

Wes shook his head, his hands balled up into fists in a way that reminded her painfully of Alder.

"There was another prophecy given to me, passed on by two children in Boneshire."

Luna said nothing.

"I'm certain of its veracity," Wes insisted.

"I don't doubt your judgment."

"This prophecy referred clearly to me," Wes said, his voice rising in frustration. "It told me that I would bestow a crown. What in the Wrathlands does that mean, if not that I am to marry a woman and make her queen?"

"You still don't understand," Luna said, her voice just as calm as before. "I heard about what happened in Kingsvier Landing. Our friend Aelrie used the power of the darkness to defeat the Gorok."

"What does that have to do with anything?" Kessara snapped. Aelrie had been hurt enough. She would not tolerate another ill word spoken against her, no matter who it came from.

"I do not mean to criticize," Luna said softly. "Or, if I do, I criticize all of us. If any of us had even the slightest faith, we could command the mountains of Umrym to collapse into rubble right now. The power of the High One would have been enough to defeat the Gorok. The power of the High One is enough to defeat this army. Don't you see?"

Without quite meaning to, Kessara found herself taking a step toward the woman before Wes placed a restraining hand on her forearm.

"Clearly, we do not *see*," she said, her voice a harsh whisper that she hoped Luna would have to strain to hear.

"Aelrie did what she felt she had to do because she did not lean upon faith. None of you did. And most of the time, those of us in the remnant don't either. We're consumed, consumed with our own ideas, our own stubborn ways in which we think things need to be done. But it's an illusion. It's hollow, it's—it's pride. Nothing but pride."

Kessara looked at Aelrie, expecting to find her own confusion mirrored on her face, but instead, she saw something else.

"Wes," Aelrie said softly, not lifting her eyes from the ground. "Tell us the prophecy you received from Holga and Gohr. The whole thing."

Wes glanced around at the assembled audience, clearing his throat, and for a moment, Kessara was certain that Celesyria would have to fill in the gaps in his memory. Instead, he recited every word, his voice never wavering.

"Stripped of all help, stricken with thirst, he will come. His tongue will be as sharp as his antlers, his eyes cast down with grief. He will leave his token to the earth, he will set the hopeless little ones free. He will bestow a crown, he will reverse the oath. He will bring the bread of hope to all Kaveryth, even to a Kingdom long thought dead. The usurpers will be cast out, the mighty will be brought to lowliness, and the High One will rule forever."

Kessara understood at once what Aelrie had to have been thinking, and fear gripped her chest, so intense that for a moment she thought she might faint.

She stumbled a little, but Wes caught her arm, and she rested on him, waiting for Luna to speak.

Instead, it was Celesyria who spoke, her gentle voice still managing to rumble through the crowd.

"My race was brought from the Farplace to help the elves," she reminded them. "That's the only reason we're here fighting for the people and dwarves of Kaveryth. It was certainly not the plan of the elves. Their own lust for power backfired on them."

She glanced at the crowd for a moment before continuing on.

"Wes and I always assumed that bestowing the crown and reversing the oath were two separate commands," she said. Wes affirmed her words with a nod. "But we were wrong. The prophecy is clear, just as we thought. The elves had assumed that there would always be an Elf-queen in Kaveryth. They were certain that one day, when they had complete dominion over all races, they would be able to banish the dragons if they chose to. It never crossed their prideful minds that it would be they who are desperate for the dragons to leave."

"And now their monarchy is lost," Jaconial said, wrinkling her nose. "Even in Nox, they cannot rule as queens. There's no way for them to change their minds now."

Kessara glanced at the crowd, listening as people turned to one another, talking in low voices.

"Exactly," Luna said, raising a hand as she noticed the crowd's confusion. "Any person would look at this situation and believe it to be a blessing. We have the most powerful race in the world on our side, compelled by an oath to protect us."

"But with the eyes of faith, everything is different," Wes finished, his tone unreadable. "We need to do what the High One asks of us, not what makes sense to our fallen minds. We need to do what the elves want. We need to set the dragons free so that they can fulfill the purpose that the High One created them for."

"I always knew it would come to this," Celesyria said quietly. "I always knew that we would have to go back."

Kessara felt her heart would shatter as she caught the dragon's eye.

Celesyria had known for a long while that her race was made for the Farplace, but this was different.

This felt real, immediate. Their dear friend would have to leave everyone she had ever loved, and go to a destination that no one knew even how to describe.

Kessara couldn't fathom it, but Wes' words rang true.

Luna was next to speak.

CHAPTER TWENTY-EIGHT

"So do you see why a marriage between the two of you would not work?"

Kessara felt numb, and she could not read any emotion on Wes' face.

Celesyria and Jaconial glanced between one another, and the rest of the crowd continued to speak in hushed tones.

"There is only one way to reverse the oath," Aelrie answered finally. "It must be done by an elf. A human queen will not suffice."

Kessara felt the ground slipping away from beneath her.

Wes moved to catch her, but before he could, she collapsed onto the sand.

Alder.

Her heart pounded in her chest. Someone was speaking to her, but she could not make out the words.

Red haired children, running across the moors.

The tears were flowing now, her throat tight with gasping sobs.

It's not me. I'm not the one who has to marry him.

I'm free.

We're free.

Chapter Twenty-Nine

WES

No one spoke for a long time.

Wes stood firmly in place, looking down at Kessara. She was still sobbing, more quietly now, hugging her knees to her chest. He longed to do the same, to feel the relief of spilled tears, but he would not cry.

I can't let myself believe it's real.

This is impossible. This is madness.

Aelrie stood mere inches away, but he couldn't bring himself to look at her. At any moment, Luna could correct her, tell them that they were wrong, that he had to marry the Princess of Galeharbor after all.

Instead, it was Celesyria who spoke. He took a couple of steps toward her, placing a hand on her flank, steadying himself.

He felt his breathing begin to slow as he felt the familiar ridges of her scales beneath his fingertips.

She was safe. No matter what happened, he had her to lean on.

Unless they had to send her away.

He couldn't bear to think of it.

"I always assumed that the ancient kings did wrong because marrying elves was evil," the dragon said. "But there was more to it than that, wasn't there?"

"Yes," Luna said. "The men who married elf-women in the beginning were only interested in their physical appearance. They were not content with the human women that the High One had given them. They saw the otherworldly beauty of the elves, and they wanted to possess it for themselves, for their own lowly ends."

Wes forced himself to lift his head, glancing over at Aelrie.

Her eyes met his, but he could not read her face.

Joy? Sorrow? Longing? Hope?

He could see it all there, a thousand emotions etched in her silver skin.

She was more than beautiful. She was fascinating, dazzling.

It was enough to drive a man mad. The ancients had proven that.

But there was so much more that he loved about her.

He knew what he had to say, but he hesitated, suddenly very much aware of all of the people that surrounded them.

She gave him a small smile, and it was enough.

"If I marry Aelrie, she will be Queen of Silverfell. The House of Cervos would live on," he said, forcing himself to speak loud enough for everyone to hear. There was nothing left to hide, even if he wanted to. "We would be able to gather more men for the war. And she would be able to reverse the oath."

"Yes," Luna said. She looked over at Kessara, who had gotten to her feet and wiped her tears. "I know it's a lot to take in for both of you. This will be difficult. But the High One—"

Wes caught Kessara's eye, and all of a sudden, the emotions

were too much.

He started laughing, and soon he couldn't stop.

Most of the crowd was staring at them in bewilderment, including Luna, but he could see a gleam in Celesyria's eyes as she gave him a sharp grin.

Kessara rushed over to embrace him, and he held her tight to his chest, barely noticing the sand that stuck to her dress and hair.

"I know there's a lot you need to deal with," she said, pulling back, her blue eyes bright with energy. "But I need to go. As soon as possible. I need to try and make it to Rill. He might still be there."

Luna stood with her arms crossed, confusion written on her brow, but she said nothing.

"Of course," he said to Kessara. She looked nothing like her usual calm, regal self. It made his heart swell to see her so filled with joy.

Could the High One really have given them this gift? Was it truly possible?

"If you have to meet someone in Rill, I think there are a few of my people who would be happy to escort you, Princess," Luna chimed in. "It will be a long hike on foot, and food will be difficult to find. You need to take precautions."

Wes remembered where they were, alone in the middle of the Boneshire desert with a couple dozen people to feed, but the thought barely registered.

They would be alright, and so would Kessara. The High One would make a way, just as He always did.

He couldn't believe how many times he had doubted it.

Within a few minutes, the camp was abuzz with activity as everyone helped to prepare Kessara for her journey. They had little to offer her by way of supplies, but Wes had no doubt that everyone would be generous. They had been through so much together in such a short time.

Even in the face of war, he knew it would be foolish to underestimate the power of a good love story.

Soon, he and Aelrie stood alone.

"Will you walk with me?" he said, placing a hand to his forehead to block the blinding sun. He doubted he'd find much shade, but they could try.

"Of course," Aelrie breathed, taking a couple of tentative steps toward him.

Without a word, they made their way toward the calm river, glancing behind them every so often to be sure that no one could hear.

"Are you okay?" Celesyria asked in his mind, and he shook his head, smiling to himself. Real privacy was difficult to come by.

"Yes. I'm just talking to Aelrie. Say a prayer for me."

Mercifully, the dragon said no more, and they found a large rock to sit on, surrounded by strange flowers.

"These are pretty," Aelrie said after a pause, plucking the pink bloom gently from its prickly stem.

"Hmm," he muttered, bending down to pick a flower of his own. Hot pain rushed through his hand as he realized his mistake.

"Careful," Aelrie said, smiling as she took his hand into her own, glancing at the long thistle that stuck into his palm. He didn't feel it as she yanked the spine free, pressing the edge of her sleeve against the wound to stop the bleeding.

He didn't feel the headache he'd had all day, either. His body had no room for pain amid so much joy.

"Thank you," he said when she let go of his hand.

"Any time."

They said nothing else, leaving only the gentle rustling of the wind over the sparse grasses to break the silence.

Wes felt heat rising to his cheeks again. He had been alone with her many times, but this was different. There was so much he wanted to say, and he was certain that he'd never find the right way to say it.

Staying silent was easier, but he wouldn't make her speak first.

"I'm sorry for making that whole thing back there so awkward," he said quickly, before he could lose his nerve. "Especially in front of so many people."

To his surprise, Aelrie laughed.

"Mentioning marriage before one has confessed their affections is generally bad form."

"In my defense, my feelings were obvious."

"Really? I thought you were rather coy," she said, rolling her eyes.

His anxiety melted away, and within a moment, he found the courage to reach for her hand.

She hesitated, her eyes searching his.

"I—I don't want to hurt you," she said, her face falling. "Not again. I couldn't bear it."

He remembered the way she looked then, dark and dangerous, commanding the sea.

He remembered the rush of pain as he touched her, worse than anything he had ever endured, coursing through every nerve in his body.

And he knew that he would endure it all again for her.

It wasn't even a question.

He shook his head.

"The High One is with us, Aelrie," he said, reaching out to clasp her small hand within his own. "This is what He wants for us. He knew it all along. Even before we met. We were always supposed to be husband and wife."

Saying those words aloud filled him with joy and fear in equal measure, but he did not regret them.

"Aren't you afraid?" she asked, her voice small.

He gripped her hand more tightly, pulling her to him, feeling her body soft against his chest. He could feel the hot rush of her breath as she breathed in and out, and her dark hair tickled against his nose, but he had no desire to move.

"I'm terrified," he said honestly, stroking the back of her head. "But I'm yours. If you will have me."

She didn't need to answer.

The pounding of her heart was enough.

ALDER

Alder sat straight in his chair, listening.

Somewhere outside, he could hear a commotion, the sound of shouting voices growing louder with every second that passed.

The other patrons in the inn looked at one another, confusion crossing their faces as the midday chatter quickly faded away into silence.

Alder glanced down at the remains of his sandwich, which was sitting on the rough wood of the bar. It was a simple lunch, to be sure, but much better than anything he'd eaten on the road.

The pleasant barkeeper he'd met upon arriving in Rill had kept her word, and always made him feel welcome despite his mysterious appearance. Even her cat liked him, taking to curling up around his feet and yowling good-naturedly whenever he stopped in to eat.

"Fira!"

The barkeeper turned, tucking a lock of escaped hair back under her headscarf. "Yes?"

"Do you know what's happening?" the man said, sounding suddenly meek as the eyes of everyone else in the room fell on him.

He gestured in the direction of the grimy front windows, where Alder could just make out a current of people–nearly half of the town's population, it looked like–heading toward the center of the village.

"No idea," Fira said, shaking her head and retreating behind the heavy bar as half of her customers got to their feet, abandoning their tankards. She eyed the scene warily as she dusted the liquor shelves.

With a final glance at Fira, Alder hurried down from his seat, kicking himself for letting Holga and Gohr out of his sight.

Holga had made no secret of the fact that his anxiety over their safety drove her mad, and he had done his best to let them have some of the freedom that they were used to.

He regretted it.

"I suppose we should find out," Alder said, heading over to the man who had spoken to Fira and tugging at his sleeve.

The man looked like the sort who spent more time drinking than laboring, his belly spilling out over his belt, but he didn't hesitate to follow Alder to the door and calling his other friends to join them.

The shouts had quieted now, replaced by hushed voices. Alder felt his chest tightening as he strode up the street.

CHAPTER TWENTY-NINE

Bandits? Or something worse?

He increased his pace as the men from the inn came up beside him, brandishing knives and urging the women and children they saw to stay off of the street.

When he'd first come to Rill, he'd been worried that someone would recognize him, or that his Aridmoorian coloring would cause trouble.

As it turned out, he fit in better than he thought. He had only needed to give the place a chance.

It was a dangerous town for dangerous men, and at moments like this, he was glad for it.

As they turned the corner of the street, relief coursed through him. He could see no Blackmasks, no Red Army soldiers, and most importantly, no elves.

The crowd was thick now, everyone pushing and shoving, trying to get a look at the people who stood on the patch of scrub grass that formed the town square.

"Step aside!" one of the men he walked with shouted, lifting his knife, the crowd parting as he walked through. Alder followed suit, though he kept his sword holstered at his belt.

He did not need the threat of sharp steel to make these people do as he commanded, if it came to that.

"Who are you?" someone shouted toward the center of the crowd.

"What tidings do you bring?" asked an old woman, her eyes brooding beneath the lace of her black shawl.

"You're far from home, ain't you?"

He used his shoulder to force his way to the front.

Standing there was a group of five people dressed in rags, their wrists ringed with red marks, their hair looking nearly red with dust.

Slaves.

He felt a wave of disgust as he noticed their prominent ribs and sunken abdomens. His hand fell to his sword automatically as his eyes scanned the crowd, looking for their master.

Did they dare conduct this wicked business in the middle of the day?

If so, where were they?

The rest of the residents of Rill looked just as angry as he was. Even in a town accustomed to crime, man-selling was still seen as a particularly heinous act.

Seeing no one else of note, he returned his gaze to the people standing in the square.

Four of them were obviously Vilzanian, all men, trying to calm the crowd as they continued to pelt them with questions.

The other person was facing away from him, but he could tell that she was a woman.

Most of the crowd seemed content to ignore her as she walked toward the other side of the square and settled down on a rock, gazing off into the open desert beyond.

She wore a dark-colored cloak, though he could not discern the exact color beneath the clinging dust, and her posture was different from the others. Her back was straight, and even from behind, he could see that she held her head high.

He felt his stomach flip.

No. She wouldn't be here. Foolish.

His heart continued to pound insistently, but he looked down at the ground, not wanting to allow himself to dream any longer. She would be with Wes, Aelrie, and the dragons. She would be safe, not out here in the desert, sold into slavery. It was impossible.

He took a few steps toward the Vilzanian men, his hand on

the hilt of his sword as he called out to them.

"Your master? I'd like a word."

One of the men shook his head, the sun gleaming on the brown skin of his bald scalp.

"None, sir. We were rescued. We traveled here from the Dread Ruins."

"You were given your freedom, and you chose to come here? To the middle of nowhere?"

The man shook his head. "I came here as an escort, as did my friends. The rest of the captives with us were headed for Auranth, last I heard. Our rescuers are with them."

Alder's stomach twisted again.

High One, please.

Do not give me hope that I cannot keep.

"Who rescued you? What happened?" he demanded, the words coming out more harshly than he'd meant them. He glanced around at the other slaves, and at the townsfolk, searching their faces.

"I will not give their names away so freely," the man said, glaring at one of his companions who had looked about to open his mouth and answer. "Not to strangers. Who are you?"

"We have a right to know the business of strange folk who show up in our town," one of the men from the inn chimed in, gripping his dagger. "Rill is not a gentle place. We are cautious here."

"Please," Alder said, ignoring him and turning to the Vilzanian once more. "I am simply looking for news about my friends. A human called Wes, an elf called Aelrie, a dragon called–"

Before he could finish, a smile broke across the man's face.

"Wait here."

Alder did as he asked, and several other townsfolk crowded in beside him, gossip filling the air like the buzzing of late-summer cicadas.

"Rescued slaves," one of the few remaining women said, her eyes crinkling up at the corners as she smiled. "Not a story we hear often, these days."

"In your day, there were few slaves who needed rescuing," a younger boy chimed in.

"The whole continent has fallen to barbarism," a thin older man added as he came up beside the boy, clapping him on the shoulder with what looked like a good deal of force. "Boneshire has been bad for a while, I'll admit as much, but Vilzan? What are we coming to? People have changed since I was a child. Those were better days, I'll tell you."

"I heard tell of slaves taken from Galeharbor, right under King Manta's nose! Can you imagine? Not even safe on the front stoop of Windshear palace. Not that they tried to stop them. Worthless peasants in the eyes of the royal House, I suppose."

"We had no choice," Alder snapped, tightening his fists. "They rigged their mounts with calesca bombs."

The woman with the wrinkled eyes gave him a strange look, but before he could decide whether or not to explain himself, he saw the Vilzanian man returning.

Kessara was with him.

His head swam, and for a second, he was certain that he would pass out flat on the sand.

No. A trick of the light.

It's impossible.

It can't be.

Her blonde hair was hidden beneath the hood of her cloak,

and her face was so tanned that she nearly matched her companion, but he could not doubt her bright blue eyes.

He opened his mouth to say something, but no words would come.

She rushed toward him then, the Vilzanian man waiting behind her, a broad smile on his face.

The crowd parted as Alder stepped toward her, forcing his feet to slow. He remembered how he'd left her, alone on the sand, broken. He wanted to kiss her, to make everything okay, but he couldn't.

Nothing had changed, and it would be cruel for him to let her think that it had.

Still, when she jumped into his arms, he did not push her away.

They stood there like that for a long moment, the sun burning on the top of their heads as they embraced, their faces shadowed by their cloaks as the crowd looked on.

The gossip continued, but the sound of Alder's own heart-beat drowned it out.

I'm sorry, Kessara Manta.

I'm sorry for hurting you. I'm sorry for walking away.

He expected her to cry, but he heard nothing but the steady inhale and exhale of her breath against his chest.

"You've lost your mind, coming here like this. You should know better, Kessara. Boneshire is dangerous," he found himself saying instead, pulling her hood away, not caring who saw them.

He'd kill anyone who dared to touch her.

"What in the Wrathlands were you thinking? You could have been killed."

He stroked the back of her hair as he continued to scold her, cradling her body against his racing heart. He felt hot tears on his cheeks, but he didn't move to brush them away.

She pulled back and looked at him, resting her gentle hands against the sides of his face, not caring who saw them. He knew he should push her away, but he couldn't. Not yet.

Her eyes looked into his own, blue and burning with such a fierceness that he almost looked away.

"Alder," she whispered, moving closer, her fingertips warm against his skin. "We're free. Wes and I aren't supposed to marry. It's over."

The rest of the words tumbled out in a rush.

"Wes has to marry an elf. An Elf-queen needs to reverse the oath. We were wrong. If I'd married him, it would have ruined everything. Alder, it can be us. We can be us. The High One is allowing it. Everything is different now."

Her own tears came then, and he raised his own fingers to her face, brushing a strand of dirty blonde hair away from where it had fallen against her forehead.

"That's impossible," he said.

His lips were on hers before she could reply.

The kiss was gentle, but he forced himself to stop after only a few seconds had passed, wrapping her in his arms and pulling her tight against his chest, his heart hammering.

He could kiss her forever.

He wanted to, however cruel he had been in trying to convince her otherwise.

And so did she.

Somewhere behind them the crowd of freed slaves and the townspeople must have been watching, but his eyes couldn't focus on anything but her.

"Alder, listen to me—" she started, her voice muffled by his tunic.

He hushed her, stroking the back of her head, letting the rest of the world fade away into nothing.

This was dangerous. Every second that they touched, every moment of false hope as he pulled her close, all of it.

But he wasn't ready to face reality.

Not yet.

For a few more blissful seconds, he wanted to feel her heart beating against his own.

He wanted to believe that the miracle was real after all.

"Don't shush me," Kessara said, slipping out of his grip and turning to face him, eyes flashing. "For once, maybe you should listen to me. Brute."

She was smiling.

Why is she smiling?

His legs felt weak.

She wouldn't lie or play a trick. Not about something this important.

He searched her face. Her cheeks were flushed, and her teasing smile did not falter.

She misunderstood. She must have. It can't be—

She grasped his hand, her small fingers curling around his own, looking up at him. He leaned down to kiss her again, but before he could, she lifted a finger to his lips.

"Soon enough, you can kiss me properly," she said, her voice so small that it was almost lost on the wind.

She wasn't smiling now. Her gaze held his own.

"Kessara—"

"You will be my husband, and it will be allowed."

His heart was racing, a giddy feeling spreading through his chest that made it difficult to sit still. He waited, holding her hand more tightly now, realizing in that moment that he would rather die than ever let her go again.

"Everything is different now, Alder," she said. "So I can tell you this."

She smiled up at him, her eyes locked on his.

He held his breath.

The words waiting to be spoken hung in the air like storm clouds, heavy and dangerous and beautiful.

She did not make him wait.

He was terrified, nearly shaking, wondering how he would find the courage to tear open his heart for her even more than he already had.

But she was not afraid.

And for her, he would find whatever strength he needed, even if it destroyed him.

It was worth it.

She was worth it.

She spoke slowly, savoring each word.

"I love you, Alder. And I promise that I will love you for the rest of my life."

Chapter Thirty

WES

Wes never wanted to move.

Aelrie rested against him, her hand in his own, her breathing slow and soft.

He had lost track of time since they had sat down. Every time a fresh minute passed, he expected his nerves to settle, but they didn't.

Each stroke of her thumb against his own, each gentle hum of contentment against his chest, and each whisper of wind that caught the scent of her hair was enough to set the butterflies in his belly dancing again.

For the first time in days, clouds had rolled in over Boneshire.

They were thick and gray, heavy with rain, and even though he knew it would ruin the moment, he was thankful. Soon enough, they would have to go back to camp and continue on a long journey with few supplies, but at least the High One was going to grant them water.

The sun was hidden now, and Aelrie's eyes had fallen shut.

She was so vulnerable, so small and gentle in her repose, trusting him completely.

He rested a gentle finger on her cheek, feeling her soft silver skin, his stomach flipping over once more.

He knew that, in time, the physical sensations of his affection would fade.

His parents had warned him long ago that the heart was wicked and deceitful, prone to mistaking lust and infatuation for true devotion. At the time, he had not understood what they meant, but now he knew.

His love for Aelrie would change, and it would grow, and sometimes that change would be painful for them both. But the High One had given them a great gift, and he was not going to waste it.

He would fight for her, no matter what it took.

A fat drop of rain landed on his cheek, followed by another, and another.

"Aelrie," he whispered, shaking her a little, not wanting to push her away from where she had huddled against his chest. "We have to go. I'm sorry."

"It's okay," she said, stretching her arms over her head as the rain continued to patter against the sand below. She shivered as a gust of wind rushed over their damp skin. With the sun hidden, the autumn chill had overtaken the desert in an instant.

"Wes, I hope you're on your way back," Celesyria's voice sounded in his head. *"Not that we're going to be dry here, either, but at least Jaconial and I should be able to get a fire going. It'll be cold tonight."*

"We're coming," he said, taking Aelrie's hand and leading her back toward the river.

For a moment, neither of them spoke, pulling the hoods of their cloaks over their heads. The rain was gentle but steady, and he imagined the fresh desert flowers that might yet grow before winter came.

They walked on, picking their way through the stone and mud that lined the edge of the river. The desert smelled different, and several lizards who had hidden themselves away to escape the hot sun were making their way out of their holes, their leathery gray skin slick with water.

A howl sounded in the distance, followed by several others in reply.

"Everyone's excited for rain," Aelrie said, smiling. "Even the wolves."

"Aren't you cold?" he asked, pulling his sodden cloak more tightly against himself. As much as he dreaded the loss of their privacy, the promise of a warm fire was enticing.

"No. Not with you."

He was still coming up with something romantic to say in response when she stopped, tugging at his hand, beckoning him to wait.

"Do you feel sick?" she asked, letting her hand relax in his. "When my skin touches yours?"

He held her hand firmly.

"No. I thought I would, and I do have a headache today, but no. Your touch doesn't seem to affect it."

Aelrie let out a slow breath.

"How has it been lately? The pain?"

He considered withholding the truth, but he knew that he couldn't.

He owed her the truth, but truth had a way of being painful.

All he wanted was her happiness, to keep her safe from any hurt, but that was impossible.

"Aelrie," he started as they began walking again, the rain

running in rivulets between their boots. "About what I said–marrying you–"

He paused, swallowing, the words tripping over each other.

I have to get used to this.

She waited.

"If you marry me, you're going to find only pain."

"I–"

"I need to know that you understand what you're choosing," he said, meeting her eyes with his own. "The sickness has been getting worse, even over the past couple of weeks. It's slow, but I can feel it progressing. I've been terrified to tell the others, but if you're going to be my wife, you need to know everything."

She nodded, her gaze unwavering.

"I'm the Envoy. The High One has plans for me, and they are going to involve danger. Danger that I may not survive."

"And you're sick," she said matter-of-factly.

"And when the elves invade Kaveryth in greater numbers, bringing their darkness with them, it's only going to get worse. If I did not have faith in the High One..."

He let his words trail away. She knew what he meant.

If the sickness got much worse, he'd be crippled.

There would be no battles, or even trips to the top of the great spire. He'd be confined to his bedroom in Auranth, watching as his friends risked their lives for what he believed in.

"I'm going to live a lot longer than you," Aelrie added after a moment. "I will have to watch you die of old age."

Her expression was stoic, unreadable.

"I thought that elves could only extend their lives through working darkness. I thought your immortality was lost."

She glanced down at their hands, watching as droplets of rain pattered against their skin.

"The High One gave my race a gift, all of us, even those that He knew would betray Him in the end," she said, squeezing his fingers more tightly.

"And he gave the same punishment to all of you. You are no longer immortal. If I make it to old age, you'll be old too, right there beside me."

"I want to believe that, Wes," she said, her brow furrowing. "But the darkness...it affects all of us. All my life, I've been surrounded with it. It changed me, shaped the way I saw the world, gave me weaknesses that I may not have had otherwise. Every other elf I've ever met has lived far longer than a human would. I've already lived nearly two hundred years. I have no reason to think I'm going to start aging properly any time soon."

"They live so long because they channel darkness," he said firmly, trying to convince himself as much as her. "You don't. Not anymore. You made a mistake with the Gorok, but that was it. You're not like them, Aelrie."

He could see tears rolling down her cheeks now, mingled with the rain, as she stared down at the ground.

"I don't want to be like them," she said, the words catching in her throat. "But what if I can't escape their evil? What if I've already fallen too many times? It's too late."

Wes stopped short, turned toward her, and took her face in his hands.

As always, her beauty hit him like a blow to the chest. It was almost dangerous to look at her head on. It made him lose sense.

He wiped a tear from her cheek with his thumb, looking into

her eyes, even as she tried to pull back.

"It's not too late for anybody," he said fiercely. "Especially not for someone as strong as you are."

"When I'm scared, all I want to do is turn to the darkness," she admitted, her chest shuddering with sobs. "I think about it all the time. Resisting takes up so much of my energy, and I'm terrified that one of these days I'm going to slip up. I could kill you, and if that happened…"

She didn't finish her sentence, but Wes could see the haunted look in her eyes.

He held her gaze, not allowing her to turn away.

"You're right," he said, ignoring the pain in her eyes. "Without the High One, you're never going to be strong enough to overcome the temptation. Without Him, you're going to slip up, and you're going to hurt the people that you love. But with him? You will move mountains, just as Luna said. With him, the strength you have to offer will be magnified. You will die when you are meant to, and I will hold your hand until the end. I promise you that."

He felt his own tears rolling down his cheeks then, but he didn't feel like looking away.

He was not ashamed. Not any more.

Not when it came to his faith, and to the woman he loved with all of his heart.

Lightning lit up the sky, making Aelrie's eyes sparkle.

The thunder came, loud enough to make the ground shake, but Wes did not flinch.

"What if He won't accept me?" she asked, her voice only just loud enough to carry over the rain. "What if I'm not good enough?"

"You're not. Neither am I, and neither is Celesyria, or

Kessara, or Alder, or any of the others."

"So how do you know that He accepts you?"

Wes paused, considering, as another bolt of lightning seared the desert sky.

"I guess I don't," he said with a shrug. "But I trust that He does. I trust that no matter how many times I mess up, He wants me to come back to Him. Celesyria told me once that sometimes we find greater faith when we fall. It reminds us that we are nothing, and He is everything. It gives us no choice but to take His hand, and let Him pull us back up. I think she's right."

For a long moment, she didn't reply.

She stared into his eyes, and he forgot how cold he was getting, forgot the damp, forgot the storm.

He wanted to kiss her.

Even if, in the end, she walked away.

But before he could lean into her, she spoke.

"I've longed for forgiveness for so many years," she said softly, a sad smile tugging at her lips. "Long before you, or the Gorok, or any of it. Before I even knew who to ask. I just knew that I was lost, and that somehow, there was Someone greater who wanted to find me."

"And He has," Wes cut in, returning her smile. "He has found you, Aelrie, and He will forgive you. You just need to ask. You just need to step out in faith. Come on."

"Now?" she said with a laugh. "Here in the pouring rain? I'm not sure that's how these things are supposed to be done."

Before he could say more, another sound split the sky, louder than before.

He grabbed hold of Aelrie and pulled her to his chest, terrified that lightning would strike them where they stood, but there was no flash of light.

They heard the sound again, and this time, Wes looked up.

Dozens of dragons flew over their heads, their roars loud enough to overtake the thunder. There were adults and hatchlings, their colorful scales bright and gleaming despite the dull gray of the sky.

Wes felt as though he couldn't blink, or the scene would fade away.

It was like something out of one of his mother's paintings, a sight not seen in Kaveryth for hundreds of years. And yet, here they were, flying over a desert scattered with the remains of their ancestors.

Aelrie pulled back, staring at the magnificent sight, the intensity between them broken for now.

"Why do you think they're here?" she asked, squinting as raindrops caught in her eyelashes. "Are they coming to help us fight the elves?"

Once again, Wes wanted to lie.

Wanted to tell her something good, to spare her worry, to protect her from yet more pain.

Even if it was only until they made it back to camp, where Jaconial and Celesyria would no doubt demand answers from the company of dragons.

But he didn't.

"If these were Guardians, they wouldn't have hatchlings with them," he said, not meeting her eyes. "No. The Guardians probably stayed behind, to protect Umrym. These dragons are evacuating. And I suspect that there are other groups fleeing elsewhere."

"Evacuating," Aelrie said slowly, as though the word didn't quite make sense. "Now? Why?"

He reached over and pulled a rope of wet black hair out of her face, letting his fingertips linger on her cheek.

"I'm sure we'll find out more soon enough. Assuming those dragons will talk to Celesyria the traitor, anyway."

"Tell me what it is you think," she said, her voice firm, her eyes on his.

"I could be wrong."

He doubted it, but maybe they still had some time. Maybe there would be a chance to get to Auranth and regroup. It was something to hope for.

"Tell me anyway."

She held his gaze, and he let out a breath. He could tell by the fear in her eyes that she knew what he was going to say already.

For a moment, they searched each other's eyes, looking for a shred of hope that they could hold on to.

He found nothing.

"Luna's information was out of date," he said gently, wiping rain from his brow. "The dragons are not turning a blind eye any more."

Aelrie sucked in a breath as realization dawned.

"The elves are taking over Umrym, Aelrie," he said gently, glancing back up at the sky as several more dragons passed overhead. "Perhaps they already have."

TO BE CONTINUED

Read *Manifest*, the final installment in the Storm & Spire series, coming 2023.

Dear Reader

Thank you so much for reading *Maker*, the fourth book in the Storm & Spire series.

If you enjoyed this book, I humbly ask you to consider leaving an honest review. It can be just a sentence or two if you like. Thank you from the bottom of my heart for your support & encouragement.

If you want to stay up to date with my writing (including the release of the final book!) please consider signing up for my newsletter.

You can sign up at https://authorstefanielozinski.com/newsletter

In Christ,

Stefanie Lozinski

Behind The Scenes

Without a doubt, *Maker* was the most difficult book in the series to write (so far... though I have the outline of book 5 done at the time of writing this, and I feel good about it). I don't even have accurate "stats" for this book like I usually share - partly because I messed up in the app I use to track such things, and partly because the whole thing was just such an **absolute mess to get through.**

Stressful. Confusing. Convoluted. You get the idea!

Okay, don't get me wrong.

I loved a LOT of the process. For sure. It was hardly a misery. And I REALLY love how the book turned out. But goodness, this book was my 'problem child'...

As some of you know, this book was supposed to be the end of the Storm & Spire series. I held onto that hope even as I was drafting, for an embarrassingly long time. I have been working on this series since (I believe...) January of 2022. I love it. I love Wes, Celesyria, and all of the other characters. I love seeing their journey unfold.

But here in the "real world", I am also tired. Ready to try new things. Ready to wrap up the old and move onto the new. I had PLANS for 2023. Plans that did not involve a whole new book in this series. ;P

Needless to say, after the struggle Maker put me through, I fought hard against the idea of writing a book 5.

I was not at peace. I felt off-kilter and shaken. Until one day – as I was nearly finished drafting *Maker* and realizing that the ending was NOT going to fit in the amount of space I had left – when I truly felt God bring conviction to my heart.

Though my faith is a huge part of my life and my author journey, I tend to pray about my writing in a more general way. I'm a pretty decisive person, so agonizing over this decision was a pretty new and stressful experience.

Fortunately, Jesus knows us, and He knows when we need Him to step in. ;)

I realized that all of the reasons I had for not wanting to write a book 5 were based on fear.

Fear of not having enough story.

Fear that no one cares.

Fear that I'm a crummy writer and won't be able to do it again.

Fear of missing out.

Fear I could be getting more readers and sales with another project.

Etc.

But God was nudging me to step out in faith.

And when I finally made the decision to give this series the ending it deserves, it was like a torrent of peace rushed through me. I am so thankful!

As much as I think my type-A tendencies are very helpful as a writer generally, sometimes I need to remember that I am ultimately not (and can't be) in control of everything.

Even my career as an author.

I look forward to seeing what God does with the final book, which I'm calling *Manifest*. I cried multiple times just writing the outline. It's so surreal, after all this time, to know how it ends.

I can't wait to start drafting. =)

About the Author

Stefanie Lozinski lives in Ontario, Canada, with her husband, two young children, two cats, and a whole lot of books. When she isn't homeschooling her little ones, you'll find her on a long walk, drinking coffee, praying a Rosary, or working on her next novel.

You can connect with me on:

🌐 https://www.authorstefanielozinski.com

📘 https://www.facebook.com/authorstefanielozinski

Subscribe to my newsletter:

✉ https://authorstefanielozinski.com/newsletter

9 781738 873104